"This is one of those series that is worth getting attached to."

—Books & Culture

"Gritty and chilling."

—Publishers Weekly

"Roland March is a great character, driven by a moral code, haunted by his past, and struggling with questions about God, good and evil. . . . He is not perfect. He can be stubborn at times. But ultimately he wants to see justice prevail."

—Eric Wilson, author of One Step Away

"Bertrand's got a pitch-perfect ear for dialogue. The cop-talk, for fans of the tough guy genre, hits the right note every time. . . . Each sentence builds anticipation; each scene leads deeper into the distinct but converging crimes."

—Comment

"Bertrand's well-plotted and tightly written novel offers glimmers of a world beyond the gritty Houston streets his cop must roam."

—World

"One of the strengths of this excellent novel is the credibility of this rogue detective's voice."

—CBA Retailers+Resources

NOTHING TO HIDE

Books by J. Mark Bertrand

THE ROLAND MARCH NOVELS
Back on Murder
Pattern of Wounds
Nothing to Hide

*Beguiled**

*with Deeanne Gist

NOTHING TO
HIDE

J. MARK BERTRAND

A ROLAND MARCH MYSTERY

BETHANYHOUSE
a division of Baker Publishing Group
www.BethanyHouse.com

© 2012 by J. Mark Bertrand

Published by Bethany House Publishers
11400 Hampshire Avenue South
Bloomington, Minnesota 55438
www.bethanyhouse.com

Bethany House Publishers is a division of
Baker Publishing Group, Grand Rapids, Michigan

Printed in the United States of America

Library of Congress Cataloging-in-Publication Data
Bertrand, J. Mark, 1970–
    Nothing to hide / J. Mark Bertrand.
      p.   cm. – (A Roland March mystery)
    ISBN 978-0-7642-0639-9 (pbk.)
      1. March, Roland (Fictitious character)–Fiction. 2. Murder–Investigation–Fiction.
3. United States. Federal Bureau of Investigation–Fiction. 4. Houston (Tex.)–Fiction.
I. Title.
PS3602.E7686N68 2012
813′.6—dc23   2012004895

This is a work of fiction. Names, characters, incidents, and dialogues are products of the
author's imagination and are not to be construed as real. Any resemblance to actual events
or persons, living or dead, is entirely coincidental.

Cover design by Faceout Studio
Cover photography by Yiu Yu Hoi/Getty Images

Author is represented by MacGregor Literary, Inc.

12   13   14   15   16   17   18   7   6   5   4   3   2   1

For Laurie

SHOOTER'S

PART 1

PARADISE

Però, se 'l mondo presente disvia, in voi
è la cagione, in voi si cheggia.

If the present world goes astray,
the cause is in you. In you it is to be sought.

When an ulcer of the soul is to be probed,
naturalism can do nothing.

—JORIS-KARL HUYSMANS

CHAPTER 1

It's the uniform's fault, my fall, for shining his light past my feet to the edge of the gully, flicking the beam back and forth in a skeptical circuit, saying, "Careful there, Detective," in a cautious, solicitous tone, the same one he'd use if his frail granddaddy reached on tiptoes for a too-high shelf. Hearing the voice, I ignore the distance between the two sides of the gully, ignore the muddy banks and the buzzing mosquitoes and the ripple of ditchwater down the middle. I kick my lead leg out into space, flashlight in one hand and notebook in the other.

Nothing but net, I think, clearing the gap, but then my foot lands just short of the other side. The ground gives a little, goes all slick, and I'm aloft again, dipping backward, flailing the air until my body crashes spine-first into the mud.

I glance up into the dark pines, illuminated by moonlight and the Fenix still gripped in my hand. The damp seeps through the back of my shirt, through my pants and up against my hot skin. My gun, torqued by the fall, digs painfully into my flank. I blink a few times, taking inventory, and then the uniform's up above me, shining his light down.

"You okay there, Detective March? I told you to watch out."

I roll a little onto one hip, then wrench myself over to the other side of the gully. No pain at first, not until I put weight on my left leg, at which point a knife blade runs up the back of my thigh and buries itself in my lower back.

"You all right?"

I wince a little, then shake it off. "I'm fine. Now leave me be and get back over there. I don't need your prints tracking up my scene. My own are bad enough."

He smiles at my irritation. I have to wave my hand to get him to go. Don't mind me, that hand says. I should have known better than to reach for the top shelf.

After surveying the ditch one last time—it's just a couple of feet deep and maybe three and a half, four across—I straighten my holster and limp a little deeper into the woods.

Back there behind me, gathered in the parking lot under the mist-haloed streetlights, a row of cruisers cast blue and red filters over the night, along with the obligatory crime scene vans and support vehicles. Beyond the scrim of officialdom, the news crews are arriving, too, setting up their tripods and adjusting their lamps. There's nothing for them to see but the coming and going of uniforms and plainclothes detectives. The body's already been screened off by a tent enclosure erected on the free-throw line of the park's covered basketball court.

Whoever dumped our John Doe, he had a sense of humor.

Between the parking lot and the court, a path runs along a sandlot where several tetherball poles stand with severed cords dangling from their top loops, the balls carried off long ago. Big lights hang under the basketball court's corrugated roof, but according to the first officers on the scene, they're no longer operational. To light things up, we had to bring our own equipment, something we're accustomed to from long experience. Past the court, a cluster of lopsided picnic tables, weathered and sunbaked, separate the park from a thick perimeter of pines, and beyond them the poorly lit gully, and beyond that me.

I scratch at a fresh mosquito bite on the back of my neck, then limp through the trees a ways, testing my leg. There's still a twinge. I wipe my waterlogged shoes against a nearby trunk, trying to scrape off the clumped mud. Then I head in deeper, tracing an imaginary line all the way from the body under the tent to here. The brush gets higher, the ground firmer, until finally I hit a tall hurricane fence half threaded with weeds. Beyond it a curving side street, with Allen Parkway in the distance.

There's nothing out here. I pass my light over the ground once more to be certain, then hit the treetops with it just in case. Gotta think outside the box. But no one's been back here in a while. Another false lead.

It won't be the last.

Back under the tent, Jerry Lorenz crouches a few feet from the body, rubbing his chin in contemplation. He holds a ballpoint in the other hand, clicking out a preoccupied beat. While the photographer works, our bosses hold a confab in one corner—Captain Hedges, sweating through his summer-weight wool suit, briefs a uniformed assistant chief while my shift commander, Lt. Bascombe, nods in the background. Only the lieutenant seems to notice my arrival, giving me the slightest of nods.

As I approach the body, he comes over.

"Where you been?" he asks, not waiting for an answer. "I assume you feel okay about this?" He tilts his head doubtfully in Lorenz's direction.

"Compared to the rest of the guys on our shift, he's practically an old-timer."

"Even so, I want you on top of this one, March. You feel me?"

"I'm all over it, sir."

He gives my shoulder a pat, then pulls his big hand away, noticing for the first time that I'm caked in mud. Before he can ask, I limp over toward Lorenz.

Jerry glances up, eyebrows raised. "You find it?"

"There was nothing out there."

"Find what?" Bascombe asks.

The hunch that led to my fall had been Jerry's idea in the first place, so I let him explain. The body was dumped, no question about that.

If the killing had taken place here, there would have been a lot more blood. But whoever made the drop took the trouble to arrange the corpse, settling it down all neat and tidy like a body in a coffin, except for one arm extending in the direction of the woods, the skinned hand shaped into a fist apart from the index finger.

"Like it was pointing," Jerry explains. "I thought if we followed the line, we might find . . ." His voice trails off. "You know. The head."

The three of us stare down at the nude, headless corpse of a Caucasian male, several days dead—though the medical examiner has yet to render an opinion on the exact time. The gray-green pallor of the muscled trunk leads to a jagged line over the neck, all crusted and glistening. Decapitation. A fine Latinate word for distancing ourselves from the mortal shock of the sight. The cap being the head, presumably, so the literal sense is something like having your cap removed. A polite-sounding way of describing a brutal—no, a feral act.

We have a whole vocabulary for such offenses. The crushed jumper doesn't plunge to his death from a high window, he's defenestrated. The teenaged abductee isn't raped and butchered, she's simply dismembered. And this particular victim, our headless John Doe, has suffered a further indignity. It wasn't enough to doff his cap. Whoever did this went to the trouble, starting above the wrists, of slicing through the back of the hand and peeling the skin back, revealing the now-black muscle, bone, and cartilage underneath.

What we call de-gloving.

Presumably this was to make identification harder, though once you've seen it, it's hard to imagine any motive other than sick delight. Whether it was done pre- or postmortem we don't yet know, but I hope for his sake it was after.

The early evening cyclist who called the body in, not taking a close enough look, had told the emergency dispatcher that the hands were burned. He'd been so shocked by the sight that he failed to mention the body's lack of a head. Maybe he hadn't even noticed.

Gazing down at the victim, Bascombe's voice is hushed. "Okay, so look. This goes without saying, but I want you both to put everything else on the back burner. We're working this and this only until I say otherwise, and any resources you need, you bring them to me and I'll make it happen. Nobody drops a body on our back porch and goes on about his business. That's not how we roll, all right?"

He wanders off once the pep talk is done. Ordinarily it would be Captain Hedges giving the speech, but the captain's been distracted of late, spending more and more time shut up in his office, working the phones. Even now, he's here without being here, bending the assistant chief's ear in an effort to impress, to look like what he hasn't been in a couple of months: in charge.

But I can't worry about Hedges now.

"We've got our work cut out for us, Jerry," I say. "It's not like our squad is brimming with experience at the moment. If we leave anything important to somebody else, odds are it won't get done right. So you and me, we've got to follow up on everything. If one of us doesn't sign off, then it didn't happen."

"You're preachin' to the choir, man. I don't trust these new kids any farther than I can throw 'em."

I nod, feeling the same way, but not without appreciating the irony. A couple of years ago, Jerry himself was a Homicide cherry, a high flyer from the outside who still couldn't be trusted to add two and two at a murder scene. He'd come in thinking he would soon be running the place, even gunned for my job at first. Then he crashed and burned, had a kid, put on some pounds, and watched his hairline start to recede. Now he's all right. He has to be. A lot of the veterans on the squad have moved on.

Mack Ordway finally retired, after threatening for years to do it, finishing the night of the party with a Bushmills in one hand and a Jameson in the other, declaring his love for all men and the end of every grudge. He slept for a week after that, then started up a blog to post photos from his fishing excursions on the Gulf. Then José Aguilar, my sometime partner, a quiet and efficient detective with a pockmarked,

15

expressionless face, got pulled into some drug task-force work, where he impressed the right people and was headhunted by the DEA.

He calls me sometimes just to brag about their budget, which seems to have no bottom.

As Ordway and Aguilar left us, new detectives joined the squad, until one day I looked out over my cubicle wall and realized I was the old man of the unit. Bascombe started treating me like it, too, not wanting anything important to go without my say-so. And I'd taken an unlikely shine to Jerry Lorenz, who just about knew what he was doing these days, except when he didn't.

"What happened to you anyway, March?" he asks. "You go for a swim?"

"In heat like this," I tell him, "a man's gotta keep cool."

Behind the driver's seat, the pain shifts into my left thigh, just above the knee. It feels like a nerve, a thin, taut strap of numbness running up the leg, around the hip, and into my spine. No matter how I sit, the pain's still there, only it moves sometimes like it's determined not to be pinpointed. Inside the glove box there's a bottle of generic ibuprofen. Jerry shakes a couple of pills into my hand and I down them with bottled water.

"Better?" he asks.

"Not yet."

JD, which is Jerry's nickname for our John Doe, will be transported, sampled, and run through the system. It could take some time to get anything back, assuming there's anything *to* get. If there's no criminal record, no government work or military service in his background, then JD might elude us for a while. We've kept others in cold storage for years without being able to name them—and they reached us with head and hands intact, dental work, fingerprints, every option open. JD didn't even have the courtesy to pick up any unusual tattoos or scars before meeting his end. He won't be easy to identify.

"We can cobble together a physical description of sorts," I say. "Maybe there's a missing white guy of approximately six feet and we're already looking for him. Theresa Cavallo would know about that."

"I'll give her a call," Jerry says.

"Let me do that. We're pretty close. She might check a little harder for me than she would for you."

"What are you talking about? Terry's one of my biggest fans."

"Fine, you do it." My leg flares up on me again. "But tell her I'm the one who's asking, just in case you're wrong about the size of your fan club."

He flips his notebook open in his lap and scrawls a new item at the end of the list he's been making. The past couple of months we've settled into a kind of rhythm. I make the assignments and Jerry does the legwork whenever I let him. He functions well with a little direction. Left to himself, he can't always think what to do next.

If Missing Persons doesn't have an open case on JD, then we'll be stuck waiting for a DNA match. Since the Houston Police Department's DNA section tends to be overwhelmed and still somewhat embattled after years of public controversy, results can be slow in coming. And when they do come, I prefer if the case is important to have them double-checked, usually with the help of my brother-in-law Dr. Alan Bridger over at the medical examiner's office. Since Bascombe said to pull out the stops, I ask Jerry to add this to his list, as well.

"So I don't forget," I tell him. "But I'm the one who'll make that call. Maybe you're right about Cavallo, but I know for a fact that Bridger thinks you're an idiot."

"You know for a fact."

"That's right," I say. "'Cause all he knows is what I tell him."

Jerry laughs and puts the notepad away. A certain amount of ribbing is good for him. Makes him feel like he's worth the effort.

It's almost midnight and the streets downtown are relatively empty apart from the occasional car heading home late and the occasional homeless guy pushing a cart along the sidewalk. Jerry leans against the passenger door, silent, and I gaze up at the forest of skyscrapers overhead, thinking about my ill-judged leap across the gully, my pointless ramble through the pines. I may be the old man of my homicide squad, but I am not an old man. Just middle-aged, a few years shy of fifty. But my throbbing leg tells a different story. You are old, Roland March, far too old to find yourself—how does the saying go?

In a dark wood wandering.

CHAPTER 2

Operating on two cups of coffee and three hours of sleep, I meet Lorenz outside the medical examiner's office at half past eight. He already looks haggard, his brow damp with sweat. The June sun crouches on the horizon, bringing the blacktop to a boil, and as we cross the lot the heat radiates up through the soles of my shoes. My leg, still sore from last night, drags a little. On principle I'm fighting the urge to limp.

Bridger quizzes us for a few minutes in his office before the autopsy begins. Lorenz fields most of the questions, consulting his notes when in doubt. Once he's satisfied, Bridger leads us down the hall, where one of his many assistants is already prepping our John Doe.

It takes a couple of hours, with Bridger working slowly, methodically, making crisp clinical observations, occasionally translating them into layman's terms for our benefit. He keeps hedging on time of death, noting signs that the body was kept on ice. This means it could have been transported from some distance, and as long as a week after the killing.

"There are a lot of variables," he says.

On cause of death he's much more precise. Pausing over the open chest cavity after removing the heart for examination, he declares that our thirty-something victim died of cardiac arrest, probably brought on by torture. There are ligature marks on the wrists, he points out, as if the victim strained mightily against the bonds as his hands were sliced up.

He pauses to let the image sink in.

"And the head?" I ask.

"The decapitation was postmortem. Probably done with a small axe. It took more than one blow—but, see, they all seem to come from the same direction." He chops his gloved hand in the air, matching his slow-motion strokes to the cuts in the neck. "There's none of the sawing back and forth you'd get if it were a knife or something like that."

"So you're thinking he was tied up?"

"In a chair, maybe, with his wrists secured to the arms. That's my guess."

Lorenz stands at the foot of the autopsy table, writing it all down. "And the murder scene could be pretty much anywhere. On the other side of the world, for all we know."

Once the procedure's done, Bridger leads us out, stripping off his gloves as he shoulders through the swinging door. He washes up, then runs a damp hand through his regal, prematurely white hair.

"Walk with me," he says.

We follow him down the stairs and out a side door to the concrete landing designated for smoke breaks. How he can stand it in this humidity, I don't know. I put my hand to the steel railing and it's hot enough to scald.

"Here's what won't be in the report," Bridger says, lighting up. He exhales a lungful of smoke before continuing. "Pure speculation on my part, but don't you think this has a Mexican mafia feel to it? The torture and beheading. Things are going crazy down there."

"I was thinking of those al-Qaeda videos," Lorenz says.

"In Houston?" I shake my head. "Anyway, when al-Qaeda cuts your head off, you're alive to see it happen. They post the video online, too. They don't drop off the body at the nearest basketball court." I turn to Bridger. "Neither do the cartels, for that matter. If this was Brownsville or Laredo, then maybe. But who would this guy have to be for them to do him this way, then dump him on our doorstep? There's no tats on him, so I doubt he's in a rival gang—and if he's just an innocent bystander, why carve him up? Why bring him all the way up here?"

"Like I said, just speculation. It could always be some nut job serial killer."

After a pause, I ask him to rush the DNA lab work.

"Everything is rushed these days, which means nothing is." He stares at me through a cloud of smoke, pleased with this pronouncement.

We stand around for a bit, soaking up the UV rays and the secondhand carcinogens; then I thank Bridger for the help and get going.

"That wasn't much," Lorenz says.

"No. But just to be thorough, let's check with the Mexican Consulate. Maybe somebody important's gone missing south of the border. If this is the cartels, they don't seem to think twice before dusting cops and politicians."

Lorenz adds yet another task to the end of his lengthening list.

At the Consulado General de México next to I-59, no one seems sure what to do with us at first. We have to explain ourselves to a series of increasingly senior officials until a small, elegant man in a dark suit and gold watch suddenly appears, ushering us into a small, elegant office. From behind the desk he makes a number of phone calls, swiveling his chair so we can only observe him in profile, speaking softly into the receiver.

"I am sorry," he says finally. "But leave your card with me, Detective, and if I am able to obtain any additional information . . ."

Outside, Lorenz pulls at his shirt collar. "Was that the runaround?"

"No," I tell him. "That was Old World charm."

We stop for an early lunch, wolfing down burgers at a Five Guys chain under the highway—the default choice for Lorenz unless I beg for a change.

Back downtown we check in on the sixth floor. The daily news has already prompted a respectable quantity of joggers and cyclists who passed through the park yesterday to phone in their details. I glance over the sheets, but there's nothing out of the ordinary. No one spotted a suspicious-looking man lugging a headless body. Nobody wrote down the license plate of a van with blood dripping out the back door. We'll have to compile an index of vehicle makes and models, following up any leads we get, but I have a feeling this won't add up to much. A project for one of our rookie homicide detectives.

Lorenz comes back from the restroom with his tie loosened and his shirtsleeves rolled up.

"I'm gonna go hit up Terry Cavallo," he says.

"I'll come along."

He shakes his head, but doesn't object.

Cavallo is the raven-haired, dark-eyed beauty of Missing Persons, her mess of exotic curls the result not of Hispanic descent—my first assumption—but Italian, which I should have figured out from her aquiline nose. Her boss, Lt. Wanda Mosser, used to be my boss once upon a time, and a couple of years ago Cavallo and I found ourselves partnering up on a missing persons task force that turned into a homicide investigation. In addition to being easy on the eyes, Cavallo's a sharp detective, sharp enough for Captain Hedges to notice and offer her a position. But she decided she much preferred hunting the living to avenging the dead.

When we turn up, Cavallo's in a conference room talking to the parents of a long-missing kid. Through the blinds I see her on the far side of the table, her hair pulled back, her olive-skinned arms exposed by a short-sleeved blouse. At her throat, the flash of the silver cross pendant she always wears. One of her colleagues invites us to wait. After ten minutes, Cavallo ushers the parents out, following them all the way to the security door, maybe even as far as the elevator.

"You think she's coming back?" Lorenz asks, checking his watch.

"Not if she saw you."

But she does come back after another minute, briefly staring us down. "The two of you together? This can't be good."

"We might surprise you," I say. "Do you happen to be looking for any unscarred, untattooed, mid-thirties white boys at the moment?"

"When am I not?" She frowns at her own joke, then forces a laugh. "Just kidding. You wanna come to my desk and take a look?"

"Lead the way."

Maybe she's still on edge from the conversation with the parents, but there's something constrained in Cavallo's voice. The cheap joke, the forced laugh. There's always been a certain reserve about her, an aloofness—a necessary defense mechanism looking like she does in a shark tank full of red-blooded cops. But we've worked together enough for her to drop that around me. In my book, we're friends. Maybe having Lorenz here with me is ruining the vibe.

"Everything all right?" I ask under my breath.

She brushes the question off. "Everything's fine."

The last time I saw Cavallo was months ago, when her husband came back from his last tour in Afghanistan. They threw a party at their new house, which she'd finally managed to unpack. Smiling and brown from the sun, her husband struck me as a great guy. And she hung from his broad shoulder like a schoolgirl showing off her first boyfriend.

Sometimes, though, in the middle of conversation, he'd stare blankly into the distance while she talked. Not looking haunted exactly—he'd volunteered for tour after tour—but like he might still be over there in his mind, like he might go out on patrol once the rest of us had left, his cheeks black with face paint and his .50 caliber Barrett slung for action.

Later in the evening I got Cavallo alone and asked how things were going. She let out a long and satisfied sigh, but then her eyes clouded. "I'm just happy he's finally home." Her voice sounded like it did just now when she told me everything was fine.

After Lorenz explains about our John Doe, she sits at her terminal and punches up a couple of files. None of them look like a match. Either they're too old or the descriptions aren't right. Cavallo's missing persons, unlike JD, do have distinguishing marks, tattoos, and other identifiers. Just to be thorough, she digs through the filing cabinets near her cubicle and shows us a few more photos. Nothing.

"Well," Lorenz says, "it was worth a shot."

As we head out, I fall a little behind him, pulling Cavallo closer. "Are you sure everything's all right? You seem a little—"

"What?"

"I don't know. Tense."

She repeats the word, tight-lipped: "*Tense.*"

"Is everything all right at home? We haven't seen you guys in a while—"

"March," she says. "What's the deal? You walk in out of nowhere and decide I'm acting strange? You're the one who asked for help, not me. As always."

"Is that what this is about? It seemed like a good lead to follow up, if you ask me."

"Never mind." She touches my arm. "Forget I said anything. You're right. I'm all worked up. It's nothing to do with you—and it's nothing to do with my personal life, okay?" She smiles. "But your fatherly concern is duly noted."

"Fatherly. Ouch."

"Anyway, how is Charlotte? You're right, we haven't seen each other since . . . It was the party, right?"

I nod. "Charlotte's out of town again. The new job."

"Ah."

My wife, Charlotte, after nearly a decade of working from home, marking up legal documents for her old partners, accepted a new position at one of the big law firms, almost doubling both her salary and the amount of time she spends on the road. She's traveled so much in the last six months that we went to the Galleria on her birthday and bought all new luggage, a shiny set of ribbed aluminum rolling cases like something out of a sixties science fiction movie. And we bought new phones as well, with cameras front and back so we can talk face-to-face from opposite ends of the globe, something we tried once or twice early on before lapsing into the occasional old-fashioned phone call.

Over by the exit Lorenz taps his watch.

"The clock's ticking," Cavallo says.

"It always is."

I catch up with my partner, giving Cavallo a last look from the threshold. She's standing where I left her, but with her back resolutely turned. Something's not right between us.

The afternoon grinds on, one false lead after another. Then the shift ends and the next one starts and it's the same all over again. We have a body without an identification, no witnesses, and no likely avenues to pursue. So we pursue the unlikely ones, roping in the rest of the squad in twos and threes, exhausting leads, exhausting detectives, exhausting the patience of my long-suffering lieutenant.

"There's always the DNA," Lorenz keeps saying.

Yes, there's always that. The long shot chance that somewhere in the FBI's massive computerized index, there's a strand of chromosomes waiting to be matched. Even that would only get us so far. Knowing a victim's name doesn't automatically unmask his killer. It might, though. Why bother making the identification so difficult, removing the head and mutilating the hands, if having a name won't make any difference?

By the end of the week I'm starting each day with a conference in Bascombe's office.

"Whatever you need," he says. "Anything at all. 'You have not because you ask not.'"

Which is the first time I can remember him quoting anything other than the criminal code.

"All I need is a hit on those test results."

"You're making the calls? I'm making them, too. Believe me, the pressure's on to push this thing through the system. I don't know what the holdup is, but I'll call again right now if you think it'll help."

He reaches for the phone, then waits for my answer.

"It can't hurt," I say.

But it doesn't help. He puts the phone down five minutes later, giving me a shrug. "We'll get the results when we get the results. Maybe something by shift's end."

So I check back with him a few hours later before clocking out, just to see if anything's come through. He looks me up and down, deciding what to say. "Get a good night's sleep. We'll go at it fresh again in the morning."

"All right."

He glances at the monitor on his desk. "I'm thinking, while we're waiting on the DNA to come back, it's not a bad idea if you and Lorenz catch up on your other open cases. We're not giving up on this, March. We just need to use our time as efficiently as possible."

"Yes, sir."

In other words, barring intervention from on high, JD will keep clocking time in the refrigerator while Lorenz and I move on to other cases. It's not the first time I've had to put a victim on the back burner, not the first time a case has gone cold on me. They say there are things you don't get used to, like seeing a headless corpse or an autopsy in progress, but the fact is you get used to them just fine. They even become a little fascinating from a professional standpoint. What I can never get used to is this: giving up. Gathering all the paper and filing it away for what might be the last time.

Whoever he was, this man was strapped to a chair and tortured, was put through such agony that his young healthy heart finally gave out. What would he have thought if he'd known in those final moments that after a handful of days, I'd be consigning him to a cardboard filing box and preparing myself mentally to move on?

I take the elevator down to the secure garage, tracing the way back to where I left my car. Sliding between two vehicles, my foot catches on a drain grate and twists. The old pain, fading steadily every day since the night of my fall, stabs through me. I steady myself against the hood of a car and try to shake it off. It feels just like a knife, or maybe a surgeon's scalpel. And then it dulls down to a throb. I take a step and it's still there. There, but manageable.

Not so bad that I can't function.

A pain I can live with.

CHAPTER 3

When I'm not working, I don't know what to do with myself anymore. The house is too empty, too quiet with Charlotte gone. The first time she left—a weeklong stay on the East Coast—I'd find myself opening drawers and checking that her things were still there. An hour later, one of her silk slips would still be clutched in my hand, or a little piece of jewelry, and I'd be sitting in the dark thinking about . . . nothing.

"Go visit the Robbs," Charlotte would say over the phone, sensing something wasn't right, but not wanting to probe too deeply into what. Her new position made her happy, more than she'd ever anticipated, and by instinct she steered away from any conversation which might call the decision into question.

In front of the muted television I try calling Charlotte. She's in London now for some kind of high-level negotiation meant to last through the weekend, after which her plan is to pick up her sister Ann, Bridger's wife, who's flying into Heathrow for a couple of days of sightseeing. It's hard to imagine what the two sisters will do alone together in a foreign land. They can hardly get through dinner together without some kind of argument flaring up. My call goes to voicemail, but I don't leave a message. She'll get back to me when she can.

I check the time, then try to watch the History Channel for a while. Back when they ran Hitler documentaries all the time, I could tune out in front of the tube for hours. Now there are too many reality shows with only a tenuous connection to the past. I switch off the TV and go to the bookshelf, taking down the thick middle volume of Shelby Foote's *The Civil War*, which I've been reading intermittently for about ten years, hoping to finish before I'm dead. Not tonight, though. After flipping a few pages, I put it back.

In the old days on nights like this, when I wanted desperately to shrug off the pressures of work, I'd end up in the parking lot of a bar called the Paragon, wondering what it would be like to take a drink. Sometimes I'd go inside and order one, then let the glass sweat untouched on the table, testing myself. But the place changed hands a few times and finally closed. Now there's just a darkened storefront.

So I grab my car keys and the black gym bag I keep next to the gun safe. The weight feels good in my hand. In my new empty life, there is one way I've learned to forget everything. And it's early enough in the evening for me to catch up.

On the way I stop over to see the Robbs. The couple who used to live in our garage apartment started looking for a bigger place once Gina's pregnancy started to show. They took their time, hoping to find something large enough for a growing family but not so expensive that Carter couldn't afford it on his ministry salary, since Gina hoped to quit teaching once the baby was born. He worked in Montrose at something called an "outreach center," splitting his time between helping the destitute and proselytizing the heathens. In his off-hours he'd try proselytizing me, too, but it's not so easy when the heathen has a badge.

With my wife's help, the Robbs found a rental bungalow not far from Carter's work, a tiny cottage of maybe nine hundred square feet, no garage, with a tear-down on one side and an incomplete glass-and-steel domicile on the other, the kind of place a *Miami Vice* drug lord would have been proud to call home. When the market tanked, the architect-builder went broke and left the site mothballed in temporary fencing and plastic wrap.

I'd gone over to see them a few times, bearing gifts, but without Charlotte things were never as smooth. Any day now, that baby would arrive, throwing their lives into rhapsodic turmoil. The thought makes me a little sad. I guess I'm starting to miss them.

Carter comes to the door in a T-shirt and shorts. He doesn't look happy to see me.

"Is this a bad time? I was just passing through—"

He shakes his head. "No, come in. I could use the distraction."

"I was heading over to Shooter's Paradise. You should come some time." Catching his expression, I pause. "What's up, Carter?"

From the sidewalk I'd noticed a bluish glow from the front window. Carter nods his tousled head toward the living room, the source of the strange light. Stepping through the arched entryway, I find the furniture pushed into the corners, stacks of books and paper teetering on every available surface, making room for a bubble of empty space at the far side of the room, ringed by light boxes and a lithe and shadowy brunette hoisting a huge-lensed camera. Gina Robb, swathed in some kind of bedsheet, sits perched on a stool, arms and legs bare, frowning intently into the light.

She's let her hair grow out a little, and tonight it hangs in self-conscious ringlets. I'm more accustomed to seeing it tucked behind a vintage barrette. Her ironic cat-eye glasses are gone, too. She looks beautiful, honestly, almost radiant, her hands on her belly in an earth goddess pose. I feel like I shouldn't be here.

I give Carter a look and he shakes his head. I expect him to say something, but he lopes down the hall to the kitchen. Before I can follow, Gina squints my way and gives a nervous giggle.

"Oh boy," she says. "This will take some explaining."

The photographer introduces herself, shifting the camera so she can shake my hand. Long, cool fingers. Black-rimmed eyes. Gina tells me she's some kind of artist, that the photos are for a "study," whatever that is, and they met in one of her night classes at the University of

Houston, where Gina's been working on her master's degree in English Lit off and on while teaching at a private school out in the suburbs. To prove her point, she indicates a stack of textbooks on the arm of the couch, then adjusts the draped fabric at her shoulder.

I glance at the books. "That's a lot of reading."

"It's, like, crazy," the photographer says.

"And you . . . paint pictures?" I ask.

"Something like that. I'm working on a series called 'Madonna and Child.'"

"You're starting early."

She bites her lip, confused.

"I mean, the baby's not here yet. You have a madonna, but no child. Never mind. Just an attempt at humor. I should stick with my strengths."

Gina starts to get up, but the photographer waves her back into place. "No, no, I need a couple more. Don't move."

"Go ahead," I say. "I'll find Carter."

While they snap photos, I find myself lingering near the couch. The first time I met Gina Robb, it took me two seconds to pigeonhole her, and she's been surprising me ever since. Modeling for an artist during the countdown to having her first kid? I didn't see that coming. Down the hall I can hear Carter moving around in the kitchen, closing the fridge, scooting things along the counter. I don't know if it's the bedsheet that makes him uncomfortable or the whole idea or just the thought of me walking in on the scene.

I find him in the crook of the counter, between the stove and the sink, downing a glass of some kind of sugary orange stuff, his eyebrows cocked upward in shock.

"You seem a little put out by all this," I whisper. The camera clicks and the cold blue light barrels down the hallway, strobing over the kitchen appliances. "You shouldn't be. It's not so bad, having a wife who can still surprise you."

"It's not that," he says. "It's the artist. Gina's doing this to try and help her, to be supportive. But she's got some baggage. I think she's bad news."

"That's funny, coming from you. You go out of your way to support people, right? It's your job. So what's the harm in her doing the same thing?"

"Yeah, I know." He shakes his head. "It's just . . . Ever since, you know, the baby . . . I just want to keep her safe. To look out for her."

I put a hand on his shoulder. "Well, that makes two of us. But I think this will be all right. She's having a good time with it. If it were Charlotte in there and I was sulking like this, I wouldn't hear the end of it. Now come on, let's go back in."

He puts his glass in the sink and follows me.

"All done," Gina calls to us, sashaying up the stairs holding the sheet at the back. In the living room the photographer is packing up her things. Carter puts on a smile and goes to her assistance. While they chat, I check my watch and survey the mess. I should get going, but I want to say hello to Gina first.

I'm going through her stack of schoolbooks when she returns wearing a knit dress that clings tight to her belly, both her hands on her hips for support. Her hair is clipped back and she makes a show of wiping sweat from her dry brow. "You're still here," she says. "I was afraid you were going to disappear on us."

"I was just in the neighborhood and wanted to stop in and say hi. Make sure you guys aren't missing the old garage apartment and want to move back."

"Tempting," she says. "In my condition, stairs aren't a girl's best friend."

Carter and the photographer start carrying gear out to her car. Gina eases herself into an empty space on the couch, then starts moving books over so I can sit, too. The one on top is Dante's *Inferno*, the Robert Pinsky translation. It's dog-eared and sticky-noted and creased down the spine. Gina is nothing if not a good student.

"Let me do that." I move the stack for her. "You like the Dante?"

"I'm only halfway through."

"If that's halfway, I don't think the book is going to survive the experience."

"You've read it?"

"Don't sound so surprised," I say. "As a matter of fact, I haven't. But I knew someone once . . ." My voice trails off. "Let's just say, I have a special relationship with that thing."

As I speak, the stack I've just moved topples of its own accord.

I lean over to straighten the books. One of them is an old paperback with a Norman knight on the cover. The nasal piece on his helmet juts out and he presses a curved horn to his lips. "Well, well. This looks like my kind of reading."

She rolls her eyes. "*The Song of Roland*. Don't get me started. That was the first one we had to read. If that's chivalry, then you can have it. That book infuriates me."

"Really." I flip through the pages, many of which are underscored. I'm familiar with the story, of course, though I can't recall having actually read the poem. In fact, before now I'm not sure I realized it *was* a poem, with all the stanzas and verses. "He's supposed to blow the horn to signal the ambush, is that it?"

"He's supposed to blow it if they need help. Only Roland's too proud for that, so he waits and waits until everybody's basically dead. Does that sound like heroism to you?"

"Actually, it kind of does."

She snatches the book in mock outrage. "It's not bravery, though. It's stupidity."

"Don't let your professor hear you. That book's a classic."

"It's all right," she says. "We're allowed not to like them. It's even encouraged."

I could sit and argue about books I haven't read for hours. I want to stick up for my namesake, for the whole tradition of chivalry, for the stupid pride that would lead a man not to give his enemies the satisfaction of blowing the horn. At the back of my mind, some history stirs, something I saw on television or maybe read years ago in college.

"Sir Francis Drake," I tell her, "when he was sailing into some Spanish port or other, and all their cannon started firing at his ship—or maybe it's Walter Raleigh I'm thinking of. Anyway, when the Spanish artillery opened up, instead of shooting back, he got his trumpeters on deck and had them blow a note."

"What?"

"That was his reply. His way of putting them in their place."

"That sounds stupid, too." She shakes her head at the ways of men. "If he was smart, he should have fired his guns at them. Unless those were really nasty trumpeters or something."

"It was like he was saying, Your efforts are beneath my contempt. He was insulting them."

She gives me an indulgent smile.

"Hey, I'm just saying, that stuff speaks to me. Don't dismiss Sir Roland out of hand. You weren't there."

"Okay," she says. "Just promise me you're not going to follow his example."

"You sound like Charlotte."

"I'll take that as a compliment."

"It *is* a compliment, kid."

After the last of the gear is packed, the photographer leans down to touch Gina on the tummy and kiss her cheek. "New life," she says under her breath. Gina beams up at her, a bookish, impish, argumentative and glowing earth mother at the height of her charms.

The uncle who raised me, after leaving the Houston Police Department on disability when a stray truck jackknifed his cruiser during a pursuit, used some settlement money to buy himself a modest gun shop on Richmond. He'd give his former colleagues deep discounts on their purchases, which ensured the place was always filled with cops. When I was a teen, I used to work with him behind the counter, learning everything there is to know about firearms. And every time a tropical storm blew through, dumping so much rain into the parking lot that we and the little jewelry shop next door would end up with an inch of standing water on the floor, it was me who mopped up the mess.

The Shooter's Paradise on I-10 couldn't be more different than my uncle's establishment. Vast and brightly lit by shining fluorescents, its spotless glass cases are packed with an endless variety of pistols and revolvers, from entry-level Glocks and SIGs to exotic race guns with fancy anodized frames. If longarms are your preference, they have those, too, along with a selection of custom leather holsters that would normally require months of waiting to obtain. As I know too well. Every surface gleams, every item is displayed with the care of a museum exhibit. It's a pistoleer's boutique, a lifelong NRA member's idea of what heaven will be like.

But the attraction for me is in back.

One of the managers recognizes me from behind the counter, motioning toward the double doors at the rear of the shop.

"They've already started," he says, "so you better get moving."

I nod my thanks.

An acquaintance on the SWAT team first tipped me off to the league, suggesting I might want to brush up my skills. The Shooter's Paradise, in addition to the showroom, boasts a state-of-the-art pistol range with twenty lanes, excellent ventilation, and even a soundproof observation gallery so you can watch the action without having to wear ear protection. On Thursdays, a loosely organized club gets together, arranging a series of tactical targets and running one member after another through the course. At the end of the night, the shooters compare rankings and head over to the *taquería* next door.

In the vestibule I run into a couple of latecomers.

"Hey, Roland, how's it hanging? We thought you were bailing on us this time."

We shoot the breeze as we strap on our gear. Meaningless small talk. There are a couple of law enforcement types in the club, but no one who knows me. I keep pretty much to myself. I'm here to blow off steam, not make new buddies. Still, there's a charm to it all—the macho camaraderie, the obsessive focus on performance, the specialized vocabulary. Egregious rule-breakers, when they're penalized, are charged with a "failure to do right." I like the term. What is a homicide detective if not the living embodiment of such a charge. Do right and you'll never tangle with me. Fail to do right, and there I am.

"I see you dropped some dollars on a new rig," one of the guys says.

I pause in the midst of adjusting my new holster, the new matte-silver Browning inside. "I didn't plan it. You just get sucked in, you know?"

When I started the league, I was shooting with my off-duty piece, a .40 caliber Kahr with all the sharp edges melted away. Long ago, the Kahr went to Teddy Jacobson for some work, coming back with an action slicker than glass. It's a flat, short-barreled hideaway pistol, but I can hit targets with accuracy much farther out than you'd expect.

But after a couple of weeks, all the club's magazine changes and malfunction drills had me yearning for a full-size pistol. Instead of bringing my duty gun or springing for one of the usual plastic-framed, high-capacity numbers, I'd toured the glass cases at Shooter's Paradise and gone a little crazy, ending up with a custom Novak Browning Hi-Power. Compact for its punch, slender, and all metal, with a crisp single-action trigger pull. It's also a natural pointer, which I appreciate.

In addition to the standard thirteen-round mags, I'd bought a bunch of hi-cap South African magazines, bringing the total up to eighteen with one in the spout. And I'd picked up a couple hundred dollars' worth of saddle-tan holsters and mag carriers, keeping it all in the new gym bag ready to go.

I feel a little guilty at all the expenditure. When Charlotte lays out money like this, I can't help giving her a lecture. But she's not here to return the favor.

Out on the range I add my name to the sign-up sheet, then file to the back of the line. Already the air smells of gun smoke. I put my things in an empty lane, locking the Hi-Power's slide back and slipping it into my belt holster, one of the club's safety requirements.

"Hey, man, how's it hanging?"

I turn to find Jeff, another new guy, unloading his gear next to me. He wears jeans and a tight-fitting linen safari shirt with epaulets and button tabs securing the rolled-up sleeves. The look is more fashion than function, but he's the only shooter here I've really warmed up to. Maybe because, unlike most people here, we both know what it's like to be shot at.

In Jeff's case, the experience was racked up doing private security work somewhere in Iraq—"outside the Green Zone" is as specific as he's ever gotten. He's in his mid-to-late twenties, square-jawed, and sarcastic. His Glock 19 has a gunmetal shine where the finish has rubbed away from use. Compared to my chromed new toy, his gun is a battered workmanlike tool. I like that about him, too.

It's hard to have a conversation with ear protection on and guns going off a few feet away. We lean through the lane openings, watching shooters work through the course. Tonight there's a cardboard wall with a window in the middle. Downrange, two IDPA cardboard bad-guy targets are staggered on the left side of the wall, one at five yards and the other at ten. Through the window, a bad guy becomes visible, most of his body shielded by a hostage target, and on the right side of the wall a crowd of three bad guys stands between five and seven yards away. The shooter takes cover on the left, puts two rounds on each target, reloads, then puts one in the head of the hostage taker through the window. To finish, he angles around the wall's right edge to put two rounds each on the three final targets. All this with the stopwatch running.

"Right," Jeff says. "This would happen in real life."

I shrug. "It's just a game, but you wouldn't be here if you didn't like it."

He smirks and turns back to the range. One of the hardcore shooters is getting ready to run the course. He wears a white germ mask over nose and mouth, marking him as one of the club's several handloaders. For economy, since they're sending so many rounds downrange, these guys make up batches of their own ammo at home. When they get together, they brag to each other about their "lead count"—not the number of bullets they've churned out of their presses, but how much lead has infiltrated the bloodstream as a consequence.

Jeff sighs. "Watch this guy."

The shooter stands still, waiting for the buzzer with his hands raised. Once it sounds, he pistons his arm down, clears his holster, and starts firing. Before the spent brass of his initial shots reaches the ground, he's already reloading and lining up the hostage shot through the window. The speed and economy of motion is something to behold. After the last round is fired, he keeps his weapon leveled, scanning back and forth like he's expecting one of the cardboard adversaries to get up. Then he unloads and re-holsters.

"Perfect round," someone says.

Glancing down the lanes, I see the timekeeper shaking his head in admiration.

But Jeff looks amused. "I wouldn't want him on my side."

"Seriously?" I say. "He looked good to me."

"I doubt that, Roland. You saw the way he uses cover? Just enough to satisfy the rules. If those targets could shoot back, believe me, he wouldn't be leaning out that way."

A couple of shooters in front of us glance back, not liking what they're overhearing. I know better than to try and shut him up, though. A little experience combined with the arrogance of youth is a potent combination.

"Now *you*," he says. "You I'd take with me into combat."

"You would, huh?"

"Maybe not with that fancy gun." He smiles. "But yeah, I would. I can tell who'd keep his head when the flare goes up and who wouldn't. You can handle yourself, I bet."

"I'm flattered."

"Whatever."

The line advances and we get closer to the front, with members crowding behind us once they're done. The middle shooters are mostly citizens. They joined the club after getting their Texas CHLs, concealed handgun licenses, or maybe they grew up in the gun culture like I did and the club offers an escape from the banking or lawyering or used-car dealing.

The club draws a strange cross section of Houston society. It's all male, but apart from that fairly diverse. Hispanics and Asians, whites, blacks, some with money to burn and others scrimping to afford the gear. Meticulously law-abiding to a man, though not without some grumbling about the ATF and the administration. There are short-bar-reled, high-capacity assault rifles on sale up front, with thirty-round clips, flash suppressors, and collapsible stocks thanks to the lapse in the assault-weapons ban. But most of the guys out here seem to think that'll all disappear at a moment's notice. At least they tell themselves that to justify the next big-ticket purchase. I know the type from working for my uncle.

As the shooters progress, Jeff keeps a running commentary on their technique, half of it lost to the muffled noise. He can't help it. Whenever the rules don't match up to his take on reality, he has to open his mouth.

"Don't you think you're stating the obvious?" I ask. "The point isn't to replicate a gunfight; it's to have some fun while working on the repetitive skills that would come in handy in real life—reloads, clearing a jam, whatever."

A couple of shooters nearby grunt their approval. They're a little tired of what they see as his bragging. Noticing this, Jeff concedes with a good-natured shrug. "I hear you, but what can I say? I run my mouth under pressure."

Now it's my turn to say, "Whatever." I have a good sense how Jeff would operate under real pressure, just like he has of me.

When his turn comes, he gives me a *watch this* look. He approaches the start line, crouches slightly, and raises his hands. At the buzzer he goes into action. It takes me a moment to realize what he's doing. Every movement mimics the masked shooter from before. The timing is identical, like he's imitating a film running in his head. The bullets even perforate the targets in more or less the same places. At the finish he scans back and forth.

"Wow," somebody says.

"He's just a show-off."

"If he can shoot like that," I say, "then who cares?"

Muscle memory is one thing. Reproducing someone else's action like that, after an interval of time—I've never seen anything like it. The timekeeper notes the scores on his clipboard without giving anything away. From this I gather Jeff finished a hair quicker than the man he was copycatting.

"That was amazing," I tell Jeff when he files back.

He pats my shoulder. "Get 'em, killer."

I toe the start line and take a deep breath. The buzzer sounds. I draw and move forward to the edge of the cardboard wall, double-tapping each of the targets. At the window, though, a needle of pain shoots up into my back. I try to ignore it. During my reload, I fumble one of the fat Browning mags, watching it bounce to the ground. I leave it, slotting the fresh one into place, then take the hostage shot. Everything's a blur, and then I'm at the right-hand side of the wall, blazing away at the final trio.

I put my gun away, embarrassed.

"You've got a failure to neutralize," the timekeeper says, meaning I missed one of the bad guys entirely.

The safety officer, standing off to the side, adds: "Also got a hit on a non-threat target."

I turn around and glance through the window. Sure enough, the hostage has been clipped in the region of the right shoulder.

Returning to the lanes, dragging my sore leg a bit, I smile awkwardly and feel the heat rising in my cheeks. Since I started, I've never dropped below the top third of shooters. This is a disastrous showing. I want to get out of here. Back at my spot I begin packing my gear.

"Don't let it bother you," Jeff says.

"I think I'm done for tonight."

He watches me. "Hey. Roland. You wanna get a beer or something."

"Maybe next time."

"Seriously," he says. "I'd really like to talk."

The guys around us give me pitying looks, apart from a couple of underperformers who just look satisfied, and one or two who won't meet my eye.

"Better luck next time," one of them says.

"I'm getting out of here," I tell Jeff. "We'll hang out some other time."

He looks like he might insist, but seeing my agitation, relents instead. "No problem. We'll do it another week."

I sling my bag and get out of there, not even bothering to wait for the final scores to be calculated. With my penalties I'll be at the bottom.

I don't need anybody to remind me of that.

Driving home, I check my phone for missed calls. Maybe Charlotte tried to return mine from earlier in the evening. There's nothing from her, but Bascombe called and left a voicemail, telling me to get in touch no matter what the time. I hit the redial button and wait.

"You and me have a special errand to run in the morning," he says.

"And what's that?"

"Search me. After you left, I got a strange call from a special agent at the FBI. You ever heard of Bea Kuykendahl?"

"Kuykendahl like the road?" There's a stretch of road in the northwest suburbs by that name, pronounced something like *Kirk-en-doll.*

"Apparently so. She's the one who called."

"Never heard of her. What did she want?"

"What she wants is for us to meet her at the field office. She wouldn't say what it was about, but I have a good idea."

"Are you going to share, sir?"

"Well, I got this call maybe half an hour after I checked on your John Doe's DNA test results. And it came on my cell, March, not my office line. Agent Kuykendahl made a point of asking us to be discreet."

My mind whirls with possibilities, the humiliation on the range all but forgotten.

"If I didn't know better," he says, "I'd guess that we've got a hit on our identification. And whoever our victim is, he had something to do with the Feds."

INTERLUDE : 1986

After the passage of years, I can't recall whether or not Sgt. Crewes gave Magnum his nickname, but he was certainly the first to use it in my hearing. On a rainy Friday afternoon, as I sat at my desk watching the clock tick down, mentally planning my fifty-odd-mile drive over to Alexandria, where I hoped to meet a girl and catch a movie, Crewes appeared in my doorway holding a fierce-looking plastic gator. Without any explanation, he shifted my stapler and tape dispenser around to make room for the animal.

"You prefer it with the jaws facing you, or facing the door?"

"Facing the door," I said. "What's the deal?"

"I believe it's intended to instill fighting spirit. Everybody's getting one."

I reclined in my chair, smiling. "I'm going to miss all this."

My four years were counting down quickly, and while I'd originally planned to re-up for life, making a career of the U.S. Army, somewhere between getting my commission after ROTC and my most recent assignment to the MP battalion at Ft. Polk, Louisiana, all that had changed. At the time, I couldn't have put my finger on the inciting incident. Looking

41

back, it was probably the ball I had reluctantly attended in Austin the year before, invited by a fellow officer to make up the numbers, instructed to wear my dress blues. There I met Charlotte for the first time. Several years would pass before we saw each other again. But it was a fateful night.

Sgt. Crewes, who'd put in eighteen of his twenty years, including a wild and well-remembered tour as an MP in Saigon, looked at me like I was crazy. However surreal military life could get—and he made no excuses on that score—compared to the insanity of the outside world, it all made sense. But then Crewes had come back from Germany with a cherished Audi coupe, which he lovingly detailed every other weekend, and a foulmouthed, chain-smoking bride he called his Marlene Dietrich. He was no judge of normality.

Something about the tail end of the plastic gator didn't look right to me, so I rotated him so that the painted white teeth and the red mouth growled up at me.

Crewes stood at ease in the doorframe, arms crossed. "When you've got your gator squared away, sir, you're wanted in Major Shattuck's office on the double."

"Why didn't you tell me?" I jumped from my chair, excited to be called and equally anxious that whatever duties the major had in mind would make me late for my evening plans. As I passed, the sergeant shook his head and smiled for the millionth time at the irrationality of the officer class, the way a misogynist smiles at the ways of women. I liked Shattuck, but for the sergeant's benefit I called over my shoulder: "What does he want this time?"

The sound of Crewes chuckling made me happy.

"Don't complain," he said. "You'll get to meet Magnum face-to-face."

On the stairwell between floors, I paused, but not to wonder who Magnum was. I felt ashamed, as I often did after an encounter with Sgt. Crewes. I'd made a cheap crack in hope of pandering favor. He'd laughed, but the joke was on me. Didn't the silver bar on my shoulder mean anything? Not for the first time I cursed myself for being such a bad, such a *weak* officer, then took comfort in the thought that I wouldn't be one for much longer. Life had other plans for Roland March.

Though he'd never seen combat, never fired a single shot in anger, in his sharp-creased woodland camo BDUs, Maj. Shattuck looked the part of a battlefield commander. Whenever Shattuck arrived on scene, men fell naturally into line. I'd seen generals who couldn't boast the same. The way he carried himself reminded me of a fishing line with a little slack left in, ready at the first sign of action to be pulled taut. I'd actually practiced this stance in the mirror, hoping I might become a better officer by looking the part.

I found him at his rain-streaked window taking in the gray skies, his hands clasped at the small of his back. The air-conditioning formed condensation at the four corners of the glass. Before I could announce myself, he turned and motioned me to stand at attention in front of his desk. I could perceive from the corner of my eye a second man in the room, a slack civilian seated on the stiff vinyl couch beside the entrance, his arm draped languidly along the back of the sofa. This, presumably, was Magnum.

"Now," Shattuck said, addressing the man on the couch, "I'd like you to repeat what you've just told me in the presence of this officer."

The iron in his tone was unmistakable. Shattuck was angry.

Magnum answered with a snort, a response so unexpected that I turned my head to look. He wore a charcoal suit and a black knit tie, his thick eyebrows balanced by the full mustache. A long, pale face with a hint of a smile on the lips. Laugh lines that bracketed the mustache in parentheses. He wasn't cowed by the major's authority. Instead, he seemed amused.

"You're not going to say anything?" Shattuck demanded.

"Hey," Magnum said. "No offense." He raised his hands in a gesture of surrender. "I guess I'll get out of here and leave you to it. Just thought maybe I could spare us both some trouble."

He eased himself off the couch.

"I'd like you to repeat your offer in Lieutenant March's presence."

"Is that his name, this witness of yours?" Magnum peered at the name above the breast pocket of my fatigue jacket, like he doubted the major's words. "Well, now, Lieutenant"—he patted my shoulder in a familiar way—"I expect we'll be seeing more of each other."

And with that, he walked out. The major let him go.

"Close the door," he said.

I did.

"If you see that man, if he asks for anything or seems to be engaged in any activity out of the ordinary, I want you to inform me immediately."

"Sir."

"I'm serious, Lieutenant March. Whatever you may think, men like that are nothing but trouble."

"Sir," I repeated. I hadn't been thinking anything at all.

The major dismissed me and I went downstairs in search of Crewes, finding him in the corridor outside my office. Waiting for me, I realized, which sent a slight thrill through me. Crewes was as anxious to hear what had happened as I was to talk about it.

"Well? What happened in there?"

I stopped myself. Maybe I shouldn't say anything.

"What happened in there, *sir*," I said, channeling Shattuck for an instant, then immediately feeling stupid.

"All right." The sergeant narrowed his eyes. "What happened in there, *sir*?"

Then I told him, ignoring my inner disgust at my own weakness, the words coming out in an eager rush. Once I'd spilled, it was his turn. "So you wanna tell me what's going on?" I asked. "Who is this Magnum guy? And where does he get off disrespecting the major like that?"

"What do *you* think he is?"

"How should I know?"

"Really?" He shook his head at my ignorance. "That's your best guess?"

He led me into my office and closed the door. Before saying anything, he took me to the blinds for a look at the parking lot and, beyond it, the parade grounds. Magnum was crossing the lot with a newspaper to shield him from the rain, heading toward a big Buick with tinted windows. Slouched elegantly on the bumper, a brown-skinned man in woodland camo smoked a thin cigar, indifferent to the rain.

"There are about a dozen of them," Crewes said, pointing to the smoking man. "The generalissimos of tomorrow. Supposedly the course they're on is something to do with logistics, but you don't have to be a rocket scientist to know that's just a euphemism for counterinsurgency. And get this: none of them have last names. It's just Juan and Pedro and Carlo and Jaime and Jesus. That one there is César—they pronounce it *say-czar*—so I reckon he's the boss man."

"Maybe that's just his name."

"Maybe," he said. "They don't wear their own uniforms, either. We have guests on base all the time—those West Germans, for example—but they don't wear BDUs from the PX, Lieutenant. These boys are special."

"Meaning what?"

"Meaning they're from some Latin American banana republic, and they're not here to learn how to service their country's newly purchased helicopters. They're learning how to throw Marxist rebels out of them."

I gazed down at the man leaning against the Buick. From this distance it was hard to tell, but he seemed to be conscious of my presence. He flicked his cigar away and said something to the approaching Magnum, who paused to glance in my direction. Magnum smiled, then ditched the sodden newspaper and got behind the wheel of the Buick. Before joining him, the generalissimo of tomorrow aimed a mock salute at my office window.

"All right, then," I said. "So what does that make Magnum?"

"What else?" Crewes said. "CIA."

CHAPTER 4

In front of the shaving mirror, over weak coffee of my own making, weaving through early morning traffic on my way downtown, I keep trying to convince myself that a summons from Special Agent Bea Kuykendahl might be a good thing. Maybe my case is already in the air, arcing toward the end zone, and all I have to do is make the catch. Bascombe's already waiting for me in the garage, and I imagine he's going through a similar thought process in his mind.

"I'll drive," he says, motioning me toward the passenger door of his car.

"This might turn out to be positive, you know."

Bascombe's long arms and six-foot-four frame hunch behind the wheel. His knees barely fit under the console. He sighs. "Anything can happen."

The reality is, I've never put a request into the system and gotten a phone call from the FBI. That's not how it works.

What I'm anticipating is something like this: a bunch of Feds in dark suits lined up on one side of a conference table, a lot of bureaucratic doublespeak passing for interagency cooperation leading up to an assertion of jurisdiction. Bridger's hunch about the Mexican mafia comes back to me, along with what Lorenz said about al-Qaeda cells.

"This is a homicide," I say. "The body's on our patch. If they have something to offer, fine, but that's where I'm drawing the line."

"Hey, if we *could* unload this on 'em, I'd be more than happy to. It's not like we're making any progress. Unfortunately."

"Yeah, I know."

To reach the field office, we have to take I-10 to the Loop, then drive up the Northwest Freeway to 1 Justice Park Drive. As we approach, there's a run-down looking donut shop on W. 43rd, so I suggest stopping off to pick up a box for our FBI colleagues. The lieutenant just shakes his head. "You're always trying to win friends and influence people, aren't you?"

Bascombe uncoils himself and we check through security, joining a crowd of arriving government workers at the elevators. My stomach rumbles—donuts don't sound half bad at the moment—but thanks to a random assortment of over-the-counter painkillers I found in the medicine cabinet this morning, my bum leg feels pleasantly numb. The doors slide open and we shoulder our way in. Just as the elevator closes, a voice calls from outside.

"Lieutenant Bascombe, is that you?"

"Hold the door," he says.

We push our way back out, ignoring grunts of frustration from our fellow passengers. Outside, a serious-looking blonde, maybe five-foot-two without her heels, in jeans and a fatigue jacket, extends a hand to the lieutenant. Her rolled-up sleeve reveals a man's diver watch, worn backward with the face inside the wrist. FBI credentials dangle around her neck.

"I'm Bea Kuykendahl," she says.

The lieutenant introduces himself, then turns to me.

"I'm familiar with your work," she tells me. "I did a little digging when your name cropped up."

"Okay."

She pats my arm. "Don't worry, it was mostly good."

"That's a relief. Should we go up?"

She looks us both over, as if making a decision. "No, actually, we're heading somewhere else. I have something to show you."

Bascombe and I exchange a look.

"Lead the way," he tells her.

At first it looks like she's taking us back outside, but before we reach the security scrim, Bea Kuykendahl guides me toward a secure door, using a key card to pass through. A flight of concrete stairs leads down to another door, then into a long, bare corridor. She keeps a few feet ahead, her heels clicking on the hard tile. My stereotype of FBI women includes pinstripes, pearls, and law degrees. They're well put together, with a bit of attitude to go with it. To be honest, my wife Charlotte fits the mold.

Bea Kuykendahl, by contrast, has a short-haired, gamine look—half butch, half kid—her side arm jutting incongruously from her hip. Pale skin, fair hair, blue-gray eyes, and broad cheeks. She has more earrings in her ear than I thought the G-Man rulebook allows. She can't be much older than thirty, and she dresses like an undercover agent on TV.

"Where exactly are you taking us, Agent Kuykendahl?" I ask.

"You've never been down in the basement before? This is where they keep the troublemakers. And call me Bea."

We round a corner into another hallway, this one lined with doors. Bea uses her card again, ushering through an unmarked entry into a separate office suite.

"This is the bullpen," she says, waving her hand to encompass a large open space with a long table at the center. On the walls, banks of computer terminals, maps, and a couple of whiteboards covered in scrawls of various colors. "We coordinate operations from here. You won't be meeting the rest of the team, I'm afraid. I thought it would be better to keep things simple."

She takes us through the open room pretty quick, like she doesn't want us paying too much attention to the papers lying around. In back, there are several glass partition walls separating individual offices from the main area. She shoves open the one on the end, motioning us inside. The lights come on automatically, motion sensitive.

Bascombe sits in the available guest chair and I move to the corner. Bea grabs a rolling chair from outside and scoots it my way, then goes around the desk. In front of her, there's an inch-thick stack of paper hidden inside a report cover. She drops it into a drawer, then edges her chair forward, clasping her hands in the empty space where the papers had been.

"Well," she says. "Thanks for coming."

Bascombe nods.

"You're probably wondering what this is all about."

Neither of us replies.

"Okay, let's get the tough stuff out of the way first. As you can see, I'm not making you jump through any hoops. I could've made this hard, but that's not my style. There aren't any supervisors here to get in the way. No liaison officers or anything like that. I could've done this the usual way, but to be honest, I don't think there's time. I wanted to talk face-to-face, to lay all my cards out on the table. This seemed like the best way."

She waits for a reply.

"Maybe you should start by putting us in the picture," I say.

"All right."

She opens another drawer, pauses, then shuts it. Then she rolls her chair to the side like she's going to reach for something in the stack of files on her credenza. But she doesn't.

"The thing is . . . Let me go back a little. . . ."

Under the fluorescent light, her face seems impossibly unlined, the skin taut as a child's.

"Early yesterday morning," she begins, "I got some unfortunate news. Your department submitted DNA samples to NCIC and they came back with a hit—"

"That's news to us."

She holds up her hand. "Bear with me. I delayed the results. I wasn't sure what to do. What you have to realize is, the person you got a match for wasn't dead."

"I have a headless body in the morgue that begs to differ."

"Yes, *all right,*" she snaps, her hands clasping again. A vein appears in her smooth forehead. "I understand that. But at the time, I wasn't aware that he was dead." She takes a deep breath, lets it out. "I knew your victim, Detective March. He worked for me."

"What?" Bascombe says. "You mean, here?"

"He wasn't an FBI employee, Lieutenant. He was an asset. He was working undercover as part of this operation. The last contact we had with him was two weeks ago, and at that time everything was fine. So you can imagine my surprise when your test results popped up."

"So you *can* identify my victim?" I ask.

The implications are electrifying. My John Doe not only has a name, but his death has a context. Under the circumstances, the FBI might be able to name not just the victim but his likely killer.

"I can identify him, yes."

"Why do I sense a 'but' coming?" Bascombe asks, creaking forward in his chair.

She responds with a pained smile. It dawns on me that Bea has more than a name to give. She knew this man. She felt responsible for him, at the very least. To her, this is more than just a case to solve.

"I'm sorry if I was a little blunt before," I say. "I realize what a shock this must be. But you're in a position to help. Not only can you identify the victim, but I'm guessing you might have a good idea what happened to him—and where. If we're putting all our cards on the table, the fact is, we don't have much to go on."

"I figured as much," she says. "There's a problem, though, and that's why you're here. Like I said, I could identify him . . . but I can't."

"You don't really have a choice. You can't obstruct a homicide investigation."

"If I don't," she says, "then you'll have another homicide on your hands."

I start to answer, but Bascombe puts a hand on my arm. "Let her explain, March. Stop interrupting."

Another deep breath. "Like I said, he was working undercover. It seems obvious that something went wrong, that somehow his cover was blown. If you release his identity to the media and start investigating his murder, then we'll be confirming to the people who killed him that they were right."

"Does that matter at this point?"

"It does," she says. "He's not the only person we have undercover. Someone had to vouch for him, and if his cover was blown, that someone is in a lot of danger."

After a pause, Bascombe edges forward a bit more. "If they killed one, what makes you think the other isn't already dead?"

"I know for a fact he isn't. We've been in communication."

"And he said he was in danger?"

"That's why we're here," she says. "Let me spell it out. I can't let you have an ID on your victim, because it would put the life of my last remaining asset in jeopardy."

"So what are you asking me to do? Leave him in the freezer?"

She blinks. "I'm not asking more than that. You're not going to like this, Detective, but I don't see that you have any choice. Not unless you want to be responsible for a man's death."

"Go on."

Bea's hand goes back to the files, removing one from the top of the stack. She hands it across the desk to me. Inside, there's a glossy photo of a Caucasian male in his mid-thirties, a curly-haired man with thick eyebrows and the hint of laugh lines on either side of the mouth. There are also photocopies of a Texas driver's license, a CHL, and a U.S. passport. Behind a stapled stack of typed pages, there's also a Federal Firearms License—an FFL, required for gun dealers.

The name on all the documentation is the same: BRANDON FORD.

"This is him?" I ask. "Brandon Ford."

"It is as far as you're concerned."

Bascombe snatches the file. "Let me see that." He flips through the pages quickly. "This is his cover, is that what you're saying?"

"Correct."

"What we're looking for is a positive identification. This doesn't do it. Brandon Ford doesn't exist. We're not in the business of investigating people who don't exist."

"Well, you are now."

They stare each other down, the big lieutenant and the slender, slight FBI agent. Her eyes shine with—what? Anger? Determination?

At least it's obvious now why she didn't bring in a bunch of supervisors and liaisons. She doesn't have any institutional authority to assert. She knows what she's doing is, at best, unorthodox, probably unethical, and possibly illegal. Not that things like this don't happen. They just don't happen officially. The only authority she can call on here is moral. Work with me or you'll get somebody killed.

"It's not that I don't want to help you," I begin.

"Detective, here's what I want. You have to leave here determined to investigate the murder of Brandon Ford. He's a licensed gun dealer, he's underwater on his mortgage and in danger of foreclosure, he's got an ex-wife and two kids who need support every month, and he's desperate for cash. So desperate that he'd be happy to supply anyone who asks with any quantity of AK-47s they require. That's who's in your morgue, and that's what you have to tell the media. When you do, the people responsible for . . . Brandon's death will second-guess themselves. They'll think their suspicions were wrong."

"With all due respect," I say, "this man wasn't just executed. He was tortured. Presumably they were trying to make him talk—"

"I'm aware of that."

"Don't you think, under the circumstances, that you'd be better off pulling out your other asset? There's no way of predicting what might happen."

She glares at me, stony-faced. "That's not an option, I'm afraid."

Though she may look young, though she may look like a pushover, Bea Kuykendahl has a spine. She's not about to give ground, which means we're at an impasse. I can feel it, and so must Bascombe. He shifts uncomfortably, not too pleased with the choice before him.

"I can take this?" I ask, rising to my feet with the file in hand.

She waves her hand in permission.

"Ready, sir?" I ask.

I'm afraid he'll say something. Afraid he'll commit us to a course of action. I want more than anything to get him out of the room before that happens.

"Listen—" he says to her.

"We need to think this over," I say.

Bea squeezes her clasped hands. "Fine. Just remember what I told you. You're playing with a man's life, Detective."

She doesn't move to escort us out. As we leave the bullpen, the door opens and a couple of agents who look as young and disheveled as their boss file in. They lock eyes with us, clearly knowing our purpose here. I push past them, ignoring the hard looks.

Bascombe and I don't talk until we're outside, back in the car, sitting with the engine running and waiting for the air-conditioning to cool us down.

"That's not what I was expecting," I say. "I don't know what she expects me to do."

"You know exactly what she wants."

"Yeah, I just don't know how to go about doing it. How do you investigate someone who doesn't exist? Leaving him on the slab is one thing—that's bad enough—but going through the motions, pretending I'm on the case. That's just a waste of time."

"I don't know," he says.

I look at him, but he doesn't look back.

"It wouldn't require much. Just put the story out there, make a little bit of an effort. If that's enough to get her insider off the hook, maybe it's worth doing."

"You're serious, sir?"

He grips the wheel thoughtfully. "I think I am. That girl, I like her spunk. She's putting it on the line and I don't feel like disrespectin' that, not if we don't have to."

"I'd rather know whose murder I'm really investigating."

"You're a detective, March. Go find out."

The file feels heavy in my hand. Bending the rules doesn't bother me, and in a good cause I don't mind a little trouble, but I can't think when I've ever been in a situation like this. It doesn't feel right.

"What do I tell Lorenz?" I ask. "What do I tell the captain?"

He sighs. "Listen here. I wasn't gonna say nothing, but since keeping secrets is the order of the day. The captain's turning in his papers."

"*What?*"

"You remember last year, during the runoff elections? He got sucked into the politics and started making alliances. Well, Drew Hedges is a good man, but he's no kind of politician. What he did is, he alienated a lot of people. Burned himself good. And the result is, his job is up for grabs. There's a shakeup coming, and he's out. That's all there is to it."

"Hedges is out? But he's a cop's cop."

"Between you and me, he's ready. He told me after Ordway's retirement party that he felt like a dinosaur, and if he was never moving up, then what was keeping him from moving out?"

"That's ridiculous."

"That's the job. It got to him."

"So what does this mean?" I can hardly keep up, hardly process it all. "Who's moving into his office—you?"

He gives a mirthless laugh. "That what you think? No, man, it's not gonna be me. Maybe when Lee Brown was still mayor . . . but no. I don't have no idea. All I can tell you is, you need to ready yourself. And don't dump any of this on the captain now. He doesn't need the headache."

The sun beats down on us the whole drive back. I can feel myself getting hotter and hotter. Maybe the air-conditioning's giving out. Maybe the ozone up above is spread particularly thin. Or maybe I'm out of my depth for once, not sure what I'm about to get myself into. A man's life is at stake, Bea said, and for me that's new territory. Avenging the dead is my job. With this new mission I don't know where to begin.

And now the ground underneath me isn't solid anymore. Hedges gave me a second chance when everybody else—Bascombe included—wanted to kick me to the curb. One thing I never imagined was that I'd outlast Drew Hedges in Homicide.

CHAPTER 5

The file from Bea Kuykendahl's office rests in my battered leather brief-case along with my old Filofax, a couple of digital audio recorders, a camera, some cuffs, a spare mag, and a mess of loose pens and paper clips and plug-in chargers. When I reach my desk, I transfer the file to a locked drawer for safekeeping, then hang my sport coat—an unlined, lightweight hand-me-down from my wife's father—on the back of my ergonomic chair.

Lorenz pops over the cubicle wall, a satisfied grin on his face.

"What?" I ask.

"Take a guess."

"Come on, Jerry."

He produces a stack of paper from behind his back. "While you've been off doing whatever it is you do, I've got a name for JD. The match came back a half hour ago, and I've been doing some research. Guy's name is Brandon Ford. Age thirty-four, six-foot-one, and there's a Houston address. And guess what he does for a living. No? He's a gun dealer."

I take the printouts from his hand, flipping through the pages. Agent Kuykendahl is sure making this easy. But what kind of strings do you have to pull to seed the criminal database with false information? I wouldn't have credited her with having this kind of pull. And if she does, what was the point of bringing me into the picture? Handing the stack of pages back, I sink into my chair.

"Don't get too comfortable," he says. "We need to get moving on this. I found a number for the victim's ex-wife, so we can start with the death notification."

"Right."

But there won't be an ex-wife, of course. Brandon Ford only exists on paper. That's why Bea Kuykendahl needed to clue me in. She realized that with a little digging, we'd discover soon enough that we were investigating a lie.

"You ready to roll?" he asks.

"I just got here."

"What's the deal? You don't seem too jazzed about the big break. Yesterday we had nothing and now—"

"Okay, okay. Just give me a second and I'll catch up."

While he grabs his gear, I head to Bascombe's office to let him know what's going on. The computer match doesn't sit right with me. The more I contemplate the matter, the less I believe a special agent in the Houston field office can snap her fingers and make something like that happen. Whatever's going on, I know Bea wasn't straight with us this morning.

The lieutenant's office is empty. I ask around, and one of the new detectives points in the direction of the captain's door. The blinds are shut, so I approach with caution, tapping lightly on the doorframe. No answer.

Just leave it.

I turn to go. Heading out, I see Hedges coming from the break room with a steaming mug of coffee in hand. He gazes at his feet like he's afraid of tripping or possibly lost in thought. Based on the news Bascombe shared, I'm sure he is. As I pass, I'm almost afraid to interrupt.

"Sir?" I ask.

He pauses, steadying his mug with his free hand.

"I'm looking for the lieutenant. He's not with you?"

Stupid question. He glances side to side and cracks a halfhearted smile. "I don't see him. Do you?"

"Never mind."

"Is everything all right?" he asks.

I should be asking him the same question. "Fine, sir."

I get a few steps away, then he stops me. "Hey, March, you sure you're okay? You're walking kind of funny."

"It's nothing," I say. "I must have twisted something the other night when I took that spill."

"Get it looked at," he says, turning away.

All during the runoff election last year, he'd been an absentee boss, present in body but absent in spirit. Things got better, but never back to normal. Now there's a hollowness to him I don't like to see. Maybe it's just knowing that he's not long for the job.

"I'll do that, sir," I say. "Thank you."

His eyebrows raise a twitch at the thanks, but he doesn't say more. He heads back to his shuttered office as I run to catch up with Lorenz.

———

The sign pushed into the grass in front of Brandon Ford's house says FOR SALE, so the first thing Lorenz does is snatch a flyer from the plastic dispenser. The address has taken us all the way out to Katy, to a neighborhood offering LUXURY LIVING STARTING IN THE 300s, so new it could have been thrown up overnight. The brick-fronted houses squat massively on their lots, their wide concrete drives free of cracks and unspotted by grease. Instead of the typical suburban grid, they hunch beside gently curving streets arranged concentrically around a man-made lake. I see ducks swimming out there, and a spout of water that shoots up thirty feet.

"Price is a little high," Lorenz says, handing me the flyer. "But at least there's a pool."

To my surprise, the flyer gives the construction date as four years ago. In all that time, the surrounding properties have managed to stay pristine. Only half the houses along the road yield signs of habitation—a freshly waxed Tahoe, some abandoned toys, a yard card in the shape of a soccer ball giving the jersey number of the child within. One or two in addition to Ford's have Realtor signs, and even some that don't sport the empty drives and naked aluminum windows of homes completed but never occupied.

We walk to the front door, peering inside through the unobstructed side window. Past the carpeted stairway, there's a high-ceilinged great room with a gas fireplace and rustic-looking twisted iron chandelier and French doors that open onto the back patio. There's no furniture inside, no decoration on the towering walls.

"If he ever lived here," I say, "he doesn't anymore."

Lorenz heads around one side of the house and I take the other, glancing in windows, testing doors. The house is locked tight, but the garage door isn't. I push through into the stifling heat of the enclosed space. There are no vehicles inside. A wall of cardboard boxes three deep and five or six high occupies one side of the garage, each one labeled in black marker: OFFICE, CLOTHES, SHOES, CHINA, BEDROOM, TOYS. The list goes on. I run my finger over one of the boxes, leaving a trail in the dust. They've been in storage for a while.

Using my lockblade, I open a couple of the boxes to see if the labels and contents match up. They do. There's a box marked PHOTOS, which contains baby albums, framed wedding portraits, and stacks of loose pictures. I grab some and start sifting. The man in the tux kissing the bride, the man cradling the newborn in the crook of his arm is the same one in the photo Bea Kuykendahl gave me along with the file. This is a lot of trouble to go through to build a cover. Too much.

"What did you find?" Lorenz asks.

"A bunch of photos."

I'm about to toss them back when one of the images catches my eye. It's a photo of Brandon Ford flanked by two other men, his arms draped over their shoulders. Behind him, an older woman looks into the camera, her eyes red from the flash. There's something about the expression on their faces—maybe the confidence of youth, maybe the camaraderie—that speaks to me. Here's my victim, alive and happy.

Seeing him that way helps to humanize him. I tuck the picture inside my jacket and close the box.

"I'm gonna call the ex-wife, since she doesn't seem to live here."

"I'll make the call," I say. "You drive."

I dial the number from the front seat of the car, the air-conditioner blasting. She answers after five or six rings, sounding frazzled and breathless. I can hear cartoons in the background, children's voices. I keep it brief, identifying myself and asking for a location where we can meet face-to-face. She gives me the address of an apartment complex on Westheimer outside Beltway 8, maybe halfway between our present location and downtown if we swing down south a ways. I tell her to expect us within the hour.

"What did she sound like?" Lorenz asks.

"She sounded young. She sounded confused, maybe a little worried. I could hear kids in the background. There were two in the photos."

While he drives, I kill time going through his research. Brandon Ford has a gun dealer's license, but he doesn't seem to have a storefront. Instead, he works out of a rental office on a by-appointment basis, special-izing in exotic longarms for collectors, everything from elephant guns to high-powered sniper rifles. According to his website, which Lorenz printed in its entirety, he also travels to a variety of Texas gun shows where he operates a booth.

"I printed out pictures from the site," he says.

"I see that."

They are low-resolution images. One depicts a tall curly-haired man in a blue polo shirt standing behind a table laden with imported tactical rifles. Not the AK-47s that Bea mentioned. These appear to be top-dollar European models. In the second photo, the same man wearing the same shirt poses with an old school FN FAL battle rifle mounted with a massive starlight scope, cutting edge in the seventies and eighties and no doubt highly collectable now.

"I'm surprised you can make a living that way," Lorenz says.

"Was he making a living? His house is on the market."

"What I mean is, it's weird people buy and sell this stuff."

"It's weird people buy guns in Texas?" I ask.

"This kind of gun, yeah. I mean, I'm on the front lines every day and I don't have an arsenal like that. I couldn't afford it, for one thing. Can you imagine knocking on this guy's door? He'd have the SWAT team outgunned."

I'm not interested in getting into an argument about guns. That's something I don't do anymore. I grew up with them, and to me you either get it or you don't. And if you don't, fine. Brandon Ford, if he really existed, would have gone through enough of a background check to put my mind at ease. He wouldn't worry me any more than the club members at Shooter's Paradise do. But I wonder what Lorenz would think of my extracurricular activities. All those armed citizens might freak him out.

Then again, maybe not. He surprises me sometimes. But there's no point in getting into all that. Brandon Ford doesn't exist. The photos, along with everything else, were staged. That's what I'm meant to believe, anyway. The question is, for whom? The way Bea made it sound, somebody wanted a big shipment of assault rifles, which suggests the Mexican cartels. The headlines have been full of Federal cases against dealers shipping their wares down south, profiteering from the drug war. The only problem with that theory is that a sting operation making use of a fake gun dealer would be designed to snare the buyer. If the buyer's a Gulf Cartel drug lord, what's the point? It's not like the Policía Federal or the DEA don't have enough on those thugs already.

"Is there something wrong?" Lorenz asks. "You've been funny all morning."

"Everything's fine."

Leaning over, he opens the glove compartment and shakes the ibuprofen bottle in my face. "Are you off your meds, is that it? I thought the leg was doing better."

"Just keep your eyes on the road," I say, shifting in the seat. "It's not my leg, anyway. It's something in my back. The pain is just a symptom. I must have pinched a nerve."

"All right." He tosses the bottle into my lap. "I just wish you'd get your head in the game. I can't be carrying you on this."

I flip on the radio, scanning the dial for some music.

"Hey, man. I'm just kidding. I'll carry you as far as I can."

He smiles and I smile back just to make him stop.

The woman comes to the door barefoot, wearing cuffed shorts and a white T-shirt. She says her name is Miranda Ford and she has a driver's license to back it up. She ushers us into a cramped apartment, a real step down from the house we've just seen. In the living room, a dark-haired toddler I recognize from the box of pictures scribbles on construction paper while a younger kid in a playpen watches him. She walks us past them to a kitchen table that's been set up as a home office. Underneath the table, there's a box like the ones stored in the garage, this one labeled CRAFTING, its flaps gaping. The table itself has been converted into work space. At one end there's a big flat-screen computer, and at the other a sewing machine lit up by an adjustable work lamp clamped to the table's edge. Lorenz asks and she explains that she makes purses and other bags and sells them online.

"That way I can stay home with the boys."

"And that's your only income?" I ask.

"I get money from my ex," she says, "and I work part-time for a friend of mine who opened her own shop."

I keep stealing looks at her, half expecting a wink of the eye or some other acknowledgment that this is all a sham. But if it is, they've gone through a lot of trouble. You don't stick a woman in an apartment with a fake ID and two prop kids on the off chance someone will go digging into a cover story.

She offers us something to drink—the options include water, Diet Coke, and apple juice—then clears some chairs for us to sit. I glance back at the children, not wanting to make a scene in front of them. For her part, Miranda Ford gives no sign of anxiety. As if the police are always dropping by and she's only mildly curious about our reasons.

"I wonder if we could talk somewhere private?" I ask.

"Of course." She looks around, then frowns. "Only there's not really any place besides the bedroom or the boys' room."

"Why don't we go out on the steps?"

She follows us reluctantly, telling the toddler she'll be just outside. He goes on ignoring our presence, scribbling hard with his crayon. On her way out, she turns up the volume on the cartoons.

The apartment's on the second floor. Lorenz and I descend the stairs a little ways, letting her sit on the top step. I show her the photo I took from the house.

"Can you identify this man?" I ask, tapping Ford's face.

"It's Brandon," she says. "My ex."

"And when was the last time you talked to him?"

She stops to think. "Maybe a week ago? I'm not sure. I can find out, though." She digs a phone out of her pocket and thumbs through the menu. "No, it was more like two weeks ago. He was doing a show and called from the road."

"A gun show?"

She nods. "Down in Corpus Christi. He wanted me to go pick up the house keys from his mother, in case the Realtor did any showings. We've been trying to sell our house. When there's a showing I go over and bake some cookies so the house smells good."

"Was he planning to be out of town long, then?"

"He travels a lot."

"And you haven't heard from him since that call?"

"If you're trying to find him," she says, "I'm not really the person to ask. You should check with his mother—that's her in the picture." She takes the photo and holds it toward me, her finger on the older woman with the red eyes. "Hilda. That's where I drop the kids when he's supposed to take them. The two of us don't really keep tabs on each other. We have our own lives. It's better that way."

Lorenz crouches down and takes his sunglasses off. "Ma'am, I'm sorry to have to tell you this, but we have some bad news."

As he goes on to break the news, Miranda's lip starts to tremble. A thick tear slides down her cheek and she wipes it away. I watch her, convinced the reaction is genuine. He explains when the body was found and where, but doesn't go into detail about the mutilation or torture. He doesn't need to. The shock of her ex-husband's death is enough.

Lorenz glances my way, gives me a questioning shrug. I nod for him to continue with his questions. Like a trouper, she endures them, answering in as much detail as she can. After a while, I tune them both out. I'm back in Bea Kuykendahl's office, reviewing everything the FBI agent said and left unsaid. None of it really makes sense. There's no way Brandon Ford isn't real, no way this shaken, bereaved girl isn't really his ex-wife.

I need to get out of here. I need to think. I need another talk with Agent Kuykendahl, too, and I want real answers this time around.

Miranda clears her throat, wipes her eyes one last time. "Am I—? I mean, is it me that's responsible for the arrangements? I don't know how it's supposed to work, but if we're not married anymore . . ."

"You mentioned his mother?" Lorenz says. "Hilda . . . was that her name?"

She nods and gives him an address and phone number, looking very relieved. But then her face clouds again. "What am I going to do? I *rely* on him to make ends meet."

"How long were you married?" I ask.

She stops to think. "He proposed after Tate was born. It lasted three years almost. We weren't happy, though. Brandon saw other women."

As we start to go, she watches us from the top step, her entwined hands pressing down against her stomach. She's looking at us, but I don't think she sees us. Her eyes are focused on the past. She seems to have forgotten us entirely, so I'm surprised when she calls down.

"Other women," she says, like she's finishing her thought from before. "There was somebody with him the last time. Somebody new. She waited in the car while he dropped off the kids. This was at Hilda's, and I'd been waiting inside for almost an hour. When he showed up, he didn't say anything about *her*, but I knew she'd been with my kids."

I climb the steps again, pausing beside her.

"This was a new girlfriend?" I ask.

She shrugs. "While we were talking inside, I looked through the window and saw her. She got out of the car and was standing on the curb, talking on her phone." Her eyes moisten. "That's who you should track down. She'd know better than me where Brandon's been."

I ask her to describe the woman.

"She wasn't pretty," she says quickly. "Kind of small and bony. Androgynous. She had choppy blond hair, and kind of dressed like a man . . ."

"Did you ask your boy—Tate? Did he know her name?"

Her face hardens. "She told them to call her Trixie."

"Like in *Speed Racer*?" I ask, showing my age.

She just shrugs. I thank her for the information and promise to get back in touch if we learn anything more.

On the way to the car, Lorenz scribbles down the name. "It's not much to go on."

"No, it's not," I say.

But it is. Given the fact that I met the woman she was describing just a few hours earlier, and that Trixie must be a preferable nickname for a woman whose parents saddled her with a name like Beatrix.

CHAPTER 6

As biker bars go, this one's pretty tame, sandwiched between a supersized Spec's Liquor and a retail chain cantina. The crowd packed onto the outdoor deck doesn't look particularly tough, mostly white suburbanites. The only cowboy boots are on the miniskirted ladies, the only motorcycles plastic imports with bold racing stripes. I pick my way through, dodging a waitress loaded down with sweating Dos Equis and Coronas.

The music inside is live. That's all it has going for it. Even the early evening drunks are having a hard time with the dancing. There's a lot of neon on the walls, a lot of yelling from table to table. It takes me a moment, scanning the darkness, to single out Bea Kuykendahl.

She may be small, but she knows how to take up space. She sits in a lazy sprawl, one arm draped over the back of her chair and her crossed legs resting on the opposite seat. Thick-soled work boots, faded jeans, and a tight, cap-sleeved black T-shirt revealing more muscle definition than I would have expected, reinforcing my earlier impression that she looks more like a teenaged boy than a grown woman.

Circling around, I approach her table from the side. I grab the back of the chair her feet are under, then yank it free.

"Hey, that seat's taken!" she barks. Then: "*Oh.*"

I spin the chair around and sit, crossing my arms over the back. "You can say that again, Bea. Or do you prefer to go by Trixie?"

"You followed me here?"

"I'm a man of many talents. I think we need to have a talk. I figured we might be able to converse a little more freely outside the office."

She leans forward over the table. "In case you haven't figured it out yet, I don't intimidate very easily. Throw your weight around all you want, Detective. Just be careful you don't throw your back out."

For a crazy moment I wonder if she's heard of my fall. But there's no way that could have reached her. Just a lucky jab.

"That story you told me, it doesn't add up. When I got back to the office, we had a match on Brandon Ford. I have a hard time believing you've got enough pull to make the computer spit out false identifications. If you could, why bother bringing me and my lieutenant into the picture at all?"

"You tell me," she says.

"At first I thought you had to, because with a little digging we'd have poked enough holes in the cover story to realize Brandon Ford wasn't a real person. But he is real, isn't he? I spoke to his ex-wife today, then I walked through his house. After that I did some asking around. The local gun dealers say he's been around on the scene a couple of years. Either this is the most elaborate cover story in history, or . . ."

"Or what?"

"Or you lied to us this morning."

"I lied to you? Knowing that you'd see right through me the moment you did a cursory check. Give me more credit than that."

"Ford's ex-wife gave me a description of a woman who was with him before his death. This woman told Ford's kids to call her Trixie. That was you."

"And?"

"And I want to know the truth about what's going on."

She glances around. "You really think this is the place to do this? I'm actually meeting people here. Why don't we handle this in a professional way—"

"This is a professional courtesy. You asked for a favor and you got it. You said there was a life at stake—fine. But now I think you were spinning us a tale, and even if I don't know what your angle is yet, I'll find out. I'm giving you a chance to clear things up right now, before it's out of your control."

Up onstage, the song ends, prompting desultory applause and a few tipsy hoots from the dance floor. The singer tips his straw hat back and says they're taking a break. The clapping intensifies.

"You're making a mistake here, March."

"That's all you're gonna say?"

"You're making this complicated when it ought to be very simple. Is it so hard for you just to follow my lead? If you go along and don't screw this up, at the end of the day you'll have a high-profile clearance you can add to your resumé. The alternative is, you get a man killed and torpedo a Federal investigation."

"I already heard the pitch," I say. "I want to know what's really going on."

"You know as much as you need to. More than that, actually. Tell me this, if what you say is true and Brandon Ford is too real to be a cover, then why would I bother handing you the file? If I knew you were going to get his name from NCIC and when you checked him out you'd be convinced, what was the upside for me?"

"I don't know. I was hoping you would explain that."

She shakes her head. "You're a piece of work. Now, will you get out of here? I've told you everything I'm going to tell you. Do whatever you want."

All the replies that come flooding to my lips would only sound ridiculous. The set of her jaw says she's unmovable.

"You've had your chance," I say, in spite of myself.

She greets this with a smirk.

On my way out I glance back. Bea still sits alone at the table. I'm tempted to hang around and see who's joining her—a friend, a colleague, someone I might be able to place?—but then the band members start climbing onstage again, reaching unsteadily for their microphone stands. I push my way through the loiterers at the door, glad to be back in the balmy night air. From the smell on the breeze I'm guessing we're in for more rain.

———

While I'm driving home, Charlotte calls from London. It's good to hear her voice, though she sounds too close to be so far away. She tells me about the people she's met, the places she's been taken to eat. She asks if I've been watching the news, because there are demonstrations on the streets. I haven't. She sounds disappointed.

"When things wrapped up in the city," she says, "the boys took a flight up to Scotland to play a few rounds at St. Andrews. I ditched them and went on my own little adventure. You really should have come, Roland. I went to Cambridge and to Ely Cathedral—it's the oldest Norman cathedral in the country—and I met a real-life vicar's daughter, if you can believe it."

I make the appropriate sounds at the appropriate intervals. I'm still preoccupied by the conversation with Bea, and getting angry about it. I need to focus.

"And what about you?" Charlotte asks. "What have you been doing with yourself?"

"Working."

"Just working?"

"We caught a nasty one after you left. But we don't need to talk about that."

"Are you all right? You sound kind of funny."

"It's nothing," I say. "I fell down the other day. I think I pulled something."

"You should go to the doctor, Roland."

"That's what Hedges told me. Speaking of which—" But no, there's no point in getting into that, either. "Never mind. I don't want to bore you with the office gossip. When does Ann get there? I saw Bridger the other day but forgot to ask."

"Tomorrow." Again, she sounds disappointed, like I should already know the answer. She went over her plans with me more than once before leaving. It feels like a lifetime ago.

"You should go see the Robbs," she says.

That old standby. I must really sound bad.

"I'll do that," I tell her. "Oh, by the way, I saw Cavallo the other day, too. She says hello."

"That's nice. How was she?"

"I think there might be some trouble at home."

"Really?"

The words are out before I can stop them. I'm as surprised as Charlotte is. I try to hedge a little, saying something about the stress Cavallo's husband is probably under, reintegrating into civilian life after so many tours overseas. She must sense my discomfort. She doesn't ask anything more.

"Was it hard for you," she asks, "when you first got out of the service?"

"That was a lot different. I spent my time at Fort Polk, Louisiana, not Bagram. In my day, we considered Grenada quite a military operation."

"Those were the days," she laughs. "Such an innocent time."

"Right."

I reach my exit on I-10 but I keep driving. I listen to her voice, cruising absently through the cones of light arcing down onto the highway. Just talk, baby. Talk. Let me hear the words crash in my ears like waves on the beach, so much reassuring white noise. When she's said all she can think to say, we sit together silently. I listen to the road under my tires and the sound of her breath over the international line.

"What can you tell me about Brandon Ford?" I ask.

The man across the counter crosses his hairy arms, the jeweled dial of his Rolex catching the morning light. His name is Sam Dearborn, proprietor of Dearborn Gun and Blade. He helped me on a case last year, proving himself to be a source of all kinds of knowledge.

"What makes you think I know more than the other guys you've talked to? Brandon's all right in my book. He's a small-timer, though. For the most part, he goes after the black rifle market, the weekend warriors with money to spend. Those guys aren't so interested in the craftsmanship or the history. You tell them this is the rifle Delta Force is currently using to punch holes in the mullah's turban, and all they wanna know is, 'How much?' I think he was also selling some big-game rifles to fellas daydreaming about going on safari."

"I already know all this."

He rolls his eyes. "What did I just tell you? You don't need me for this."

"That's not why I'm here. I just wanted to get it out of the way."

"Okay, then. Shoot."

"Here's the real question, Sam. What do you know about the Mexican cartels buying rifles in bulk from Texas dealers?"

At first he doesn't react, like he didn't hear the question. Then he glances down the length of his counter, scratching at the gold necklace dangling in the opening of his shirt.

"You're serious?" He snorts the words out. "This is for real?"

"Relax. I'm not accusing you of anything. If anybody knows what's going on out there, it's you. If anybody's got his finger on the pulse—"

"Yeah, yeah," he says. "Spare me. You just took me by surprise, that's all. That kind of business, it doesn't go through guys like me. Just so we're clear."

"Understood. So how would it work?"

The simplest way, he says, is for a straw purchaser to walk into a gun store from off the street. Flush with money from the cartel, he buys five or ten assault rifles in his own name, then hands them over once he's taken possession.

"A straw purchase is illegal, but if I'm the one selling the guns, how do I know you're not buying them for yourself? You pass the background check, you get the weapons."

A gang making straw purchases, even in small quantities, can amass quite an arsenal over a short period of time, stockpiling the rifles for transport to Mexico. Assuming they spread the activity out, it might go unnoticed. If they hit the gun shows, buying from private sellers to take advantage of the so-called loophole, then they can fly under the radar longer.

"But if a guy wants twenty rifles," I say, "and he's covered in tats and takes a rubber-banded wad of cash out of his pocket to pay for them, that's gonna raise some red flags, right?"

"You ever heard of racial profiling? That's against the law." He chuckles at his own joke. "Sure, common sense dictates that if a gangbanger walks in wanting twenty-five identical assault rifles, some-thing's up with that. But you'd be surprised how many people don't have common sense. And honestly, even a gun dealer's gotta feed his family. You know how it is. Didn't you say your uncle used to be in the business?"

"My uncle wouldn't have sold to somebody he got a bad vibe from. He reserved the right not to serve whoever he didn't like."

"Those were different times."

"And anyway, you don't make a living by arming the cartels."

He shrugs. "The guns may flow down, but the drugs are flowing up. We may be hurting them a little, but they're hurting us a lot."

I hold up my hand. "You're not helping yourself with that argument. They're not just killing each other down there. They're killing cops."

"I'm not saying it's right. You wanted to know how it works, so I told you."

"Let me ask a different question. If I was a gun dealer and I wanted to get in on the action, how would I go about it? The way you're talk-ing, it sounds like that initiative's on the cartel's side. What if I wanted to make a big score?"

"And by 'you,' you mean Brandon Ford?" He shakes his head. "I think you've got the wrong end of the stick. Brandon doesn't hustle the cheap stuff. If you want a Romanian AK, which sells for four hundred, you don't call in a specialist."

"For the sake of argument, though, assume he wanted to sell to the Mexicans."

"He'd have to know somebody, I guess. They're not a number you can call to volunteer your services. I assume he could have made a contact. If you're asking me for a name, I don't have one. This is pure speculation."

A name is exactly what I want. If I push too hard, I know he'll dig in. Before Sam Dearborn will cooperate, he needs a little time to think it over. I decide to give it to him.

"I appreciate your help," I say. "And if you think of anything else, you've got my number. It never hurts to have a cop in your debt."

"If you say so."

Back in the car, I unsnap my briefcase and pull the Filofax out. I keep a plastic divider tucked in next to the blank note sheets. Before I forget, I write down everything Dearborn told me. Looking at the process on paper, I'm baffled. The FBI operation must be about guns and the cartels, otherwise what would it have to do with Brandon Ford? What I can't figure out is why they would need him. The straw purchaser scenario doesn't fit here. Like Dearborn said, Ford would need some kind of contact with the cartel, someone he could approach with an offer to supply guns. But then I'm back to the original problem: what's the point of a sting operation targeting a notorious cartel? Is it really so hard to make a case against the drug lords?

I dial Lorenz on the phone.

"How'd it go?" he asks.

"Nothing here. But I just had a thought. Where are the guns we're thinking Ford wanted to sell? I didn't see a gun safe when we went through the house."

Silence.

"Maybe you should swing by that office he rents. If there are crates of AK-47s lying around, we might want to know."

"I'm on it," he says. "You wanna meet me?"

"I trust you, Jerry."

He sounds gratified as he hangs up. The fact is, I already know what he's going to find. There won't be any guns in the rental office, just like there weren't any at the house. Whatever Brandon Ford was up to, however it connects to Bea's Federal operation, it doesn't have anything to do with assault rifles, and maybe nothing to do with drug dealers, either. There's something here I'm not seeing. A connection I have yet to make.

Maybe what I need on this is a fresh set of eyes.

CHAPTER 7

I shoulder my way through the entrance to Homicide and sense right away something's going on. The detectives stand clustered in groups of three and four, conferring in hushed tones. The ringing phones go unanswered. Lorenz has already left, so after slinging my gear into my cubicle, I raise my eyebrows at a passing colleague. He raises his back but says nothing. Not good.

Through the open door I can see Lt. Bascombe poised over his desk, all the weight on his fingers like a runner in the starting blocks. He looks up at me without acknowledging my presence. When I start over, he comes around the desk, intercepting me outside the door. He puts a hand on my chest.

"What's up?" I ask.

He scans back and forth across the room, still looking through me. Like he's making sure I'm alone. Then he pulls me inside and closes the door.

"It's official," he says. "The captain's pulling people in one at a time to break the news."

"He's leaving?"

"That's the story. But like I told you before, what's really happening is, he's getting the push. I wasn't expecting it so soon."

Remembering my encounter with Hedges the day before, I shake my head. "He seems like a shadow of his former self."

"Yeah, well, that's not entirely his fault." He sits on the edge of his desk, motioning me into a chair. "I can't believe they're rushing him out like this. It's the politics, March. You end up on the losing side in this department and, I swear, they'll cut your throat."

"Maybe I should go see him."

"Don't be in such a rush," he says. "It's depressing. When they do you like this, they don't just can you. They also write the script. Not only do you have to leave, but you leave on their terms, giving their reasons, or else."

"Who's 'they'?"

He looks at me like I'm stupid.

"Anyway, can I run something past you, boss? I think that FBI agent is spinning us a yarn."

"You're one of those people who tells jokes at funerals, aren't you?"

"What do you want me to do? I think she lied to us."

Bascombe goes around the desk and slumps into his chair. The cushion hisses as it takes his weight.

"Go ahead, then."

I bring him up-to-date on everything, including Miranda Ford's description and my after-hours confrontation with Bea. As I talk, his expression goes from bored to mildly interested. By the time I'm done, he's leaning forward, elbows on the desk.

"Well, something's not right," he says.

"I know. So what should I do about it?"

"What *can* you do? Seems to me the only thing is to ignore what she told us. Pretend that meeting never happened. What does it actually change, after all? You got a hit on your victim, the identification's made, and he's a real person with a real history."

"Yeah, but Bea's working some kind of angle—"

"So what? If you take her story and set it aside, what are you left with? Some forward movement on your case. Whatever the FBI is or is not up to, we do one thing here and that's clear homicides. So that's what you do."

"You make it sound so easy."

"Unless something changes, I don't see what else you can do."

"I was hoping you would make some phone calls and see what you can find out about Bea and her operation."

"It was making phones calls that got us into this." He sighs. "Leave it with me, okay? I'll see what I can do. Don't expect any miracles, though, because I have my hands full at the moment. For the time being, ignore the FBI and just do your job."

On my way out I pause at the door. "Who's moving into the captain's office?"

He raises his palms. "I still don't know. And that right there should tell you something."

When my turn comes, I file into the captain's office, surprised to find his personal belongings—the books and knickknacks, the framed photos and diplomas—already packed into a row of boxes along the credenza. The skin on his head shines through his flinty close-cropped hair, making him seem older to me than he ever has before.

"I should have done this a long time ago," he says.

The euphemisms flow, and I sit there receiving them passively, not daring to question the script Bascombe says "they" have prepared. I owe this man. If it weren't for him, I wouldn't be here. Out of respect, I don't question anything he says. I nod in agreement, like I'm happy for him, like this is the best news he could have shared. Any other reaction would risk humiliation.

"Sir," I say, reaching across the desk to shake his hand. "It's been a real pleasure working for you. It won't be the same here without you."

He holds my hand a beat longer than is required, fixing his piercing eyes on me.

"Thank you, March. You know you've always had my respect."

I pull my hand back. "You've always had mine, too."

It's not fair.

Closing the door behind me, I walk out of Homicide and take the elevator down to the ground floor. A man like that, with the years he's put in . . . I go through the lobby past the front desk, pushing through the revolving doors out onto the sidewalk, into the searing brightness of midday. To go out like this, a whimper not a bang, and for what? For being ambitious. For getting on the wrong side of people who play the game better than him. But they don't run homicide squads better than him, because no one does. I take a deep breath, let it out. Take another. I close my eyes and try not to think. He doesn't deserve what they've dealt him. I'd pay them back if I could, if I even knew who they were.

Cars rush by, leaving the smell of exhaust in their wake.

I will know soon enough. When someone else takes his place.

My phone rings before I get back inside, Lorenz calling from Brandon Ford's office.

"There's a safe here," he says, "with a couple of rifles inside. There's something else down here, too. I think you should come take a look."

"What is it?"

"I'm not sure . . . a shrine? Newspaper clippings, photos, kind of a psycho wall."

"Snap some photos of it *in situ*, then bring it all down here."

He hesitates. "I'd rather you meet me. You'll see what I mean."

Instead of heading upstairs again, I go straight to the garage. It takes twenty minutes to get there, and another five to circle around, retracing my path along Westheimer until I figure out which of the half-empty low-rise office parks is the right one. The building's storefronts house a couple of pawnshops, a check casher, and a seedy-looking lingerie boutique. A sign in the parking lot lists the businesses inside. Brandon Ford's name doesn't appear.

I park next to Lorenz's car and go through the glass doors into a small air-conditioned entry with a row of mailboxes on one wall. Down a tiled corridor I hear the splash of a water fountain. As I follow the sound, the air grows humid. The corridor opens into a cathedral-like atrium, open in the center, its terra-cotta expanse filled with blinding sun from the overhead skylights. Around the shadowy perimeter, two floors of office space face the lobby like the split levels of an old-fashioned motor court.

The smell inside reminds me of when I was a kid and my aunt would lock me in the car on a hot day with the windows cranked down just an inch. As my eyes adjust, I see the water fountain, hedged in by thirty-year-old plastic bushes.

After ascending a flight of stairs, I find the right door. Lorenz answers on the first knock, like he's been waiting at the threshold all this time.

"It's like a time warp out there," he says.

The space Brandon Ford rented consists of three rooms. The reception space up front houses an empty desk. On the right, there's a hallway that leads to two offices. The front one contains the gun safe, its thick door hanging open to reveal a couple of black rifles. I peer inside. Tucked in back I find a short-barreled AK with a folding stock. This particular variant is called the Krinkov. To possess a short-barreled rifle of this sort legally, Ford would have had to jump through some NFA hoops, and it would only be transferrable to others willing to qualify the same way. I detach the banana mag—which is empty—and pull the breach open to make sure it's unloaded.

"Is there any paperwork on these?"

Lorenz pulls open a file cabinet in the corner. "There's a bunch in here, depending on what you're looking for."

On the shelf inside the safe, twenty-round boxes of Wolf 5.45 x .39mm hollow points are stacked on top of each other.

"It doesn't matter now," I say, putting the rifle back. "But we should probably make a call to ATF. I'm not sure what the procedure is when a gun dealer is deceased, but I don't think leaving these here is a good idea. How'd you open the safe?"

"Same combo as the one at the house. I found it in his bedroom nightstand."

"So where's this psycho wall?"

He points the way to the back office. I go inside, flipping on the lights. This is where Ford must have conducted business. The desk wraps around one corner with custom cabinets overhead, the doors ajar from Lorenz's search. The computer hums inside the footwell, but the twenty-inch monitor on the desk is dark, an add-on camera clipped to one side. On the opposite wall there's a corkboard covered in news clippings.

"Take a closer look," he says.

Some of the clippings are from the *Chronicle*, some are from the *Houston Press*. Some are printouts from the Internet, the URLs stamped on the outer margins. All of them concern the same story, and they are covered in ink underlining and bright yellow highlighting.

"You remember that incident?" Lorenz asks.

I nod silently.

Earlier this year, an HPD patrol car pulled over a man speeding on Allen Parkway after midnight. The uniforms—a rookie and his training officer—handled everything by the numbers. The rookie went to the driver's window while the trainer approached the other side. After shining his light into the car, the rookie exchanged words with the driver and then returned to the patrol car to run the license. All of this was captured on the dashboard cam.

While the rookie was out of the way, his trainer approached the driver's window. On the video, which was played over and over on the local news, the trainer suddenly backpedals and starts to reach for his side arm. There's a flash from the window, an orange tongue of flame, and the trainer rolls backward onto the pavement. He draws and fires while the rookie runs forward with his own weapon drawn, also firing.

He approaches the driver's window first, making sure the threat is neutralized, then goes to the trainer and helps him up. Thanks to his vest, the trainer is bruised but otherwise fine.

Watching the footage, things happen so fast. It's all straightforward and undramatic, the way fights mostly are. If you weren't paying attention, you might mistake the trainer's motion for a clumsy fall. The stakes were life and death, but they don't look it on camera.

When the uniforms made their report, the story got strange. According to them, the driver had refused to give his identification, claiming he had immunity. He told the rookie he worked for the CIA. Then he'd changed course and handed his license over. His name was Andrew Nesbitt, aged sixty-one, a well-off retiree with a house in River Oaks. When the trainer approached, sensing something wasn't right, Nesbitt grew combative and paranoid. He accused the officers of pulling him over without justification—and then, without warning, he produced a gun. It was a .32 Walther PPK, weapon of choice for James Bond.

"The guy wasn't just delusional," Lorenz says, lifting the corner of one of the clippings. "He was some kind of con man. He was, like, the president of the retired intelligence officers' club. Even the real spooks believed he was one of them."

"That's a theory. It's always possible he was telling the truth. There's no law that says retired case officers can't go nuts like everybody else. I bet they're more prone to it than most."

"But the government denied he'd ever been in the CIA."

I crack a smile. "They would, wouldn't they?"

Judging from the Internet printouts, the usual conspiracy theories must have started proliferating the moment the story broke. Ford tacked up a forum post providing an ersatz history of the former spook's club in Houston, claiming that dozens of high-ranking officers have retired to the oil capital over the years, putting their experience to good use advising on overseas operations. According to one blog, Nesbitt was a prime recipient of drilling dollars, while according to another he had a well-documented history of mental-health issues. The *Houston Press* had run a feature that summarized all the possibilities, and the annotated spread made up the center of Ford's psycho wall.

"This is all pretty interesting, Jerry, but I don't see why I had to come down and view it in person. I've heard of this shooting. I've seen the video. Our guys were in the right. No matter who this Nesbitt dude was, he drew down on a cop. End of story."

Lorenz goes to one of the open cabinets and pulls out an orange-covered, spiral-bound Key Map. A scrap of paper marks one of the laminated pages. He opens it on the desk and turns the map to face me. His finger thumps down to a green patch near the middle.

"That's the park where we found Ford's body," he says.

"Let me see that." I study the map. "And it was marked like that when you got here?"

He nods his head.

"So Brandon Ford marked the page where his body was dumped? Like he knew in advance that's where he'd end up."

"You'd think so, right? But no, that's not what it is. Here—" he takes the book back—"*this* is why he marked it."

I lean closer. He taps on a section of Allen Parkway curving through the map grid. When he moves his hand, I can see an X drawn over the road.

"That's where Andrew Nesbitt was shot?" I ask.

He nods again. "And that's not all, March. Remember when I sent you out into the woods and you had your fall? I thought if we followed the direction that finger was pointing, we'd find the severed head. But I was wrong. The fact is, if you follow that pointing finger—"

"You end up on Allen Parkway."

And I'd seen it, looking through the weedy hurricane fence that night. I'd seen it without realizing the significance. The pointing finger had not led me astray; it guided me. I just didn't know enough to make the connection.

Now I'm beginning to.

What I have is this: an unorthodox FBI agent telling me lies about the death of a man whose skinned finger, when his body was discovered, pointed straight to the site where another man, claiming to work for the CIA, had died in a gunfight with the Houston Police.

"So what's the next step?" he asks.

"Let me think."

The guns in the safe. The story that Ford was down in Corpus Christi. Bea Kuykendahl, a.k.a. Trixie, riding shotgun while he dropped off his kids. While that was going on, he kept a room here at his office

81

dedicated to the shooting death of Andrew Nesbitt and the many conspiracy theories swirling around the event.

It all fits together somehow, assuming I have enough of the pieces. The bloody finger is pointing, the finger is guiding, the only question is where. I have to follow it. I have to think. It all fits together if I can only figure out how.

CHAPTER 8

Camped in Brandon Ford's office, I tell Jerry everything: the early morning meeting with the FBI, my suspicions about the match on Ford, the ex-wife's description of Bea. He listens silently and doesn't ask any questions. When I'm done, he just looks at me.

"Well?" I ask.

"I feel like you just showed me *your* psycho wall. No offense. It just sounds a little crazy, that's all." He cocks his head toward the clippings. "And this is crazy enough."

"This doesn't make the hair on the back of your neck stand up?"

He smiles. "It does now. Look—are you hungry? 'Cause I'm starving. I skipped lunch coming out here."

"Jerry, will you stop and think a minute? I need your help putting all this together. This Agent Kuykendahl, my gut tells me she's trying to hide something big."

"Maybe you're right, I don't know. I can't do this on an empty stomach. Lemme run down the street and pick us something up, okay? I think there's a Five Guys—"

"Not again."

"Come on," he says. "You can choose the next place."

There's no chance of getting him to focus, so I let him go. He promises not to take long, and I can hear him chuckling to himself as he heads down the hall. Like he's happy to get away. It occurs to me he hasn't had a sit-down with Hedges yet. He doesn't know there's already a cloud over the day.

The door shuts behind him and I get down to work. I left my briefcase at the office, so I have to use my new phone to take pictures of the wall. They come out good, better than my three-year-old point-and-shoot, in fact. Maybe it's time to upgrade.

With that done, I start pulling the clippings down one at a time. I read through the content, especially where Ford underlined and high-lighted things, then stack pieces on the desk. Lorenz had called this a psycho wall, but it's really a mind map, a visual scheme illustrating Brandon Ford's obsession. Or to be more precise, his investigation. He was compiling information about the Nesbitt shooting, about the man's alleged background—but why? Whatever his motives, this inquiry of his must have led to his death. Which means that if I can understand the wall, it might lead me to his killer or killers.

Once the wall is dismantled and stacked, I go to the computer. We have an excellent forensic computer specialist named Hanford, and he'd probably want me to leave this to him. I take a look anyway. The screen comes to life with a shake of the mouse. In Ford's email inbox, there are more than fifty unopened messages. I scan them quickly. Mostly junk. Nothing from Bea Kuykendahl.

There is, however, an email from Sam Dearborn, sent after my visit to him, asking Ford to give him a call. Strange, since he already knew that Ford was dead. Reviewing the conversation in my head, though, I realize I never made my interest in Ford clear to Dearborn. A sign of my misgivings about the case? Perhaps.

The door opens down the hall.

I check my watch and call out: "I thought you were coming right back."

Silence.

I wheel around in Brandon Ford's chair, my hand moving to my holster.

"Don't," a voice says.

The only things visible in the doorframe are part of a man's head—mostly hidden by a black balaclava, only an eye showing—and the barrel of a pump shotgun.

"Draw that gun and you're dead," he says.

My hand wants to move. My heart's racing, my vision tunneling, my aim fixing on him. The voice in my head saying *Go, go, go*.

But he's holding that shotgun steady, using cover like he knows what he's doing. I will my hand to relax. I move it away from my side arm.

He leans further into the doorway. The fluorescents raise a shine on his synthetic mask.

"Stay calm," he says. "Lift your hands. Put them flat on the desk in front of you."

As he speaks, a second man crosses behind him and enters the room. He levels a black pistol in my face, circling to my left so as to leave the shotgun's line of fire open. If I drew now, there'd be no way of taking them both, assuming I could beat the twelve-gauge in the first place, which is unlikely.

"I'm a cop," I say.

"Do what I tell you and you'll still be a cop when we walk out of here."

"You're in charge."

"Good. Now, keep your hands flat on the desk, and without lifting them I want you to stand up. If you lift your hands, you're dead."

He delivers the instructions calmly with just the hint of an accent—East Texas, maybe, or Louisiana. The man with the pistol says nothing. He just stands in the corner of the room, covering me. I glance his way, trying to burn the details into my memory. He wears a tight balaclava, too, and a gray T-shirt that leaves his nut-brown arms bare. There's a gold ring on his left middle finger. A metallic skull with red stone eyes. Jeans and tan lace-up boots. I catch a smell of musky cologne on the air, the scent intensified by his stress.

"Don't sit there all day," the man at the door says. "Get up."

Keeping my hands flat, I rise into a crouch. The pain in my leg flares up. I try to ignore the sensation. It feels wet, like if I put my fingers to my thigh, they'd come away bloody.

"Okay. Now you're going to stay like that while my associate takes your gun. This is for our safety and yours. If you try anything, I won't hesitate."

"I won't try anything."

The second man lowers his gun and tucks it into his waistband behind his hip. He approaches obliquely, removing my SIG from its holster in a practiced motion. Then he rests the muzzle against my back while his free hand roams over me.

"Where is it?"

"Left ankle," I say, my throat tight.

He stoops slightly, tugs my pants leg up, and slides the .40 caliber Kahr out of my molded ankle holster. A tremor runs up my spine. My skin feels clammy with sweat.

Once he has both guns, the man fades back into the corner. The one with the shotgun finally reveals himself. He steps toward me, bringing the muzzle almost to my face. All I can see is that gaping hole, but I get the impression of a broad chest and thick forearms all blurred behind it.

"We understand each other," he says. "Now here's what we're gonna do. I want you to come around the desk and go over to that corkboard. I want your nose in that corner and your hands on the wall. When I say go, you lift your hands over your head and do it."

A drop of sweat runs down the side of my nose, hitting the desk.

"Go."

I lift my hands off the desk. They leave damp prints. I raise them and straighten up, ignoring the needles in my hip and back. Unsteady on my feet, I shuffle around the desk, past the stack of clippings to the bare corkboard. In the corner I rest my hands on the two walls, staring into the crevice where they meet.

"This is a mistake—"

"Don't bother with the speech," he says. "We're taking what we came for, then getting out of here. If you don't move, everything will be fine. If you do . . ."

The second man, the one with the skull ring, sniggers.

"Shut up," the Shotgun says. "Open the desk and find a folder or something to put all this stuff in."

I hear them moving behind me, gathering the clippings and putting them away. Then there's a sound of moving furniture, metal scraping metal.

"Are we taking this whole thing?" Skull Ring asks.

"Just pop it open and take out the hard drive."

"You got a screwdriver?"

"Just do it, okay?"

A sudden crash makes me jump.

"Don't you move!" Shotgun yells.

More crashes—they're banging the computer on something, trying to break open the housing. Skull Ring huffs with the effort, but finally wrenches away the metal and starts digging inside. My shirt sticks to my chest. All I can think about is not moving, keeping calm, storing every detail away in my head. Not the sound of a trigger pull, not the explosion, the stench of blood, the darkness, the death and the nothing.

Live to fight another day. Live to fight another—

"Keep your hands on the wall. Don't try to follow us."

I hear them backing into the hallway.

"Leave my guns," I say.

"Yeah, right. You're keeping your life. Be content with that."

Footsteps in the hall. I turn my head. They're gone. With effort I take my hands from the wall. The front door of the office slams shut.

I let out a breath. I crouch down, hands on knees. Gotta get myself under control. Gotta do something. I stare at the carpet between my shoes. The pant leg rucked up over my empty holster.

The switch flips. I go cold.

I poke my head into the hallway to be sure it's clear. Then I race into the next office to the open gun safe. I torque the banana mag out of the Krinkov and grab a box of ammo. I start jamming rounds past the mag's sharp metal lips. My hands are scraped, torn, but I keep loading. When the box is empty, I fit the mag into the little AK and pull the charging handle. The folding stock is already in place.

Running now, confident, invincible, with the assault rifle's butt in the pocket of my shoulder, I push through the office door, scanning left and right with the muzzle. They're already downstairs, disappearing into the corridor at the end of the atrium.

Adrenaline pumps through me, dispelling all pain. I glide ahead, descending the stairs in twos, sprinting past the fountain and into the corridor, with no thought but catching up to them, no thought but making them stop.

I reach the entry. I can see the parking lot outside. The bright sun. Gunshots ring out.

I throw myself into a crouch, slamming into a wall of mailboxes. But there's no shattered glass. No one's firing at me. I get up and take a few steps forward. Through the glass I see them outside. One of them, the muscled shotgunner, disappears behind an open car door on the far side of the lot. The one with the skull ring is just standing closer, between my own vehicle and the one next to it. His mask is hiked up over his eyebrows, his right arm extended toward the pavement.

Outside, I advance in a crouch, my finger alongside the Krinkov's trigger. His back is to me. Looking over the cars, I can only see his head and upper torso. As I hook around the back of my car, I see him clearly. My Kahr shines in his hand, the muzzle pointing downward. On the ground between his feet, lying in a tangle with his gun in one hand and a Five Guys bag in the other, Jerry Lorenz spits blood and glares upward at the *coup de grace*.

"Police!" I scream.

Skull Ring turns. We're maybe four feet away from each other. I mash down on the Krinkov's trigger.

His gray T-shirt erupts in a pink haze, his body jerking wildly. He staggers backward, rolling, and I advance. The thump of the gunstock against my shoulder feels good and right. The man falls. The gun goes silent. It's empty and smoking.

A car screeches past us and I glance up in time to see the driver. Through the window I can see the outline of his unmasked face framed by a curly mane of hair.

"March."

I throw the Krinkov down. Get on my knees beside Jerry.

His chest.

Two—no, three wounds. Thick, bright blood coming out in tidal surges, soaking his shirt. A line of blood down the side of his mouth.

"Don't talk," I say.

I put pressure on the wounds as best I can. I call for help. Traffic races past on Westheimer, oblivious to what's happening.

Underneath me, Jerry's gone pale. His eyes have an unnatural brightness. He's going. I scream for help again, afraid to take my hands off of him, afraid he'll slip away if I do.

"Come on, Jerry, don't do this. Don't leave me. You're gonna be okay."

He tilts his head and spits, trying to clear his mouth.

"Don't talk. You don't have to say anything."

He looks up at me. "My *kid.*"

"I know, Jerry. It's gonna be okay. Just stay with me."

His eyes bore into me. I keep talking, keep reassuring, and then my eyes cloud and my throat fills with phlegm.

"Jerry, no."

Under my hands, his body is still.

Behind me, I hear footsteps on the blacktop. A hand touches my shoulder.

"We saw everything," a man's voice says. "We called the cops and an ambulance. They gonna be here soon. You better get out of here, man. The cops are on the way."

I shrug free of him. I slump against the car.

"I *am* a cop."

He steps back, showing me his palms. "It's cool, man." Glancing down, his face goes blank and he starts retreating.

I sit there, sticky with my partner's blood, watching his wounds glisten in the harsh shine of the indifferent sun. My head tilts back. My eyes close.

I long for the sound of sirens until they come.

CHAPTER 9

They find me in the long antiseptic breezeway, where the nurses left me half an hour earlier, working on my hands with a reddened towelette. I see them in my peripheral vision. Only one of them advances, his footsteps echoing on the glossy floor. The shoes come into view. Black wingtips with a military shine. He settles his weight next to me and sighs.

"Getting yourself cleaned up," he says. "Good."

He rests his hand on my shoulder.

"I'm sorry, sir."

"You don't have anything to apologize for."

"Just when you were saying all your goodbyes—"

"Shut up," he says gently.

"You didn't get to talk to him."

"March, shut up." The hand on my back feels so heavy. "He was a good man. A good detective. We all had our doubts in the beginning, but he worked out all right."

I can't answer him. All I can do is nod. The silence between us is full of understanding. After a while he squeezes my shoulder and begins to rise.

"There's some people who need to talk to you. Some questions that need answering."

"I have a question," I say. "What did Lorenz have to engage them for? Did the people on the scene say anything about that?"

An air of hopelessness comes over him. "I don't think anyone saw what led up to the initial shooting. We just don't know . . ."

More footsteps. I look up to find Bascombe there along with an assistant DA and a couple of plainclothes men I assume are from Internal Affairs. Behind them, several detectives from a different homicide shift. They'll carry the ball on this, our own people being too close.

As we walk down to the elevators, I'm wrapped in an inviolate bubble, nobody alongside or too close, like they see me as a piece of evidence at a crime scene, something not to touch unless you're properly gloved. I don't care.

I don't want them getting close.

"This is not good," the ADA says. "Not. Good."

Bascombe bristles. "Of course it's not. It never is when we lose a man."

"I'm not talking about that, Lieutenant. One of your detectives walked up to a suspect and unloaded on him with a full-automatic weapon. They won't even know how many holes are in him until they can search him during the autopsy. And there are witnesses who saw it all. There might even be footage from the pawnshop surveillance cameras."

"This isn't an interrogation. Detective March is answering questions to help with the hunt for the suspect who got away. Anyway, the guy whose ticket he punched was about to shoot Lorenz in the head." Bascombe looks my way for confirmation. I give him a mute nod. "Under the circumstances, what was he supposed to do?"

For the interview, they've commandeered the ground floor all-faith chapel, positioning me on the front bench and taking up a semicircle of positions between me and the door. The other homicide detectives—the ones who actually need this information—stand in back, staring down at their notebooks, fully aware of the awkwardness of the situation.

One of the Internal Affairs investigators breaks in. He's in his mid-fifties and sports a healthy golf-course tan with light circles under his eyes and light stripes on his temples where his sunglasses rest.

"My understanding," he says, "is that your partner was actually killed with your side arm, Detective March. Is that correct?"

"It was my backup. They took my weapons. That's why I went after them."

"With an automatic weapon."

"I didn't know it was full-auto. I'd seen it earlier in the gun safe, so that's where I went. I had to load it first or I would have been quicker." I glance at the cuts on my finger from pushing the rounds into the magazine.

"You didn't call for assistance."

"It all happened so fast."

The ADA interrupts. "This is not good. Did you have to shoot him so many times?"

"I pulled the trigger once. I wasn't expecting to empty the clip. Like I said, it happened real fast. If it's any consolation, he was on his feet with a gun in his hand. The ballistics will confirm that, too. I didn't shoot him once he was on the ground." *Which is more than he had in mind for Jerry—*

"That's it," Bascombe says. "I think we're done for now, unless you guys need anything more." He glances back to the homicide detectives, who shake their heads. "Fine. We'll do this for real once everybody's had a chance to process."

But the IAD investigator isn't finished. "One more thing, Detective. I know a lot of people are going to applaud your actions here. I'm sure you'll get a few pats on the back for this. Whatever you were feeling at the moment, though, seeing your partner there on the ground, there's such a thing as overkill. If you're expecting us to rubber-stamp this, you've got another thing coming. That was *your* weapon used to kill Detective Lorenz. And if what you did to that shooter isn't excessive force, then I don't know what is."

He waits for an answer but nothing comes. I don't have it in me to fight. All I can give him is a shrug and a shake of the head. It was my weapon. It was excessive force, at least in the sense that seeing your partner shot up in front of you is excessive. Seeing one of the assailants drive away without injury is excessive, too.

Bascombe chases the others out of the chapel, turning at the door to face me. He claps his hands on my arms a couple of times, like he's trying to impart his own strength to my sagging frame.

"Stay strong," he says. "We'll get through this."

"There's something I need to tell you."

"It can wait."

"I didn't say anything to the first responders. And I wasn't going to bring it up in front of those jackals just now."

His eyes narrow. "All right. What is it?"

"I did get a look at the second suspect, the one who got away. He took his mask off in the car. As he drove past, ours eyes locked."

"And?"

"I can't swear to this," I say. "He was behind a tinted window. But remember the photo we got from Bea Kuykendahl? In that file on Brandon Ford?"

"Yeah, I remember."

"Well, that's who it looked like to me."

When you're put on administrative leave, they tell you it's for your own good. You've been through something traumatic. It takes time to recover.

Don't worry about the job. Just focus on you.

But none of this is true.

The last thing I need is this. Time to reflect. Time to replay what happened over and over in my head. Time to dream it's still in progress. Time to wake up in a cold sweat, my hands tensing as if I'm still firing the gun.

It's not for you. It's for them. So they don't have to see you. So they don't have to think of something comforting to say. In grief you're like the sun to them. In disgrace they cannot bear to look at you full on. So they tuck you away somewhere out of sight, telling themselves that one problem at least can be solved, if only for now.

At home I lock all the doors and switch off the ringers on all the phones.

I go to the stereo with a stack of CDs and a half-formed intention of choosing something appropriate to the moment, music to feed the rage in me, or alternately to quench it. The discs end up strewn in a half circle, their liners unfolded. Portishead first, quite depressing, but it's too sterile and electronic. Too artificial. So I play Tom Waits full blast for two minutes until the gates of hell open up under me. Then I switch it off and pull the plug from the wall.

Upstairs, I run the shower on cold until my whole body shivers and convulses. I stick my face under the spigot and imagine the water blasting it away like porous stone.

I can't do nothing.

I won't do nothing.

Dressing in jeans and a black pullover and a pair of steel-toed Red Wings, I grab the gym bag from the closet safe and dump its contents on the bed. Two high-caps loaded with Speer Gold Dot hollow points slip into the spare mag holder, which clips to my belt. The holstered Browning, loaded with another high-cap, tucks inside the waistband behind my right hip, my shirt hanging over the butt. In front of the mirror I check to make sure the rig doesn't print, then I draw the gun, punching my arm forward, making sure my hand doesn't shake.

Outside, it's dark already, the night thick with cicadas and the smell of citronella and steaks grilling on the other side of the neighbor's fence. In the back of my head, a thumping, cauterizing wail. Maybe from the album or from my roughed-up soul.

I don't know where to find Bea Kuykendahl now. She won't be at her office, and I doubt she'll be at her suburban country biker bar, either. If she's heard about Lorenz, maybe she'll be expecting me. Maybe she'll make herself scarce. I will find her no matter what and I will make her reveal the truth.

A man's life is at stake, she said.

She'll eat those words.

I wrench open the car door and drop behind the wheel. The sharp edge of the Browning's cocked-and-locked hammer digs at my side. The spare mags on my left do likewise, and when I try to adjust them—there it is. The pain I've been fighting since the fall. The blade goes in deep and starts twisting. It saws back and forth in my vertebrae, slices down the back of my left thigh. Whatever I do to ease the pain only makes it sharper. I try climbing out of the car only to end up frozen in a crouch, the small of my back hollowed out.

Whimpering, I stagger inside, making it up the stairs on fingers and toes. I unsnap the holster and pull the Browning out of my belt. I strip off the spare mags and leave them on the floor. On the bed, I inch my way up, straining my arm toward Charlotte's nightstand where her old prescription sleeping pills are kept. I swallow two of them dry, feeling the capsules scrape down my throat.

I roll over onto my back, wincing with every minute adjustment. The overhead fan is still. The room feels close and warm. Somewhere nearby I hear a faint sniffling, a soft wet gasping sound like a kicked and broken dog might make. Somewhere nearby, maybe even in this room. Maybe even on this bed.

The IAD man was right about one thing. People I don't know, mainly in dress uniforms, go out of their way to clasp my elbow, to pat my back, to whisper encouragement. They do it on the sly, and not just because of the funeral. We live in different times, when even if you reach the end zone, spiking the ball is no longer done. But the consensus is unmistakable. The man with the skull ring got what was coming to him.

"I wish they would stop," Charlotte whispers.

She's a vision in black, clinging to my right arm like at any moment she might have to hold me up single-handed. I stare at her until she frowns. She's only a few hours off the plane and already back on duty. A cop's wife. Bridger called her in England and she cut her trip short. I never would have asked her to, but I'm not complaining. I've been floating, all my ballast poured out on the ground. Now there's someone here to grab my ankle and pull me back.

I have no role to fulfill here, no casket to carry and no eulogy to give.

I prefer it that way, though I was not consulted on the matter. From experience I know that tragedy has a way of marking a person, setting him apart, making others as reluctant to approach him as they would be to enter some awe-filled holy place. I should be invisible in this crowd, unnoticed, and if it weren't for the fact that I'd riddled Lorenz's killer with bullets, I would be.

We file down one of the aisles—the anticipated crowd is so vast, the event was moved to the auditorium of one of Houston's smaller megachurches—and disappear down a long, padded pew. As I stare down at the folded program, Charlotte spots people she knows in the crowd, wondering aloud if we should go and join them.

"There's Theresa," she says. "She looks pretty torn up."

I glance up briefly. Cavallo is half hidden under her husband's arm, her eyes damp and sparkling, her mouth hidden under her hand. Maybe Lorenz had been right and she did think highly of him. She'd told me once they went to the same Bible study, though he'd never given any evidence of piety in my presence. While I'm watching her, José Aguilar catches my eye. He raises an eyebrow in acknowledgment, then nods. Hang in there. I nod back.

It takes a long time for the mourners to enter, there are so many. All the brass is up front, and so is the new mayor and most of the city council. The shocking death of an HPD detective will not go unheralded, not on their watch. I realize for the first time that there will be speeches. I shift in my seat.

"Are you still in pain?"

"I'm fine."

"If you can't sit through it all, we can always slip out."

"I said I'm fine."

I'm not going anywhere. I owe him that much at least.

Near the front, weaving between the public officials, I see my old boss, Lt. Wanda Mosser, her white hair radiant. She shakes a few hands, managing to smile and look appropriately sober all at once. Two years ago she presided over the media fiasco that was the Hannah Mayhew task force, and even though it failed to find the girl alive, Wanda managed to use the opportunity to burnish her own reputation. Back in the day, when she'd come through the ranks, a woman couldn't hold her own and be successful in this man's world unless she was even tougher than the boys. Wanda had no trouble delivering. When she was angry, she had a way of looking at you like she might just slit your throat. I've been on the receiving end of that look, so I should know.

Today, though, she's just one of the brass. Nothing to prove except that she knows how to lend decorum to a solemn occasion. Which is not such a bad skill to have.

The funeral lasts more than an hour, but it's a good one. The politicians keep their remarks brief, relinquishing the spotlight to Lorenz's family. His widow does not speak. Instead, his younger brother reads from a prepared script, mostly recounting how proud Jerry was to be a homicide detective and the only thing he loved more was his wife and their two-year-old son. I manage to get through this stony-faced, though Charlotte doesn't. Then there's music, an aria of some kind from a famous requiem I've never heard of, performed by a woman from the Houston Masterworks Chorus without even a hint of accompaniment or artifice. Her voice rings through the church, austere and beautiful, the words incomprehensible to me, most likely Latin. When she finishes, I realize for the first time that I've been holding my breath.

"I want that at my funeral," I whisper.

"Don't even joke about it."

I feel strangely detached from the spectacle. I shouldn't, but there it is. No voice, no matter how haunting, can bring me ritual closure. No endearing anecdote, no volume of tears. If I want, I can conjure Jerry in my mind, blood-spattered and choking, whispering his final confession. *My kid.*

None of them will ever have that moment. I wish I didn't. But I do, and because I do, all this does nothing to stir me. I can't bury him, not yet. I can't shovel the dirt onto his coffin and move on. For everyone else, this is a great trauma, something that happened and can't be reversed.

For me, it's still happening. The guilt trip from the IAD investigator sees to that. It was my gun that killed Lorenz. For me, his death feels utterly reversible, too.

I retrace the moments, following them back, then push play and do it all over, gaining valuable seconds in the process. I can move faster, load quicker. I can get down the stairs in time. When the shots rang out, I was in the vestibule just feet from the building's entrance. As the pallbearers approach either side of the casket, as they take up the weight of their burden, here I sit, working out how to shave a few seconds off my time. Like I'm back at Shooter's Paradise, watching the others run the course so I can learn from their mistakes. Only it's myself I'm watching, my own mistakes, and eliminating just one of them could make the difference.

We stand as the casket makes its exit. Charlotte presses a tissue to her eyes. As the bearers approach, I drop my eyes, hoping to go unnoticed by the passing mourners. All at once, the pews around me go silent. I look up to find Jerry's widow standing before me, the whole procession paused behind her. Her composure astonishes me. She reaches for my hand, the skin still nicked from my rushed loading of the AK magazine, then starts to say something. Suddenly the brittle surface of her pale, drained face is like an opalescent egg—first smooth, then dented, then cracking all to pieces. She presses herself into me, clinging to my arms, balling my sleeves in her fists.

"That *scum*," she sobs into my chest.

My cheeks burn. With every eye on me, I start to wilt. Looking over her shoulder, I see the two-year-old riding a relative's hip, looking confused by his mother's actions, perhaps by everything that's going on around him.

Jerry's brother advances to take her by the arm and ease her back into place. His expression is fraught and apologetic, perhaps not realizing who I am.

She looks me in the eyes again. "*Thank you for what you did.*"

Once they've gone, I glance down. The lapel of my jacket is wet and glistening. I cross my arms and tuck my hands into my armpits to stop them from shaking.

The mourners move on. I take my emotions and stuff them way down, struggling to get control. Wanda Mosser pauses beside me and leans to whisper in my ear.

"Tomorrow," she says. "I want to see you in my office."

I nod, trying to hide my confusion. Whatever help she imagines she can offer—a self-help lecture of some sort, presuming on our past relationship—I don't need it. Charlotte asks what she said and I just shrug.

Finally we join the procession, Charlotte taking the lead.

Someone behind tugs at my sleeve. Bascombe.

"What did she want?"

"She thanked me for what I did."

"No," he says. "Mosser."

I tell him and his mouth twists.

"That's her," he says. "The new boss."

"Who, Wanda?"

"*Captain* Mosser. They announced it today."

I file out, staring at Charlotte's slender back, the curve of her shoulders. Behind me I can hear the lieutenant muttering. I can hardly believe it. Wanda Mosser? She's a good cop. She's not a conniving political—well, she's got her ambition, obviously. But I'd never have thought Wanda would put the knife in the captain's back.

Out in the sunlight, mourners huddle in small groups on the lawn, waiting under a mockingly beautiful sky as the pallbearers slot the casket into the long black hearse. Cavallo comes over, tucking a stray lock behind her ear, her face blotchy from crying. She speaks to Charlotte a while, asking about her trip to England and if she's heard whether the Robbs have chosen a name for their baby yet, or found out if it's to be a boy or a girl. Then she glances sideways at me, like she's only just seen me there. She must sense the distance between us.

I step closer. "You knew about Wanda?"

"I couldn't say anything," she says. "I wanted to."

"It doesn't matter."

The hearse doors shut and it begins to roll forward, a line of cars edging into procession behind. Time for bystanders to decide whether attending the church service was enough or if they will continue out to the gravesite.

"That was the last time I saw Jerry. When the two of you came to see me. Was that the same case you were working on . . . when it happened?"

"It seems like such a long time ago."

Cavallo's husband, who's been standing with a couple of cops in dress uniform, makes his way over. She bites her lip with indecision.

"What is it?" I ask.

"Wanda's move. She wants me to go with her. I said I would."

"You passed up the opportunity when Hedges offered it."

"Well," she says, "things are different now."

She leaves us to meet her husband halfway. Charlotte raises an eyebrow: are we going to the gravesite or not? I mull it over a second, watching Cavallo depart. Things are different now. There's no doubt about that.

"We're going," I say. "I owe it to him."

CHAPTER 10

The first time I reported for duty to Wanda Mosser, I was a different man, a newly minted detective with a happy marriage and a little girl at home, an up-and-comer with prospects and connections. Though my law enforcement experience up to then had been in uniform, unlike most officers getting their first plainclothes assignment, my resumé included a stint with CID while I was in the Army. Military service is always a plus, but having been an MP was golden. Not only would I shine in my new position, but my colleagues would be lucky to have me.

It took Wanda maybe ten seconds to cut me down to size.

"The question is whether I can make anything of you. With most of the boys they send me, even I can't turn 'em around."

We were always boys to Wanda. Even the women under her command, when referred to in the aggregate, were boys. And after a while, if you could endure her constant scrutiny and her blistering lectures, if you could earn every so often one of her reluctant smiles, then you counted yourself fortunate to be one of Wanda's boys. She tore you down only to build you back up. Wanda was a master of *esprit de corps*.

No one called her Lt. Mosser. No one called her boss or sir or ma'am. She was Wanda to everyone, and yet you never felt like you were using her first name. I remember a veteran detective, a mustachioed old bull trying to stay young by dyeing what was left of his hair an unnatural black, telling a story that pretty much summed the situation up. He'd gone to a family Christmas party, this man of perhaps fifty, where his widowed mother sat in a wheelchair receiving kisses from a line of kids and grandkids. When he approached and planted a kiss on her forehead, he whispered under his breath, "Merry Christmas, Wanda." Then, realizing with embarrassment the mistake, he corrected himself. "I mean, Merry Christmas, *Mama!*"

He told that story once in my hearing, but Wanda must have repeated it a hundred times. Supervising the Missing Persons section wasn't enough for her; she wanted to be our matriarch, too. Fierce and protective as a mother, amongst her children Wanda also played favorites, pitting us against each other in the struggle for favor. The force of her personality was such that, once you were sucked into the familial mindset, there was no getting out. She dominated your thoughts, provoking fierce loyalty and simmering anxiety at the same time. You'd cry into your beer after-hours about how Wanda didn't appreciate you, didn't even notice all the sacrifices you made, and then she'd bestow an "attaboy" and leave you beaming with pride.

I rode that roller coaster awhile, earning my way into her good graces, getting close enough to see how the Cult of Wanda worked. None of it, I decided, was premeditated. She plied her divide-and-conquer strategy by instinct, unaware she was doing anything at all. Realizing that, I admired her even more. I just didn't want to work for her.

In my experience, Wanda was not above departmental politics. She even excelled at mid-level intrigues and interagency skirmishes. Before now, though, I would have said she only indulged in the squabbles to protect her territory and back up her people. Necessity drove her rather than ambition.

Last time I walked into Homicide, the captain's awkward leave-taking had spoiled the atmosphere. The morning after Lorenz's funeral, the shift hasn't recovered. If anything, the detectives hunkered down in their individual cubicles give the impression of being shell-shocked. Only a few bother to look up as I pass. My own work space has been tidied by hands other than my own, my briefcase tucked under the footwell, and the one where Lorenz worked is entirely vacated.

I go to the break room for coffee, spend a few minutes at my desk getting my head straight, then lift my briefcase onto the desktop, opening the limp leather flap. From my drawer I transfer Bea Kuykendahl's file on Ford into my case, along with every bit of paper I can find related to the investigation. The keyed lock on the flap is broken, so I pull the wraparound straps taut before tucking the briefcase back under the desk, ready for a quick exit.

A loud thump on the other side of the cubicle wall gets my attention. Glancing over, I find Cavallo dumping a second cardboard box onto Lorenz's old desk. The rest of her things are secured by bungee cords to a collapsible luggage cart.

"Moving in?"

"Don't start in on me, okay? It's hard enough—"

I lift my hands in surrender. "No offense intended. I've been called to the principal's office, that's all. I don't look forward to it. What's she got in store for me? I'm guessing you already know."

"Come on, March, you can't ask me that. My loyalties are complicated enough. I can't go behind her back. You know that."

"Just tell me this: should I be worried?"

"If I played the game your way, I'd always be worried."

I have to smile at that.

The clock is ticking, but before I obey the summons from Wanda, I take Cavallo through the office and introduce her to some of the newer detectives, the ones who weren't around to witness her work on the Hannah Mayhew case firsthand. I let them know Hedges wanted her in Homicide back then, trying to head off any potential ill will. It's the least I can do for a friend who's put her career on the line for me more than once.

While I'm breaking the ice for her, the captain's door opens and Bascombe peers out. He beckons me with a crook of the finger.

"Wish me luck."

I don't know what this place will look like once Wanda's put her stamp on it. In a lot of ways, it's changed already. The old stalwarts are gone. Hedges is gone. Lorenz. Of the old guard, there's just Bascombe and me, and our relationship has always been tenuous. The squad as I knew it is over and I'm turning the page—as always—with a blot on my book.

The captain's office proves unrecognizable. Everything's changed, right down to the carpet. The sterile, businesslike style Hedges preferred has been replaced by tufted chairs, warm earth tones, and blond wood. Even the cheap metal blinds have given way to thick white plastic ones with faux grain molded into the slats. Instead of waiting behind her desk, Wanda occupies a wing chair in a new seating area, while Bascombe sits rigid on the low couch, his knees halfway to his shoulders.

"Come in, March," she says. "Have a seat."

I take my place beside Bascombe. Wanda crosses her leg and consults a notebook resting in her lap, reminding me of a therapist.

"I feel like I should be lying on the couch."

She smiles faintly while Bascombe just shifts his weight.

"I've asked the lieutenant to sit in," Wanda says. "I'm sure you know what this is all about. You've worked for me in the past, so you know how I like to run things. I expect a lot from my people and they expect a lot from me."

"I understand."

"Lieutenant Bascombe has already briefed me on your case load. While you're on leave, we will be reassigning the open investigations. Theresa Cavallo will pick up the slack, so I'd like you to brief her on anything outstanding."

"Is that really necessary?" I ask. "Nothing against Cavallo, but the thing is, I'm ready to come back to work."

"You've been through quite a trauma."

"Regardless, I don't want to sit on the sidelines any longer."

"There's the question of the IAD investigation. Until that's concluded—"

"I'll be riding a desk. I understand."

"You keep saying that, but I don't think you do understand. Until further notice, you are on leave. We'll review the situation periodically and reassess. In the meantime, I want you to hand everything over to Cavallo and bring her up to speed."

"What are you trying to say, Wanda?"

"I think I said it."

"That sounds like indefinite suspension to me."

"Not at all."

I turn to Bascombe for intercession. He's busy counting the tiles in the suspended ceiling. Clearly Wanda has already clipped his wings.

"Listen," I say. "My partner was murdered practically before my very eyes. I was held at gunpoint while they removed important evidence from the scene. We don't have the luxury of sitting back and waiting, Wanda. This needs to be our top priority."

"Are you really going to fight me on this, Roland? On my first day in the saddle? Frankly, I'm insulted that you feel the need to lecture me on my priorities. If you had your head on straight, you'd realize that the second you decided to shoot a man in half with a machine gun, your involvement in the case was basically over. At best you're a witness, at worst—I don't even want to say it."

The problem with having history between us is, it gives me liberty to say more than I should. At a certain point, in an argument with Hedges or Bascombe, I'd know when to shut my mouth. Not with Wanda, though. In a family squabble you speak your mind, even when it's suicide.

"You know something," I say, "it *is* your first day, and with all due respect I'm only lecturing you because you seem to need it. One of our people is dead. We should be out there making our presence felt. There are some serious irregularities in this case and—"

Bascombe cuts me off, coming to life so suddenly he makes me flinch. "Now you listen to me! You're *way* over the line. Now you either shut your mouth right now or you *will* be on indefinite suspension. Do I make myself clear?"

"Lieutenant," Wanda says calmly.

I stare at Bascombe, still surprised. And then it dawns on me what's going on. Despite what Wanda said, he hasn't briefed her on the case, not entirely. He jumped in to prevent me from enumerating the irregularities—namely the FBI runaround and the fact that, unless he has a twin brother, my decapitated victim is very much alive and well and wielding a shotgun.

"You were saying?" Wanda asks me. Not that she really wants to hear it. She's just giving me more rope.

My first impulse is to get everything out in the open. Why hold back? But Bascombe chose not to say anything, and he must have his reasons. I can feel the tension coming off him in waves.

"Nothing," I say. "Never mind. If you want me to take a couple of days off, that's your call. You can imagine the stress I'm under, so please disregard what I just said."

She lifts her hand. "Don't say another word. Lieutenant, let's have Detective March come back in two weeks—"

"Two *weeks*?"

"—for a reassessment. Assuming he's up to it and there are no new developments, we can look at the option of restricted duty." She makes a note on her pad, then rises to escort me out. Again, like a shrink whose client's hour just ran out. Bascombe starts to follow me out, but she recalls him to the couch, saying they have a lot of work to get through. "I'm sure March knows how to find the exit by now."

After I've summarized my open cases for Cavallo and answered questions to the best of my ability concerning a couple of Lorenz's files, I hoist my briefcase and make for the door. With every step I expect to be called out for trying to leave with the Brandon Ford paperwork. But I make it to the elevator without incident, then down to the lower-level garage.

Charlotte calls from her office, asking if I'm interested in lunch. I start to agree, but I really don't feel up to it. I want to be alone, to lick the fresh wounds the morning has inflicted on my pride. Sensing my mood, she backs off.

"I did make you an appointment with a doctor, though."

Before the funeral, I'd confessed to her about the constant pain that followed from my fall in the woods. Then she threatened to call a doctor, making me regret saying anything at all.

"I don't need to see a doctor."

"Yes, you do. If it's nothing serious, he'll give you a prescription and you'll have some relief from the pain. And if it is serious, Roland, then the sooner you do something about it, the better. You're not as young as you used to be."

"Thanks."

"I'm not trying to hurt your feelings, baby. Just stating the facts."

Which is how I end up, a couple of hours later, perched on a blue vinyl examination table wearing nothing but a stiff cotton gown. X-rays of my lower spine glow on the light board across the room, placed there by a nurse with appliqué crystals on her fingernails. As she departs, she estimates the doctor's arrival time at three minutes.

Twenty minutes later, a short, handsome Asian man in his mid-thirties appears, wearing mint scrubs and a modish pair of black plastic glasses. He launches into a speech about the mysteries and complexities of the human back. His tone sounds a little defensive, as if I've suggested there's an easy fix. "Have you ever known anyone who's had back surgery?"

"Not surgery," I say. "Surgeries, yes."

He laughs. "I'll have to remember that one. There's some truth to it, for sure. You don't want to go down that path, assuming you don't have to."

The vertebrae could be compressed, he notes in a dubious tone, pinching the sciatic nerve, but there's no herniation. "The symptoms you describe, though, sound consistent with a herniated disc." He says a lot more, most of which I don't catch. In my case, he says it's possible we might do nothing and the pain will go away. Or we could take action and inadvertently make it worse. The thing to do is to wait and see.

"For now, I'm going to recommend rest," he says. "And I'll write you an anti-inflammatory prescription to bring the swelling down. No heavy lifting."

In other words, no gun, no cuffs, no lugging that thick leather briefcase.

"I'll see what I can do."

When I get home, I swallow a couple of pills and start running a bath. Just as my toe touches the water, the doorbell rings. I slip on a terry cloth robe and grab my Browning before descending the stairs. Through the peephole I see Bascombe, his eyes hidden behind a pair of Ray-Bans.

"Open up, man."

I welcome him inside. He smirks at the gun in my hand.

"Can't be too careful," I say.

We go through to the kitchen. He's never been to the house before. He pauses to appreciate Charlotte's marble counters and stainless appliances. Then he pulls out a barstool and sighs. "You didn't make things easier on me this morning."

"I didn't know I was supposed to."

"You and me, we're the last of the old breed. If we don't stick together . . ."

"I hear you, Lieutenant. I guess I felt a little blindsided. I mean, with Hedges, I got shot in the leg and was back on the job within twenty-four hours. He knew when to bend the rules."

"Well, he's gone now." He shakes his head. "You might think you and Mosser have some kind of relationship, but let me tell you, she's ready to throw you to the wolves. There's a lot of pressure being put on her, March. I don't know where it's coming from. Somewhere higher up, maybe even from outside the department. They want to come down on you for this shooting."

"The guy murdered a cop."

"You don't have to tell me. But these IAD guys, they're treating Lorenz's death and your shooting as two separate events. To them, you might as well have walked up to the man at random and lit him up. And they didn't come up with that on their own. Somebody's telling them how to play this. Somebody with a lot of pull."

"You're freaking me out."

"I hope so. Now tell me one thing: are you absolutely sure that the man you saw at the scene was the same one in the photo Bea Kuyk-endahl provided?"

"I'm not absolutely sure. How can I be? But it looked like him. When I saw him, the voice in my head went, *That's the guy.*"

"I don't know, man. I don't know what to make of that at all."

"It means the man the FBI says is on the mortuary slab is really alive and kicking. Which makes you wonder why they'd want us to think otherwise. There's some kind of connection to Andrew Nesbitt's death, too—the guy who claimed he was working for the CIA. That's what all the stuff they took from the scene was about. Lorenz put it all together. That finger was pointing at something after all. It was pointing to the stretch of Allen Parkway where Nesbitt was shot. You may not know what to make of it, but to me it looks like some kind of cover-up."

"A conspiracy," he says. "You sound crazy."

"Maybe. Do you have another explanation?"

He shakes his head.

"So what are we going to do about this?"

"*We* aren't doing nothing. Wanda Mosser's keeping tabs on me like nobody's business. She barely let me leave her office for bathroom breaks. And you're done. If she so much as suspects you're working this case, she'll come down on you like bricks. You were about to spill everything to her, too. If she'd found out about the file Agent Kuyken-dahl gave you, trust me, you wouldn't have walked out with it."

"What?"

"I'm not stupid, March. The point is, whatever your suspicions are, they're just that: suspicions. You don't know anything concrete, and you certainly can't prove it. Right now, you've got to go with the flow. Stay under her radar, and she won't feel like she has to do anything more to you for the time being."

"So just rest," I say. "Just relax. You sound like my doctor."

"You should listen."

The sound of a car outside. I glance through the kitchen blinds and see Charlotte pulling up to the garage. Bascombe rises, making for the front door.

"What about the ID on the guy who killed Lorenz? Have they gotten anything yet?"

"Nothing," he says. "Nothing on the prints, nothing on the DNA. He wasn't carrying any identification, just cash, and it turns out you can buy those skull rings pretty much anywhere. It's like he never existed."

"Or his files were erased."

"Man," he says, "I'm getting out of here. Pretty soon you'll have me believing it."

He closes the front door just as Charlotte comes through the back. She drops her purse and keys on the side table.

"Was somebody here?" she asks.

I stand there, uncertain what to say. The conversation fills my head like so much cotton wadding, muffling the sound of her voice. Then I flip the switch. I take the fears and suspicions and I bury them.

"Bascombe," I say. "He just left. And now my bathwater is probably cold."

She kicks her shoes off. "A bath sounds good."

It's a pleasure just to be in the same room with her. To be able to reach out and touch her. To have more in my life than her disembodied voice.

"You can join me," I say.

"Tempting." She tilts her head to one side, her expression an alloy of mischief and concern. "I would, baby, but I'm afraid you might hurt yourself."

INTERLUDE : 1986

One morning, already late and breathing hard, a lather of sweat on my skin, I veered off the path of my usual run, cutting through a stretch of parkland on base. I passed through clusters of empty picnic tables set in clearings draped with camouflage netting. Going this way, I could slice five minutes off my time and avoid the hard glare from Sgt. Crewes.

Rounding a corner, I wiped my brow on the sleeve of my olive drab T-shirt. When I looked up, a group of men were staring my way. Magnum and his death squad trainees sat huddled at one of the picnic tables. My sudden appearance had interrupted some kind of lesson. Magnum said something in what sounded like fluent Spanish, eliciting a laugh from his men. I should have kept jogging, but instead I pounded to a halt, doubling over to catch my breath.

"Don't let us interrupt you," he called. "It's Lieutenant March, right?"

I nodded. A couple of weeks had passed since our first meeting, and in that time I'd mostly forgotten about Magnum and the so-called cabana boys. I'd even wondered whether Crewes had made all the cloak-and-dagger stuff up, having fun at the expense of a credulous officer. Now I knew better.

He held a long whippy reed in one hand and an open lockblade knife in the other, and he looked to be carving as he spoke. He held the reed at eye level, appraising the beveled end. Probably wondering if it was thin enough yet to slide under a fingernail.

At the table I noticed César, the man who'd been leaning against Magnum's Buick. Once again he was smoking a panetella, and once again he gave an ironic salute. Up close, his courtly smile reminded me of young Omar Sharif. There was a dark mole on his cheek. While his fatigues, like all the others, bore no insignias of rank, his manner combined with the deferential way the others hedged around him backed up Crewes's idea that he was the boss man. I held his gaze a moment before looking away.

Magnum glanced over his shoulder to see what was attracting my interest. Then he turned and gestured with the knife. "I'm sure you have somewhere to be."

I nodded again, then got going.

I had some speed back then. For a couple of years in high school I'd gone out for track. The 440 was my race, and though I was never good enough to compete seriously, for a while I fancied myself quite a runner. Thanks to that conditioning I had aced my PT requirements, making it clear throughout ROTC and OCS that I could lead from the front.

Unfortunately a good officer needs more than physical courage. He must be someone that other men can look up to and follow. Having grown up a loner, I always had trouble with that part. The Army figured this out long before I did, sorting me to one side for staff and administrative work, tasks that didn't require too much personal charisma. After my assignment to the battalion, where my duties consisted mainly of office work, I began to worry that I was getting soft. Which is why, every other morning, I'd drive in early to jog around the base before showering and reporting.

Brief as it was, my encounter with Magnum stirred something in me. By the time I reached my office I was half an hour late, still wrapped up in my own head. Crewes appeared at the door looking stern.

"Don't you have somewhere to be?" I snapped, echoing Magnum's words to me.

The sergeant stiffened at the unaccustomed rebuke and disappeared.

The next day I took the same route, slowing my pace through the park trail. As I approached the netted picnic table, Magnum appeared. He sat by himself on the tabletop, his soft loafers resting on the seat. He seemed lost in the pages of the fat paperback clutched in his hands, but he saw me as I passed and gestured me over.

"I thought you might drop by," he said.

I paused, jogging in place.

"No, really. Have a seat. Let's exchange a few words, Lieutenant."

He closed the book and thumped it down on the table. Dante's *Inferno*. After what Maj. Shattuck had told me, I should have bolted. But I wouldn't have come in the first place if I'd intended to do that. Besides, running away would be an unworthy response for an officer. I posted myself a few feet from the table, arms crossed, keeping a wary distance between us, trying to look hostile rather than defensive.

"Suit yourself." He fixed me with a disarming smile, a smile that lit up his face and said he was my friend and only wanted what was best. "What I'm wondering," he said, easing the words out, "is whether your commanding officer put you up to this. Don't try to lie to me, either. I can always tell when I'm being lied to."

"Nobody ordered me to run," I said.

"I'm pretty sure *that's* not true."

"What I mean is—"

"Never mind." The smile broadened. "So if you're not spying on me, what are you doing here?" He patted the table next to him, inviting me to mount up. I stood my ground. "All right, then. What exactly did you see yesterday? I'm assuming you don't speak the language?"

"I'm from Texas."

"So you don't."

He chuckled at his joke, then slid off the table. At the edge of the perimeter, he passed a hand through the draped netting and plucked a cattail from the bushes opposite. Then he dug a knife out of his pocket and cut the ends off, making toward me.

"If you're forcing me to guess, I will. What would I assume if I were you, stumbling onto a scene like that? I know—" He sliced one end of the stalk into a crude spear. "Maybe you figured I was teaching these boys to make punji stakes. Or how to make shoots to stick under people's fingernails." He tossed the reed away. "Or *maybe* I'm just one of those people who likes to whittle things as he talks."

"I know why you're here," I said.

"Do you?" He slipped the knife away. "Or do you just *think* you do?"

"Everybody on base knows."

I could hear my voice wavering. Nothing good could come of this conversation and I knew better than to continue. But I was weak. And frankly I was also intrigued. Whatever Crewes thought about the spooks, I'd grown up in the last phases of the Cold War. In college I'd dutifully attended Russian language classes, which in those days were populated almost entirely by ROTC students learning not to appreciate the culture or the literature, but how to interrogate prisoners. I'd grown up watching James Bond, too, and now here I was, in the presence of a real-life secret agent. Anxious as I was, I was excited, too. And Magnum had no trouble picking up on this. He gave me another one of those smiles.

"Let me tell you something," he said. "Everybody on base may think they know what's going on, but they have no idea."

"What are you doing, then?"

"Put it this way: I'm a talent scout. These guys you see me with, they may not seem like much today. They aren't, and most of them never will be. Some of them will go nowhere, some will end up blindfolded against the wall. Some will end up jumping out of an airplane with no parachute." He laughed. "Don't worry, though, not all of them will sink. A couple will swim, and one of them? He might even fly."

"And when he does," I said, "you'll already be his friend."

"You're smarter than you look. But no, I won't be his friend. *We* will. The United States of America. And right here is where it all will have started. There are names I could mention—powerful men today—who are friends to this country as a result of relationships forged just like this. I'm not looking for quick results here. I take the long view."

I stood there not knowing whether to be appalled or electrified, whether to judge Magnum's long view as ruthlessness or just common sense. Despite the Buick and the boxy suits, there was a glamor to the man. While the rest of us were playing soldier, he was fighting the secret war—the *real* war—and didn't that lift him above our standards of judgment? Whatever Shattuck might think, I knew why I'd come, and it wasn't to judge. I was here to be noticed. I was here to make my availability known. Here am I, send me.

"It's César, isn't it?" I asked, hoping to impress him. "The one who's gonna fly?"

"You're sharp, you know that? I spotted it right off. Like I said, I'm a talent scout. I don't need much time to get the measure of a man. Now, tell me something . . ." He leaned closer. "Can you keep a secret, Lieutenant March?"

I stepped toward him, the hair on the back of my neck standing up.

"Yes," I said. "I can."

"Good." He patted my shoulder for the second time. "Prove it."

He got up and walked away.

THE
PART 2
VESTIBULE

... credo ch'un spirito del mio sangue pian-
gala colpa che là giù contanto costa.

*... a spirit of my own blood laments the guilt
that brings so great a cost below.*

Dante accepts the idea of neutral agents
in the quarrel between God and Satan. And he puts
them in Limbo, a sort of vestibule of his Hell.
We are in the vestibule, *cher ami.*

—ALBERT CAMUS

CHAPTER 11

Saturday in the Heights. Johnny Cash on the stereo and steaks on the grill, the neighbor's automatic sprinklers *wick-wick-wicking* on the far side of the wooden fence. I'm stationed, spatula in hand, comfortable as a lizard in the sun, trying to tell myself this is the life and I could get used to it. Charlotte, who's flowering now that she's practicing law full-time, has lectured me twice already about a man being more than his job description.

I'm trying to take it in stride.

Behind me, Carter Robb is trapped in a conversation with Cavallo's husband, Dean, who gulps down Shiner like water and has none of the veteran's stereotypical reticence when it comes to boasting about wartime exploits. Robb slips in the occasional yeah and uh-huh. Most of Dean's stories seem to involve some combination of exploding goats and friendly fire, and I suspect he plays up the details, testing the young reverend.

"If there's one thing I've learned, though, being over there," he says, "it's that people are more similar than they are different."

"Uh-huh," Robb says. He must know, judging by what's gone before, that there's more to Dean's heartwarming pronouncement than meets the eye.

"Take this, for example. The Arabs, they think all the bad stuff that happens to them is the result of some international Zionist conspiracy. The family goat walks into a minefield, and they blame the Jews. Crazy, huh?"

"Yeah," Robb says.

"Then I come back here, and Terry says we're going to church. And I meet this old guy there, and when he finds out where I've been, he starts in on how the president won't produce his birth certificate and steel doesn't melt just because some jet wrecks into it. See what I mean? Different players, same idea. Somebody's running things behind the curtains. Nothing ever just happens." Dean chuckles to himself. "Although this guy, he really seemed big on Israel."

Cavallo's husband may be a bit of a blowhard, but I figure he's earned the right. And it's not like he doesn't have a point.

"Don't get me started on conspiracy theorists," I say.

Dean perks up. "Oh yeah?"

"I've got this cousin who thinks her brother was murdered by Dean Corll—you remember him? He was a serial killer here in the Heights back when we were kids. The Candy Man, they called him. Anyway, she devoted a website to all this, convinced all these other fruit loops that she was right—"

Charlotte brings out a bowl of tossed salad from the kitchen, her sundress fluttering in the breeze. "Who are you talking about?"

"Nothing, dear." I smile ironically and Dean starts to laugh.

"Don't talk bad about people behind their backs." With a wink she rejoins the women inside. A moment later, they all emerge, their arms laden with plates, glasses, pitchers—Cavallo in white shorts and oversized sunglasses, Gina Robb pink-skinned and waddling, looking ready to pop, but still as radiant as she was in front of the camera.

Carter rises to make room around the patio table, probably relieved for the deliverance.

Over lunch, Dean fades a little, not having much to contribute to a discussion of baby names and due dates. The Robbs have settled into their new place, but they've had to suspend their planned repainting because the fumes are giving Gina headaches. She lights up as she describes the nursery's two perfect marigold walls and the two untouched sides that still sport the hideous original flocked velvet wallpaper, dating back to before either one of them was born. "When I'm at the hospital in labor," she says, "I told Carter he has to run home and finish painting the room."

Cavallo gives Dean a few meaningful looks during the baby talk, which he either doesn't pick up on or chooses to ignore. According to Charlotte, Theresa's gone a little baby crazy: "She's tired of snoozing the biological alarm clock." A hard image for me to square with her flinty work persona. It would be strange if she rode Wanda's coattails into Homicide only to take a time-out for maternity leave.

"So how are you settling in at the new job?" I ask.

Charlotte makes a threatening motion with her steak knife. "No work at the table!"

"I'm just asking."

"It's fine," Cavallo says. "They think you're some kind of legend, the other detectives. They ask a lot of questions about . . ." She pauses, glancing over at the Robbs. They actually knew Hannah Mayhew, the subject of my recent comeback case, whereas for us she was just another victim, albeit an all-important one. "About the task force," she finishes.

Dean jumps in. "I'll bet you're a legend now, the way you put that shooter down. Terry told me all about that, man. That was righteous."

Cavallo gives him an elbow. The rest of them ignore the remark.

Yet I find his approbation strangely satisfying. Dean strikes me as the type who's a boor on principle, the kind of guy who tramples social conventions like he wouldn't know what else to do with them, but would carry a wounded buddy out of enemy territory, humping fifty miles if he had to. When he met Cavallo, he was a cop and an Army reservist, and he'll probably end up working on one of the city or county tactical response teams once he's considered all the options. I like him, but I've never quite figured out the attraction between the two of them. I have a theory it was mainly physical, intensified by Dean's long absences, and now that they're together things aren't going particularly smooth.

Trying to segue, Cavallo produces her new business cards and starts showing them off. I take one, turning it over in my hand, remembering the first time I'd seen my own name and the word HOMICIDE on the same card. I gave those cards out to everyone.

"So you're keeping your maiden name?" Robb asks.

Next to me, Charlotte deflates. Doesn't anyone besides her know anymore what questions are appropriate to ask? I try not to smile. Dean makes a show of turning in his chair to face his wife, like it's a question he's wondered himself and he can't wait to hear the answer.

"We haven't really talked about it," Cavallo says, not looking at Dean. "For me, it's sort of like how celebrities, once people know them by a certain name—"

"But it's not like you're famous or anything," Dean says.

"I know that."

"Is it maybe a *feminist* thing?" He grins at the dig. "Now, Charlotte, you're a professional woman. Did you change your name when you two got married?"

Charlotte sputters, caught on the horns of a dilemma. She doesn't want to side with Dean against Theresa, but on the other hand she's about as traditional as they come. Her father was a conservative kingmaker in Texas politics back in the day, and as the elder daughter, Charlotte took after him, leaving her wayward sister to drift toward the other extreme.

"I did," she finally admits, "but I can understand what Terry's saying. Anyway, what's in a name? The important thing is that this girl right here waited for you a long, long time, and now that she's got you, I've never seen her happier."

"And *that's* the truth," Cavallo says, raising her glass.

Satisfied, Dean puts his arm over her shoulder, squeezing her tight.

Dean and Theresa leave midafternoon with thanks and promises to do it again soon. Charlotte walks them out with Carter in tow, leaving Gina to rest in her chair. I scoot around to the one beside her, asking how she's been.

"I was really sorry," she says, "hearing about your partner. That must have been terrible."

I nod without replying.

"I just kept thinking about the last time I saw you, and all that stuff I said about Roland and chivalry and Francis Drake or whoever. That was stupid of me. It's just an abstraction for people like us—the danger, I mean—but you live it, don't you? I'm very sorry."

"You weren't being stupid at all," I say, patting her hand, which is warm to the touch and swollen. "That Roland guy really was an idiot. Besides, I thought you'd moved on from him to Dante now."

"I finished him, too."

"What did you think?"

"Well, this wasn't my first time, you know. I was surprised by some of the things I never picked up on before."

"Like what?"

"It turns out that to exit hell, you actually have to climb over the devil's back."

"For real?"

She nods.

"That sounds about right."

Charlotte returns, decides the sun is too warm and takes Gina into the air-conditioned house to show her sightseeing photos from England, having just discovered that the data card from her camera will plug straight into the flat-screen television. Left to ourselves, Carter and I start cleaning up.

"What's your take on Dean?" he asks. "One-on-one I find him kind of aggressive."

"I guess you shouldn't have said anything about Cavallo's name."

"Before that even. Did you hear some of the stuff he was saying?"

"Honestly? I think he was sizing you up. He wanted to get the pecking order out of the way, trying to get a rise out of you. Don't you get a lot of that in your line of work?"

"A little, I guess."

"Don't take it personally. I'm sure Cavallo's talked you up a lot. He was probably jealous."

"Do they seem . . . *happy* to you?"

I shrug. "You gotta remember, they were engaged all that time long-distance; then after the wedding he went back to Afghanistan. They've been together a long time, but they've really only been living together since he got back. It's a different dynamic."

While he ruminates on this, I'm struck by how much Carter has grown up since the specter of fatherhood reared its head. He's retired the ironic tees in favor of shirts that actually button down the front. Instead of flip-flops, he wears canvas lace-ups. He's been through a lot, this young man, but life hasn't marked him. I feel a quasi-paternal pride, though I've never been anything like a mentor to him, let alone a father.

"You're gonna be a dad," I say, stating the obvious.

He smiles.

The outreach center where he works is undergoing a transformation, he tells me. The man behind it, Murray Abernathy, bought a building in Montrose and spent a pretty penny doing renovations. That was a couple of years ago, and until now the facility has remained mostly empty. Originally, Abernathy envisioned sharing the space with charity and social justice organizations, but the partnerships never materialized. "It's the way Murray embraces things," Carter says. "He gets so excited that people are afraid he's going to take them over."

Now that's starting to change. Thanks to the recession, there are plenty of nonprofits looking to economize. In addition, the need for shared infrastructure and coordination has increased. "There are more people in crisis, so why not create a single place where they can go for whatever kind of help they need?" Robb's time has been increasingly devoted to cultivating these partnerships, keeping Abernathy's intimidating enthusiasm at bay.

"It may sound shallow," he says, "but I finally feel like I'm doing something. You can only have so many open-ended theological arguments with people before you start feeling it hasn't amounted to much."

"Is that right?" I've been on the receiving end of those arguments before, so I can relate to what he's saying. "I'm glad you're finding your feet there. I know you had your doubts for a while."

When I'd first met him, Carter had a comfortable job at a suburban church shepherding affluent teens. Then one of his charges, Hannah Mayhew, disappeared and suddenly the bubble he'd been living in burst. Since then, he's been on a kind of journey, looking for a simpler, more authentic way to minister. Living in Houston, I've run into all kinds of religious leaders, from the staid and respectable to the firebrand nut jobs, and I try to respect other people's callings even when I do not share them. With Carter that has never been hard. The authenticity he claims to seek is something that, to my mind, he already possesses, though for some reason he cannot see it for himself.

"I want you to know," he says, "you've been a big help to me. You probably won't even remember the conversation, but last year, when I'd just found out about Gina being pregnant, we got into an argument in the car. Do you remember?"

In the middle of the Simone Walker case. I remember it well. My mind was on other things at the moment. "Don't worry about it."

"We got to talking about evil, and you said God wouldn't stand by and do nothing if he had the power to stop it. Because if you had the power, you'd stop it, and isn't God better than you?"

I don't recall my exact words, though I remember the gist of the argument. Something about free will.

"Dean made me think of it. That thing he said about the conspiracy nut he met at our church. I think I know the guy he's talking about." He shakes his head. "People need to put a face on what happens. That face used to be God's. Christians called it providence, the idea that God was behind everything that happened, working it all out according to his will. I grew up in church, though, and that's not what I was taught."

"Really?" I say, thinking of my Presbyterian aunt. "Because I'm pretty sure I was."

"No, what I was taught was that line I tried to feed you. God wants to do the right thing, but his hands are tied. Anyway, Dean's right. Since God isn't in charge anymore, we invent conspiracy theories to replace him. We know there's some kind of driving force—"

"There's always chance."

"Is there?" He's on the verge of taking the bait, then pulls up with a grin. "I won't rehash an old argument. I just wanted to show you I'm willing to admit when I'm wrong."

I pat him on the back. "I knew that already, Carter."

When the dishes are squared away and the grill looks spotless, we head inside to rejoin Charlotte and Gina. There's some truth in what he said about people inventing conspiracies. But the fact is, sometimes the powerful do conspire. Lorenz said I was showing him my own psycho wall. Bascombe thought I was crazy even to suggest something sinister's going on with Brandon Ford's supposed death. Everybody knows that conspiracy theorists are idiots. So what can you do when confronted with evidence of a conspiracy? All this is jumbling around in my head, along with what Gina said about crawling over the devil's back.

"What's that quote you told me once," I ask Carter. "Something about Satan's biggest lie?"

He grins, no doubt happy that at least one of his proselytizing attempts has stuck in my mind. "It was this: 'The greatest trick the devil ever pulled was convincing the world he didn't exist.'"

"That's it."

A good line. If conspiracies don't exist, they're just a fantasy of simple minds, then blowing the whistle is tantamount to confessing your ignorance. I know better than to believe in such things. I should walk away. I should forget.

"What's that from, anyway?" I ask. "The Bible?"

"No," he says. "It's from *The Usual Suspects*."

When they've gone, Charlotte and I go back on the deck. The sun sits low on the horizon, casting an orange glow, but the air remains thick with heat. Sometimes a Houston sun can be a malevolent thing. Other times that warm blanket brings nothing but comfort. We recline side by side on the chaise chairs, our hands joined. Charlotte's bare feet stray over to my side, running down along my calf.

"I could stay out here forever," she says.

"I'm not sure I could."

"Roland. That's not very romantic."

"I just mean, if I don't get back to work soon I'm gonna go crazy."

"That's funny," she says. "I was going to bring up the possibility of retirement again. I know we haven't talked about it in a while, but you've put in your years. With Hedges moving on and all the . . . changes at work, maybe it's time to reconsider?"

"The way this conversation used to go is, you'd say we should both quit our jobs and buy an RV to tour around the country."

"I'm pretty sure I never said anything about a recreational vehicle. In my sixties, maybe, but not in my forties."

"What about your job, though? You seem to enjoy it."

She pulls her foot back, but leaves her hand in mind. "Do you have a problem with me working full-time again?"

"Of course not. But if you're working and traveling the way you have been, what am I supposed to do if I chuck the badge? Take up gardening?"

"This yard could use it. But no. There are other things you could do. You know what I've always thought you'd be great at? Teaching. You'd make a good history teacher, and then I'd know when you were coming home each day. And *if* you were coming home."

"Don't be so sure. The public schools these days . . ."

"It's just a thought," she says. "The main thing is, I want you to be happy."

"Who says I'm not?"

"I've . . ." She takes her hand away to flick her hair back, then returns it with a squeeze. "I've found something, Roland. A few years ago, we were both so miserable. There were so many things we didn't even talk about—"

"Yes, I know."

"—but things have changed for me. I found my faith, Roland, and that really helped me. I wanted to share that with you. I still do. But I'm not going to drag you kicking and screaming—I already tried that, right? And now, with my new job, I've found this inner strength I didn't even know I had. I feel like I'm finally back on course, finally doing what I'm meant to do. And it worries me, baby, because we're not on the same page."

Charlotte and I, we're good at fighting. We have some experience. Inside me I can feel the old anger stirring. This could go in so many directions, most of them bad. If we're not on the same page, then maybe it's because she turned hers. I could say that, but I don't want to.

"We're not so far apart."

"In some ways—and this sounds terrible, I know, but in some ways I feel like we're more apart than we were. We're living separate lives."

This hits me like a blow.

She moves her other hand over, clasping mine in both of hers. "Don't take that the wrong way, baby."

"It sounds like you're leading up to something."

"I'm not. Don't even say that. But I am worried about you, Roland. I'm not going to hide that. And the thing that prevents me being happy with what's happening in my life is the fear that, in doing all this, I'm leaving you behind. I'm not—but I'm afraid you feel that way."

"I don't feel that way," I say.

"Baby," she says, "at least try to sound convincing."

Her talk has drawn a curtain on the evening, which might have turned out so well. I'm not a big believer in talking. Maybe I'm just weak. Confiding my secrets, even with the woman who's endured so much by my side, does not come easily. Not that I try particularly hard. Silence does come easy. It's when I open my mouth that the trouble starts.

But she deserves more than silence.

"I think you're wrong," I say, "but I don't want to argue. You're happy with the job and that's fine with me. I'm glad for you. But I miss you, Charlotte. What else do you expect me to say? I wish you were around like you used to be—and I realize how hypocritical that is, considering the hours I work."

"It is," she says softly.

"The truth is, I worry about myself, too. Jerry died in my arms. I was covered in his blood, Charlotte, from trying to save him. And you know what? I don't feel anything. I'm angry, sure, but what else is new? Something like that, it should scar me for life, right? They made me take leave because, given what I've been through,

I'm supposed to need it. But I don't. I really don't. Now, what does that say about me?"

She leans over, presses her lips against my cheek. "It says you're hurting. You just don't want to admit it. You think you always have to be strong, but you don't."

"I'm not going to let it rest," I say.

She sits up. "Let what rest?"

"The case. Bascombe told me I have to lay low until the Internal Affairs investigation blows over. He seems to think that if I do, they'll eventually drop it. Think about that. If I go after the people who killed Jerry, then I'm in trouble—"

"The man who killed Jerry is already dead."

"—but if I let it go, then I can move on with my career. And I get a vacation, too. A reward for looking the other way."

"I'm sure that's not what Bascombe meant."

"The reason I'm telling you is, I want you to be prepared. I'm not planning to leave the job, but they might kick me to the curb all the same. And then we'll buy a shiny silver Airstream and drive to Santa Fe like a couple of old-timers, because I'll finally be ready to shake the dust of this city off my shoes."

She likes the sound of this and lets me know. We go inside, pulling the back door closed, and the hem of her sundress is already in her hands, and she's not thinking anymore about the possibility of my hurting myself.

But she should be.

CHAPTER 12

According to the plaque, eleven thousand gallons pour over the sixty-four-foot-high Water Wall every minute, crashing down in sheets onto the angled steps below. To approach, you pass under a gabled archway "reminiscent of an ancient Roman theatre stage." (That spelling of *theater* makes me smile.) The landmark fountain went up around the same time as Philip Johnson's Transco Tower, which looms nearby, and ever since it's served as a backdrop for countless tourist snaps and wedding portraits. I remember Mack Ordway once saying that the ideal Houston suicide would consist of a dive off the Tower culminating in a face-plant before the Water Wall. In addition to a death wish, you'd need a set of wings to cover that distance. But gazing up with the massive fountain at my back, it almost seems possible.

I pace along the edge of the water, letting flecks of cool water dissolve on my face. It feels good in the morning heat. Apart from a couple of office workers in shirtsleeves and loosened ties eating breakfast burritos under the gables, I'm alone for the moment. I gaze upward at the slice of sky framed by the top of the circular wall, the voluminous edge of a smoke-white cloud backed by the clearest of blues.

"You're here early."

I turn at the sound of Bea Kuykendahl's voice, barely audible above the roar of the water. She wears jeans and a cotton blazer to cover her gun. A gust of wind agitates the short blond spikes of hair into a temporary ridgeline.

"I've got nowhere else to be," I say. "I'm on an involuntary vacation."

"I see you're still strapped." She nods at my own jacket.

"I'm still a cop, after all."

She has to get close for us to hear each other without shouting. It would be too strange, standing face-to-face, so we end up side by side, gazing into the water with our backs to the outside world. I have a feeling I know why she chose this as a meeting place. It would be hard to get good sound if you were trying to listen in. Maybe she thinks I'm wired. Maybe she thinks one or both of us might have been followed here.

Or maybe I'm letting my imagination run free.

"When you told me NCIC spit out a match on Brandon," she says, "I didn't believe you at first. I had to double-check it for myself."

"I find that hard to believe."

"Believe what you want. The only reason I brought you into this is because I expected . . ." Her voice trails off. "My information was different."

"What's that supposed to mean? I thought the whole point was that you saw we were looking for a match with your undercover agent. We got it, so you had to intervene. If you could rig the results so that the cover story was confirmed—"

"You really think I have that kind of power? A special agent at the Houston Field Office?"

"Maybe," I say.

After doing a little checking, I've come to have a new appreciation of Bea Kuykendahl. Her age and appearance are deceptive. According to my sources, she's something of a prodigy, wielding more influence in the world of Gulf Coast criminal intelligence than I would ever have imagined. Her latest assignment included carte blanche when it came to picking her own personnel and putting them into action.

"I'm flattered, but really, that's not even funny. What I'm saying is,

I had information that the computer would come back with Brandon's real identity."

"Who says it didn't? Everything about this guy checks out."

Everything but the main thing, namely, the link between Brandon Ford and the headless corpse left in the shadow of Allen Parkway. But I say nothing about that. I'm here to get information, not dole it out.

"You're making a fundamental mistake," she says, cutting off my objection with a flick of the hand. "Listen to me. You're assuming that if somebody's undercover, then the story will be flimsy and won't check out. If it was thrown together at the last moment, then maybe. But exactly how far back did you really go?"

"I talked to the man's ex-wife. I saw his kids."

"And she's known him for how long? A few years?"

"His mother does the baby-sitting." I take the photo from the garage out of my pocket: Brandon and his two friends, with his mother in the background. "*She's* known him since he was born."

As she studies the image, the corner of her lip curls down. "Oh, I know her. And there's more to the situation than you realize."

"Let me lay something out for you, Bea. This started off as a murder investigation, and now a Houston police detective, my partner, is dead. From where I'm standing, I'd say there's more to this situation than *you* seem to realize. You're withholding information, pure and simple. Now either start at the beginning and tell me everything you know, or I'm gonna walk."

"You'll walk? You're the one who called me."

I shrug. "I'm not gonna stand here and be lied to again."

She's mad, that much is obvious, even though she tries to keep it bottled up. Maybe she thinks I'm not showing her enough respect. Whatever illusion she had of controlling the situation is starting to crumble.

"This is off the record," I say, giving another little push.

"Here's what I can tell you. I inherited Brandon. I inherited the whole operation. Another agency put it in place, and for some reason had a change of priorities. This thing goes back years. But I was only put in charge of it four months ago."

"When exactly?"

She does the math in her head. "Early February. Going on five months, I guess."

In other words, not long after Andrew Nesbitt's death.

"And the other agency that was responsible for putting the operation in place?"

"I can't tell you that. Seriously. I have my suspicions, but there's a certain . . . imprecision to the way things like this happen."

"But we're talking about the CIA, right?"

"Maybe," she says. "Or somebody working with them."

"Earlier, you said you had information that the computer would blow Ford's cover. Where did that come from?"

"A phone call," she says. "A tip."

"From?"

She stares into the water, not wanting to give it up.

"Bea, who tipped you off? You realize whoever it was set you up, right? We wouldn't be here if it wasn't for that call."

"You said Brandon's mother baby-sits his kids. Did you actually talk to her?"

That was on Lorenz's list, but we never got that far. I shake my head.

"Well, you might have a hard time finding her now. That's who called me. Hilda. And she was Brandon's handler, not his mother. What a piece of work." She shakes her head. "I haven't been able to reach her since that call."

"This operation," I say. "What's it all about?"

She takes a half step toward me, touching her right arm against my left. She talks so softly I have to bend closer to hear. "This cannot go any further than you and me. I'm telling you this in good faith."

The story she tells concerns a war between the powerful Gulf Cartel and the renegade enforcers called Los Zetas, now a cartel in their own right. Los Zetas was originally from the Mexican special forces, recruited by the Gulf Cartel's then-leader, Cárdenas Guillen, to take out the competition. After defying the FBI and DEA, Guillen is now doing time in a U.S. prison without possibility of parole. A Federal judge in

Houston sentenced him not long after Bea was handed her undercover operation. "Suddenly I had an inside man in Matamoros, home base of the Gulf Cartel."

The volume of good intel coming up from Matamoros was staggering. The first report to come across her desk read like a soap opera digest of cartel gossip. Some of this she routed to contacts at the DEA, some she delivered through channels to the Mexican government. Everything came through the woman posing as Brandon Ford's mother. She gave Bea the initial rundown on the organization and introduced her to Brandon, who would make the 350-mile trip to Matamoros every couple of weeks to collect information.

"Brandon had ideas of his own," she says. "He wanted a larger role in the operation. He was tired of being the courier."

So with the help of their cartel insider—Bea won't share the man's name, or even his code name—they set up the scenario she'd hinted at in our first interview. Brandon would use his gun-dealer cover to offer arms to the cartel. The plan was to expand his business until he had deals in place with the rival outfits, too.

"It would have been a delicate operation," she says. "We'd have to set up new deals before the original ones were fulfilled, then arrange the deliveries close enough together to where the initial arrests wouldn't tip the others off."

There was another side to the sting, which made it appealing to Bea's higher-ups. With a bankroll from the FBI, Brandon would purchase guns from U.S. dealers. With luck he'd be able to rope in manufacturers or importers, too.

"How far along had all this gotten?" I ask.

She sighs. "He had the money."

"And what about the arms?"

"I don't know," she says with a shrug. "This first deal had already been worked out. Things were going smoothly. The last time we talked, he was heading to Matamoros for the final arrangements. I guess something went wrong."

There's a tremor in her voice.

"Bea, look at me."

She turns. Her smooth face twists into a knot. She puts a hand over her nose, like she's trying to stifle a sneeze. But it's more than that.

"What's wrong?" I ask.

"Nothing," she says, shaking her head. She chews her lip and wraps her arms tight around her body, squeezing herself still.

"You and Brandon . . . ?"

"Whoever did this, I want them as bad as you do."

"The two of you . . ."

"I don't want to talk about it. But, yes."

The idea forming in my head puts all my earlier conspiracy theories to shame. Suppose this fellow, Brandon Ford, finds himself running information back and forth across the border. He's looking for a payday and suddenly finds himself working for Bea, who's not as tough and streetwise as she'd like to make out. He insinuates himself into her life, and pretty soon she's going to her superiors for the cash to fund this sting operation.

"How much money did you actually sign out?"

"Not much to begin with," she says. "Two hundred and fifty grand."

Is that enough? I guess it depends on the situation. If Brandon Ford was ready to decamp before the opportunity came along, an extra quarter million to jump-start his new life wouldn't have gone amiss. And if he was ready to leave behind an ex-wife and kids, then saying goodbye to a new love interest—and leaving her in the lurch—would not have presented any problem. How this connects with Andrew Nesbitt's death and the way the dumped corpse was arranged, I'm not sure. A message to his so-called mother, maybe? Given time, I suspect I can work it all out. But Bea still seems oblivious.

"You're not going to like the sound of this," I say, "but I suspect you've been played. He wasn't in this to hand you a sting operation. All he wanted was the money."

She walks away from me, then turns. "You didn't know him."

"Neither did you, Bea. I think he was using you. Once he had the money, it was only a matter of time."

"You. Didn't. *Know*. Him."

She punctuates each word with a jab of the finger, speaking loud enough for the breakfasting office workers to turn and watch. I close the distance, put a hand on her arm. She shrugs free but stands her ground.

"You can at least do me the courtesy of not questioning my professional judgment!" Her words come out in a hiss. "I thought I was doing you a favor, putting you in the picture. I could get in serious trouble even for talking with you."

"Bea," I say. "Calm down. There's something you need to know."

She starts to go. "I've heard enough from you—"

"Wait." I take her by the arm. Her eyes flare with outrage, and for a moment I'm afraid she'll lash out. "Wait, Bea. You need to hear this."

She glances at the office workers, who start gathering their things and moving on. She looks at the sky, her whole body trembling with rage. Then she takes a deep breath and bores into me with her eyes. "What is it?"

"There were two men. They got the drop on me in Ford's office. For some reason, they wanted the evidence—he'd covered a wall full of clippings related to Andrew Nesbitt's death." Her face is blank. No reaction to the name. "They took the computer hard drive, too. One of them, the man I killed, was tall and lean. He wore a gold ring shaped like a skull. The other one did all the talking. He had a faint Texas accent, stood about six feet and had a broad, muscular chest. They wore hoods so I couldn't see their faces. When I shot him, the one with the skull ring had pulled his hood up. The other one got away in the car. He'd taken his mask off, so as he went by I got a good look at him."

"And?"

I nod at the photo still clutched in her hand.

"What?" she says.

"That's who I saw." I point to Brandon Ford. "That face."

"Then you saw a ghost."

"We'll see." I take the photo back. "I want you to go somewhere with me, Bea. We'll figure out which one of us is right."

"Go with you? Where?"

"The morgue," I say. "You'd know Ford's body, wouldn't you? I want to see if we can make a positive identification."

Bridger waits outside, not looking too pleased by our sudden arrival. He senses something's wrong between Bea and myself. I close the door gently, then walk to the cantilevered platform where the body waits, draped by a sheet.

"I don't want to see this," she says.

She stands a few feet back, her hands gripping the fabric front of her blazer, pulling it tight. The room is cold to begin with, but the open refrigerator forms a chilly draft. She's breathing hard, loud enough that I can hear it. Her eyes stray to the depression in the sheet where a head should be.

"What other choice is there?"

"Are you *sure* about what you saw? Absolutely sure?"

"You're not going to believe me if you don't see for yourself."

Maybe it's cruel, what I'm putting her through. If I could be absolutely sure, then I would stop. But I only glimpsed the man with the shotgun, only got a snapshot impression of his features. This is the only way to be certain.

"I'll start at the feet," I say.

She extends one of her hands as if to stop me.

"You have to do this, Bea. You have to face up to it."

She drops her hand.

I lift the sheet in stages, folding it back on itself, revealing the feet, the shins, the thighs, the genitalia. The mutilated hands appear, and there's a catch in her breathing. I reveal the torso with its autopsy incisions. At the height of the clavicle, I rest the sheet and step back.

"Is this Brandon?" I ask.

Bea edges forward slowly. She takes her time with the body. When she's finished, she straightens up. The expression on her face is unreadable.

"Bea?"

She doesn't look at me. She turns for the exit, her heels clicking across the hard floor.

"It's not him."

She disappears behind the swishing door.

CHAPTER 13

Bea is a quiet passenger, uninterested in anything I have to say. Legs crossed, arms folded, face turned toward the window so I can only see her expression in chance reflections. Blank. The muscles slack. Signifying nothing. The extent of her contribution is to point the way to Hilda Ford's house at the opposite end of Westheimer from Brandon's office. When we pull up in the driveway, she's out the door before I can cut the engine, advancing up the driveway with her side arm drawn.

"Bea!"

She keeps advancing, halted only by the locked door. I coax her gun back into the holster and try to calm her down. But she already seems calm, preternaturally so. It's hard to judge whether I'm getting through to her.

We circle the house, peering in through the windows. I half expect to find the place cleared out. But no, it's fully furnished, even a little cluttered with knickknacks. Through the kitchen door I can see the white fridge covered in layers of children's artwork and alphabet magnets. I try the handle, but it's locked.

As I check the nearby windows, Bea rears back and kicks the kitchen door. She can't put enough weight behind her foot to force the lock, but the wood gives a satisfying crack. She tries again before I can stop her.

"Have you ever heard of a warrantless entry?" I ask. "Anything we get will be unusable without probable cause."

She glares at me. "We're past warrants."

"No, Bea, we're not. I'm not. The people responsible for my partner's death, I plan to put them away. And I can't do that if you go nuclear on the scene."

"March," she says. "*March*." She clutches my arms in her hands, shaking me, looking up at me like she's gone crazy. "Are you listening to yourself? Are you serious? Don't you get it?"

I grab her wrists and pull her hands away. She tries to twist free, but I hold her.

"Get control of yourself," I say.

"Let go."

"Bea, I mean it."

Her shoulders slump and the mask falls over her features again. "I'm fine. Let me go."

I release her wrists.

"We're going in there," she says.

After a long, silent standoff, that's what we do. There's no way to stop her, and I need her cooperation. Without that, I don't have a next step. If I go along with her this time, the forced entry will hopefully burn up some of her rage and I can reason with her before we move on. She gives the door a final kick while I look on.

We clear the house, which is unoccupied, then work our way back through the various rooms. While all the furniture, appliances, and clothing are still in place, there are no computers or phones. The garage is empty, too. Nothing I see suggests this is anything other than the home of a lone woman in her fifties with a fondness for her grandchildren. There are even toys strewn across the living room floor.

"Look at this," Bea says, beckoning me over to an upright piano tucked against the wall. On top, a line of framed photographs, mostly of the two kids I recognize from the ex-wife's apartment. There are two gaps in the row. Missing photos. "There used to be one of Brandon here. And there was one of him and Miranda with the children."

She finds a pack of plastic bags in the kitchen and starts filling them with random small objects, anything that might yield fingerprints or trace evidence. Then she goes into the master bathroom in search of combs and brushes for stray hair.

"We're going to find out if Hilda's in the system," she says. "Maybe we can get a real name on her."

Given the fact that her supposed son was in the database, I seriously doubt that. But it's worth a try. When she's finished, we go out the way we came in, pulling the busted door shut. She stores her samples in the trunk of my car.

Back on the road, I ask if she wants to talk.

"What I want to do is find him," she says.

We hit a series of locations, places she thinks he might be: a chain of bars and restaurants and cigar lounges along the Sam Houston Tollway, Hempstead, and Tidwell. She shows his picture around, but gets nothing. She has me drive slowly through the parking lot of several hotels along the Northwest Freeway without explaining why she'd expect to find him in these particular spots. None of this is likely to bring results, of course, but I'm humoring her in the hope that once she simmers down, she'll be forthcoming with information.

"He's going to be anywhere associated with his old life," I finally tell her.

"You think I don't realize that?"

"What next, then?"

She thinks it over. "We should have a talk with Miranda."

"And tell her what? Her husband's not dead? I think she's the last person who's gonna have a line on his whereabouts."

"I don't know," she says. "He loved those kids."

She turns her face back to the window, elbow on the sill, her balled fist pressed against her lips. Then it all catches up to her and she doubles over. She doesn't cry, doesn't sob out loud. She just tenses up like a woman in labor, only instead of giving birth, she's trying to hold something inside. The gravity of the betrayal, the weight of her own misjudgment—whatever it is, she's overcome. I put a hand on her back.

"I want to help you fix this," I say, "but I need you to work with me."

She sits up, burying her face in her hands. "I can't do this. Take me back."

"Bea, I need you."

"Just drive me back. I can't think. I can't even breathe."

I point the car in the direction of the Water Wall, trying to argue her out of it the whole way. She's determined, though. Whatever force was driving her to the brink, overcoming all her instincts toward secrecy and self-preservation, now it's gone. Perhaps she's even a little scared of herself, afraid of the consequences of what she's learned and what she's done.

Just when I think I've lost her, pulling up to the curb behind her car, she turns in her seat and touches my arm.

"If I find anything, I will let you know," she says. "You have to promise me to do the same. And remember: you'll wreck us both if you're not careful who you talk to."

"What's my next step?" I ask.

But she doesn't know. "If you could figure out who that John Doe really is, it might help. Or get an ID on the guy you killed."

"They won't let me near the case. Is there anything you're not telling me? Anything that could help?"

"I've told you everything I know."

"What about Nesbitt? What's his connection?"

"I don't know who that is."

Near as I can guess, she seems to be telling the truth. I fill her in on the shooting death of the self-proclaimed CIA agent and the fact that John Doe's finger was found pointing toward the scene of his death.

"I don't have a clue," she says.

"Well, see what you can find out."

She agrees. And she takes the bagged samples out of the trunk, too, suggesting she hasn't abandoned the effort altogether. She just needs time, I tell myself. Once she's had a chance to process everything I told her and figure out a way to collaborate without jeopardizing herself, she'll come around.

––––––––

My first partner, Stephen Wilcox, ended the relationship by leaving Homicide for Internal Affairs. We'd been through a lot by then. He had accompanied me on my early successes and then, following a personal tragedy of mine, watched my gradual decline. As my work became sloppy, he covered for me, but when he discovered my extracurricular vigilantism—nothing illegal, though I was pursuing some private vendettas at the expense of my casework—he decided he'd finally had enough. While he never came out and accused me of misconduct, he was pretty free with the accusations in private, especially among his new colleagues in IAD.

Over the years, as I've regained my balance, I have also made efforts to reconcile with Wilcox. The problem is, no matter how friendly and forgiving he seems, the old frustration is always bubbling under the surface. He can't let go of it. As a result, I try to give him as much space as I can.

As he pulls into his driveway and sees me parked along the curb, the brakes on his Land Rover light up. He gets out, leaving the motor running and door open, bounding toward me with tight-lipped determination. I buzz my window down.

"What do you want?" he asks.

"Can we talk?"

He glances up and down the street, like he's afraid the neighbors will notice. "You really think that's a good idea? There's an ongoing investigation into your shooting."

"You're not on that."

"No," he admits, "but I still think it's a bad idea. If it's professional, I can't help you. And if it's personal . . ."

"Hey, Stephen," I say, "last time we met, you were all worked up about the Fauk case. You ever hear how *that* turned out?"

He sighs. "Yes, I did."

When we were partners a decade ago, we made headlines by putting

Donald Fauk away for murdering his wife. Last December, it looked like that conviction was going to unravel, and instead of backing me up, Wilcox was only too happy to throw me under the bus. In the end, I not only kept Fauk behind bars, but I managed to hand the Harris County Sheriff's Department the name of a serial killer who'd been flying under the radar. The detective who broke that case, Roger Lauterbach, went on record giving me the credit. And I've never heard a squeak of apology out of Wilcox in all this time.

"It gets old after a while," I say. "Me offering a hand of friendship, you spitting on it. We're on the same side, whether you realize that or not. It would be nice if you'd at least hear me out before pitching a fit."

"Fine," he says. "Let me get my keys."

Instead of inviting me inside, where I might be seen by his wife and kids, Wilcox has me drive in circles around the neighborhood while we talk. I ask him what he knows about Andrew Nesbitt's shooting, and even though he didn't conduct the investigation himself, he seems very well-informed. I imagine that one received plenty of airtime around the IAD water cooler. And since it's old news and I haven't been forthcoming about the nature of my interest, he can't see the harm in humoring me by answering a few questions.

"That one's gonna go down in the records as one of the strangest incidents in HPD history. You would not believe how many people behind the scenes are divided over it. This Nesbitt guy wasn't some random crank. He was well known by people in law enforcement. He was on the payroll of a couple of the big energy companies, where he did some very hush-hush consulting. As far as anybody in this town was concerned, before the night of the shooting he was exactly what he said he was: a retired CIA officer. In fact, a pretty senior one."

"But they denied that after he was dead?"

"Exactly."

"Which doesn't mean anything, right? They always deny it."

He shakes his head. "It's not like when a spy is caught in enemy territory. There are plenty of retired intelligence people around, and the government doesn't deny *their* existence. I mean, if they did, it would be pretty hard for these people to cash in. And believe me, they do. All those contacts built up over the years really pay dividends when you go into the private sector."

"You sound bitter."

He laughs. "In this case, though, the government went out of its way to disavow the man. It wasn't just a question of saying 'We can neither confirm nor deny.' They had people on the ground. There was a liaison to the investigation. All these retired intel folks who'd been telling us before that Nesbitt was a pillar of the community started coming forward to recant. They'd all been duped, they said. Even the ones who're on record saying they'd served with him in the past. The end result was, pretty much everybody in Internal Affairs is convinced the dude *was* a spook."

"And what about the uniforms who shot him? The video was released, and there are people on the Internet who think it was a hit."

"Yeah," he says. "People are crazy."

"There's nothing to it?"

"What do you think?" He laughs again. "Sure, a couple of HPD patrolmen are hiring themselves out as underworld hit men."

"There's such a thing as a corrupt cop," I say. "I don't have to tell you that."

"Seriously, this was a righteous shooting. Nesbitt drew and fired. Case closed."

We round the block, turning back onto his street. "I wish it was always that easy."

"You mean your own shooting?" He adjusts his seat belt so he can face me. "I was sorry to hear about what happened to Lorenz. I didn't know him that well, but he was a good man. I know that can't have been easy for you."

"Thanks," I say, really meaning it. "They're coming down on me pretty hard."

"We really shouldn't talk about that."

"What was I supposed to do—let him put one in Jerry's head?"

"It's the automatic weapon," he says. "They found something like sixteen entry wounds."

"Sixteen?" It's the first time I've heard the exact number. "It was over in a heartbeat. I didn't even know the gun was full-auto. I just grabbed what was near to hand."

I pull up in the driveway behind the Land Rover. He reaches for the door handle, but doesn't pull it.

"Listen, Roland. I shouldn't even be saying that. There's a lot of pressure on our people. We're not stupid. You shot a cop-killer in the middle of the act. Nobody wants to come down on you for that. A lot of us think you deserve a medal. But like I said, there's a lot of pressure from up top. They want every aspect of this thing scrutinized."

"It's like a traffic stop," I say. "They've got me on one thing and they're trying to turn it into something bigger."

"Pretty much. So keep your head down."

He opens the door and starts to exit.

"One last thing. You heard about Hedges, I assume? Now Wanda Mosser's in charge. I'm not sure why, but she seems to be gunning for me, too. I don't suppose you have any insight into the back-room deals?"

"All I know is this: Hedges made a big play during the runoffs, thinking he had a shot at the chief's office. I assume some promises were made, but I can't say. In the process, he put a target on his back. Meanwhile, Wanda has a lot of friends in the new mayor's office. Homicide was her reward for backing the mayor's choice for chief. I think you're wrong about her gunning for you."

"It looks that way from where I'm sitting."

"Well, you still have a job, don't you?" He gets out of the car and shuts the door, then leans back through the open window. "If she wasn't looking out for you, I'm not sure you'd even have that."

"Thanks, Stephen."

He taps the roof. "Just don't make it a habit."

CHAPTER 14

As a testament to how well our conversation went, before I'm home Wilcox calls me with the name of a contact—an ex-intelligence man—who proved immensely informative during the investigation of Nesbitt's death. "His name is Englewood and he's the real deal." Apparently the club of retirees Nesbitt had chaired appointed this Englewood as an informal liaison, empowering him to give the detectives the lay of the land, answering questions with surprising candor, though always off the record. Wilcox only met him once, but kept the man's card. He rattles a phone number off while I copy it into the open Filofax on my lap, trying not to steer into one of the parked cars on my right.

I dial while idling in my own driveway, mentally preparing myself for some song and dance. Just because he's helped the police once doesn't mean there's a permanent shingle out on his stoop.

"This is Tom," a voice says.

"Tom Englewood?" I introduce myself, mention the fact that I'm a homicide detective, and launch into a vague soliloquy about lingering questions surrounding the Nesbitt shooting. He cuts me off midsentence, leaving me to expect the worst.

"Tell you what," he says. "You know the Downing Street Pub? I'm usually there between ten and eleven, enjoying an evening cigar. Why don't you drop by this evening and we'll have ourselves a little chat."

"I'll see you then."

In the first ten minutes, Tom Englewood reveals himself as a former Northeasterner, an Ivy Leaguer who during the course of a rich and varied life sloughed off his regional identity, trading it for what I can only describe as Latin elegance. Engine-turned cuff links sparkle at his wrists, and his watch has a skeleton face that reveals the jeweled movement inside. A puff of silk erupts from the breast pocket of his glen plaid suit jacket, with a sterling clip holding his silk-weave tie in place. He wears his hair slicked back and keeps a tightly trimmed mustache.

He holds down his side of the table like it belongs to him. I wouldn't be surprised if there was a brass plaque on the edge with his name on it. When he offers me a cigar, he clips the cap himself before passing it over, like he doesn't trust anyone else to do the job right.

Before I can ask any questions, he starts lecturing me on the virtues of American bourbons, switching in midstream (after catching my glance at the band on the cigar in my hand) to a denunciation of anyone who says the best Honduran cigars don't equal or better the much-vaunted Cubans. During the 1980s, he says, he spent a lot of time down in Honduras (*wink, nod*) and during the cigar craze of the nineties considered going back to get something going on the cigar front—easy enough to do, he hints, with contacts like his.

"Mr. Englewood," I say.

"Please. It's Tom." He makes a flourish with his cigar hand, leaving a trail of smoke in the air, granting the favor of his first name with *noblesse oblige*. "I know you didn't come out tonight to hear my theories on life. You said you have questions about Andy Nesbitt, is that right?"

"There seems to be some confusion about whether he really worked for the CIA or not."

Englewood gives me a big smile. "Uh-*huh*."

"Where do you come down on that question?"

"I knew Andy really well," he says, "but only after I settled down here. That doesn't mean much, of course. My own work was more of an analytical nature—I was a big-picture guy—whereas he always claimed to have been operational. Wherever he got his experience, I can tell you he was good at putting together networks and producing high-grade intelligence product."

"He continued to do that kind of work, you mean? After retirement?"

"None of us retires. Not if we can help it."

There are two paths, Englewood explains, which he dubs the High Road and the Low Road. Returning to the private sector, a former intelligence officer can sell his services to the government, either through an existing private security company or by creating his own. Since 9/11, there are plenty of opportunities for ex-officers with Middle East experience. "And even if they *don't* have it, there are ways and means." This kind of work, suckling at the government teat, whether directly through the intelligence community or indirectly via government contractors, is considered the High Road.

"And the Low Road?"

"Corporate money," he says. "A lot of us in H-Town, we're Low Roaders, I guess you could say. The energy companies do business all over the world, so wherever you happen to have contacts, there's usually somebody you can provide with some added value. Think about it: you could spend your whole career with Langley, sweating it out at some station in Africa, a thankless backwater where you could always be kidnapped and shot just for being seen at the embassy, without any of the compensating charms. . . ." He chuckles at the thought of said charms, but doesn't elaborate. "And when you retire, there's a Houston oil maverick looking to drill wells off the coast of your old stomping ground, and only you can tell him which palms to grease. It's a beautiful thing."

All this is interesting, but it's not what I came for. "What about Nesbitt? Which road was he on?"

"Oh, I would have had him pegged as a High Roader. You know about his newsletter? You don't?" He raises an eyebrow in surprise. "Nesbitt compiled an intelligence report specifically for policy makers, drug enforcement administrators. That was his bailiwick, international criminal organizations, particularly the Latin American ones."

"The cartels?"

He nods. "The way he described it—and obviously I can't vouch for the accuracy of this, considering our government's denial of the whole thing—his career had two phases: there was Cold War Andy and then Drug War Andy. He'd cut his teeth doing the usual cloak-and-dagger, so he seemed like a good candidate for Colombia in '91. The idea was to help the military set up networks for gathering intel on the drug lords. Shut down the problem at its source. The results, unfortunately, were mixed, but Andy came away a believer."

"So he would have been interested in what's going on with the Mexican cartels?"

"Very." I wait for him to say more, but he doesn't. An impish light shines in his eyes.

"Is there something more?"

"Funny," he says. "I get the impression *you* have something more to say. I've been pretty candid, haven't I? Maybe it's time for you to show your hand."

With a man like Tom Englewood, it's hard to know how much information to share. As forthcoming as he seems, he could simply be priming the pump, feeding me just enough background to win my trust in an effort to discover how much I really know. If I tell him about the operation Bea inherited, he might be able to confirm that it was set up by Nesbitt. From what he's saying, the Gulf Cartel op sounds like the kind of thing Nesbitt did for a living. On the other hand, he might respond by clamming up, filing away the information for future use.

"You're wondering how much you should say. That's smart. But remember, it was you who called me."

"All right, then. If I were to say that, before he died, Nesbitt was running an undercover operation inside one of the major Mexican cartels, how would you respond?"

He calls a waitress over and orders a single malt, glancing my way to see whether I'll have anything. The butt end of his cigar drops into the ashtray and he reaches into his jacket for another, withdrawing it from a hallmarked silver case. It's his last, so he offers it to me first.

"No thanks," I say. "I'm still waiting for your answer."

"I'm thinking." He clips the cigar and toasts the tip with a torch lighter before putting it to his lips for a few puffs. "The thing is, I know a little bit about your situation. After you called, I made a couple of enquiries. You aren't assigned to the Nesbitt investigation. In fact, that investigation is closed."

"I didn't say I was."

"No, you didn't. So what I'm wondering is, why do you care? You're not interested in drug enforcement, and as far as I know, as bad as things are south of the border, the drug war hasn't made its way up here yet." He cuts off my objection with a wave of the cigar. "Oh, I know, I know. The drugs are here. But no one's assassinating prosecutors or snuffing police detectives."

"I have a victim in the morgue," I say. "He's been decapitated and, before he died, he was de-gloved. You know what that means?"

His eyes narrow. "Oh, I know what it means. And I have an idea the sort of people who'd do something like that."

"So you understand my interest."

"Maybe. But you're not planning to slap the cuffs on some low-level cartel enforcers. You have a different idea in mind."

"I want to know whether Nesbitt had an operation going, that's all."

"Of course he did."

"He did? You know that for a fact?"

"I don't know anything for a fact. Let me put it this way: I was under the impression that's what he was up to, or something like it. Andy had a theory. In the 1830s, the Texans set off a chain of events that led to a U.S. invasion of Mexico a decade later. A lot of people in the American government didn't want that to happen, but the Texans led out and sucked the rest of the nation in."

"More or less," I say.

"Right. I'm not intending this as a history lesson. It's just a point Nesbitt used to make. The reason Latin America in general and Mexico in particular are so unstable is that we've ignored them. We turned our attention to the other side of the world and left our backyard to fend for itself. A familiar complaint.

"Andy's theory was, only a disaster could focus our attention on doing something. Only a disaster could shake us out of the complacent notion that we can just wall ourselves off from the problem. What he wanted for Mexico was what we'd already given to Baghdad and Kabul."

"Regime change?"

He smiles. "Stability. When the border became such a contentious issue after 9/11, Andy started telling people the border would never be secure until the nation of Mexico was, and that wouldn't happen without some kind of intervention. Cooperation simply wasn't enough. The question was, what would have to happen before Americans would support such a move?"

"You mean, before they'd support an invasion of Mexico? That's insane."

"Not an invasion. What he had in mind was something similar to what he'd worked on in Colombia, only with a more effective U.S. component. And anyway, it's not *that* insane. We've invaded Mexico before, and not just when Santa Anna was in charge. Remember Black Jack Pershing?"

"What does all this have to do with the drug cartels?"

He gives a theatrical shrug. "You tell me. You're the detective. We put pressure on the Mexicans to crack down on the cartels, so they started waging war, which sent the borderlands into a death spiral. Now the headlines are full of the excesses and Americans are shocked, *shocked* at what's happening on our doorstep. Someone has to *do* something."

"That's a very cynical point of view."

"What can I say? My profession doesn't breed many idealists. What I'm telling you is this: Andy tried to convince anyone in power who'd listen that the cartels were running wild and the Mexican government was out of its depth. If you were one of the people paying top dollar for his intel reports, that was the message he hammered into you day in and day out. So, no, it wouldn't surprise me at all to find that Andy had a line into the cartels."

The cigar in my hand has burned down to my fingers and my throat burns from sucking it down. The column of white ash suggests that Englewood has good taste in smokes, but I feel compromised somehow in partaking of his largess. When he signals the waitress again, I scoot my chair back.

"You've had enough?" he asks.

"The night he was shot, Nesbitt seemed to believe those cops were planning to kill him."

"They *did* kill him."

"Right, but he thought it was a hit. He thought HPD pulled him over with the express intention of punching his ticket. What would have made him so paranoid?"

"Your colleagues asked me the same question. I'll tell you what I told them: I have no idea. In most parts of the world, though, when you do the kind of work we did, it's not so strange to assume that when the police pull you over, they intend something more sinister than to write up a traffic citation."

"Is that the kind of thing you worry about?" I ask.

"Me?" He knocks back the last of his scotch. "No, I don't. But like I told you, my line was analysis. I never got my hands dirty. Andy did. Always assuming he never worked for the CIA at all. Naturally, I take the official denials at face value."

"Naturally."

I put a few dollars on the table despite Englewood's objection. I believe in paying my own way. He leans forward a little, the mischievous glint back in his eyes.

"I forgot to mention something," he says. "You and I, we have a mutual acquaintance. I thought I'd heard your name somewhere before."

"Oh really?" I ask, thinking he means Wilcox, though why Wilcox would have mentioned my name to him—

"Reginald Keller," he says. "I think you guys called him Big Reg."

At the sound of the name, my whole body tenses.

"How do you know Keller?" I ask.

"Before his troubles, he was involved in a little business venture.

I was one of the investors. So was Andy, if I'm not mistaken. I guess you could say that when you brought Keller down, you cost us all a pretty penny." He reaches for the money on the table and pockets it. "I'll consider this as repayment."

"It's supposed to be for the tip."

"Oh, don't worry," he says. "I always leave a big tip."

As I leave, I can hear him laughing under his breath. I push through the doorway, out into the balmy night, a few cars racing down Kirby with their stereos thumping. I go to my car, fumble through my pockets for the keys, then slump down behind the wheel. Everything he told me about Nesbitt is forgotten. The spooks and the cartels, the interventions and the border wars. All of it erased by the sound of that name.

I brought him down, but I didn't bring him to justice. He disappeared into thin air as we closed in on him. With friends like Englewood, maybe that wasn't so hard to do.

Reg Keller. Big Reg. He once threatened to come back and settle the score. The name alone is enough to have me checking over my shoulder. But Keller's not in the backseat with a garrote. He's not in the parking lot taking aim. He's gone, long gone, and he'd be crazy to return. I slip the Browning out of its holster and press the slide back, touching my finger against the reassuring round in the chamber. He'll never come back again.

But just in case.

CHAPTER 15

The last time I saw Reg Keller, we faced each other in the gutted wreck of my garage apartment after Hurricane Ike knocked a tree into the roof, him pointing a submachine gun in my face and me blinded by the flashlight mounted under the barrel. He gave a rambling, self-justifying excuse for why the death of a girl named Evangeline Dyer, which led directly to the murder of her friend Hannah Mayhew, wasn't his fault. He'd put a bullet into the brainpan of one of his own men, Joe Thomson, and that wasn't his fault, either. I'd driven him to it, and someday I was going to pay for it. But not that night. He'd had his chance, but despite everything Big Reg didn't have the nerve to pull the trigger.

I turn onto Kirby and head past San Felipe, following the curve in the road around to Allen Parkway, heading home to the Heights north of Interstate 10. Somewhere along here—I slow down to try and pinpoint the spot—Andrew Nesbitt was pulled over and eventually killed. A grass verge runs down the middle of the road, separating east- and westbound traffic, the streetlights distantly spaced, alternating cones of light with stretches of shadow. Off to my left in the darkness I glimpse the headstones of the Jewish cemetery and beyond them

Buffalo Bayou, which looks lovely in the tourist brochures but in the doldrums of summer is essentially a fetid swamp with bicycle trails cutting through it.

Perhaps Englewood's job is not the only one to breed cynicism.

While I reflect on this, a pair of headlights comes alongside in the right-hand lane. It's an H3 Hummer, one of the smaller ones, just a little bit larger than a Sherman tank. I glance over in time to see the rear passenger window rolling down.

As I watch, a flash erupts and my passenger window shatters into a cloud of glass. Reflexively I jerk the wheel, running up onto the grass median, then panic and pull back onto the road with a thump. I stomp on the brake but catch the accelerator instead, jolting forward. Which is just as well. My car slides right and glances off the Hummer, forcing it to swerve and lose a little ground.

I keep the pedal down, checking my rearview. The Hummer jumps ahead. I clench my teeth for impact, holding tight to the wheel. All my evasive driving skills have gone out the window, my strategy just to go fast and hold on for dear life. Instead of ramming, which is what I expected, the Hummer makes a surprisingly agile slip. Now the headlights are on my left.

The Hummer flicks into my rear fender near the back tire, accelerating into the contact. My car wrenches and spins. The tires slide back onto the median. I'm moving sideways, my right tire in the lead, skimming the grass until I shear off a newly planted sapling. Then the car finds purchase and leaps the median into the opposite lane.

My body is rigid with fear. I try to level out the wheel, but suddenly there are headlights coming westward, threatening a head-on collision. I slice the tires to the left, overcompensating. I'm off the roadway, sucking in breath, careening down a wooded embankment with my foot on the brake.

My car slides to a stop, the wheel jerking at the last moment, tires jammed in the soft dirt. At this angle, all I can see in my rearview mirror is a towering apartment block on the opposite side of Allen Parkway. Turning around in my seat, I watch the Hummer crawl to the edge of the embankment, where the doors open and the dome light comes on. I count four men inside. They're only twenty, twenty-five yards away.

This is bad.

I turn off my engine, killing the headlights, then feel around for my own dome light and switch it off. Then I force my leg over the middle console and pull myself to the passenger seat, ignoring the sound of crushed glass. With the Browning in hand, I push the door open. I roll onto the damp ground, aiming toward them.

The men are lined up on the curb, but they haven't started down. They seem to be waiting for traffic to clear so they can descend without any passing motorists noticing anything odd. I reach back into the car for my phone, ripping it free of the charger. Glancing behind me, I spot a dark thicket of trees outlined against the sky. While they're still standing on the edge of the road, I close the passenger door and raise myself into a crouch.

There's no pain in my leg, I realize.

I dash for the trees. The sprint takes just a few seconds, but in my mind I'm moving in slow motion, silhouetted against the night, the fatal bullet tearing its way through the air. I reach the thickest of the trunks and hide behind it for cover, which only leaves about a quarter of my body exposed. I hunker down next to the roots, trying to make myself invisible. My breathing is loud and ragged and must be audible for miles.

When I look back, they're not on the embankment anymore. The bright apartment tower makes it hard to pick out their shadows in the dark. Squinting, I see them fanned out, advancing on either side of my car. They move with precision, minding each other's fields of fire, like men who've been trained in the art and have worked a long time together.

At that moment I realize I don't have a chance.

In training it's so different. The targets stay put while you pepper them with holes. All the drills, all the preparation locks your muscle memory in so you can't act without thinking. When the balloon goes up all the sudden, hopefully the training kicks in and keeps you from freezing. You draw and fire, you get a good sight picture, you're careful of your backstop so nobody innocent comes to harm.

If you have time, though, and nothing else, no one to back you up, no advantage in numbers or tactical surprise, if all you have is time to run through all the possibilities, knowing your opponents won't stand still, that they'll react unpredictably and all too fast, then the result all too often is hopelessness. Walking up to Skull Ring and mashing the trigger on the Krinkov, that was nothing. I flash back to my most recent performance on the range, when I bungled the reload in the middle of the course and dropped my mag on the ground. Just remembering that, I know I can't shoot my way out of this. These men are careful. They know what they're doing. Even if I drop one, the others will return fire. I won't make it out alive.

I pat my pockets for my flashlight, but I know it's not there. Like the rest of my things—my briefcase, my ballistic vest, the zeroed-in AR-15 locked in the trunk, everything that might have helped me in this situation—it's back there in the car. All I have is the Browning with one magazine. That and my phone. And I'm afraid to use it. The screen is so bright I'm afraid to switch it on for fear of attracting their notice. I can hear their voices declaring the car empty.

Glancing behind me, I try to make out a path. Maybe there's a line of retreat that will get me out of here. There should be parkland deeper in, and then I should hit Buffalo Bayou. Only they're so close that if I make a break, I know they'll see me, and at this range it would be hard to miss. I like my chances better hunkered down. If I fire first, I know at least that I can drop one of them. That's better than nothing.

"Tracks," a voice hisses.

The sound makes me freeze. One of the shadows points a hand in my general direction.

I have to force myself to move. I raise the Browning, lining up the Tritium night-sights over his silhouette. I take a deep breath, then let it out.

The first shot has to count.

I'm sorry, Charlotte. I should have been a better—

Up on the embankment, the Hummer's engine rumbles to life. The shadows all stop in their tracks, then turn to watch. Now they're the ones frozen in place. The back wheels spin out and the Hummer tears onto the road with a throaty roar.

Then it's gone, leaving silence in its wake.

"Are you *kidding* me?" a loud voice says.

The reply is softer: "He must have doubled around."

"And you left the *keys* in? Is *that* what you're tellin' me?"

The voice is familiar. The last time I heard it, the speaker was holding me at the point of his shotgun. Brandon Ford. I strain to listen, trying to make out which one of the men is him. If I can figure that out, then I'll know where to aim my first round.

A third speaker, loudest of all: "*Shhhhh.*"

They aren't crouched anymore. They stand flat-footed. They think they're unobserved. This would be a good time to hit them, if only I trusted my ability to pull it off. I don't. While I lick my lips in pained anticipation, one of them races up the embankment. He reaches the crest, looking hard down the length of the road, then signals to the others. The Hummer is long gone. They huddle up near the trunk of my car, conversing in subdued tones, words I can't make out. Clearly an argument, and by the sound of it, desperate. This is a development they didn't anticipate.

And they think *I* did it. I wish I'd had the forethought and the nerve.

I let out my breath. Whoever took that Hummer—a car thief seizing his chance?—is now tops in my book. By now I would probably be dead if not for his intervention. A freak occurrence, the kind of pure chance Carter Robb would attribute to providence.

Thank you, thank you, thank you.

All I have to do is stay hidden. Even better, now that they're on foot, maybe I should risk making a phone call. If the bright screen doesn't attract their attention, or if I can shield the light from view, we're in the heart of the city, meaning patrol units could swarm this place in a matter of minutes. That's what I've got to do. Otherwise, I run the risk of letting Ford slip through my fingers. I don't have a choice.

I grip the phone in my left hand, my finger hovering over the sleep button. When I press it, the screen will flash to life. If I keep it close to my chest, screened by the trunk of the tree, then it should be invisible. I can only afford to speak in whispers, they're so close.

"Hey," a voice calls, not Ford's. "He left *his* keys behind."

A man slides behind the wheel of my car. He turns the key. The engine fires up, touching off the headlights. I flatten myself against the ground, eyes tightly shut, expecting the gunfire any second. I grit my teeth as if the bullets are already ripping through me.

Nothing. I glance up, but the lights dazzle my eyes. The motor revs and the wheel spins in a long, whirring circuit, kicking up earth. The revving dies down.

"The wheels are stuck. Give me a hand."

I can't let them take the car. The file on Ford is in my briefcase. All my notes. The rifle in the trunk. There's no way. I tap the sleep button on the top of my phone, bringing the screen to life. Now that I'm bathed in the headlights, what's the risk? Emergency dispatch is on my speed dial. I punch the number.

Then I cancel the call. This is exactly the kind of situation I can't afford to be in. Exactly the kind of explaining I don't want to do. Not to Wanda, not to Internal Affairs. But if I don't call, I'm letting Ford walk away. The odds of finding him again are almost nil.

Am I making a mistake? Probably so.

I set the phone between two roots, facing toward me, ready to press redial as a last resort. As long as they don't detect me, though, I'm not going to call for help. If I lose the car and everything in it, I'll make up an excuse.

"The front left is blown," one of them announces. "Pop the trunk and see if there's a spare. We've gotta get out of here."

"*Look.*"

The Hummer has reappeared on the embankment, coming from the opposite direction as it disappeared. I feel goose bumps rise on my forearm.

"Leave that and come on!"

Without another word, they head toward the newly arrived vehicle. It's not the same one, I realize. They have a backup driver. One of them must have called for help during the whispered huddle.

I keep my position until they're all in the Hummer. The doors slam shut and they turn around on the embankment, heading off in the direction of Kirby, the way we came. Part of me wants to go after them. Ford is getting away.

I wait a few seconds, conflicted about my lack of action.

Cars pass back and forth on the parkway. Cicadas chirp in the distance. My breathing returns to normal. It's done. The decision is made. It's like they were never here, except that my car is trashed and stuck in the soft dirt. Unsteadily, bracing my hand against the tree trunk, I get up on my feet. I slip my gun away. I limp toward the car. The pain in my leg is back with a vengeance, hard to ignore.

On inspection, they've at least done me one favor by rolling the car out of the ruts the front tires had embedded themselves in. The left front tire looks shredded. Even the rim is chewed up. I pull out the jack and the spare, retrieving my flashlight to make the work a little easier. The physical task calms me down. As I tighten the lugs, I begin to wonder who those guys were and why they were trying to kill me. Before now, the question hadn't occurred to me.

The Hummer must have picked up my trail at Downing Street. That much seems certain. How would they know to find me there? Tom Englewood told me where to meet him. It follows that he made this arrangement. At the last minute, revealing his connection to Reg Keller, he must have figured he was telling a dead man.

What have I gotten myself into?

Once the tire is changed, I back the car around carefully, not wanting to get stuck again. I edge my way up the embankment, then accelerate onto the road. At the first break in the median, I swing around to head east, picking up speed as I pass the site of my near-death experience. The engine whines.

The apartment tower looms on my right again. In the next parking lot I see a black Hummer sitting with its lights switched off.

Against my better judgment I hit the brake and pull in. I roll up behind the Hummer with my high beams on. With my gun drawn I get out to investigate. Before I can advance more than a few steps, the driver's door pops open. Two empty hands poke into the light.

"I'm not armed," a familiar voice calls. "I'm coming out now."

He slides his feet down onto the blacktop, lifting his hands high. My muzzle is trained on the center of his chest, but he comes toward me, smiling.

"That was a pretty close call," he says. "I wasn't sure what to do exactly. Four to one isn't great odds, not in the real world, and I didn't know if you were in any condition to help after they ran you off the road."

"Stop right there."

He stops. He raises his hands a little higher, showing off.

"Are you gonna shoot me, March, or say thank you? 'Cause I'm pretty sure I just saved your life back there."

I lower my gun, then put it away. He extends his hand for me to shake.

"Thank you, Jeff," I say. "Now, if you don't mind, I think you'd better start explaining."

CHAPTER **16**

I don't know where I expected Jeff to take me.

Not here.

Not to a run-down auto repair lot wrapped in eight-foot hurricane fence and topped with concertina wire, where a line of rusted beaters sit rotting in the heat, and hand-painted signage on the side of the garage is sun-faded and semiliterate.

This is his birthright, he says, the sum total of his inheritance.

"And don't get your hopes up, seeing it's a car repair joint. It hasn't been open for years." The damage to my car will have to be fixed elsewhere.

He gets out to unlock the chain threaded through the gate, reattaching the padlocks once I've driven onto the lot. I swing the car into a space near the garage entrance, but that's not what Jeff has in mind. He directs me around back, where a channel of gravel runs between the back of the building and another row of dismembered Detroit muscle cars. When I switch off the engine, we're sitting in darkness.

"I don't want to be visible from the road," he says. "Come on."

The back entry has three dead bolts, shiny in the light of Jeff's key ring LED. Newly installed, from the look of them. Judging from the outside, I wouldn't have thought there was much in here to secure.

He tells me to wait just over the threshold while he flicks on shop lights strung throughout the garage. The windows all seem to be blacked out for privacy. Inside, a small corner of the space has been reclaimed from the chaos of scattered tools and abandoned auto parts, all of it covered in a film of old grease, to make room for an Army surplus cot, some folding tables—one for dining, the other for cooking—and a desktop computer rigged to surveillance cameras with a view of the property outside.

"You don't *live* here," I say.

"If you can call it living."

There's a restroom door with an EMPLOYEES ONLY sign still affixed to it, a sink, a washing machine, and some drying lines hung with Jeff's clothes. There's even an ironing board and iron set up on the edge of a gaping hole in the concrete floor where a lift must once have been installed. The iron gets to me for some reason and I feel pity for the young man who's just saved my life. Despite an oscillating fan at the foot of the cot, the whole garage is infernally hot.

"It's my base of operations," he says, sounding a little embarrassed.

"Makes sense."

It doesn't, but I feel bad for having shamed him with my initial reaction. On the table, there's an interesting mix of books and magazines. Back issues of *Skeptic* and *Combat Handguns* mixed together. A fat, dog-eared paperback whose title declares *You Are Being Lied To*.

"I know it looks strange, but everything I need is here. And compared to where I was—over there—this is luxurious, believe me. To you, this looks like roughing it. But you've never lived off the grid. Which is fine. It makes you easy to find." He drags over an incongruous-looking wooden dining room chair for me to sit in. "Me, I can't afford to be easy to find. Not anymore."

I ease myself down, making sure the chair can take my weight. Absentmindedly I take up another of his books and flip through its pages. *The Foxhole Atheist*, it's called, the content divided into daily readings like one of Charlotte's devotional books.

"And why is that?" I ask.

"Well," he says, "I used to have something for you, something I was supposed to give you . . ."

I put the book down. "To give *me*?"

"But I don't have it anymore because they found where I lived and they took it. If I still had it, this would have been a whole lot easier."

"What was it?"

He draws a rectangle in the air with his fingertip. "An envelope. I can't tell you what was in there, but it was thick. I never looked because he told me not to. My job was just to hand it over in the event that anything happened."

"Did something happen?"

His eyes widen. "Of course. And I should have given that envelope to you right then and there. But under the circumstances, I didn't know *what* to do. It was you people who killed him. I wasn't sure who could be trusted. That's why I waited, and as it turned out, I waited too long."

"You're talking about Andrew Nesbitt?" I ask.

He nods. "Mr. Nesbitt. He said you'd know what to do with the contents of the envelope. He said you were one of the good guys. I should have just done what he told me, but—"

"How did you know him?"

"I worked for him."

"So all those nights at the shooting range . . . ?"

"Partly I was trying to get a read on you. Partly I was looking for an opening. It's not like I could've just walked up and told you any of this. You would've thought I was crazy. Without that envelope I figured I had to bide my time."

"Until tonight."

He smiles. "I had an idea something like this would happen."

The only thing he'd tell me back in the parking lot was this: the men in the Hummer weren't out to kill me. They would if they had to, but the mission was more likely a snatch. If all had gone according to plan, I'd have been run off the road, pulled from the wreckage, and whisked away to an undisclosed location. The Hummers, stolen earlier in the day for one use, would be recovered far away, their interiors scrubbed clean. And as for me, once they'd found out everything I knew, then a decision would be made as to my final disposition. Based on the fact that I'd snuffed one of their number, chances are my body would never have been found. These guys think nothing of killing cops, he tells me, something I know already firsthand. They think nothing of killing anyone.

"But who are *they*?"

"I wish I could tell you."

"You didn't recognize any of them?"

"I didn't get real close."

I hand him the photo I've been carrying of Brandon Ford, the one I took from the box in the garage. "Do you recognize him? What about the other two?"

He shakes his head and starts to hand it back. Then he pauses.

"I do know *her*."

Hilda.

"She worked for Mr. Nesbitt, same as me. When I was hired, he sent me to her. She snapped my picture and asked me all kinds of questions, and a couple of days later I went back and there was a driver's license, a passport, the whole nine yards."

"A new identity?"

"Like the witness protection program. That's what she does. Mr. Nesbitt said there was nobody better in the business. But I couldn't even tell you her name. He believed in doling out information on a need-to-know basis. He believed in cell structures. If one goes down, the fact that its members only know their own role means the others can continue to function."

"Her name is Hilda," I say. He seems impressed. "Do you know how to get back in touch with her?"

He shakes his head. "When I got back, I was looking for more private security work, something that would let me take advantage of my skills. Mr. Nesbitt hired me as a bodyguard. I figured I'd be going everywhere with him, like a personal protection detail. I was cool with that. I'd done that kind of thing before. But instead, he kept me around as more of an errand boy. He wanted someone he could trust to make pickups and deliveries, to carry messages, things like that. I would've given notice—that's not what I'd signed up for—but the truth is, he was this larger-than-life character and sticking with him seemed like my best shot for going places. Plus there was something exciting about all the precautions, the fake IDs.

"I never got the impression from him that his life was in danger. But one day he sits me down in his command center, which is just this room in his house that's got all these TV monitors and computers with news from all over, and he gives me an envelope I'm only supposed to deliver in the event of his death. He gives me a file, too, that's got all your information in it. *That* I still have."

He reaches under the cot for a metal ammo box repurposed for storage. There's only one thing inside, a thin file folder. I have one just like it in my briefcase. When I open it, a photo slips out onto the floor. My own face stares up at me. In every other respect, from the trim size to the thickness of the glossy paper, the picture is identical to the image of Ford in the file Bea Kuykendahl gave me. The pages inside could have been printed at the same time, from the same computer system. The type matches, the margins, everything. As if, somewhere back in time, the file on me and the file on my supposed John Doe resided side by side in someone's cabinet, just waiting to be put into action.

"You recognize your file?" he asks, surprised.

I flip through the pages. There's a detailed resumé, tracking my progress in life all the way back to high school, the Army, and my misguided years as an undergraduate in the University of Houston history department. My rookie class when I joined HPD, and every assignment since then. My marriage is here, the birth of my daughter, the car crash with Charlotte behind the wheel, the burial.

"Are you okay?" he asks. "I shouldn't have shown you that."

"It's fine." I close the file. "I have one just like this on a guy named Brandon Ford. Have you heard of him? According to the National Criminal Information Center, his body was found in a park not far from where we had our little adventure tonight. Just the body, not the head. And the hands had been skinned. Does any of that ring a bell?"

There's a funny kind of smile on his face, like he thinks I'm putting him on. "Is this a case you're assigned to?"

"It was. The only thing is, Brandon Ford was there. I recognized his voice."

Now Jeff looks really confused. "So you knew him?"

"He was one of the guys who held me at gunpoint. He's in the picture I showed you a second ago. His accomplice murdered my partner, and I killed him. This is news to you? That's the reason I've been on leave, the reason I was talking to Tom Englewood tonight."

"Him I know. Or know of."

I'm surprised he hasn't heard about Lorenz's death or the murder investigation that lit the fuse. *Need to know.* Maybe Jeff only has a small piece of the puzzle. Maybe he knows less than I do about what's really going on.

"Tell me about Englewood, then. Those were his men, I assume?"

"Mr. Nesbitt met with him once, and I escorted him. I don't know what they talked about, but afterward Mr. Nesbitt said to watch out for him, that he was a mercenary and men like him were the problem."

"The problem with what?"

He shrugs. "He didn't elaborate. I think the two of them were in competition. When Mr. Nesbitt retired from the CIA, he started his own company. Englewood's consortium wanted to shut him down, discredit him."

"So you believed him when he said he worked for the CIA."

"You know he did."

"I don't *know* anything."

"Oh," he says, confused again. "Only, the way he talked about you when he gave me the envelope, I was pretty sure you knew each other. He actually said that, I think. That he knew you from the old days and you were one of the good guys."

"He said he knew me? Maybe from around town?" I wrack my brain, but I can't think of any professional encounters we might have had. Until now, though I've heard rumors about goings-on in the intelligence community, I don't recall ever running across these people in person. At the time of Nesbitt's shooting, when the conspiracy theories started to get some coverage, the idea that Houston was home to a club of ex-spooks seemed as quaint as it did unlikely. "I think he must have been mistaken."

"I don't know," Jeff says. "He was a pretty sharp guy. Maybe you're the one who's mistaken. If he didn't know, I doubt he would have told me you could be trusted."

"What about the thugs tonight? Have you run into them before?"

"Not until this," he says. "You hadn't shown up at the range for a while, so I decided to catch up with you. I was outside during your meeting with Englewood, and that's when the Hummers rolled up. One of them got out and put something on your car, under the bumper—" I spring out of my chair, but he calms me with a smile. "Don't worry, it's not there anymore. After they pulled out, I moved it to another car. That's why the second Hummer wasn't on the scene. It was following the wrong signal."

When they pulled alongside me and shot out the window, Jeff was taken by surprise. Trailing in his own car, he hung back as far as he could, then passed us by once I'd skidded down the embankment. He parked and doubled back, not sure how exactly to help. "I figured we were headed for the O.K. Corral." Then inspiration struck. He saw that the Hummer's keys were in the ignition and decided to take it.

"I wasn't thinking too far ahead," he says. "It didn't occur to me they'd think I was you. I just thought that without their ride, they'd be sitting ducks when the cops arrived."

"They would've been," I say, "assuming I'd made the call."

"Why didn't you?"

"Why do you think? That would have been game over for me. We've had a shakeup in my shop, and I'm precariously placed at the moment. This would have been just the excuse they needed to clip my wings down to the nub."

"Well," he says, "what do we do now?"

He leans forward, elbows on his knees, his eyes full of trust and expectation. And I look back, seeing him in a new light entirely. The feat of tactical mimicry he'd pulled off on the range, the mature cynicism that comes from battlefield experience (something I admire because, despite my hitch in the Army, I never had any), the bravery he showed tonight—all of that goes transparent, revealing the youth and uncertainty underneath. Like a spy in a Le Carré novel, he's been out in the cold and now he's looking to me for instructions, as if I have the power to bring him back into the light.

"You've got to stay out of this," I say. "I appreciate what you did tonight, but if you keep going down this path"—I wave my hand to encompass the surreal surroundings—"I'm afraid you'll get into some serious trouble."

"I'm already in. There's no going back for me. I've been in this for months, keeping my head down and my eyes open, biding my time until I can hit back where it hurts."

"You can't, Jeff. It's not your job. You've got to leave this to the police."

"*The police are who killed him.*"

"That's not . . . You're not looking at the whole picture. Nesbitt drew first. He fired first. Whatever the rumors are on the Internet, those cops didn't assassinate him."

"Yeah," he says, "and those guys tonight didn't come after you. It was just a fender bender, right? Wrong place at the wrong time. You don't get it. You still have blinders on. It's time to wake up and see what's happening in this country. If tonight didn't do the trick, what's it gonna take?"

It's so late it's early. Despite my warning that I might be out well past midnight, Charlotte will be worried about me. I should have called. If I do it now, though, I risk waking her up if she's managed to get to sleep. Look at me, finding more excuses not to pick up the phone.

I rise to my feet, tucking the file under my arm.

"Lemme see that picture again," he says.

I hand it over and he studies the faces like he's committing them to memory.

"There's one thing more I can tell you about this woman. Hilda, you called her? I liked her. She reminded me a lot of my own mom. Maybe she felt the same. After Mr. Nesbitt got shot, she did call me. Just checking to see if I was all right. This was after the others caught up to me and burgled my place. She gave me the address of somewhere I could hole up. A safe house, she said. But to be honest with you, I didn't know if I could trust her. And I already had *this* scoped out." He sweeps his hand through the air, indicating the garage.

"Do you remember where this safe house was?"

He goes to the table where his books are stacked and hands me *The Foxhole Atheist*. "You were flipping through it just a minute a go. It'll be somewhere in the readings for April."

I skim the section until I find a handwritten note on the entry for April 14, a page with the heading COMFORT IN LIES IS NO COMFORT AT ALL. Down the inside margin, scrawled in blue ink, is the address of a Midtown apartment tower.

I start to tear out the page.

"Don't," he says. "Just take it with you. I have another copy, and it's such a good book. You should read it."

I slip the book into my jacket pocket, then give the garage a final once-over. There's nothing more I can do at the moment.

"Hey," he says, "I'm still in this." Issuing a challenge.

"Give me your number." I program him into my phone, then outline the various numbers he can use to get in touch with me. Although I realize it will do no good, I warn him to keep his nose clean anyway. "Wait until I get back in touch, Jeff. Can you at least do that?"

He answers with a noncommittal shrug.

As I leave, the dead bolts start turning behind me.

INTERLUDE : 1986

I ran into Magnum on base fairly regularly after our first conversation, but we always kept our distance. Sometimes I'd pretend like I didn't see him. Other times he'd acknowledge me with a far-off nod. Though we never talked, over time we were coming to understand each other better. I was conscious of his presence even when he wasn't there.

This was some kind of test, I decided. Magnum was keeping an eye on me to see what I was made of. After all, he had told me things he probably had no right to reveal. Had he divined something in me— some kind of trustworthiness or cunning—that suggested there was no danger in opening up?

"I'm a talent scout," he'd said. And I was a willing recruit.

Whenever scuttlebutt on base touched on the doings of Magnum and his cabana boys, Sgt. Crewes reported everything in thrilling detail. He kept an ear to the ground, presumably on Shattuck's orders, though he never said as much. According to the Spanish-speaking master sergeant, Magnum's men were Uruguayans, or possibly Argentines. They were junior officers of similar rank to one another with the exception of César, who gave orders and never seemed to get his hands dirty. Unlike the others, César also had the run of the town. He'd been observed sampling the Leesville night life, such as it was, doling out hundred-dollar bills like he had an endless supply. The whole group had come direct from Ft. Benning, meaning they were School of the Americas alumni. Crewes had to explain to me what that meant.

Unfortunately the sergeant's intel was low-grade product, spiked with implausible rumors.

"One of them's missing," he revealed one afternoon. "They're keeping everything hushed up, but the word is, he took a nosedive out of a Huey."

"One of the cabana boys? He fell out of a chopper?"

"More likely he was pushed," the sergeant said, a gleam in his eye. "It's all over base."

By "all over base," he meant the tight-knit circle of long-serving NCOs who were the only soldiers who mattered to Sgt. Crewes. I was incredulous.

"You're saying one of them was thrown out of the copter—for what? To demonstrate how it's done? Let me guess. Nobody actually saw this, but they heard it from someone who did. The Huey pilot will never turn up, and neither will the crew, but that doesn't stop the word from getting around."

"What's your problem?"

I stiffened.

"Let me rephrase that," he said. "What's your problem, *sir*?"

"My problem is, you're supposed to be a sergeant, but you gossip like an old woman."

The words were out before I could stop them. I paused and swallowed hard, bracing myself from the reaction.

Crewes cocked his head like a pointer catching the scent of the fox.

"Oh," he said to the air over our heads. "I think I know what the problem is now. Somebody has a crush."

"What are you talking about?"

"It's all those secret meetings," he said, still talking to the ceiling. "Only the major already laid down the law on that point."

He knew.

Crewes looked me in the eye and grinned. "I'm just saying, you'd better watch yourself, Lieutenant. Things aren't always what they seem. And neither are people."

The next time I spotted Magnum on base, he was coming out of the PX. I made a beeline for him, still shaken by the sergeant's warning. Our paths would have crossed in the parking lot, but at the final moment I veered away, spooked. A few steps behind Magnum came a warrant officer assigned to our company, one of our criminal investigators. He looked preoccupied and nondescript, the way you would if you were tailing somebody.

Maybe he had just been doing some shopping. But I doubted it. I bent down between two cars to tighten my bootlaces, letting both of them pass. Then I headed off in the opposite direction, sweat blooming on my brow.

That night, dressed in jeans and a pullover, I made a round of the Leesville clubs. Since I'd grown up in Houston, there wasn't much Sleezville's bars and nightclubs and strip joints could do to shock me. Besides, I was moderate in my vices and preferred to indulge them outside the public eye. In the hot, intermingling crowd, the thumping music, the alluring shadows, I became too self-conscious ever to lose myself. I was an observer, an all-seeing eye. Sometimes that was all the escape I needed.

I passed the night in a series of dank settings, matte-black walls and jury-rigged stage lights, local bands offering a semblance of live music, half the crowd probably underage. Although I recognized a few faces, I spoke to no one and no one spoke to me. I thought about the girl I'd met in Alexandria and taken to the movies. I thought about the girl in the blue gown at the ball in Austin, too, her strange and lofty world so different from mine. Mostly I thought about Magnum and the way he'd led me on and groomed me. And the fact that, whatever he was up to, it was enough to infuriate an officer like Shattuck.

Past midnight I decided to call it quits. Out in the parking lot I recognized the Buick. Glancing around and seeing no one, I decided to walk over. Through the tinted glass I couldn't tell whether anyone was inside the car. As I approached, the passenger door flung open. I took this as an invitation and went for it.

I had plenty I wanted to say to Magnum. The words lined up behind my teeth like paratroopers ready for the big jump. As I ducked down, a girl's bare leg touched the ground. She rolled a little and propelled herself from the passenger seat, running smack into me. She couldn't have weighed more than a hundred pounds, but she almost knocked me over. All I got was a glimpse of streaked mascara, the smell of alcohol on her breath, and a fleeting sob. She was past me then, stumbling and confused, turning backward to see what she'd struck. In the streetlight her face glowed amber. Her hair was chopped in a bob and there was a stud in her nostril—a strange sight in those days. Then she was gone.

I watched her, then leaned through the open passenger door. As I did, the driver got out. We faced each other across the roof of the Buick. He lit one of his thin cigars.

"You," he said, exhaling smoke. "The policeman. From the base."

He spoke in a low vibrating purr, the kind of voice he might use with a woman. He rested his elbows on the car and gazed up at the night sky.

"What an evening!"

"You want to tell me what that was all about?" I asked.

"This place," he said, waving the cigar. "It's not like my home."

As he sighed, I felt an anger boiling inside me. Despite his aristocratic airs, César looked like he could take care of himself. But I reckoned he was ten, fifteen years older than me, and all those cigars couldn't have helped his conditioning. I started thinking of what I'd like to do to him, realizing this was what it felt like to snap.

"Why did that girl take off like that? What were you doing to her?"

I didn't wait to hear the answer. I was already making my move, rounding the back of the Buick so I wouldn't have the open door between us. He watched, but that was all.

"Are you upset about that *puta*?" he asked, calm as ice. "It was not me doing anything to her, quite the other way around. Anyway, that was not the reason for the trouble. There was a disagreement over the price."

My fist was half cocked. He looked at it, amused.

"You understand what I am saying?" he asked. "She was just a whore."

What was I doing here? What right did I have—? I paused, then lowered my hand. The moment was gone.

"Come," he said. "I have heard all about you. A drink, yes?"

He closed the car door and gestured toward the club. Only after he'd stepped past me and turned did I realize he was inviting me inside.

"What do you take me for?" I said. "I'm not going anywhere with you."

"For a drink, yes? There are plenty of them to go around in there. You don't get angry over just one."

"What?"

"The whore," he said, smiling. "I will show you. Come on."

It was all an act, I realized. The crossed signals, the failure to communicate. For all his smiling bonhomie, he couldn't get the reptilian calculation out of his eyes. He would put a knife in me first chance. All he was doing was trying to decide where to slide it in.

"Come," he said.

I left without turning my back on him, then spent the night dreaming of that mole on his face and the glacier underneath his smile.

CHAPTER 17

The next morning, with the sun blazing through the half-open blinds and the clock on my nightstand reading a quarter past ten, I roll over to find Charlotte long gone, the sheets cool, the damp of her morning shower all but dissipated. It's a strange feeling, sleeping in. Nowhere to be, no one expecting me. I've slept on my right side, intermittently aware of the numbness in my left leg. Now, as I test my foot on the wood floor, a dull ache radiates through my thigh and into my lower back. I swallow more pills and go downstairs.

As I brew coffee, I notice the back door ajar. In a rush, Charlotte must have neglected to pull it closed. The problem with an old Victorian house is that no matter how much of the woodwork is restored and replaced, fluctuations in temperature cause what remains to expand and contract. In the summer heat, none of our doors seem to fit their frames anymore. I shove the door closed, then use the keypad on the wall to arm the security system.

For years we did without one, not wanting to tamper too much with the aesthetic, but when the sanctity of our home was violated last year and my wife was attacked by a maniac named David Bayard in our bedroom, we decided there were things more important than the historical character of an old house. If it hadn't been for Carter, she might have been killed. I was hours away, pursuing a lead in New Orleans, while he was upstairs over the garage. Now that the Robbs have moved out, I'm grateful Charlotte spends her days away from home.

We're on the grid, in Jeff's terms. Easy to find. If the men from last night want to catch up with me, it won't be too hard.

With a mug in one hand, I settle down in front of the computer, sifting through search results until I've located the video from Nesbitt's shooting that's all over the Internet. The resolution on most of the copies is pretty poor, but after a string of misses I find one that's not too bad, complete with subtitles to help with the grainy audio, probably added by a helpful news desk. I download the video and copy it onto a USB drive, which I take into the living room and plug into the flat screen. It takes some trial and error, but within a couple of minutes I'm reclining on the couch, watching Nesbitt's death clip again and again.

I wouldn't be doing this if Englewood hadn't mentioned Reg Keller's name. Wilcox's assurance that the shooting was justified is enough for me. Even without it, I have never questioned what really happened. Nesbitt drew and fired. Case closed. Corrupt cops exist, but they typically fall into two categories: cops on the pad and cops exceeding their authority. Sometimes the lines blur. A guy taking kickbacks will compensate by going extra hard on crime, busting heads to balance his own sense of guilt. There aren't many cops, I reckon, who would cold-bloodedly execute a man on orders. Not in front of a dashboard camera.

To my eyes, everything looks right. The subtitles tag the dialogue with the names of each uniform. The rookie is Farouk, his training officer Silvestri. I've never met either one. In the opening frames, a vintage Mercedes 450SL, signature ride of the '80s oil boom in Houston, is pulled over on the curb, lit by the patrol car's powerful spotlight. The back of a man's head is visible through the rear window. Farouk advances on the driver's side, his torso stiff and upright, hand resting on the butt of his pistol. On the passenger side, Silvestri carries himself more relaxed, scanning the car with an offhand flashlight.

"What's going on here? What is this?"

Nesbitt's already edgy. Farouk glances toward Silvestri, just a microscopic turn, probably looking for reassurance. Then he launches into his patter, his voice even and reassuring. He requests identification, and Nesbitt responds by demanding to know why he's been pulled over. When Farouk asks again, Nesbitt snaps at him.

"Who put you up to this? You think I don't see what's going on here?"

He sounds crazy, frankly. Delusional. And the rookie takes this in stride, aware that people are strange and you can never predict how they'll react. Silvestri crouches down a little for a better look into the car. I can't see his face, but judging by his body language, he's still not overly concerned. He's a T.O. He's seen it all before. It would take a lot to rattle a man like him.

"I will not submit to this. I'm under no obligation to cooperate."

"Sir, if you operate a motor vehicle in the state of Texas . . ."

"Was I speeding? Do I have a brake light out?"

"Sir, if you can just cut me some slack here. License and registration?"

Something in Farouk's manner seems to reassure Nesbitt. The only part of him visible to the cameras is the back of his head. He slumps a little and sighs loud enough for the microphone to pick it up.

"You need to understand something. I want you to listen carefully. You are interfering with a U.S. government operation. I'm working directly with the Central Intelligence Agency. You understand what I'm telling you, officer?"

Farouk sends another micro-glance toward Silvestri. When I was in uniform, there were some heady late-night traffic stops, but nothing like this. If a guy I'd pulled over started telling me he worked for the CIA, I'm not sure how I would've handled it. I probably would have laughed. To his credit, Farouk stays professional. Maybe he's too nervous in front of his training officer to show what he's really thinking.

"Sir, I'm going to need your license and registration to call this in."

He doesn't come out and say that he's going to confirm Nesbitt's story, but his words are carefully enough chosen to be interpreted that way. Despite his belligerence, Nesbitt's hand appears in the window, extending his license toward Farouk. Then he reaches toward the glove compartment and returns with an insurance card. Farouk tells him to sit tight, then returns to the patrol car, disappearing from view.

My next step in this situation would probably have been to administer a Breathalyzer. Whether you smell alcohol or not, when a driver claims to be a secret agent, that's probable cause in my book. Maybe Farouk signals something to Silvestri. The training officer takes a couple of steps toward the cruiser, then stops. He seems to nod, as if to say *message received.* Then he turns on his heel and approaches Nesbitt's window.

I've watched the video countless times by now, but never on a large screen. The enlargement renders the details as boxy pixels, but even so, I notice something this time that I've never observed before.

As Silvestri makes his approach, Nesbitt's head is clearly turned. Up to this point, only the back of the head was visible, but now I can see the darkened cavity of an eye and a mouth. He is watching the training officer as he advances.

And Silvestri does something I never noted before, too. Like Farouk, he rests his hand on the butt of his pistol. As he passes across the spotlight's beam, his right hand is brightly illuminated. I can't make out the individual digits, but the gesture is too familiar for me to miss. He pops the thumb break securing his gun into the holster, then flips it free. This is the sort of thing a cop might do if he's expecting to have to draw.

I pause the video and go back to the computer, doing a search that cross-references the shooting and the term *thumb break.* Instead of the hundreds of results that came up earlier, this time there are only a few. The first one takes me to a blog post with screen captures from this moment in the video. Red lines overlay the image, illustrating the significance of the movement. The title of the post reads, EXECUTIONER COP GETS READY FOR THE KILL. So at least I'm not the only one to have noticed.

Back in front of the television, I advance the video a few frames at a time. Silvestri never lifts his side arm out of the holster. He also never removes his hand from the butt. There's nothing to suggest he's a would-be executioner. Then again, he's clearly prepared to draw his weapon.

"You have no justification for doing that!"

The tone of Nesbitt's voice sounds different to me. He's not arguing about the traffic stop. He's protesting that popped thumb break. I feel certain of that. It's the perceived escalation of force that sets him off this time.

Silvestri's reaction is a little surprising. On the big screen, it's clear that as Nesbitt speaks, the training officer's face turns. He looks away from the driver, back toward the patrol car. Back toward the camera. I pause the video and run it back. The resolution is poor, but I'm sure there is a change in the face, a momentary fullness signifying the backward glance. Why would he take his eyes off a belligerent driver at such a critical moment? To check on Farouk, perhaps? To make sure he's ready to provide backup should it be necessary? That makes sense. I can even imagine myself in the same situation making a similar mistake. But watching again, what it really looks like is this: Silvestri's about to make a move and he's checking behind him to see if anybody's looking.

It's ridiculous, of course. He's a training officer, brimming with experience. Even if the conspiracy theorists are right and he's about to attempt an assassination, a glance over the shoulder isn't enough. He would know the camera was filming everything he did.

The muzzle flash from Nesbitt's pistol looks huge on screen, out of all proportion to the tiny size of his .32 caliber ammunition. The flash is caused by unburned power hitting the night air. Erupting in Silvestri's face, it must have been blinding. He reacts like a blindman, stumbling backward, falling on his backside. Only after he's on the ground does his gun clear the holster. I remember it differently, the training officer firing from the ground, but watching closely this doesn't appear to be the case. It's Farouk who flies into action, Farouk who's already rushing forward, his bullets shattering the windows of Nesbitt's Merc. As far as I can tell, the training officer never even fires. Nesbitt slumps forward, just the top of his head visible on camera. He's dead, struck in the neck by one of Farouk's .40 caliber rounds.

When the footage ends, I sit with the controller pressed against my cheek, contemplating a replay. I thought I knew what I was going to see. For the most part, I did. But that gesture of Silvestri's, the backward glance, coupled with the release of his thumb break . . . I'm starting to have my doubts.

Nesbitt was clearly worked up. Based on the way things actually went down, there's no question he was also in the wrong. If I'm right about him seeing Silvestri release the thumb break, though, it helps explain why he thought his only course of action was a preemptive strike. And that backward glance really bothers me. It looks like the unconscious action of a guilty man.

Troubled by my new doubts, I shower and shave. The water makes the scrapes and nicks on my hands and legs burn, scrapes and nicks I didn't realize I even had.

"You're getting too old for this," I tell the reflection in the steamy mirror.

I towel myself dry and do some stretching exercises on the bedroom floor, trying to limber my leg for the day. Bending over, I can just touch the ground without bending my knees, but there's a nasty pull all down my leg. It feels like a bamboo shoot has been jammed down through the muscles. All I have to do is push the stretch a little further and the pain grows intense. The way it travels along the sciatic line, I imagine digging my hand through the tissue, grabbing hold of the nerve, and yanking it out.

The stretch exacerbates the discomfort at first. After I walk it off, I can feel the leg relaxing into a prickly numbness, about as functional as it gets.

I've known cops who had to retire based on back injuries. There's so much weight to carry, so many demands that even a plainclothes detective can't keep up. In my mind, there's always been something pathetic about such cases. I've always wondered if the guys whining about their bad backs weren't goldbricking. Now I'm one of them.

And the stupidity of the fall still gets to me. A man urges me to be careful, and because he's younger than me and I'm feeling conscious of my age, to defy his expectations I take a leap that ends up confirming both his assumption and my worst fear.

Given time, a man can adapt to just about any pain. I can live with this if I have to. That's what I tell myself. I can live with it until the day that I can't.

After I'm dressed, I head downstairs again. Part of me wants to call Wilcox back and get him to watch the video with me. Either he will tell me I'm crazy or he'll see what I see. If it's the latter, I reckon he will feel duty-bound to take a second look at the case. I'll warn him about giving out Tom Englewood's number, too. *That's a good way to get people killed.*

Not that I want to put ideas in Wilcox's head.

Seeing him again stirred up some feelings. Maybe I'm yearning for the old days when we were still partners and the world seemed so uncomplicated.

The old days.

That was a phrase Jeff used last night. He had insisted that Nesbitt and I were acquainted, that we knew each other from "the old days," whatever that means. Once the thought lodges in my head, I can't get it out.

The only photos I remember seeing of Nesbitt were in the newspaper just after the shooting. They didn't ring a bell at the time, but I wasn't expecting them to. It's always possible we knew each other by sight or that—considering his penchant for cloak-and-dagger—I knew him by a different name.

Back to the computer, back to the interminable search results. I click around until only images are displayed, then only the ones with decent resolution. There seem to have been two pictures of Andrew Nesbitt circulating at the time of his death. The more common one depicts a jowly, balding man of sixty with capped teeth and crow's-feet. His button-down collar bulges at the sides, framing the knot of a regimental tie. I stare at the picture, but there's nothing familiar.

In the second image, which appears only on a few sites and seems to have been produced in an effort to verify his intelligence claims, a younger Nesbitt stands in a receiving line, shaking hands with the first President Bush, former Director of Central Intelligence. The photo appears to date during Bush's reelection campaign, so there's no direct tie to the CIA. His face is leaner and more handsome, his hair thick and jet-black. He sports a full Tom Selleck mustache.

It's the mustache that does it.

Old days is right.

The summer of 1986, to be exact. I was just twenty-four years old, younger than Jeff is now. A first lieutenant assigned to the Criminal Investigation Division at Ft. Polk, living off base in nearby Leesville, Louisiana. We all knew we had to assist him with whatever he requested, but none of us knew his real name. One of the sergeants, taking into consideration the facial hair, dubbed him Magnum.

I knew Nesbitt after all. And what I remember, I do not like.

INTERLUDE : 1986

The housing block where the cabana boys were quartered wasn't difficult to locate, not once I started looking. The trick was making do without the help of Sgt. Crewes or anyone likely to report back to him. The man had ears all over the base. I spent a few hours each night camped out in my car, keeping an eye on the block with a starlight scope, all without the sergeant's knowing. My first surveillance.

I never saw Magnum there, but I spotted a couple of guys I took to be handlers. They escorted the group when it left the building, functioning more like tour guides than guards. Occasionally they went out on errands, returning with groceries or beer or, on one occasion, a vanload of women in high heels and skimpy dresses. Through the scope I couldn't make out any features—either of the men or the prostitutes they'd procured. That night in particular I left with a sick feeling in the pit of my stomach.

"Good-time girls on base?" Crewes said in mock horror. "Something's gotta be done. Next thing you know, there'll be dancing."

"I'm just asking."

I'd brought up the subject without explaining my interest, saying I'd heard from some of the investigators that it was getting to be a problem.

"You never struck me as the puritanical type, sir."

"Last time I checked, it was illegal."

"So it is," he said thoughtfully. "So it is."

A day later I was standing at attention in front of Maj. Shattuck's desk, with the major looking right through me. He didn't need to say a word, but he did anyway.

"March, I thought we'd gone over this. I told you to steer clear of the man. I told you to have nothing to do with him, that he was dangerous. Do you know something I don't?"

"No, sir—"

"Because you must *think* you do, otherwise why go against me on this? I was looking out for you, son, and you're throwing it in my face."

"No, *sir!*"

"What other explanation is there?"

A long silence.

"Explanation, sir? For what, sir?"

Shattuck gave me a withering look of disgust. He opened a file folder lying on the desk before him, wrote a note inside, then slid it away. "From now on, Lieutenant March, you will follow my instructions. You will not have any contact with that man. You will not go anywhere near the housing where his people are quartered. Do I make myself clear?"

"Yes, sir."

"You must have a pretty high opinion of your abilities," he said, shaking his head. "Do you have anything to say for yourself?"

I did, but I kept my mouth shut. I wanted to ask who'd informed him, though I knew the answer had to be Sgt. Crewes. Subtle as I'd attempted to be, I'd given the game away with my questions. I also wanted to know what harm it did to keep an eye on things. Something was going on under our noses that the major didn't like any more than I did. In fact, while my feelings had been conflicted, he knew that Magnum meant trouble from the start. So why warn me off like this?

"You have nothing to say?" Shattuck asked.

"No, sir."

"Dismissed."

I was tempted to drive by the housing block that night, not to stop but to roll by casually and give the place a glance. But I thought of all the other cars parked on the street and remembered the warrant officer who'd been trailing Magnum from the PX. There was no point in bringing aggravation down on my head.

I managed to clock César a couple of times on base, though. Whenever I did, tagging along to see where he was heading. In the mornings I jogged through the picnic tables in search of random encounters, but the cabana boys had moved their party elsewhere.

The one time I spotted Magnum, it was at a bookstore off base. He was browsing through the high-tone foreign policy journals shelved by the newspapers, the ones nobody ever bought, so I ducked into the history section to avoid being spotted. It didn't work. When I looked up from a volume on warfare in the classical world, Magnum was staring at me from across the store. He winked, then disappeared out the door.

I dropped the picnic detour from my morning path, returning to my old route. On the sidewalk at a quarter past seven, I jogged past a couple of parked cars in front of an officers' housing unit, swinging wide to avoid a woman who was slipping an overnight bag into an open hatchback. A few steps later I stopped and turned. She shut the hatch before noticing my presence. Her hand went unconsciously to the stud in her nose.

"Excuse me," I said. "You remember me, don't you?"

"Of course," she said, smiling, though I could tell she didn't. "Good to see you."

I shook my head. "I'm not a customer, ma'am. We ran into each other about a week ago. You were bolting out of a car, and there I was."

"Oh." The smile faded. "That was you? Are you all right? I didn't— no, of course I didn't. How could I? Hurt you, I mean."

"You didn't hurt me. But I was concerned. You got out of there in a hurry."

"Yeah, well . . ."

"The man in the car. His name is César, right?"

She shrugged. "If you say so. Look, I should probably get out of here." She nodded at the houses behind me. "This is supposed to be a surgical strike, you know? In and out. No witnesses."

"How old are you?" I asked.

It was the wrong question to ask. Her cheeks flushed and she started digging in her purse for the car keys.

"No, wait. I'm just trying to help. I want to know what was going on in that car."

She got the door open, then paused to laugh. "You really are sweet, you know that? I could tell you what was going on, but I wouldn't want to corrupt your morals . . . or put any ideas into your head."

"You should be careful around that guy."

"No kidding," she said. She slammed the door and drove away. For the second time I watched her go. She couldn't have been more than twenty. A student, maybe. She had a nice car, wore decent clothes, didn't look at all like my idea of a prostitute. Not that I subscribed to any heart-of-gold hypothesis. Not that I romanticized the underworld or its inhabitants. She just seemed too . . . something. Too *real* to do what she did.

I hadn't gotten her name. I hadn't written down her license plate number or anything like that. There was no way of tracking her down after the fact, declaring my identity and giving her some kind of warning to stay off base. With nothing but a sense of confusion, a sense of uneasiness to go on, I took a few steps and kept on running.

I should have tried harder than that.

CHAPTER 18

My union attorney, no stranger to officer-involved shootings, meets me in advance of my official sit-down with Internal Affairs, telling me he's expecting a walkover. "You're in the clear on this, no question. If they want to make out that excessive force was used, the fact that you were unfamiliar with the weapon should answer that." I wish I could share his confidence. As we file into the interview room, I scan the IAD office for Wilcox. He's nowhere to be seen.

The detective with the tan lines on the side of his head conducts the questioning, with a colleague waiting in the wings to take notes. I brace myself for a grilling, remembering his demeanor at the hospital, but my attorney's assessment proves prophetic. We work through the events leading up to the shooting step-by-step, without hostility. He asks the questions, I answer, and he moves right on without challenging what I've said. After a few minutes, we're in a comfortable rhythm. My attorney relaxes into his chair.

"Let's take a break," the detective says once we've gone through the story beginning to end. He sends his colleague out for coffee, then splits for a bathroom break.

The attorney smiles. "I think that went well."

"I'm just waiting for the other shoe to drop."

When the interview resumes, three more IAD personnel sit down across the table, bringing their total to five. The newcomers are armed with old case files, every shooting I've been involved in going back to my days on patrol.

"You're no stranger to this process," the tan-lined detective says. "Some cops go through their whole careers without firing a shot in anger. You're not one of them."

The attorney's done his homework. "All of those shootings came back clean according to this very department. You're not suggesting Internal Affairs dropped the ball, are you?"

"I'm not suggesting anything. It just seems like, if you're accustomed enough to the process, maybe it gets easier and easier to pull that trigger."

"It's hard to imagine any officer in Detective March's situation acting differently."

"Perhaps. We're just concerned that what we're seeing here is a pattern."

The lawyer suggests this is something to explore in post-trauma counseling, not an IAD interview room. They spar back and forth in a passionless, technical way, like chess players making well-known moves, fully anticipating each rejoinder. I'm not sure exactly what purpose is served. After ten minutes, they arrive at a draw and agree to suspend the match—for now.

"What was that all about?" I ask in the hallway.

The attorney shakes his head. "What they're saying is, We've got nothing, but we're not ready to let it go. I was hoping we could get you back to work. Unfortunately they're going to drag things out as long as possible."

"And how long is that?"

"It all depends," he says.

"On what?"

"On whether they find anything or not."

Wanda receives my update on the Internal Affairs situation without surprise, thanks me for dropping by, and dismisses me with a wave of her hand. "Until they give you a clean bill of health, I don't think you should be seen around here." I ask halfheartedly about administrative duties, not wanting to be stuck at my desk. She doesn't even respond.

"I'm just gonna check in with Cavallo," I say. "Make sure she doesn't have any questions about the case load."

Cavallo's work space looks serene and tidy, all the paperwork stacked just so. She motions for me to wait as she finishes up a phone call. From her end of the conversation I surmise she's going back and forth with the crime lab about the priority of evidence. She hangs up the phone with a satisfied smile.

"The thing I love about homicide is all your requests go to the top of the list."

"Theoretically," I say.

There hasn't been any progress on the Ford homicide, she tells me, and the last she heard from the team investigating Lorenz's death, they hadn't come up with an identification on the man with the skull ring, either. "Your open IAD case is the only thing keeping them from declaring victory. If they could, I think they'd just as soon call it even and go home."

"Theresa, I need to bring you into the loop."

Her eyebrows rise. "Meaning what? You've been holding something back?"

"We can't do this here. Can you get away sometime? And I need you to do me a favor, too. I'm a little wary about approaching Wilcox directly, but you two got along when we were all working to bring down Reg Keller. I want you to set up a meeting with him so I can crash it."

"You're asking for a lot."

"In return I'll give a lot back. I have some new information that leads me to believe we missed something the first time around with Keller. It might have a bearing on your case. Since Wilcox did all the digging into Keller's finances, we need his cooperation."

"You think ambushing him is the way to get it?"

"I tried knocking on the front door."

"He wouldn't answer?"

I catch Wanda watching us through her open door. "I'll tell you later. Just set something up and call me, okay? I'll be eternally grateful."

To her credit she doesn't make me beg. We've been down this road before. Without losing any of her skepticism or even bothering to hide it, she still agrees to help out. "But if you have been holding back on me . . ."

The meeting takes place in a downtown deli, one of the many that serves the lunch throng before closing up shop at three o'clock. They've commandeered a table for two and pulled up a third chair as if expecting someone. Wilcox doesn't look surprised to see me. Cavallo must have tipped him off to the plan, uncomfortable with the idea of luring him under false pretenses. The fact that he's still showed up is a good sign.

"You want anything?" Cavallo asks, lifting a half-eaten sandwich.

I shake my head. "There's a question you have to answer, Stephen, before we can go any further. The other night after we talked, when you called me back with Englewood's number, were you telling the truth about remembering him after the fact?"

He shifts in his chair. "Look . . ."

"Just answer the question."

"Yes and no," he says. "Why do you want to know?"

"Because Englewood tried to have me killed."

They both freeze.

"*What?*"

"After I left him, some guys in a black Hummer ran me off the road on Allen Parkway. They came down the embankment with guns drawn, and I had to hide in the bushes or they would've shot me. The only person who could have tipped them off is Englewood, and you're the one who sent me to him."

"You think *I* set you up?"

"I don't think anything. I'm just asking the question."

Cavallo sips her drink through a long straw, her eyes darting back and forth like she's watching a show.

Wilcox gives her an incredulous look. "Are you hearing this?"

"There were shots fired on Allen Parkway," Cavallo says. "Patrol responded, but nobody was on the scene. They did find some skid marks. That was *you*?"

"Off the record, yes."

"Well, I had nothing to do with it," Wilcox says, "and I'm shocked you would even have to ask. All the time we worked together and you still don't have a clue about what makes me tick."

"I could say the same thing. But you said 'yes and no.' So explain the 'no' part."

He curls in on himself, crossing his legs, tightening his arms over his chest, like the diagram labeled CLOSED in the body-language handbook. But he does talk. After our conversation, he says, it occurred to him to phone a colleague who'd worked the Nesbitt shooting, not to pump the man for information on my behalf but to report the contact. "I figured they'd want to know if questions were being asked." Less than five minutes after that call ended, Wilcox got a call from Englewood, asking that his number be passed along. "Explaining all of that back and forth would have been too complicated."

"So you lied to me instead."

"I didn't lie," he says, his cheeks flushed. "I paraphrased."

"Can one of you tell me who this Englewood guy is?" Cavallo asks.

We exchange a look and Wilcox shrugs. "You go ahead," he says.

I summarize what I know about Tom Englewood, repeating his metaphor about the governmental High Road and the corporate Low Road, and that leads into an explanation about Andrew Nesbitt and his contested shooting.

"Why this matters to you," I tell her, "is that when we found our headless John Doe on the basketball court, Lorenz noticed that the body was arranged with the finger deliberately pointing. He thought maybe if we followed the dotted line, we'd find the head. But just before he was killed, he worked out the real significance of that pointing finger."

"Which was?"

In answer I produce a page from my own Key Map, identical to the one taken from Brandon Ford's office, indicating the crime scene, then tracing the direction of the line until it intersects with Allen Parkway. "This," I say, tapping the map, "is where Nesbitt was shot."

She takes the map, studies it, then does her own impression of closed body language. "That's a pretty big thing to omit from your report."

"I didn't," I say. "Bascombe knows."

"Well, he didn't say anything to me."

I tell her about our visit to Bea Kuykendahl's basement office at the FBI, then produce the file on Brandon Ford, opening it up to the photograph.

"There's something else. You told me they haven't identified the guy I shot. The fact is, I got a look at the other one without his mask. The same man was there the night I was run off the road. He seemed to be the group's leader."

"And you have a description?" Wilcox asks.

"I have more than that. I have a photo." I tap the picture on the table in front of me. "It was Brandon Ford."

"But . . ." His voice trails off. "What?"

Cavallo doesn't say a word. She just glares at the photograph.

"So what you're saying . . ." Wilcox struggles with his thoughts, not wanting to speak them out loud. "Didn't the DNA come back with a . . . ?"

"The lieutenant knows all this?" Cavallo says. "Wanda's gonna crucify him."

"You can't say anything to Wanda."

"March, I can't *not* say anything."

"This has to stay here. It can't go beyond this table. I wanted you both here because I feel like I can trust you, and you both have a stake in this."

"Not me," Wilcox says. "It's none of my business."

"According to Englewood, it is. He told me something interesting as we were saying goodbye. He figured I wouldn't live to share the information. He said we had a mutual friend, Reg Keller, and that he was an investor in Keller's operation. Now the three of us brought Keller down, but it was you, Stephen, who uncovered all the financial shenanigans related to his shell company. So yes, you do have a stake, because in all that work you seem to have missed something. I think we all did."

"What do you expect from us?" Cavallo asks.

"Very quietly, without raising any suspicion, we have to reopen that case. We need to know what the connection between Keller and Englewood was. And we need to see if anyone knows where Reg Keller is now."

Wilcox shrugs. "Argentina, I thought. That's the rumor."

"That's old information," Cavallo says. "And it was never more than speculation. The guy who swindled Keller out of his money—Chad something—"

"Chad Macneil," I say.

"Right. When he turned up dead in Buenos Aires, people thought it was Big Reg settling the score. I don't think there was anything more to it than talk."

"We need to find out. Can you check into that?"

She gives me a frosty look. "I think my days of carrying water for you are pretty much done, Roland. This was the last straw. Jerry was my friend."

"Mine, too. I mean that."

Neither one of them looks very convinced. I knew it would be hard, and I knew there would be some resentment to overcome. Somehow, though, I'd imagined that my revelations were strong enough in themselves to win both Cavallo and Wilcox over. Now I begin to wonder.

"I don't know what to do with this," Cavallo says. "I'm going to have to think it over. Frankly, I can't imagine a scenario in which I'd feel comfortable withholding information from Wanda. You told your boss everything, so why shouldn't I tell mine?"

"Do you think she'll listen?"

"That's not the point."

"If I were you," Wilcox tells her, "I wouldn't say a word. The one part of this story I can attest to is this: there's an enormous amount of outside pressure on the Internal Affairs investigation. I don't know where it's coming from, but I'd say there have to be some powerful interests involved. If it's true that Ford, your homicide victim, is alive and kicking, and the database still came back with a match . . . well, I don't know what to think about that. But I'm not gonna breathe a word about it, if you know what I mean."

"Because you don't believe it?" she asks.

"Because I don't know what to believe."

"Listen," I say. "I'm not asking either one of you to walk out on the limb with me. Only I can't do this alone, not from the outside. What it comes down to is this: do you trust me?"

Silence.

"I'm serious. Do you trust me?"

Cavallo frowns. "It's not that I don't—"

"Then help me. Simple as that. Theresa, you can find out if there's anything concrete linking Keller to the murder in Argentina. Stephen, you can search for the connection between Keller's finances and Tom Englewood."

"And what about you?" Wilcox asks.

"Me? I'm on leave."

"Yeah, right."

"I do have a lead to follow up," I say, thinking of the safe house. "There's a guy who used to work for Nesbitt who's turned me on to something. According to him, there was a package Nesbitt wanted me to have, only it was stolen. But look at this." I reach into my briefcase for the file on myself. "It's identical to the one on Ford, so they come from the same source."

Cavallo picks up the folder and flips through its pages thoughtfully. The thoroughness of the dossier seems to make an impression. When she's done, she sets it on the table.

"All right," she says. "It stays between the three of us for now, but only because if I took it to Wanda, she'd think I was crazy. Maybe I am. But to answer your question, I do trust you."

I turn to Wilcox.

"You don't want my answer. But I'll take a look and see if I missed anything with Keller's finances. I have an idea now what I'm looking for."

"I appreciate what you're doing," I say, extending my hand.

After a pause, he shakes it.

Once he's gone, I launch into my apology to Cavallo. She doesn't cut me off or tell me there's no need. She sits through the whole speech, warming slowly to the theme, nodding in agreement when I tell her how wrong I was to withhold information from her.

"With the static between us," I say, "all the stuff with Wanda taking over, I just didn't know how much you'd want me to share."

"Next time, just be honest with me. Don't make me feel like I have to prove myself all over again before you'll respect me."

"I do respect you," I say. "A lot."

"Then act like it."

I extend my hand to her. "Deal."

Afterward, limping back to the garage where I left my car, Cavallo's frustration settles over me like fog on damp grass. When it comes to ticking off the many flaws in my personality, she's never held back. I withhold information, obviously. I suppress painful truths to the point of denial. I don't talk about my feelings. I take an instrumental view of people, which apparently means I use them to achieve my own ends. These are all terrible faults in her mind, even though to me they sound like virtues, things I not only value about myself but wish I could see more of in others.

When she lectures me, I tend to write it off as her thing. Some people can't help psychoanalyzing others, projecting their own concerns onto the world around them. Honestly I don't think I've ever reflected on the criticism. Maybe I should. Maybe these really are blind spots, forcing me to repeat the same patterns, to fight the same battles over and over again.

Before I can talk myself into an epiphany, I reach the safety of the car. To my chagrin, as I settle behind the wheel, I realize I am breathing hard from the walk.

What is happening to me? I'm falling apart, that's what.

But that's another epiphany I'm not interested in having yet. I reach for the radio dial to drown out my inner monologue. Then I pick up the phone and dial.

"What do you want?"

Her voice is cold.

"Hello, Bea. It's good to talk to you, too."

"Listen," she says, lowering her voice almost to a whisper, like she's afraid of being overheard. "What happened the other day . . . it *didn't* happen. Understand? And whatever I might have said, I didn't say it."

"I'm guessing you didn't have any luck testing those things you took from Hilda's place."

Silence.

"Well, guess what? I have an idea how we might be able to get a line on her. Only it will require a little ingenuity. Since you seem to have a flair for coloring outside the lines—"

"I can't talk right now," she says.

"But you'll call me back?"

After a long pause, she relents with a sigh. "Give me an hour."

CHAPTER 19

There's a chain coffee shop across the street from the apartment building where women in sports gear meet for soy lattes while telecommuters in shorts and hands-free earpieces compete for the tables next to the wall plugs, and the remixes piping down from the ceiling are always available for purchase at the register. When Bea arrives, she gives the place a good scowl, as if I've compromised her with this choice of venue. Once I've explained about the safe house, the attitude evaporates.

"How did you find out about this?"

"I have my ways," I say, reluctant at this point to apprise her of Jeff's existence. "So let me explain the plan."

The whole point of a safe house is to have a place where you can stash people and still keep tabs on them. You can find them, but no one else can. So there will be some kind of link, some means of communication between the safe house and Hilda. The landlord will have a contact number, someone to call in case the rent is late or there's a mishap in the building, like a flood or a fire.

"I'm not suggesting we set the place on fire. But suppose we get the manager or concierge or whatever to say the apartment on the floor above was flooded, and there's water damage she needs to inspect?"

"If she's blown town, what makes you think she'd show up at all?"

"Maybe she won't. Let's give it a try, though, and see what happens."

"And you're comfortable doing this without a warrant, without any kind of backup?"

I smile. "You're the one who said the time for warrants was over."

We cross the street on foot, dodging a dog walker with three canines on the leash. Entering the lobby, we're enveloped by cool air. The manager's office is tucked into a compact but stylishly appointed suite of rooms just off the elevator on the first floor, immediately behind the tenant mailboxes. Bea dazzles the manager, a slender and serious-looking woman in her fifties, with a flash of her FBI credentials, and within five minutes we're all three peering down at a computer screen with all the rental information on file for the seventh-floor safe house. The name on the lease is Hillary Mendez.

"Oh yes," the manager says, "I remember her. She lives down on Galveston Island and wanted a *pied-à-terre* here in the city."

"You have a number where you can reach her?"

She points to the screen. "And her home address, too."

I copy the information down, even though the address is likely to be a sham. As I write, Bea starts explaining how we're concerned that something might have happened to the apartment's occupant and so we need to take a look inside. Without asking any questions, the manager opens a key box on the wall.

We take the elevator up and head down a thickly carpeted corridor, pausing at the apartment door. Before trying the key, the manager knocks three times and calls out. There's no response, so she opens it up.

The apartment is quite small, just a studio with a kitchenette and bath, sparsely furnished, with a breathtaking view thanks to the fact that the back wall is entirely glass. Bea motions the manager to stay put while we have a look around. There are two rolling suitcases on the floor next to the bed, their panels unzipped, and toiletries scattered on the bathroom sink along with a blow dryer and an unplugged curling iron.

"Somebody's staying here," Bea whispers.

Now comes the tricky part. I turn to the manager and start to improvise some kind of halfway convincing story. Bea cuts me off.

"We're going to stay here and wait for her to come back," she explains. "And we need you to keep this entirely confidential. It's a matter of homeland security. Thanks for your cooperation."

The woman teeters on the threshold, looking simultaneously dazed and excited. Then she springs forward and presents Bea with the key.

"If you need *anything*—" she begins.

"We'll let you know."

When she's gone, we close the door. Bea goes straight for the luggage, looking for anything packed away underneath the clothes. She finds nothing in the first case. From the second, she produces a zip-around pouch full of passports, currency, credit cards, and driving licenses, all bearing Hilda Ford's face but with different names including Hillary Mendez. She puts everything back in place, then shakes the bag over her head in triumph. I motion for her to keep looking. In one of the internal pockets, wrapped in a silk slip, she finds a stack of file folders identical to the dossiers on Brandon Ford and myself.

"Look at this."

We spread them out on the bed, open to the photos. There are five in total, all of them men in their mid-twenties to late-thirties. I pat my jacket pocket, removing the now-familiar photo. Brandon Ford flanked by two buddies, with Hilda in the background. I lay it on the bed among the folders.

"This one here," I say, tapping the man on Brandon's right. "That's him." I show her the folder with his photograph. "And the one on his left, that's him over there." I slide another folder alongside.

"They're all using false identities."

I lift one of the folders, holding the image close up for inspection.

"You recognize that one, too?" she asks.

"Yeah." I hand her the folder. "That's the one I killed."

A brooding silence descends as we wait. I sit at the window, listening to the rumble of traffic on the street below, the sun warm on my hands, my face, my closed eyelids. I can hear Bea perched on the edge of the bed, quietly browsing through the dossiers, trying to make sense of what this means. I haven't told her about my run-in with Ford on Allen Parkway, about the voices of the men who came after me, no doubt the same ones whose files she holds on her lap. If they were Englewood's team, as I assumed, why does Hilda have their dossiers? Obviously she created their new identities, just as she created Jeff's. That's her specialty, he said.

"I should have known about this," Bea says. "I should have dug deeper to begin with. I just accepted everything they told me. I made it easy for them."

"It won't be easy for them anymore."

"No," she says. "Not if I can help it."

I open my eyes. She's holding all the files in a thick stack, her knuckles white. From across the room, her sinewy, boyish muscularity and the random twists of hair spouting around her temples make me think of a kid in school, stumped by the test.

Sometimes my thwarted fatherly instinct comes out. I'll find myself connecting, albeit awkwardly, to substitute children like Carter Robb, maybe even Cavallo. Not that I'm old enough to have fathered either of them, but I can imagine Carter as the grown-up son I never had, imagine Cavallo as the daughter who was taken from me. It's stupid, I know, but maybe it explains some things.

Looking at Bea, I feel none of that. Her broad, unlined face is just a cipher. She could just as easily be carved from stone. And the funny thing is, I bet if I asked about her job, how she gets along with her colleagues, what they think of her, I'd hear a story not unlike my own. We're a lot alike, I suspect, and that's why we can sit in a room together and both feel alone.

"You know something—"

She silences me with a finger, then tilts her head toward the door.

I rise quickly, moving across the room, positioning myself inside the bathroom while Bea sets aside the stack of files and slips into the corner to the right of the door. We make eye contact. Bea holds a collapsible ASP baton in her hand, a wicked smile on her lips.

Here we go.

The door swings open. A short, plump woman laden with plastic shopping bags walks through, heading straight to the kitchenette. She hoists the bags onto the counter, peels off her sunglasses, and pauses. Her head turns toward the bed, toward the stack of files.

"Hello, Hilda," Bea says, pushing the door shut.

In the photo I've been carrying, Hilda Ford is a hard-looking, ashen-faced woman with demon eyes. In real life, she has a dimple on one cheek and a crooked smile. She gives off a comfortably aged, grandmotherly vibe, and if she's shocked to find two unexpected visitors in her safe house, she doesn't let on.

"Hello yourself," she says, dragging the words out like she's trying to recall a forgotten appointment. "Bea. And you—" she turns my way—"I recognize you. You're Roland March."

"That's right. You made a file on me."

"And I see you've been sneaking through my files."

"You got careless, Hilda," Bea says, moving forward, slapping the baton against the palm of her hand. "You thought I wouldn't find you."

The older woman shrinks back at Bea's approach, and I have a terrible premonition of sudden violence, Bea's arm lifting and the baton crashing down. I edge myself between them to head off the possibility. Seeing this, Bea smirks.

"Why don't you have a seat, Hilda?" I ask. "We need to have a little talk."

"You set me up," Bea says. "You lied to me."

"That's not true—"

"*You told me Brandon was dead.*"

Hilda smiles sweetly, her palms turned up. "I thought he was. I only told you what I believed myself. I was trying to help."

"Then why did you disappear?"

"Not because of you, dear," Hilda says.

She trails past the bed, glancing around as if the room is unfamiliar, finally settling herself on the chair I recently vacated by the window. She wears a flowery capped-sleeve top, stretched tight across her thick arms, and boot-cut jeans with little sparkles down the side. There's nothing threatening about Hilda, nothing to even suggest the sort of work she's done or the secrets she must have been privy to over the years.

Bea puts the tip of her baton on the arm of the little sofa and makes a show of collapsing it back to its original size. Then she slumps onto the cushion, leaving the last chair for me. I scoot it over, positioning myself between Hilda and the door. It's force of habit. I don't anticipate her making a run for the exit.

"I knew Andrew Nesbitt," I tell her. "Were you aware of that?"

"Yes, I was. But I'm surprised you are. He went looking for you a couple of years after your first meeting, to see if you had ripened up. And lo and behold, you were out of the military and working as a Houston cop. He didn't have any use at that time for a Houston cop, but he kept you in mind. He told me he figured he could make something out of you."

"I'll bet. Do you know what it was he wanted to give me?"

She strokes thoughtfully at the fold of skin beneath her chin. "I have an idea what it might have been, but no more than that."

"Can we back up a minute?" Bea says. "Who are you talking about?"

"I'll let Hilda explain."

"Andrew Nesbitt was my boss," she tells Bea, "before you were my boss." She's using the slow, clear enunciation of a first grade teacher. "It was Andy who brought our little family together, and Andy who gave us work to do."

"He worked for the CIA," I say.

Hilda tilts her head, acknowledging this might be so.

"And so did you?" I ask.

She smiles. "I've done some things here and there. I give people new lives. I've been doing it a long time. It's gotten harder in some ways and a whole lot easier in others. Documents are a snap. It's all the computers that pose the challenge now. That's why I called to warn you, Bea, because I knew that my work for Brandon was only going to hold up for so long. If the police dug past the middle of 2002, things would look a little fishy. And if they ran his DNA, well, like all my boys, Brandon was ex-military. They were sure to find out who he was."

"Only we didn't," I say. "The database came back with the fake identity."

"Which is why I had to disappear. There are people who can fiddle things like that, and I don't want to have anything to do with them. You shouldn't, either."

"You're talking about Tom Englewood? I've met him."

Her smile hardens and she doesn't reply.

"Again," Bea says, "why do I feel like I'm the only one who's not in the picture?"

I explain to her about my meeting with Englewood, watching Hilda's face for any reaction. For context, I have to bring in Nesbitt's shooting and the investigation that followed, along with the official denials and the conspiracy theories. Hilda sits through this placidly. When I start talking about the headless body in the park, she leans forward a bit. The pointing finger puts a frown on her face. Once I've traced the line between the finger and the stretch of road where Nesbitt was killed, her jaw is hanging open. I've got Hilda's attention.

"On that same stretch," I say, "on the same night I met with Englewood, Brandon Ford and the other men in those files of yours took a shot and me and ran me off the road. They were either trying to kidnap me or kill me, and I imagine either scenario would have ended up the same way."

"In that case, you're lucky to be here."

"What Bea and I both want to know is, what's going on?"

"Where do you want me to start?"

"At the beginning."

CHAPTER 20

After 9/11, Hilda says, Andrew Nesbitt offered her good money and steady work if she would relocate to Texas, where he'd set up a private security company and started selling his services back to the government. He needed her particular skill set because one of his sidelines involved putting together a team of ex-military operators for contract work, men whose records were dubious enough to raise red flags on a background check. He was also keen to keep a low profile, and not just because secrecy came second nature to him. His presence in Houston would draw resentment from a much larger and longer-established rival, Tom Englewood's firm, which had for years offered the benefit of his rich network of international contacts to the city's oil oligarchs. The more successful Nesbitt was, the more pressure Englewood could be expected to exert. If the new company intended to operate under his nose, they would need to be discreet.

During his time spearheading U.S. efforts to suppress the drug growers and traffickers of Latin America, Nesbitt had done a lot of talent scouting in the pool of military and intelligence personnel. Having once observed the man who would become Brandon Ford whip a handful of Colombian conscripts into a ruthlessly efficient counterinsurgency squad, Nesbitt decided to build the new team around him.

Because he was paranoid by nature, Nesbitt also chose to limit his face-to-face exposure, instead using Hilda as the go-between. For convenience, she wove her own new identity and Brandon Ford's together. No one on the outside would question constant contact between a mother and her son. Ford's profession as a dealer in exotic firearms served a similar end. He could legally acquire whatever equipment was needed without raising undue suspicion. Plus, he enjoyed the work. The rest of the paramilitaries were fixed with similarly flexible occupations, jobs they could leave for weeks, even months at a time without making a ripple.

Hilda became their de facto den mother, organizing their living arrangements, seeing to their needs. She'd never married or had children, but when Brandon indulged his ill-fated relationship with Miranda Ford, fathering two kids whom he subsequently abandoned, she embraced the grandmotherly role.

"I was a better grandmother to those boys than he was ever a father," she says, but with a smile that reveals real affection for her pseudo-son. I can only imagine the strange emotions at work in that chain of relation between the true and false parents.

Hilda's feelings about Brandon became very conflicted. On the one hand, she grew fond enough of him to run interference with Nesbitt whenever there was friction between them. On the other, she resented the source of that friction, which was Brandon's ambition. Where Nesbitt wanted him to operate in a clearly defined cell, he aspired to larger things. There was more opportunity, he told her, in the intelligence side of the company, building networks and selling the information gleaned in the form of reports and analyses. Nesbitt jealously guarded that aspect of the operation, however. The more Brandon pushed, the more suspicious his boss became.

"These arguments could be very awkward for me," she says. "What I wanted was to keep everyone in our little family happy."

Listening to her describe what sounds to me like a criminal organization or at the very least a mercenary one, I am struck by how normal it all seems to Hilda. For her, the nature of the work never changed, only the employer did—and even there, it was more a change in status than degree. She had worked for Nesbitt when he was government-sanctioned, and she continued after he went freelance. Not that different, I suppose, from a cop who retires only to hang out his shingle as a private investigator. Not that different apart from the secrecy and the lawbreaking, that is.

For Hilda's "little family," the status quo was disrupted not by conflict but by opportunity. Nesbitt was presented with a chance to bring down the competition, Englewood's firm, and this led him to overreach.

"What kind of opportunity?" I ask.

"He never confided the details to me. What I gathered, though, was that someone had information to sell, and he wanted to be paid in services. If Nesbitt would do a certain job, he would get the information. What the job was, I never knew. Whatever it was, Andy kept me out of the loop and he kept Brandon out, too. The first effort failed, so he had to come up with Plan B, and that's when we got involved."

Plan B resulted in the creation of an intelligence network. Why this was necessary, or even relevant to the quid pro quo deal that inspired it, Hilda doesn't know. But Nesbitt managed to place someone deep inside the Gulf Cartel, using Brandon as an occasional courier to collect reports. And what reports they were! The quality of this intelligence stunned them all, as did the appetite for it in government circles. Nesbitt's insider mapped the internal workings of the cartels with so much precision it began to seem that no aspect of their operations was off-limits to him. Needless to say, his reports became a hot commodity.

Although he was the natural person to use, Brandon turned out to be a bad choice to use for courier. His first taste of intelligence work whetted his appetite. He started coming up with a host of new angles, insisting that Hilda pitch each one to "the Old Man" only to have them shot down. Selling weapons to the cartel and then selling intelligence about the transactions to law enforcement was Brandon's big idea, one that he revived once Nesbitt was out of the picture.

"And now we come to the point," she says. "Andy's death."

He was a victim of his sudden success. There was no way to keep what he was doing quiet once every decision maker in Federal drug enforcement was on the distribution list for his reports. With the exposure came increasing paranoia. Nesbitt brought new people into the organization. He took extra precautions when making contact with Hilda and discussed the possibility of cutting Brandon out of the loop entirely. He was preparing a new courier, he said, and taking measures to guarantee that his network wouldn't get away from him.

"Why was he so concerned?" I ask.

"Because someone put it into his head that he was going to be assassinated. And he was convinced it was the police who would carry it out."

"That's absurd."

"Even so," she says, "look what happened."

"I have looked. I watched the video over and over."

"Whatever you think really happened, Andy believed his life was in danger. So did Brandon. He told me someone was gunning for all of us. All I know is that Andy was murdered, and then when Brandon tried to take over, he was murdered, too. At least that's what I was told."

Before his death, Nesbitt entered into a negotiation with a contact at the FBI, essentially offering to hand his network over in return for protection and a financial consideration. Hilda waited two weeks after the shooting to get in touch with the contact herself to renew the offer. She handed over herself, Brandon, and the anonymous insider in Matamoros, who was known only by the code name Nesbitt had given him: INFERNO. She kept the rest of Nesbitt's operation, including the men in her files, out of the spotlight.

"Your people have a lot of faith in you," Hilda says, turning to Bea. "They told me we'd be in good hands, that your record with drug intelligence operations was unparalleled. You were an iconoclast, a rule breaker. I liked the sound of you right away."

"Great."

"If I had realized what Brandon was up to, honey, I would have warned you. I guess he saw the opportunity to expand his role, so he took it."

Bea clears her throat. "He told you about . . . *us*?"

"Eventually. I suspect what attracted you to each other was what you both have in common: ambition. You could use each other and neither one of you really minded. It would have been better, though, for all of us, if your bosses had put somebody *less* ambitious in charge. Somebody who could've shot Brandon's ideas down instead of falling for them."

"Who told you March's headless victim was Brandon?" Bea asks.

"One of them," Hilda says, nodding toward the stack of dossiers. "He called me in a panic, sounded very convincing. I actually cried—which I didn't do for Andy. He told me Brandon was dead and that the rest of them were going to disappear. They didn't need my help, which I thought was strange and a little ungrateful, but then I'd been guilty of leaving the boys in limbo since Andy's death. Of course, we were all in limbo after that."

"So you called Bea to warn her—?"

"I called her because Inferno, the insider, had stupidly vouched for Brandon to the cartel. If they were watching the investigation, and it came out that Brandon wasn't really who he'd said, if you made his real name public along with his military record . . . well, let's just say that Mr. Inferno would have found himself in some hot water. I owed it to him to prevent that, if I could."

"And then you disappeared yourself."

"Partly," she says, glancing across the room. "I am on my way. If you had shown up here a week from now, you would have found the place vacated. I'd tell you where I'm headed, but . . . You understand."

"We already found your bag of passports," Bea says.

"Those are old lives," Hilda replies. "I'm moving on to something new."

"You're not going anywhere, not anymore."

"You can't arrest me, dear. I haven't done anything. And besides, if you did slap me in cuffs, there are parts of my story I don't think you'd want your superiors to hear."

To my surprise, Bea doesn't respond to this. She buries her face in her hands, shaking her head. She is ambitious, and Hilda is right. A story like this would end her professional rise, if not her entire career. Losing some expense money, even such a big chunk of it, hardly compares to jeopardizing a major intelligence asset like Inferno.

"Whatever anxiety Bea might have," I say, "the fact is, I didn't track you down for a history lesson. I'm looking for a murderer. I want to know who took the skin off my John Doe's hands and cut his head off, and I want to know where I can find the men in your files—your 'boys.' They killed a good cop, and tried to kill me, too."

"And what, I'm supposed to do your job for you?" There's a flash of anger in her eyes, the first I've seen, a glimpse of the cornered animal behind her innocuous act. "I've already told you more than you could ever have figured out on your own. This is not something you can drag into a courtroom, Detective. This is not something you could ever document, let alone prosecute. And even if you could, before you got that far, there are people who would stop you. That's not a threat. It's a simple fact."

"Maybe," I say. "But I can't let you walk out of here without giving me more. Where do I find Brandon Ford, for example?"

"How would I know? I think we're both aware of the fact he's switched allegiances. You should go and ask your new friend, Mr. Englewood."

"Not good enough."

"Your guess is as good as mine."

"Tell me about this courier business. He was traveling down to Matamoros, you said? Where'd he stay down there? What kind of transport? Where did he like to stop for gas? There are all kinds of things I bet you could tell me, and we have plenty of time."

"In return for what? You'll let me go?"

"Possibly."

"If I give you what you're asking, then I can walk out of here. That's what I'm asking."

"You're not walking out of here," Bea says.

"Hold on a second," I tell her. "I think Hilda wants to help us out. There must be some kind of agreement we can come to, right?"

The two women glare at me, then at each other. After a while, Bea nods. Hilda shifts in her chair, draping one arm over its back.

"All right, then," she says. "Where was I?"

DOWN THERE

PART 3

Lo 'mperador del doloroso regno da mezzo
'l petto uscia fuor de la ghiaccia.

The emperor of the realm of grief protruded
from mid-breast up above the surrounding ice.

He had had his chance to blow his horn
at the beginning and save all those lives,
but for his own glory he would not blow.

—GRAHAM GREENE

CHAPTER 21

As the days pass and Wanda Mosser's confidence in her grip on Homicide increases, the question of my work status remains ambiguous. My legal counselor subscribes to the "no news is good news" school, insisting that if Internal Affairs had anything concrete, they would be acting on it. What's going on, he explains, is that the department is holding its breath. If I had shot the man only once or twice, if I had shot him with my own side arm, then I would be back on the job already, a hero who put down his partner's killer, even if it was too late to save his life. But because I used another weapon, a cut-down assault rifle converted illegally for automatic fire, and because I riddled his body with bullets, a total of sixteen entry wounds, there was enormous political risk in signing off on the shooting.

"All it would take is one cry of police brutality," he says, "one outraged demagogue to lash out at the department. There could be bad publicity, lawsuits, even protests at city hall. So they're gonna do nothing until they're sure it won't backfire."

This is Bascombe's opinion, too, which he gives in a late-night phone call prompted by the discovery that his newest detective, Cavallo, is for some reason making international phone calls to the *jefatura* of the Argentine

215

Federal Police. I'm tempted to keep everything from him, remembering that we haven't always seen eye to eye. But the bond of trust that's developed between us recently outweighs any conflict from the past.

So I tell him everything I know about the case. I tell him about Englewood and the attempt on my life. I tell him about Bea's relationship with Brandon Ford and how we managed to track down Hilda. I recount the whole convoluted tale of intelligence networks and couriers and false identities. He listens without interruption. Maybe he doesn't know what to say.

"There are more dossiers," I tell him. "Including one for the man I killed. According to that, his name is James Lodge. I wrote down the info. There's an address in Meyerland."

"You have a *file* on him?" he asks, incredulous.

"Bea has all the files. And the informant. She's using her resources to try and locate the men on that team."

"But when they tried to run his DNA, they came back with nothing?"

"Hilda created the false IDs, but she's not the one who gave us the match on Brandon Ford. That had to be Englewood pulling the strings."

He lets out a long sigh, then goes quiet for a while. I understand how crazy it all sounds. I realize, too, the complications that all this unsubstantiated, unverifiable information introduces to the black-and-white world of a homicide investigation. Is he supposed to walk into Mosser's office and declare that the John Doe we have identified as Brandon Ford really isn't, because the real Brandon Ford is still on the loose—only he isn't really Brandon Ford? Is he supposed to assign the name James Lodge to the second unidentified corpse on my say-so?

"I'm putting you in an awkward spot, I know. But that's the spot I'm in. I don't know what else to do."

"You're not supposed to be *doing* anything. And I'm worried about you dragging Cavallo into this. You're not doing her any favors."

"She'll be fine. Wanda likes her. How is the new captain doing, anyway?"

He sighs again. "She's riding me, March. Making sure I know who's the boss."

"That's just her way. Don't let it get to you."

"When she gets wind of what's going on, things are gonna be bad. She'll want your head and mine if we're not careful."

"So we'll be careful," I say. "It would be nice if you could get Internal Affairs off my back."

"Listen, I'm worried about this Englewood character. If he's as all-powerful as you're making out, why have I never heard of the man?"

"They know who he is in Internal Affairs. Maybe you should ask around over there, kill two birds with one stone."

"Maybe. In the meantime, try not to drag Cavallo down with you, all right? I'm already shorthanded as it is."

The next morning, my throbbing leg wakes me up while it's still dark. I swing my feet onto the floor, try to do some stretches. There's a spot in my lower back, just to the left of my spine, where I can dig with my fingertips and with enough pressure force the muscle to give just a little, to start to relax. The floor creaks under my weight and Charlotte turns in bed.

"Are you okay?" she asks. "Here, let me do that."

She has me lie flat on the bed, then, kneeling beside me, works her finger into the nerve.

"Breathe out," she says. "Try to relax."

Her hands are cool against my skin.

"Does this hurt?"

"It's fine," I whisper, though it does hurt some.

After a while she adjusts her angle, pushing deeper. I feel the tightness at the back of my thigh. As she leans down, her hair brushes against me.

"There," she says, "I just felt it let go."

I let out a long breath, lying as still as I can. She sits back, then sinks onto the mattress beside me, running a finger up the length of my arm.

"I could stay home today," she says. "We could spend it together. It's been a long time."

"I thought you had a meeting."

"Meetings can be rescheduled."

The idea sounds appealing, spending the morning in bed, dragging ourselves up for a late lunch, maybe getting in the car and just driving. Escaping. I bend my leg at the knee, bringing my foot up as high as it'll go and there's no pain anymore, just a pleasant numbness. I straighten my leg out, close my eyes, and lapse back into sleep.

When I open them again, a faint light filters through the blinds. Through the open bathroom door I hear the drum of water against the shower wall and feel the humidity in the air. I can just make out Charlotte's form behind the foggy, spray-flecked glass. I throw the covers back and go downstairs to make coffee, then bring her up a steaming mug. Wrapped in a white towel, her hair clinging in damp tendrils to the side of her face, Charlotte takes the coffee with a smile and asks what we're going to do with our day.

"I thought we would sleep late, but I guess not."

On my nightstand, my cellphone starts to buzz. The ring grows progressively louder until I pad across the room.

"It's Cavallo. I better take it."

Fifteen minutes later, I'm dressed and out the door. Charlotte walks me out, still nursing her mug. "Maybe next time," she says, and I peck her on the cheek. She puts her hand on the back of my neck, pulling me down for a proper kiss.

"I don't have any sympathy for you," Cavallo says. "I've been up for hours already. Buenos Aires is three hours ahead of us, and he sent this stuff over first thing. It's lucky for you that he called to let me know or it would be still sitting on the fax machine."

She stifles a yawn, then glances at her watch. Her hair is still damp and her makeup, applied in the car, is minimal. With a cop's instinct for greasy spoons, she has commandeered a booth at a diner on Yale just a few minutes from my house, where she's spread out official-looking faxed pages, all in Spanish, and some crime-scene photos—printouts muddy with toner. Her Español runs rings around mine, so I leave it to her to translate.

"I'm impressed you got anything out of them."

"The Federal police were no help at all," she says. "Too many hoops to jump through. This is all courtesy of a journalist down there. Turns out there's an English-language newspaper and Brad Templeton knows one of the reporters. I dropped his name and here we are."

Brad Templeton, a former journalist turned true-crime author, is an on-again-off-again contact of mine. Since our falling out last year, the relationship has been decidedly off. But Cavallo's better than I am at maintaining lines of communication.

"I'm impressed," I say. "It wouldn't have occurred to me to even ask him."

I turn the crime-scene photos to face me, peering down at the body of Chad Macneil.

For two innocent weeks in 2008, in between updates on the presidential elections, before word of the impending worldwide financial crisis broke, the nightly news in Houston obsessed over the disappearance of Chad Macneil, a former Arthur Anderson exec who had transformed himself post-Enron into a freelance money manager with a rumored net worth in the tens of millions. He sat on a couple of boards, but otherwise kept a low profile, devoting himself full-time to the creation of wealth. As his privileged clients whispered to each other over cocktails, Macneil worked wonders with other people's money.

What those clients didn't know was that for months Chad Macneil had been the subject of a fraud inquiry and that investigators believed the case was so strong they were on the verge of making an arrest. In the middle of lunch at The Houstonian, Macneil received a tip-off by phone, probably from his attorney. He excused himself and wandered off in the direction of the restroom. The last he was seen was on surveillance video, collecting the keys of his Maserati from a valet. Macneil disappeared, and so did a sizable chunk of his clients' money.

"The *Herald* reporter had photos from the scene, the autopsy report, everything. Unfortunately some of the pages have been redacted. Somebody got a little heavy-handed with the permanent marker."

"I see that."

At the time, Macneil's disappearance meant nothing to me. It only became relevant when I discovered that one of his cheated clients was Reg Keller, who at the time headed up an elite team inside the police department dubbed Comprehensive Risk Assessment, derisively renamed the Golden Parachute Brigade, since its sole reason for existence seemed to be to guarantee a bright future in security consulting once Keller made the long anticipated move into the private sector. To further that end, Keller had wooed some outside investors into creating a company to bid on port-related Homeland Security contracts, keeping his own involvement a secret until the groundwork was laid for his retirement. Chad Macneil, who helped put it all together, held the purse strings. When he disappeared, so did everything Keller had built.

The golden parachute was gone, leaving Keller on the hook with the investors. If he had been a businessman himself, Keller might have sought new investment or figured out some other way to keep the enterprise intact. Despite his rise through the ranks, Keller remained a street cop at heart. On his team he had officers with tactical ops experience, and he also had Tony Salazar, a former gang homicide unit detective who knew the city's drug infrastructure better than most anyone. They started jacking drug dealers, amassing cash and product both, spreading the damage across different gangs and different parts of the city so that no one could pinpoint who was responsible. In the process they managed to put a small crimp in the supply lines and stir up rivalry and suspicion on the street. They could tell themselves they were helping the city and themselves at the same time.

It all came to an end at a house off of West Bellfort. An informant gave Salazar some bad intelligence, which led to a raid on a loan shark named Morales. There were no drugs, no stash of bills, but there was a teenaged girl strapped down on the bed. In the confusion of the gun battle, one of Keller's men accidentally shot the girl. Investigating her murder fell to me, and the cop who shot her, consumed by guilt, wanted to confess to everything. He was a liability to the team, and Keller had gone too far to allow himself to be exposed now. So he put a bullet into one of his own men.

That didn't stop me from finding out what had happened, but by the time I did, Keller had followed Chad Macneil's example and disappeared. Cavallo, Wilcox, and I raided his apartment with a team of detectives. He was long gone.

It was a year later that police in Argentina responded to a call from a Buenos Aires luxury hotel, where they found a guest dead in the bathroom of his suite. He was kneeling on the tile floor, his body arched over the rim of the half-filled bathtub, his head submerged under the water. Although no one was ever charged, the rumor in Houston among people familiar with the case was that Reg Keller had caught up to him and taken revenge.

"There's a lot of black ink here," I say. "What are they trying to hide?"

"It's not unusual to keep things from the press. We do it all the time."

The tone of her voice tells me there's more to the story than that.

"What are you not telling me?" I turn a few of the autopsy report pages toward me, scanning the text around the marked-out passages. "Help me out here."

"Well," she says, lifting her purse onto the table. "There was one thing that got my attention and that's why I thought we should meet." She unzips the purse, reaching in to produce a folded sheet. She opens it facedown on the table, smoothing the crease with her fingertip. "It's hard to tell from the report what they're hiding. But when I saw this photo, I think I figured it out."

She flips the page and slides it across to me.

It's another crime-scene photo, but unlike the others in which Chad Macneil's nude body is photographed from the rear, with the head and arms disappearing over the rim of the tub, this one was taken from above so that the entire corpse is visible. The cloudy bathwater, which obscures the body in other shots, has been drained for this photograph. Only the back of his head is visible, the hair damp. The outstretched arms, bent at each elbow, intersect at the wrists, which would place his hands about six to eight inches above his head.

The hands are not visible, however. Around each, someone has drawn a square in black marker and then heavily shaded in the boxes.

"They're hiding the hands," I say.

"And why would they do that? Maybe something was done to them, the same thing that was done to Brandon Ford—or whatever the John Doe's name really is. They could have been skinned."

"De-gloved."

"Which would suggest that the two homicides have something in common. Like maybe they were done by the same person."

If she's right, if the blacked-out hands in the photo were mutilated, the skin sliced away from the flesh, then the murder in Buenos Aires and the body found in Houston the next year could be related. The work of the same killer. Dr. Bridger needs to see this. He can tell us if what we're guessing makes sense.

"Theresa . . ." My throat tightens. "People say Reg Keller killed Macneil."

She looks at me, one eyebrow arched, saying nothing.

She doesn't have to.

CHAPTER 22

"And what exactly do you expect me to do with this?" Bridger asks. He peers at me across the top of his reading glasses, the faxed pages in his hand, with an expression of amused incredulity. "For one thing, I can barely read them. And for another, so much of it has been crossed out."

"We were kind of hoping . . ." Cavallo lets her voice trail off suggestively.

"Hoping what? That I could guess what's underneath the black ink?" He tosses the stack onto the desk in front of him, crosses his leg, and smiles. "Your faith in me is touching, but a little misplaced. As a great man once said, 'I'm a doctor, Jim, not a miracle worker.'"

"Could have fooled me," I say.

"Flattery? You must be desperate."

I know him well enough to realize that this resistance is a mask. The photo of Chad Macneil with his hands blacked out intrigued the medical examiner as much as it did me. His eyes widened the moment he saw it, and he didn't need me or Cavallo to suggest a motive for the redaction. The same thought popped into his head as mine. But Bridger's opinions are never offered without qualification, especially not when I'm the one asking. I come to him for too many favors, as he's always reminding me. When he does speculate, though, you can usually take what he says to the bank.

The reason I first introduced my sister-in-law Ann to Dr. Alan Bridger was because, whenever I tried to explain to her how airtight the forensic evidence was against the convicted felon whose innocence she'd taken up as a *cause célèbre*, she naturally assumed that as a policeman I simply couldn't admit the truth. When Bridger speaks, however, he has a way of channeling the voice of objective science circa 1950. Everything he says sounds right, which is why he's a favored witness for the prosecution, and why from the start he drove Ann crazy, leading to many passionate and protracted disagreements.

I suppose the good doctor was accustomed to people deferring to his judgment. He enjoyed their little debates so much that he started coming over regularly for dinner. Eventually I suggested that the two of them could argue without Charlotte and me having to host. Before long, they were dating, and then Bridger surprised everyone (Ann included) by proposing marriage. The funny thing is, once they tied the knot, the debates pretty much ended. They can be very serene in each other's presence.

"I figured that if you looked at the autopsy report, maybe the context alone would suggest something to you. And maybe there are other similarities between the two cases, things they didn't suppress."

He takes up the pages again, mouthing the Spanish words to himself. Cavallo glances my way, risking a faint smile. The doctor is hooked.

Bridger helped me greatly when I first joined the homicide squad, explaining details of forensic medicine in a way that didn't put me to sleep, and teaching me that, despite his manner, the science could be far from objective. So much depends on interpretation, and on the context investigators provide. And we rely so much on the science, myself included, that common sense sometimes takes a backseat. The answers, more often than not, aren't waiting in the laboratory. They're out on the street. You have to ask the right people the right questions, simple as that.

When you need an expert, though, there's no substitute for a thorough, analytical mind like Bridger's. If something's there, he'll find it.

"Did you bring a copy of the other autopsy report?" he asks. "No, of course not. Fortunately I have it handy. I had a visit from your FBI colleague yesterday, asking for a similar kind of miracle."

"Bea was here?"

"She brought some interesting files along, several men the approximate age of the victim. Despite the identification, she seemed to think he might be one of these others."

"She knew Brandon Ford," I say. "Intimately. When we came here before, she said that wasn't him."

"You might have shared that information."

"Were you able to find a likely candidate?" I ask, ignoring his remark.

"I did recognize one of the men. It was the one you shot. Interesting that she has a file on him and no one's made that connection public."

"Yes, interesting. Maybe there are some questions about the reliability of those files."

Cavallo scoots her chair closer to the desk, distancing herself from me. "If you're feeling left out, Alan, you're not alone. Roland operates on a need-to-know basis, and he seems to think the people who put their careers on the line for him don't need to know. Everything I get, I have to pull out of him. It gets old after a while."

"I can relate," he says.

"Considering how explosive some of this stuff is, maybe I'm doing you both a favor by not burdening you with too much. Have you considered that?" They clearly haven't, and I know it's a lame excuse to make. I concede as much with a smiling shrug. "But hey, the important thing is, we may have linked these two cases, assuming you can find something concrete to go on."

Bridger goes over the John Doe autopsy report quickly, refreshing his memory, then returns to the Argentine report, squinting through his glasses and mouthing more words. Tense with anticipation, I have to force myself to breathe. He goes back and forth again, comparing lines, examining photographs, keeping his thoughts entirely to himself.

"The suspense is killing me," I say.

He doesn't look up. After another minute, he pulls a photo from the John Doe report and compares it to the one with Macneil's hands blacked out. His lips part.

"Yes?" I ask.

"Come with me."

He leads us back to the cold storage, where I'd had him take Bea the morning she looked at the body. He hands me the photos before donning a pair of gloves. After consulting the register, he opens the right refrigerator unit and cantilevers the sheeted corpse out for examination. He glances at Cavallo before pulling the sheet back, forgetting that she's seen worse, much worse.

Glimpsing the corpse again, I get a flash of memory, a snapshot of the concrete basketball court where we first encountered him, Lorenz and me. The wounds had seemed fresher then, more shocking to behold. The stylized pose, the skinned finger extended.

"Are you okay?" Bridger asks.

"I'm fine."

"This is what we're looking at," he continues, lifting the left arm. Using his pinkie, he draws a semicircle in the air above the wrist, indicating the discolored flesh where some kind of restraint was used to secure the hand during torture. "Tied to an armchair, most likely. See underneath? The marks are on the top of the wrist, but not the bottom, like it was resting on something. Now take a look at the Argentine photo. See that mark there, just below the part that's blacked out? What does it look like?"

"The same," Cavallo says.

"You'd want to make a real comparison, obviously, or at least work from a better photograph, but what that suggests—and this is only speculation—but it *suggests* Macneil may have had similar injuries to his hands."

I look at the picture again, then the body. Once the ligature mark in the photo has been pointed out, it's impossible not to see it, not to interpret it as a restraint. Before, it was invisible, bordering so close to the black box. Cavallo double-checks the comparison, too.

"It's really there," she says.

"I think so."

Bridger puts the sheet back in place, rolls the body back into storage. Halfway in, he stops and rolls it back out. "There's something else," he says. "Bad news, really. But since this is your case now, Theresa, I thought you should know. Detective Lorenz, before his death, had asked about the marks on the back of the victim's leg—"

"What marks?" I ask.

He cocks his eyebrow in surprise. "That's right. You weren't there. This was at the scene, after you went off on your wild-goose chase into the woods. But it's in my full report—you have read the full report, haven't you?"

"I don't remember anything about marks on the leg."

He exchanges a look with Cavallo, then extends the body tray all the way out so he can access the legs. "There are three dark streaks running parallel, here on the back of the calf. Like he swiped against something while being moved. Looked like oil to me, and I was right. It's a 5W-30 motor oil. Nothing to help you there. If the body was transported in a car trunk, maybe a van, there are a thousand ways to get marks like that. Lorenz hoped it might be something more exotic, to help pinpoint a murder scene."

I hunch down for a closer look at the marks. Three faint swipes across the back of the calf, maybe two inches in length.

"Is there anything else you're holding back?" I ask.

Cavallo laughs. "Holding back is *your* specialty, March."

"Yeah, yeah."

While Bridger returns the body to the refrigerator, Cavallo and I go into the corridor. She's biting down on her bottom lip, waiting for me to acknowledge the fact that she's done good work. I give her shoulder a pat. "Nice job. Do you think there's any chance of getting the full autopsy report through official channels? That's what we need to make this stick."

"It might be possible," she says.

"Ask Bascombe. He's good at that kind of thing."

"If I did that, I'd have to tell him what I'm working on."

Now it's my turn to laugh: "He already knows."

When I left Hilda and her files in Bea's hands for safekeeping, it was an acknowledgment that her resources were greater than mine. But I did not walk away empty-handed. Hilda gave me a detailed outline of the process Brandon Ford used for making contact with Inferno to collect his raw intelligence. She'd never made the journey herself, of course. But Ford had apparently relied on her experience when it came to making operational dispositions. I trusted that her information would prove accurate.

Setting up a watch on the route on the off chance that Ford might make a trip to Matamoros was beyond my capabilities, though. So was hunting down the men in Hilda's files. With Bea's team of experienced drug intelligence officers, she could do more on both counts. I had to take it on faith that if anything turned up, she would keep me in the loop.

Bridger's tip leaves me thinking that faith was misplaced.

I try to call Bea and find out what's going on, but I keep getting her voicemail. The last time I paid a surprise visit, she wasn't expecting me, which made following her from the field office parking garage to her suburban cowboy bar a piece of cake. I'm not in the mood to take so much trouble now. Besides, I like to shake things up.

After parting with Cavallo, I drive downtown to Bea's office, showing my badge at security and explaining who I'm there to see. Nobody bats an eyelid. Phone calls are made and a stout woman in pinstripes with an electronic earpiece assures me that Special Agent Kuykendahl will arrive momentarily. Instead, the door to her basement lair opens to reveal a broad-chested All-American with a blond crew cut and perfect teeth. He beckons me through, leading me down the same path I took the first time, explaining in the corridor that Bea is his boss.

It's a strange thing to realize that someone as young as Bea, someone who looks so adolescent, can command such men. The All-American speaks of her in hushed tones and with great respect. There's a note of pride at being a member of her team, reminding me of the *esprit de corps* that Wanda Mosser once inspired in her tough-guy subordinates.

"Did you know Brandon Ford?" I ask him.

He swipes us through the security door. "I'll let you talk to *her* about that."

Last time, the bullpen was empty. Now half a dozen officers are gathered around the conference table with Bea at the head. Behind her, a large portable whiteboard is covered in photographs and handwritten notes. When she sees me, Bea flips the board over to conceal their work, but not before I see the faces of the six paramilitaries whose new identities Hilda kept on file: the curly-haired Brandon Ford, James Lodge of the skull-shaped ring, and four others. One of the four is circled in red, a question mark next to his face.

It's a reasonable assumption that one of these men could be John Doe. Six to begin with, then subtract Lodge, who murdered my partner and was killed in turn. That would leave five, but the night they descended on me in the Hummer, there were only four, including Ford himself. So where was the missing man? Could he have been dead all along, cooling off in Bridger's refrigerator with some oil stains on his leg?

"I've been trying to reach you," I say.

"Everybody, I'm sure Detective March needs no introduction. As you know, he is assisting us on this one, though unofficially thanks to a certain altercation with one of our targets."

With the exception of one agent who appears to be in his forties, Bea's team looks as young as they do eager. Like her, they don't fit my idea of the G-man mold. Maybe that's because they work in a specialized field, or maybe she chooses underlings who resemble herself. The outlier is the older guy, who has enough starch in his shirt and steam on his creases to make J. Edgar Hoover proud. He stands to shake my hand. When Bea leads me back to her office, he follows behind us, pausing at the door.

"You need anything, boss?" he asks.

"March might want some coffee. No? Then I guess we're fine."

He looks me over before pulling the door shut.

"He seems like a very accommodating guy," I say.

She slumps in her chair like a teenager, crossing one leg over the other, stretching her hands behind her neck. "If it was up to him, he'd be sitting at my desk."

"So that's how it is." I take a seat.

"That's how it is. Now, what are you doing here? We agreed that I'd call if I needed anything from you."

"I remember our agreement a little differently, but never mind. I assume Hilda is tucked away somewhere? The thing is, Dr. Bridger says you paid him a visit. Now he's wondering what's going on. You should have included me in that conversation."

"He told you why I was there?"

I nod. "I assume, looking at your board out there, that the visit was successful."

She sits up straight, tucks her legs under the desk. "You saw that, huh? It doesn't matter. I'm not trying to keep you in the dark. In fact, I'm pretty proud of the way my people have come through on this. I doubt Houston's finest could have done any better."

"How so?"

"Dr. Bridger was not such a big help," she says. "He couldn't match any of the files up to the body on his slab, said there wasn't enough to go on. But he did throw out an idea. The John Doe died of cardiac arrest, but apparently with the kind of torture he went through, that's not a given. You can endure something like that without your heart giving out, I guess. This guy may have had a heart condition—"

"Is there anything in the files about that?"

"They're not *that* thorough. But we did some checking and we found out that one of these guys, Robert Johnson, was admitted to the hospital two years ago, complaining about an irregular heartbeat."

Johnson, Ford, Lodge. Such generic names. Designed so their owners could pass unnoticed through life.

"They put him on a monitor and diagnosed it as stress," she says. "That's good enough for me. According to his stats, he's about the same height as Brandon and they're in the same age range. I think Johnson is who you found on the basketball court."

"Then why did the database say it was Brandon Ford?"

"Here's my theory: Brandon saw an opportunity and he took it. None of his paramilitaries were on my radar screen, but he was. If that body was identified as him, he could walk away and none of us would even know to look for him, because we'd think it was him we buried. But after his 'death,' he must have gone back to his office for some reason—maybe to pick up the money we gave him. He figured out you were there—maybe you tripped some kind of signal without realizing—and he knew he had to get everything out of there or you'd realize it couldn't be him dead on the slab."

"So you're saying that Ford killed his own man and planted the body to make us think it was him?"

"I'm not saying that. I don't know—"

"And Ford on his own wouldn't have the juice to rig that DNA match."

"Like I said, it's theory."

"Here's something else to put in your hat. There's an earlier victim, a man by the name of Chad Macneil. He was murdered last year down in Buenos Aires. The cops there didn't release all the details, but we're working on that. What we do have suggests that Macneil's hands were skinned just like Robert Johnson's—assuming you're right about him. So the question then becomes, can you place Brandon Ford in Buenos Aires when that murder occurred?"

"Can you give me the dates?"

"I can do better than that." From my briefcase I produce a photocopy of the autopsy report on Macneil. "We're working on getting an official copy of this. Maybe you'd have more pull as a Federal agent?"

"I'll see what I can do."

She flips through the pages, her face clouding. Before I walked in, she was confident she had a handle on things, and now that handle's yanked itself right off. There are questions I'd like to ask her. I'd like to know how much her team knows about what's going on, if she's leveled with them about her relationship with Ford or not. From what I saw earlier, there don't seem to be many secrets in here. Maybe she's found a way to cover her exposure, or at least to limit the fallout. If it's true the old man of her team wants her job, she wouldn't put everything on the table unless she was fairly certain neither the inappropriate relationship nor the missing quarter million could come back to bite her.

"Was there anything else?" she asks.

There is, but I'm not going to ask. I already know the kind of answers she'd give and how far I could trust them. When you're in the dark and you suspect there's a brick wall, there's no point running into it just to prove you're right.

On my way out, though, I make a point of pausing at the big white-board. With a glance in Bea's direction I flip it back over, taking a long look at the man she's identified as Robert Johnson. He has a long, thin face with dark eyes and a cleft chin. His jet-black hair is cut short. A thick, muscular neck with a prominent Adam's apple. I can imagine him swallowing. I can imagine the axe falling across his throat.

"The face that launched a thousand ships," Bea says.

"Maybe so. I just want to know why he was killed." I touch the edge of the photo, some of the red marker coming off on my finger. "There's something you should know. When Chad Macneil was killed, a lot of people thought it was Reg Keller who did it. You know about Reg, I assume. If he's connected to this somehow, then I need you to realize this: he's mine."

"He's yours," she says. "Message received."

My eyes trail across the board, resting on Lodge's face. I remember him turning at the sound of my voice, his legs planted on either side of Lorenz, my pistol in his hand. I remember his eyes, the mask hiked up over his forehead, the millisecond's worth of surprise before he was hidden behind the Krinkov's flash.

Bea puts her hand on my arm. "Don't let it get to you. It had to be done."

I'm conscious of everyone in the room, their eyes on me, but when I turn, they are all looking away. All except for the outlier, the older man, who stands apart from the rest with his arms crossed, barely concealing his disgust.

CHAPTER 23

Leaving the field office and its air-conditioning via the front entrance, the sauna effect hits me outside, steaming my sunglasses at the bridge of the nose. As I walk, I'm conscious not only of a twinge down my leg but also a leftward tilt brought on by the weight of my briefcase. Even empty, the bridle leather is a handful, but now it's stuffed to capacity with all the gear and paperwork I lug around on a daily basis, mostly without being conscious of the load. Remembering the doctor's words about heavy lifting, I tell myself it may be time to retire the old bag, or at least dump some of the ballast.

"Hey, you," a voice calls.

I wheel around to find the outlier from Bea's squad breathing down my neck. "You got a problem with me?"

He gets up in my face, eyes flashing. But I see right off that I've misread the signs. He's not confronting me. He's putting an arm around my shoulder, hunching down, whispering something he doesn't want anybody to overhear.

"Listen here," he says. "What's going on back there, we're crossing all the lines. We're doing things we've got no business doing, taking risks we've got no business taking. She's sucked you into it. Don't argue with me now. I can see it. I can read the signs for myself. I know because I've been there myself."

"What are you trying to tell me?"

"What I'm trying to do is warn you. She's got her hooks in you good. She calls the tune and you put on your dancing shoes. But this is gonna end bad for everybody involved. I'm telling you right now to walk away."

"This is sour grapes," I say. "Bea somehow maneuvered herself into the job you wanted, and now you're out for revenge. What's the matter? Can't handle having a woman for a boss?"

"What I can't handle is having a *snake* for a boss. She's not the victim here, partner. She's calling the shots."

"I'm not your partner." I shrug myself free.

He throws his hands up. "Fine. You've been warned. And I won't feel sorry for you when you take the fall."

After he's stalked away, I open my car door and sling the briefcase to the passenger side. It lands on the edge and falls over. The straps that hold down the top flap are buckled loosely, leaving enough play around the opening for some of the smaller items to spill onto the floor mat. Bending over, I retrieve my digital recorder, my beat-up little camera, and Jeff's dog-eared copy of *The Foxhole Atheist*, which I'm still carrying around.

By the time everything's packed away, my forehead's beaded with sweat. I start the engine and adjust the air vents, pausing a couple of minutes just to cool down. Then I reach into the glove compartment for some pain pills.

I'm not sure what to make of that guy. He doesn't like Bea, that much is obvious. As for the rest, I may be a fool to trust her, but what choice do I have?

I let the air-conditioner blow as I dial Wilcox.

"Have you made any progress?"

"If I had anything worth sharing, I would've already called." He takes a breath. "Look, if Englewood was an investor in Keller's business, there's no paper trail I can find. Maybe that in itself says something.

The man does what he wants and never leaves a trace. He knows how to keep invisible."

"Speaking of invisibility, is it possible that Englewood made Keller disappear when we were hunting him? He'd have the connections, presumably."

"Anything's possible," he says. "Proving it, though, that's the problem. Can I be honest with you, March? Maybe we're out of our depth. You're over on the sideline, I'm coming up with nothing, and the idea that any of this is going to end up in court . . ."

"What are we supposed to do? Ignore it?"

He doesn't answer.

"I'm flailing around here," I say, "but it's better than doing nothing. So keep looking, okay?"

Silence on the line, which I interpret as consent. I'm about to say goodbye when he clears his throat. "I shouldn't say anything," he says, "but I've seen the preliminary report on your shooting."

"And?"

"They've got nothing."

"That's good. I mean, I *knew* there was nothing, but still . . . I'm relieved."

"They're sitting on it, though. Keeping their options open."

"Still," I say. "Thanks."

When I turn off Justice Park Drive on my way to the Northwest Freeway ramp, the donut shop on W. 43rd calls out to me. I steer into the lot, putting the car in park and bringing my briefcase inside with me. Inside, a couple of sun-weathered old-timers are drinking black coffee across from each other, the morning paper scattered in sections on the table between them. One of them wears a white sleeveless T-shirt over cigar-wrapper skin, a flat cap low over his eyes. The other has one hand tucked into the waistband of his powder-blue stretch jeans. They look me over with indifference before resuming their conversation.

At the counter I line up behind a couple of refill-seeking seniors, then order coffee and a glazed donut, which I take to an empty table up front with a view of the parking lot and the feeder road beyond. The coffee is weak, but the donut tastes pretty good in a soft, sickly sweet sort of way. I have to give my fingertips a good scrub to get the glaze off, and even then, as I unpack my briefcase, spreading the papers out across the Formica tabletop, my touch seems to raise sticky welts on everything.

I sip some coffee and start flipping through *The Foxhole Atheist*. The marginal note with the safe house address isn't the only annotation. In fact, many of the pages feature underlining and one- or two-word notes. Sometimes he's written GOOD or EXACTLY next to a line from the day's devotional reading. Sometimes he limits himself to an exclamation mark beside a telling passage. Clearly he's spent some hours with this book, so it's no surprise that when needing to write the address down, *The Foxhole Atheist* was at hand.

As I browse the little book, I notice pages where Jeff has underlined just a single letter in the middle of a word. On an entire page, there will be just one or two of these random lines underneath an I or an O or an F, reminding me of the way I used to mark up books as a kid first discovering cryptography, using a simple book cipher to write secret messages. The memory brings a smile to my lips.

The very first entry in the book is the most marked. It's titled THERE ARE NO ATHEISTS IN FOXHOLES, BUT THERE SHOULD BE. The first line in the second paragraph reads:

> In these cases, the very same fear that prompts the theist to doubt his faith perversely motivated the atheist toward an artificial certainty in the existence of a spiritual world.

The letters he's underlined—the I and N in the word *in*, the F and E in the word *fear*, the R in *artificial*, the N in *certainty*, and the O in *world*—they're not a cipher code, but they do spell a word. Turning the pages with greater urgency, I find the pattern repeated, not all in one sentence as in the first instance, but stretching over the length of paragraphs and pages. Always the same sequence of letters, always spelling the same word.

INFERNO.

Jeff gave the impression that he didn't know much about the inner workings of Nesbitt's company, and when Hilda spilled her own version, she never alluded to Jeff by name, only mentioning that in the grip of paranoia Nesbitt had brought new people in from the outside, people she presumably didn't know well. And yet, over and over in a strangely compulsive way, Jeff was picking out the sequence of letters that spell the code name of Nesbitt's informer.

Why?

I pull out my phone and dial Jeff's number. Evidently he knows more than he let on. Maybe giving me the book was his way of revealing this, knowing I would pick up on the underlining eventually. There's no answer. The voicemail picks up and an electronically generated voice repeats the digits.

"Call me," I say. "I've been reading your book."

Then I wait. When he doesn't call back right away, I pop the rings of my Filofax open, removing a couple of fresh sheets of lined notepaper. I make two lists side by side, the first column labeled NESBITT and the second ENGLEWOOD. Underneath the first I put Jeff and Hilda, Brandon Ford and the men in his paramilitary team. Then I relist Ford and his men under Englewood, drawing an arrow from left to right, since at some point they must have switched sides.

At the bottom of the page I write INFERNO, underlining the name.

What column should I put him in? I would write Inferno's name under Nesbitt's column, only it seems Ford is the only person in touch with the insider. If he's switched sides, maybe Inferno belongs to Englewood's team now. That's where the power seems to be, after all. The way Wilcox was talking about him, there's not much the man can't do. The phony DNA results are proof of that. And if he has the power to manipulate the NCIC database, why maybe it's not so implausible to think he could have arranged the traffic stop that led to Nesbitt's death. Maybe Silvestri, the training officer, undid his thumb break for a reason; maybe he really did intend to shoot Nesbitt, just as the conspiracy theorists online insist. The crooked cop angle strikes me as ridiculous, the stuff of Hollywood or bad television dramas, but after my face-to-face meeting with Englewood, when he dropped Reg Keller's name, anything seems possible.

I write SILVESTRI under Englewood's column, but with a question mark.

At the top of the page, above all the rest, I add KELLER in heavy block letters. Unfinished business. The way he disappeared so completely when we were hunting him, that suggests powerful interests working in his favor. Englewood again? By mentioning Big Reg's name, he as good as confirmed it. If Englewood protected him before, clearing the way for him to kill Chad Macneil in Buenos Aires, is it possible Englewood also brought him back to Houston, where he murdered my John Doe, who may or may not be one of the paramilitaries by the name of Robert Johnson?

All the names. All the interconnections.

I check my phone for missed numbers, but Jeff hasn't attempted to return my call.

Staring at the lists, going over them in black ink, making everything darker and darker, scoring deep lines into the page, I don't know, I just don't know how it all fits together.

But my sense of Reg Keller is this: he committed minor crimes for personal advantage, and when his back was to the wall, he went as far as homicide. Still, there's a difference between putting a gun to someone's head and pulling the trigger, and tying a person's hands down and methodically skinning them.

Any of us, in the grip of desperation, with fear narrowing our options down, is capable of the first kind of evil. The second takes a special kind of sadist.

Is Keller one of them? I would have thought not.

Here's the thing, though. Since we last met, Big Reg has been on an outlaw journey, traveling to darker regions of the mind, perhaps unlocking doors even he didn't know were there before. The man I went up against two years ago might not have been capable of such brutality, but that doesn't mean he isn't today.

I'm flailing, just like I told Wilcox. But there's one thing I've learned, and it's this. Even when you don't connect, even when your fist keeps slicing through air, if you keep punching, sooner or later, you're bound to hit something.

On his way out, the old guy in the flat cap peers down at the mess I've made on the table. He tucks his paper under his arm, shaking his head.

I smile up at him. "You have a nice day."

The gate outside Jeff's auto garage is padlocked and there's no sign of activity on the lot, just the row of picked-over car husks out front, the debris of tires and crushed glass, brown weeds pushing up through the cracks in the concrete. The blacked-out windows show a layer of baked-on grime, and the creases in the articulated garage doors are outlined in rust. I walk along the curb, inspecting the coils of barbed wire at the top of the fence, not relishing the prospect of making the climb.

A tall hedge separates the property from the undeveloped lot behind. I pick my way across the overgrown, potholed ground, looking for gaps in the bushes, hoping there's a back way into the alley I parked inside during my first visit. There's no opening in the fence, but the wire stops where the fence meets the hedge.

I glance around to see if anyone's watching. Across a side street is a liquor store with burglar bars over the windows. Next to it, some itinerant workers are loitering in the Burger King parking lot, but they aren't paying attention to what I'm up to—or if they are, they're making a point of not showing it.

The hedge is inside the fence on Jeff's property, so I have to shimmy up, pushing my shoes into the links for a toehold. The climb is awkward rather than difficult, and soon my leg is over the top, seeking purchase among the tree branches. It's a pine hedge, prickly and too fragile to support my weight, so there's no choice but to slide down the fence itself, scrubbing my back against the needles. Once I reach the ground, I'm sandwiched by the hedge on one side and the fence on the other, with only a pocket of space to move around in and no visible path through the foliage. Wandering again, but in a not-so-dark wood. Covering my face with my upraised arms, I push my way through.

Outside the hedge, I'm cut off by the bumper of an old Plymouth Barracuda with no glass and a stripped interior. In the dark, the old muscle cars had looked a little better than they do in the blazing daylight.

After brushing myself off, I go to the back door with its row of dead bolts, pounding out a beat with my fist. Nothing. I knock again, then try the handle. The door doesn't budge.

I call out. "Jeff?"

Silence.

I walk around the garage, trying the big bay doors, which are firmly shut, looking for gaps in the blackout that covers all the glass. The old entrance, a metal-framed glass door, is missing its bottom panel, the gap covered in cardboard. I work the corner free with my foot, but there's something blocking the other side. It feels like a heavy cart or shelf, maybe some kind of workbench. There's no space to crawl through, even if I relished the thought of forcing my way in on hands and knees, ruining my clothes on the greasy concrete.

The workers at the Burger King are stealing glances my way. It doesn't matter. They are not going to call the cops to report a suspicious prowler on a seemingly abandoned property. They're just curious, that's all.

I try Jeff's number again, listening at the gap in the cardboard in case the phone rings inside the garage. There's no sound in there and no answer on the line. I make up my mind to get inside, so I start scouring every car on the lot, peering into threadbare backseats and holed-out trunks for a stray crowbar or a length of pipe.

Then it happens.

The crowd at Burger King starts going "*Oh*" and "*Ah*," like guys in front of a football game when the quarterback is sacked, and then I hear the metallic rattling of chains and the big gate heaving on its dry hinges. I step out from behind the trunk of a catercorner land yacht just in time to intercept Jeff with his arm cocked high in the air, some kind of vicious-looking club in his hand.

I raise my arm to block, clenching my teeth for impact.

"March," he says, lowering the club. He takes a step backward.

"Where did you come from?" I ask. "Why aren't you answering my calls?"

He glances at the club in his hand, a short, studded hardwood rod that swells toward the tip, the handle wrapped in tape, and smiles with embarrassment. "I've had some trouble with people trespassing, mostly vagrants, so I made them a little something to remember me by. If I'd have realized it was you . . ."

"You haven't answered my question."

Through the open gate I see an old Camaro on the curb behind my car, its door hanging open, the finish dull enough that it could have been stored in a barn for the past decade. Parked on this lot, it would pretty much blend in, only it runs.

"Listen, let's go inside," he says. "People are watching."

"Give me that," I say, reaching for the club.

He surrenders it. "Can we go in now?"

I walk back to the garage while he retrieves his car and drives it inside the gate. We head around back, side by side and silent. He works some keys out of his jeans pocket and undoes the dead bolts. Inside, the air is stifling. He turns on the fan, then goes to a window unit air-conditioner I hadn't noticed the first time. It shudders to life with a dull hum.

"I've been reading that book you gave me," I tell him. "You made some interesting notes in there, and underlined some things."

"That's a great little book. I highly recommend it. Living down here in the Bible Belt, it doesn't hurt to inoculate yourself against all the stupidity."

"What I was particularly interested in was the word you kept spelling."

Digging through the books on his folding table, he seizes on a floppy softback with a lurid cover. "That's what I'm talking about. You ever read this one?" He fires the book across at me, forcing me to catch it against my chest. "Dante's *Inferno*. It's all in there, all the hysteria. What he does is, he writes a poem about hell, and guess what? Everybody who crossed him in life happens to be down there in torment. I mean, yeah right. That's why they invented hell, so they could send their enemies down there."

"Don't tell me you're interested in poetry."

The book is heavy in my hands. A memory surfaces. The same copy of Dante—the very same one—thumping down on a picnic table at Ft. Polk more than twenty years ago.

"Mr. Nesbitt, he gave me that book. He wanted me to read it."

The pages are brown with age. I turn them slowly. "We both know the significance of Inferno, right? Let's not make this harder than it has to be. You know more about Nesbitt's operation than you led me to believe." I put the book down. "Tell me what you know, Jeff."

"If I didn't give you everything," he says, "maybe it was for a reason. Maybe I wanted to see if you were going to keep me in the loop or not. After all, I've been working on this longer than you have, and there's more at stake for me."

"Like what?"

"Like everything, man. They're *after* me. Why do you think I holed up here? What do you think I've been doing ever since they killed Mr. Nesbitt? Twiddling my thumbs? Hardly. I've been getting on top of this thing, figuring out who they are and how they operate."

"So tell me who they are. Tell me how they operate."

"I could," he says, wagging his finger. "Oh, believe me, I could. Only there's nothing you could do about it, March. I realized that right off, even before I decided to bail you out that night. You can't help me. You're too tied up in the rules. You've got no room to maneuver."

"Try me."

His smile is halfway to a sneer. "What were you doing anyway, trying to break in here? If you wanted to rile me up, congratulations. I'm riled. I did you a favor—more than a favor—and this is what I get in return?"

"I've been trying to reach you ever since I saw the underlining in your *Foxhole Atheist* book. You gave me the book for a reason. You wanted me to make the connection."

"Did I? You took your time."

"I've been busy since last time. I caught up with Hilda, for one thing, and now I have names on all the guys who came after me that night. It was one of them who killed my partner. I'm pretty sure it was one of them we found in the park, which is what started this whole thing."

"What started it for *you*," he says.

"And I found out about Nesbitt's intelligence operation down in Matamoros, and the code name of his insider there. Inferno. But you already knew about that, Jeff."

Something I've said flips a switch in Jeff's head. He freezes a second, then turns, his eyes burning. He starts coming toward me, raising a finger in the air. Not threatening, but argumentative, like he's determined to set me straight. "You wanna know what I know? You want me to tell you what I know? You think I'm the one who's holding out—?"

As he rushed forward, my pocket starts to buzz. The ringer grows louder and louder as we stand there looking at each other, waiting. His mouth twitches. He blinks. A smile cracks across his lips.

"Are you gonna get that or not?"

I smile, too. The absurdity of the situation. I take out my phone and step away. The number on the screen is unfamiliar and I don't recognize the voice at first.

"You're gonna want to hear this," the voice says in my ear, "but first I need assurances. Just because I came by the information doesn't mean I'm in any way involved—"

"Who is this?" I ask.

"What?" He sounds disappointed. "It's Sam Dearborn. From Dearborn Gun and Blade. You said if I found out anything, you'd be in my debt."

"Right. Mr. Dearborn." I motion Jeff to sit tight for a minute. "What did you find out?"

"Like I said, I want assurances."

"Absolutely. Now what do you have for me?"

"Well," he says. "You're not going to believe this. I just got off the phone with a certain friend of mine, and what he told me I think you're gonna be interested in. You were asking me all those questions about Brandon Ford, on account of him being dead."

"I remember."

Jeff walks back to the window unit, sucking up the cool air. I turn away from the corner of the garage he's converted to living space, picking my way into the garage's dead zone, the empty lift hole and the grime-covered, long-abandoned equipment.

"Only this friend of mine," Dearborn is saying, "it turns out he'd been contacted by Ford a while back about getting some assault rifles. He wanted ten M4 carbines and . . . well, he didn't want them tracing back to him. This friend of mine, he's apparently not as ethical as me. Point is, he has the guns in his shop, but never heard back from Ford for the obvious reason that he was dead."

"So where are these guns exactly?"

Out of the corner of my eye, I see Jeff stand upright. Alert. He starts coming toward me.

"He moved them to a storage lockup he has, but that's not important. The important thing is that just a minute ago he gets a call wanting to arrange to collect them. And it was Brandon Ford on the phone."

"It was Ford?"

Jeff's eyes go wide.

"Who's supposedly dead," Dearborn says.

"And when is this collection supposed to happen?" I ask, my pulse racing.

"That's what I'm trying to tell you. It's happening right now."

Five minutes later I'm pushing my way out the door, heading around the garage toward my waiting car. Behind me, Jeff does up one of the dead bolts and runs to catch up. Later, I've already told him. We'll continue this later.

"What's going on?" he asks. "Where are you going? You've found out where Ford is, haven't you?"

"I'll call you," I tell him. "Answer next time."

"I'm coming with you."

"You're not coming with me."

"I am," he says. "Try to stop me. Besides, you're flying solo now. Who else are you gonna call for backup? You know I can handle myself, March. Come on."

He's standing at my passenger door, his hand on the latch.

"Fine. Get in," I say. Knowing I'm going to regret it.

CHAPTER 24

With Jeff riding shotgun, I take the Gulf Freeway into downtown, snaking back and forth through midday traffic, availing myself of the shoulder when necessary. Jeff wants to slam a flashing light onto the roof, *Starsky and Hutch*-style, but I've been driving my own car since my unofficial suspension began. Traffic stacks up at the Southwest Freeway exit, reducing our progress to a crawl. Once we're through it, the pace picks up and I steer to the far left lane, hurtling by at ninety miles per hour. We slow down again at the Loop, then pour on the speed through Sharpstown, past Houston Baptist, hooking a left on the Sam Houston Tollway en route to Missouri City.

Exiting the tollway, we pull into a gas station along the feeder, where Dearborn waits in the front seat of a glossy black Chrysler with a stacked Bentley-clone grill. He locks up and jumps in the back, reaching over the seat to shake hands.

"It's just up the road," he says. "I just got off the phone with him, and he says he's still waiting for Ford to show up."

"So we beat him?"

"I think Ford might have a number of stops to make."

The assurances Dearborn wanted weren't mine to give. I gave them anyway in the interest of time. His "friend" was only willing to cooperate if I would agree that he wouldn't be prosecuted.

"The past couple of weeks," Dearborn says, "this friend of mine has been filling the order, picking up one piece here, one piece there, buying from private sellers when he can find them and from dealers if he can arrange a straw purchase. This is not my kind of business—you know that. He came to me because he knew I'd been asking around about Ford, after our first conversation. From what he says, it sounds like Ford had several people freelancing for him, putting together a nice little cache of weapons."

"They're all M4s?" I ask. Military carbines, basically updated M-16s.

"Far as I know. And Ford was offering good money to make it worth everybody's time."

On the drive down I explained to Jeff what I expected of him: basically silence. You're just along for the ride, I told him, and he agreed. Now he sits there quietly, lips pursed and arms crossed as if to hold himself back from talking.

"So what makes you think Ford has other pickups to make?"

Dearborn leans forward between the seats, blocking the rearview mirror. "Because when he found out the guns weren't in the shop anymore, that they were sitting down here in a lockup, he wasn't too happy. Said he was on a tight schedule and didn't have time to mess around."

Jeff can't keep quiet anymore. "Which means when he gets here, he'll have an arsenal with him, probably some other guys. And you're gonna take him all by yourself?"

"You're offering your services?"

"I'm not even packing. But yeah, I'll pitch in."

"You don't sound as gung ho as you did back at the garage."

"I've had time to think."

Dearborn jabs a finger at Jeff, catching my eye in the mirror. "So this guy's not a cop? I guess you have, like, a SWAT team or something lined up?"

"Let me worry about that."

Neither one of them seems satisfied with that, Dearborn because he doesn't know what he's gotten himself into, and Jeff because, with his military background, he realizes there's a level of planning required to go up against armed men successfully, not to mention overwhelming force. Trouble is, I'm in no position to call on what resources I have, and even if I were, there may not be time. My plan at the moment is to see what develops and go forward from there, something I don't intend to share with Jeff or Dearborn, neither of whom would want to hear it anyway. Instead, I resolve to project an attitude of calm—in other words, to bluff my way through.

We pull up across the street from a gated plot of corrugated, subdivided longhouses, with red-painted garage doors granting access to each stall. If Dearborn's friend had an outer stall, everything would happen out in the open, but instead it's on the inside. We can watch them drive up and go inside, but whatever happens after that will be invisible.

"How are we gonna play this?" Jeff asks.

I sit and think for a moment. All that matters is that I take Ford into custody. I'm not trying to build a case against him for gunrunning. So the important question is whether he'll be more vulnerable and off guard inside the facility or out in the parking lot loading his cargo. The answer seems obvious. Once he's outside, his radar will be switched on. The only way to get the jump on him is to get inside.

"Okay, here's what we're going to do," I say, turning in my seat. "Dearborn, I want you to take me in there and introduce me to your friend. Then you can make yourself scarce while I get into the lockup. That's where I'll wait for him."

Jeff is already shaking his head. "And what about me?"

There are lines you cross without realizing, and others you step over deliberately. I pause, knowing I'm on the verge of stepping over and not feeling good about it.

"You . . ." I say. "How about overwatch?"

I get out of the car and lead him around to the trunk, conscious of Dearborn watching from the backseat. I pop the lid, obstructing the gun dealer's vision, then open up the padded case mounted into the trunk that holds my AR-15 carbine.

"You know how to use one of these, obviously."

He nods.

"And you know when not to? I mean, you're not going to do anything crazy. If this thing goes pear-shaped, then you do something about it. But not until."

"I hear you."

"Am I making a terrible mistake here?" I ask.

He looks me in the eye. "No, you're not."

"I can trust you?"

"If you have to ask, it's too late."

"All right, then. They'll have to pull up at the entrance there to load up, so take the keys and maneuver around for a clear field of fire. Ford will go inside himself, and he'll have at least one man staying with the vehicle to keep an eye on the guns they've already picked up. That's who you need to watch. If Ford comes out and I don't, then I've scrubbed it. Don't do anything."

"Check," he says.

"If the opportunity presents itself, I'll take him. Otherwise, we'll let him walk and try to keep an eye on him."

"I understand," he says. "Now get in there before he shows up."

―――――――

At the far end of the corridor, a gaunt man in Wranglers and a tightly tucked shirt stands with his back turned, one hand pressed against his ear.

"That's him," Dearborn says in a stage whisper.

As we approach, the man turns. "Uh-huh," he's saying in a cellphone, "that's fine. Like I said, I'm already here waiting. So long as you brought the money, there ain't no problem." He gives us both a nervous once-over, putting a finger over his lips for silence. "Well, I wish you'd hurry up, then. I'm ready to get this done with as much as you are. Fine, I will."

He ends the call and curses under his breath.

"This is the detective I was telling you about," Dearborn says, "and we've already discussed the conditions. You don't need to worry about any legal entanglements."

The man in Wranglers puts his phone away, wipes his hand on his jeans, and offers it to me to shake. "That's good to hear, because I tell you, this is not what I signed up for. If I'd ha' known the kind of business Ford was up to, I woulda told him to take a hike."

As implausible as this sounds, I'm not surprised he feels the need to justify himself. Even with assurances against prosecution, you can never be too careful.

"So he's on the way?" I ask.

"That's what he tells me. I done been here a whole hour."

"And this is your lockup?" I point to the sliding door next to us, with its padlock hanging loose on the hinge.

"This one," he says, hiking the door up, "and I got another one across the hall there. Inside I got a couple of safes, too. This is more secure than it might look to you."

To prove the point, he flips the lights on and walks us down a row of black gun safes, lined up like so many filing cabinets. At the back of the unit he's stored a couple of motorcycles lengthwise, one of them under a tarp and the other bare.

"What's in there?" I ask, indicating a waist-high old-fashioned icebox against the opposite wall. It looks like a white metal casket, to be honest, the lid secured in the middle with another padlock.

"That's where they are. They're in padded cases, packed up real nice, so I couldn't put them all in the safe."

"Let's take a look."

Wrangler makes a show of checking his watch, only opening up the lid when he realizes I won't be deterred. Inside, packed five across and two deep, there are ten matching black Cordura cases, the kind that zip around and have pouches on the front for spare magazines. I slide one out and open it up to find a pristine M4 carbine with a collapsable stock and a gaping mag well.

"You have magazines for them?"

"Just the rifles," he says.

"What about ammunition?"

He shakes his head. "I have some .223 in one of the safes, but he didn't ask for nothing but the rifles. Mags and ammo you can pick up anywhere."

I let him lock the lid down while I take a look around the unit. There's nowhere inside to conceal myself. If I hide behind the door, then I have no choice but to act when it opens, no matter how many men are on the other side, or what they're armed with. Dearborn sees me making mental calculations, his forehead glistening with sweat.

"You said one of the other units is yours, too?" I ask.

"That one there." Wrangler points to the unit directly opposite.

"If I wait in there, you'll have to leave the lock off, and Ford might notice. Not to mention, I won't be able to see what's going on until I throw open the door."

"I could leave it open and tell 'em I've got some other things to load myself."

I shake my head. "They'll search it."

Dearborn goes into the corridor. "What about me?"

For a moment I'm not sure what to do. So I follow him into the hall, glancing left and right. The side we came from leads straight to the entrance, a pair of glass doors that open wide to accommodate loading. The other end of the corridor stops in a T, with smaller entrances on either side of the short hallway, and two doors in the back wall. Stepping closer, I see that one is a men's restroom and the other is for women.

"That'll work," I say. "Take the women's side in case somebody needs to go."

Dearborn heads to the ladies', his heels clicking on the glossy concrete floor. I turn to his friend. "I'll be in there. If anything happens, you just hit the deck."

"If anything happens?" His voice cracks. "Something *is* gonna happen—"

"Just stay calm and keep out of the way."

He looks at me like I'm crazy. At the far end of the corridor, through the glass doors, I see something flash by. A white van pulling up.

"Gotta go."

I run to the T-intersection, pushing through the door to the women's restroom. It's a nicer facility than I would have expected at one of these places, a sink and a couple of stalls and the scent of ammonia on the stifling hot air. There's a plastic wedge on the linoleum floor, the kind the cleaners use to prop open the door. I bend down for it, thinking I might wedge the door open slightly, but first I switch off the lights. In the dark I see a beam of light shining under the door. Kneeling, I find about an inch of clearance between the bottom of the door and the ground.

"Are you okay back there?" I ask.

From inside the farthest stall, Dearborn coughs. "Tell me when it's safe to come out."

I push my jacket back, hitching the fabric behind the holster, then ease my Browning free. Dropping the safety, I press the slide far enough back to touch the chambered round through the ejection port. Then I put the safety back on and drop to my knees, pressing my cheek against the floor, trying not to think about the sanitary implications.

Down the length of the corridor I see two shadows. As they approach, I can hear their footsteps faintly, and the farther they get from the backlighting of the entrance, the more I can make out.

"What's going on out there?" Dearborn whispers.

"Quiet."

I was crouched like this behind the tree the night they ran me off the road, biding time until they spotted me. Now the advantage is on my side. They're just a few steps away from the point where my floor-level view will cut them off at the head. That's when I get my glimpse: Brandon Ford, his face framed by longish black curls, both hands in the pockets of a light windbreaker—worn for concealment in this heat, just like my jacket. The man next to him is one of the paramilitaries from the files, though I can't put a name to him. His left side is dragged down by the weight of a green canvas shopping bag, presumably containing the money.

Then their faces disappear above the horizon, followed by their chests and waists, until all I can see is two pairs of legs cut off above the knee and the bottom of the drooping bag. Wrangler steps out of the storage unit to meet them.

"I been waiting more than an hour," he says.

"Keep your shirt on, brother." Ford's voice. "I said we were coming. Now, let's take a look at what you got."

"Is that for me?"

"All in good time. All in good time."

The three men move into the unit, leaving me with a view of the empty corridor. I push my ear against the gap, straining to hear, but all I get is the hum of voices. I can't make out the words. Seconds pass, but they feel like hours. All the precautions I'd imagined them taking—searching the rest of the corridor, checking the restrooms, making sure the locks on the other doors are secure—none of it seems to matter to Ford. This could all be over quick, the money exchanged, Ford and his companion exiting with the guns. Could two men carry them all? If they enlist Wrangler, the three of them could manage.

I can't do anything from behind this door. Getting my feet under me, I rise to a crouch, drawing the door open about a foot, peering out into the corridor. They're still inside, still talking, and all I can see are shadows cast across the corridor from the lights inside the unit.

I take a deep breath and pass through the door, pausing to cushion the impact as it pulls shut. On tiptoes I cross diagonally to the edge of the T, pressing myself against the wall, getting as close to the edge as I dare, feeling terribly exposed. There are glass doors at either end of the short hallway. Anyone approaching could look right in and see me.

"They're all here," a voice says. I don't recognize it, so it must be Ford's companion. "Ten carbines. Just what the doctor ordered."

"And here's ten grand, like we said. It's all in small bills, tens and fives and ones, like you took it in at a register. Nobody's gonna look twice."

"You expect me to count all that?"

"Do what you want. But we'll need a hand first getting them out to the van."

A long pause follows. I imagine them eyeballing each other while Wrangler makes up his mind whether to count the money first or take Ford's word. If he didn't know I was out here, I'm guessing he'd insist on the count. Hopefully he'll do that anyway, so they don't get suspicious. I steal a glance around the corner, but the corridor is still empty.

"All right," he says.

I hear a dull thud, then a metallic ring followed by the sound of a padlock being threaded through a hasp and snapped shut. He must have taken the money and dropped it into the icebox where the guns had been stored, locking it up for safekeeping. I hear the Cordura cases rubbing against each other.

"I can take one more," says Ford's companion. "Lay it on me."

More shuffling, and then footsteps.

"Come on," Ford says. "You go up front so I can see you."

Three sets of heels click on the concrete. I glance around, and there they are, backs to me, silhouetted against the sunlight pouring in through the entrance. Time to move. I advance on tiptoes as far as the open storage unit, ducking inside for cover. I use the edge of the doorway to brace my arm, lining up my sights on Ford's silhouette.

I'm about to call out when I feel the vibration in my pocket. Ignore it. The phone buzzes more insistently, and if I don't stop it the ringer will sound. I reach into my pocket and mute the sound, raising the glass face high enough to check the screen—force of habit.

The call was from Jeff.

Down the corridor, Ford is halfway to the exit. Far enough now that he might think he can draw down on me, or make a run. The phone buzzes again. A text message this time. My hand is shaking as I look at the screen.

ABORT.

No, no, no, no, no. I put the phone away, drop the safety on the Browning, and edge into the corridor. There's still time. If I advance quickly to close the distance, I'll risk exposing myself and they'll have the light at their backs, making it harder for me to see their hands. But it's just two against one and I have the advantage of surprise.

I step out, gun leveled, licking my dry lips so I can shout a challenge.

The phone buzzes again, insistent. The word flashes in my head. He wants me to abort. I can't see what he's seeing, can't judge whether his call makes sense or not. Heart pounding, I start to backpedal, tucking myself behind the cover of the open unit. What else can I do?

One more look. They're at the entrance, pushing their way out into the light. Wrangler goes first, and he's scowling through the glass, probably wondering what happened to the cavalry. Ford motions him forward and the three men disappear from view, heading in what I presume is the direction of the white van.

The ringer chirps audibly and I answer.

"It's a scrub," Jeff says. "There's at least one in the van and then a separate car. I can't tell how many men they have total, but they're switched on and ready for a fight."

"What's happening now?" I ask.

"They're loading the van. The curly-haired guy is over at the car, saying something to the driver. He's going around to the other side."

"What about the good guy—cowboy-looking—?"

"Going back inside."

I peer around the corner. Wrangler comes through the glass doors, takes a few steps, then starts running in my direction.

"They're rolling out."

I take off running, too, heading to the entrance. We pass each other in the corridor and I tell him to collect Dearborn and get out of here.

"Are we square?" he calls. "What about the money?"

"I'll be in touch!"

When I reach the glass doors, I pause for a look before pushing through. The white van brakes at the edge of the parking lot, waiting for traffic to clear, then accelerates onto the street, the back end sagging. It disappears behind a stand of pines overlooking the road.

I walk outside, squinting at the glare. I rub my hand against the holster for reference, then slide the Browning in. Jeff cruises up with one hand draped over the wheel.

"Get in," he says.

I slump into the passenger seat and pull the door shut. He punches the gas, pinning my shoulder blades against the upholstery.

"Don't lose that van."

"Don't worry," he says.

We turn onto the street in time to see the lights change at the next intersection, freeing the van to proceed on its way. I rattle off a host of instructions: don't get too close, don't change lanes if you can help it, don't do anything to attract the van's attention. In reply, all Jeff does is nod. He keeps nodding until I'm done talking, then nods some more, like he wants to make it clear he knows what he's doing.

"They're heading back to the tollway, looks like."

"Just keep them in sight," I say.

I cradle my phone in the palm of my hand, looking down at the screen. Thinking. I can have them pulled over, no problem. I can call dispatch and have patrol intercept them. I can also get a tactical team in motion if I call Lt. Bascombe and fill him in. He won't be happy about it, but what's more important? Keeping people happy or picking up Brandon Ford? With him in custody, the John Doe investigation blows wide open. I can hand him over and let Bascombe and Cavallo take things from there. Or I can dial Bea's number and let the FBI take it from here.

It's not up to me to see this through. Not personally.

"Are you gonna blow the trumpet?" Jeff asks. "Summon up the cavalry?"

"I'm just working out what to say."

The van swings U-turns under the tollway and takes a northbound entrance, heading back toward I-59. As Jeff speeds up the ramp, he strains over the wheel, trying to see farther up.

"March," he says.

"What?"

"I don't see the car anymore."

"Just follow the van."

"Yeah, but Ford got into the car and now I don't see it. I thought they were ahead of the van, but they're not. It's a silver four-door, a big Toyota, with tinted windows and dealer plates. Do you see it? I think we lost them."

I crane my neck around, scanning the traffic behind us. I press myself against the window trying to see ahead of the van. No silver four-doors.

"What do we do?" he asks.

"Just follow the van."

Maybe Ford went ahead. Maybe he's planning to meet up with the van farther down the road. If we keep the van in sight, we have to catch up with him sooner or later. There's no other option.

"They're getting onto 59," he says. "Going south away from town."

"Keep following." I lean over and check the fuel gauge. We have three quarters of a tank. "They'll lead us to Ford, maybe take us to wherever they're all staying. Just don't let the van get away from us."

The white van curves off the tollway, circling onto the Southwest Freeway, and thirty seconds later we do the same thing. Once the turn is made, Jeff finds a southbound truck to settle behind, letting a comfortable distance build between us and the van.

"I'm sorry about back there," he says. "Maybe I just lost my nerve, but I could see it all going wrong right in front of me. They would've fought, and it would've gotten messy."

"It's fine. I'm sure you made the right call."

But I don't feel sure. My fist closes around the rim of my phone, mashing down hard. I had Ford in my grasp and I let him walk away. There in the storage facility corridor I had the power to end it all. Perhaps Jeff is right that I couldn't have gotten away with it, would never have gotten Ford in cuffs and taken him into custody. He was in my sights, though. I could have stopped him one way or another. Even if it all went wrong, even if things did get messy, I would have stopped him. And now I can't, and maybe I'll never have the power again.

This phone is rigid in my grip. As my knuckles whiten, my palm starts to throb. There is no one to call. Not yet. Maybe never. I was wrong before; I *do* have to see this through. That's what my gut tells me, my heart, my pain. This is my responsibility. Mine. And it has been since the last breath of Jerry Lorenz.

CHAPTER 25

The white van pulls into a truck stop on the edge of Victoria, a couple of hours outside Houston, where the driver pumps gas. The passenger trots straight inside like he's overdue for a bathroom break. I motion Jeff toward the opposite pump island.

"Let's switch seats," I say.

I top off the tank, using my credit card so there's no need to go inside. Jeff circles around the back of the car, stepping over the hose to pass behind me.

"Looks like there's just the two of them. Want me to run inside and take a look?"

"No need," I say. "Just sit down and don't call attention to yourself."

He slides into the passenger seat and shuts the door.

"We need some way to slow them down," I say. "If I could distract the guy at the pump, you think you could get over there and stick a knife in the tire? They'd have to change it, which would give me time to make a phone call and get some real surveillance up."

"You're asking me to slash his tire while he's pumping the gas?"

I let out a sigh. "There's gotta be some way to slow them down. We could have somebody waiting for them on the other end if I had an idea where the other end might be, but—"

"I hear you," he says. "But if you're making that call, it had better be a good one. You only get one shot, you know."

"What do you mean?"

He turns in his seat. "The moment you make the call, all this is out of your hands. The moment you make the call, *they* take over—whoever they are. It ends the way they want it to, not your way."

Between the pumps I watch the driver out of the corner of my eye. As he finishes pumping and screws the cap into place, the passenger returns with a couple of water bottles and a road atlas tucked under his arm. They spend thirty seconds or so consulting the map, then climb back into the van. Apparently the route is new to them.

When I get back in the car, the driver's seat is warm and too far forward. I scoot it back, realigning the mirrors, giving the van time to get under way. They pull back onto the feeder and continue south, driving just under the speed limit, taking 91 at the split and heading straight onto Highway 77, next stop Corpus Christi. Once the switchover is complete, the van speeds up to about five miles over the limit. They're driving fast enough to keep up with traffic without running the risk of being pulled over.

Jeff has a point. If I call Cavallo or even Bascombe, it'll get kicked up to Wanda's desk and I'll be cooling my heels indefinitely. Besides, we're already outside HPD's grip, which would mean bringing other agencies into the picture. There's always Bea with her Federal reach. But that underling of hers who put the flea in my ear might have known what he was talking about. I've taken a lot on trust from her. When I've had the power to check on what she's told me, it hasn't always added up.

My speedometer holds steady and the whine of the engine subsides as the gears shift. Apart from the thump of the tires on rough highway, we drive in silence. The sun sits far enough to the left that no matter how I reposition the visor, I can't block it out. I rest my elbow on the door, using my hand as a screen. This isn't silence, not when I really listen. There's also the wind hurtling around us, an invisible envelope of white noise. And the percussive pop of fresh insects against the windshield, already scabbed from the drive out, leaving behind viscous smears.

I hold the wand down, sluicing the windshield with washer fluid, then let the wipers swish back and forth.

"If I'd had more time back there," Jeff says, "I would have scraped some of that stuff off."

"What's a road trip without a few dead mosquitoes?"

He smiles. "So how far are we gonna follow them?"

Neither of us has asked the question out loud to this point, though it's been on the air since we left the city. There are many stops between here and the border—why assume they're heading straight to Mexico?

"We'll follow them until we know where they're going."

"I have a pretty good idea already," he says. "It's not South Padre. This is the delivery run. Which means they're not stopping until they hand off those guns. Are you prepared to cross the border, or are we gonna call it quits when they hit Brownsville? You've got one call to me. Is that where you'll do it?"

I don't answer because I don't know. The possibilities have been churning at the back of my mind. Along with my driver's license and police ID, in the recesses of my wallet there's a passport card, good for travel to Canada and Mexico, which I applied for at Charlotte's behest when she was temporarily obsessed with the notion of a cruise to Cozumel, a plan she dropped, much to my relief. Since I've never taken it out of my wallet, I have the option of crossing the border without any hassles. Back when I was in college and the six-hour drive to the border was a regular weekend jaunt, you could pass back and forth without anything but a Texas driver's license, and sometimes without even that. Those days are gone.

"You don't happen to have a passport on you?" I ask.

Jeff laughs. Of course not.

"What?" he says. "You do?"

I ignore him. The passport card isn't a solution. With the Browning on my hip and the AR-15 in the trunk, I can no more cross the bridge over the Rio Grande than the men in the white van. It's not a matter of simply flashing my badge. I'm out of my jurisdiction, and in Mexico even the U.S. cops who are supposed to be there must go unarmed thanks to the tight gun regulations.

"If it comes to it," Jeff says, "there are ways."

"Maybe it won't. Maybe they'll meet up with Ford somewhere along the way."

"That could happen," he says, shaking his head.

———

The landscape changes as the hours pass. We've left behind the pines for the desert-like plains, their flat monotony broken up here and there by a lonely mesquite. In Sarita, south of Kingsville, a line of northbound vehicles idle at the ICE checkpoint, waiting for the agents to confirm their citizenship and give their backseats a once-over. And this is about an hour outside Harlingen, ninety minutes from the Rio Grande, well inside Texas. The fact that the Border Patrol is operating this far north is a testament to the scale of the immigration problem. Not long ago, the agents stopped a minivan driving back to Houston and found illegals hunched between the rear seats, hiding under blankets. That arrest made the news.

The white van sticks to its southward heading. Instead of mesquites, the highway is lined by dried-out palm trees. The Gulf of Mexico is less than thirty miles from here, close enough that when I roll the window down, I imagine I can smell salt on the balmy, humid breeze.

When Hilda walked me through Brandon Ford's procedure for making contact with Inferno, she said he usually took a flight from Hobby Airport down to Brownsville, then took a taxi downtown, crossing the border on foot. After collecting whatever Inferno had for him, he'd stay overnight at the Colonial on E. Levee Street, and then fly home in the morning. If the van doesn't lead us to him, there's always a chance he will be at the hotel. When I explain this to Jeff, he repeats what he said before: "That could happen."

"This may sound crazy to you, but we might just get lucky. For days I've been feeling like there's nothing to hold on to, and now that I have something, I'm not letting go. The big breaks are always like this. Half the time you don't know what you're doing, but it feels right, so you go with it."

"So it's not about evidence and hard work," he says. "It's about luck."

"Napoleon thought so, too."

"Napoleon?" He snorts the name, like I've just made the most unlikely connection he can imagine. "You mean *him*?" He presses his hand flat against his chest, tucking his fingers inside his shirt.

"That's the one. You should study history sometime, Jeff, or you'll be forced to repeat it."

He rolls his eyes.

"Anyway, that's what Napoleon would ask about a general. Not if he was experienced or tough or a genius. He'd ask, 'Is he lucky?' And right now, I think I am. The tip from Dearborn, that van right there. The initiative is finally on my side for a change."

"Napoleon," he says, shaking his head. "'God is on the side not of the big battalions, but the best shots.' Wasn't that Napoleon, too?"

"That was somebody else," I tell him. "But I can see why you'd like to agree with that one, being such a good shot."

"Yeah," he says. "Except there's no God."

"I should introduce you to my friend Carter. He'd argue with you on that point."

"And he'd lose."

"He would argue with us both about luck, too. He'd say everything happens for a reason, all part of the divine plan." I glance over to see him react with an amused smile. "You don't happen to be a conspiracy theorist, do you? Is the government hiding the existence of aliens from us, or denying the truth about the Twin Towers? If so, you'd be playing right into Carter's hands. He has a theory about you foxhole atheists."

He answers with a snort of derision.

"When you stop believing God controls everything, Carter says, then you start making up all-powerful conspiracies to take the Almighty's place."

"This Carter sounds like a moron. Plus, some conspiracies are real."

"That's what I told him."

"And anyway," he says, his voice charged, "I happen to be a determinist. I think things happen for a reason, too, but not because Zeus or Allah or God or whoever says so. My determinism isn't top down; it works from the bottom up. We're products of our environment, March, pure and simple. Genetically determined, socially determined, whatever you like. To people like me, the God hypothesis *is* a conspiracy theory—the ultimate conspiracy."

"Still, there's something to it—"

"There's nothing to it, March. There's no heaven or hell, no angels floating on the clouds, no good, no evil, none of it. We're just animals who like to tell ourselves stories in the dark. Animals making up rules for each other to follow. And when you die, that's it. End of the line."

"You don't think there's something out there—?"

"There's nothing. Absolutely nothing. Read the book, March. You told me you did."

"I've been a little busy recently."

We sit in silence awhile. I can tell Jeff's angry, the emotion coming out of nowhere like a flash fire. All I'd intended was to rib him a little, to pass the time as we drove, but the turn in the conversation has gotten him riled up.

"You're a bit of a fundie, you know that?"

"Yeah, yeah," he says.

"Anyway. We're coming up on Brownsville. I guess this isn't looking too good. They're gonna have to stop somewhere, though. They can't just drive those guns into Mexico. The odds of the van being searched are too much to risk."

"Not if they already have a plan. Someone could wave them right through."

I laugh. "Now you *do* sound like a conspiracy theorist."

"Do I?" He doesn't even smile. "Or maybe I've happened to see some things in life that you haven't. On our side, I doubt they're searching vehicles that are leaving the country, and I'm guessing the cartels pretty much own the Mexican side."

"You're probably right," I say, trying to sound conciliatory. There's no point in stoking the tension between us. I need him focused on the situation at hand.

He points up ahead. "The van's turning off."

"Here we go."

We're just inside Brownsville, flanked by a row of chain hotels on one side and a suburban strip mall on the other. The van turns off the frontage road into a big shopping-center parking lot, cruising down the rows until it slides into an empty space. I drive past them, keeping an eye on the rearview mirror, circling the row and doubling back on the other side. The van doors open. The driver climbs out, leaving his door ajar, while the passenger makes a beeline toward the Best Buy electronics store.

"I'll follow him," Jeff says. "Any of these guys sees you, they might recognize your face. You keep an eye on the van."

I head up the row and drop him on the front curb just as the passenger walks up. Jeff pauses, then follows him inside. Then I double back and find a space halfway between the store entrance and the van.

The van's driver leans against the fender, propping his foot up. He cups his hands in front of his mouth, and then there's a flame. He drops his hands and exhales a cloud of smoke. In the twilight I can see the cigarette's cherry, if I'm not imagining it. The man seems relaxed, not bothered about the time or concerned that he has a payload of illegally obtained assault rifles in the back of his van.

I take my phone out and rest it on my lap. This isn't the end of the line for these guys, and there's a limit to what I can expect of myself. If I lose sight of them just once, if those guns disappear and end up in the hands of the cartel . . .

I dial Charlotte's number. It rings and then her voicemail picks up.

"You're not going to believe where I am." I pause, not certain what to say. "I told you I couldn't let go of this thing, right? I guess I wasn't kidding. I'm going to be out of pocket for a while. Something's come up—a lead—and I've got to follow it."

I look up and see the passenger emerging through the sliding doors, walking out past a yellow concrete stanchion.

"I'll call you later, Charlotte. I love you."

Stopping in front of a garbage basket, the man digs through the plastic shopping bag in his hand, removing the contents. He tosses the bag, then rips the package open and throws that in after it. He slips whatever he's purchased into his pocket, then starts toward the van. Jeff walks out with a bag of his own.

When he reaches the car, I ask: "What did he buy in there?"

"A GPS unit. Wherever they're stopping for the night, it's not here. Pop the trunk for me."

"What for?"

"Hurry, before they take off."

I push the trunk release, then go around back to see what he's doing, glancing at the van to make sure it's not moving. He takes the AR-15 out of its case, resting the rifle at the bottom of the trunk, then dumps the contents of his own bag out. A pack of plastic zip-ties drops out. He rips it open and stuffs a handful in his pocket. Then he takes the rifle and crawls underneath the car.

"What are you doing? Anyone could see you!"

"Are they leaving?" His voice sounds muffled. His legs protrude from under the bumper.

"The engine's running. The headlights are on. It looks like they're talking."

"Hand me your pistol."

Down on one knee, I peer under the car. He's slotted the rifle into a gap in the undercarriage, securing it in place with the plastic ties. As I watch, he gives it a tug to make sure everything's tight. Then he reaches his hand out.

"What are you doing?"

"We don't have time to discuss this. They're gonna pull out any second."

"What about the spare magazines?"

"Find something to put them in, and I'll stick them under here, too."

After scanning side to side and making sure no one's watching, I slip the Browning out of its holster and quickly drop the safety to lower the hammer. I place the pistol in his hand and it disappears immediately.

In the trunk I pull a nylon bag from my crime-scene kit, dump the contents, and jam the three spare mags for the AR-15 inside. There's enough room left, so I add the spare hi-cap for the Browning from my belt rig, along with the holster and mag carrier, then zip the bag closed and pass it under to Jeff.

"Hurry, they're leaving!"

The van pulls back, stops, then accelerates down the row. I can see the red running lights over the tops of the parked cars.

"Come on, come on."

Jeff slides out, brushes his hands on his jeans, and gives the trunk a quick search. "Is there anything else in here we need to dump?"

"It's gonna look strange, me having an empty gun case bolted into the trunk."

"Right." He reaches into the case and starts ripping out the molded gray foam. I lean in and try to help. We toss the foam onto the pavement, then slam down the lid of the now-empty case. "That's the best we can do. It's good enough."

In the car, racing to keep the van in sight, he outlines his plan. "If they do try to cross, I'll get out and you can follow them alone. The odds of your car being searched are pretty slim. They'll look inside, but they're not gonna tear it apart. Don't flash your badge or anything. Just show them the passport card like you're any other visitor. If worse comes to worse, tell 'em that van is smuggling guns. That should distract them."

"What about you?"

"I'll make my way across on foot. You'll be sitting in line, so I might even get there ahead of you. I'll call you and you can pick me up."

"And what if you can't get across?"

"Don't worry about me." He notices my phone in the cup holder. "Did you break down and make the call?"

The van exits the highway, turning onto International Boulevard. There are signs up ahead for the University of Texas at Brownsville and the Gateway International Bridge.

"I can't," I say. "There's no one I trust. With my own people it would take too much explaining, and with the Feds, I think they might be playing me. I have to see this one through. I don't have a choice."

"There's always a choice," he says.

"Then I guess I'm making it."

Brake lights flash in front of us. The traffic ahead rolls to a halt. The white van is four cars ahead, edging its way toward the Mexican border.

"You'd better let me out," Jeff says.

He crosses to the sidewalk in front of the duty-free shop, walking toward the bridge without waving, without glancing back, giving no sign that we're together. A group of pedestrians, black-haired kids in shorts and T-shirts, files in front of my car. I scoot forward toward the bridge's entrance, a line of kiosks that reminds me of a toll plaza or a drive-through bank teller. I have my passport card ready, but on the American side a man in uniform is waving everybody forward.

I can't see Jeff anywhere. As I move onto the bridge, its sides lined with hurricane fencing topped by rusted barbed wire, I try to center my mind, to think only positive thoughts. My phone starts to buzz, and then the ringer fills the car.

It's Charlotte.

"Honey, I got your message. Where are you?" she asks.

This makes me laugh. I briefly imagine what would happen if I told her the truth, that I was sitting in line waiting to enter Mexico with my guns zip-tied to the bottom of the car. The absurdity of the situation surges through me and suddenly I can't stop laughing.

"Sorry," I say. "I'm gonna be a little late."

I glance out across the brown ebb of the Rio Grande, gilded by the sinking orange sunset. I'm not sure what side of the line I'm on anymore.

"I'm calling you from the hospital," she says.

The hospital. Every dark thought flashes through my head. It's been ten years almost since the car accident that put Charlotte in the hospital and our daughter Jess in the grave, but those words drag me right back, flooding me with the same helplessness.

"Are you all right, baby? Did something happen?" I'm hours away. There's nothing I can do. My hands begin to shake.

"No, I'm *fine*," she says, the fear she picked up in my voice forcing her into her uppermost, euphoric register. "Honey, it's *time*. You need to get down here or you're gonna miss it. Carter's pacing so much he's gonna wear a hole in the floor."

The cars ahead of me roll forward. The white van disappears under the shade of the roofed checkpoint on the opposite end of the bridge.

"Baby, you got my message, didn't you? I'm working a lead. I'm not even in Houston. I'm hours away."

"Roland, they're having the baby. Gina's in labor. She was asking for you. Where are you? Can you at least tell me that?"

"I'm about to crawl over the devil's back," I say. "No, listen, that's wonderful. I feel terrible that I'm not there. I would be if there was any way in the world. You tell them I'm thinking about them, and I'll get there as soon as I can."

"Are you in trouble, Roland?"

The white van is no longer in sight. The cars move forward again. The phone is hot against the side of my face, hot and silent.

"I've got to go, Charlotte. I'm so sorry."

"Are you all right?"

"Don't worry about me. Everything's going to be fine. I love you. Tell Carter and Gina I love them, too. And I want to see that baby when I get there. I want to hold it."

The car in front of me advances under the soaring red arch that marks the end of the bridge. Half the lanes are blocked by orange pylons. Off to my right a flock of pedestrians passes through, the air around them humming with laughter. I pull my phone away, imagining a sterile hospital hallway, Charlotte standing off to the side, stricken with worry.

"Are you doing something stupid?" she whispers.

"Possibly. But get in there and be with them, okay? Don't worry about me. I can take care of myself just fine."

I should turn around and go back. But I've come too far already.

"I love you," she says.

"I love you, too."

Up above me, as my car moves forward into the shade, there's a string of words emblazoned across the entry terminal, like the motto at the gates of Dante's hell. *"Abandon hope, all ye who enter here."* Only in this case, it's a Spanish epitaph:

BIENVENIDOS A MEXICO

INTERLUDE : 1986

When the phone rang, I was twisted in my sheets, reliving old memories in my dreams. The glowing clock said it was two in the morning. The voice on the other end of the line belonged to Sgt. Crewes. He spoke quietly, with great precision, like a man who doesn't want to repeat himself. Like a man who doesn't want to be overheard. "Report to base," he said, only not to the office. I was to meet him at the special housing block set aside for the cabana boys.

"You know that's off-limits to me," I said.

"Ten minutes." He hung up the phone.

When I arrived, a couple of MPs were descending the second-floor stairs. They wouldn't answer any questions. "Sergeant Crewes is upstairs, sir. We were never even here."

I went up. The building layout reminded me of a dormitory. An entrance at either end led into a long corridor with doors on either side. Because of the hour, the common area lights were dimmed. Some of them flickered as I walked beneath them. I glanced up to see the husks of dead insects trapped inside the plastic.

Crewes stood outside one of the doors, looking pale and thin as woodsmoke.

"I couldn't put this on my men," he said. "But you know the score."

Then he led me into the suite. The front room was bare apart from the furniture and a couple of garbage bags with bright yellow twist-ties. The hallway opened into a central bathroom with a bedroom on either side.

At the right-hand door stood Magnum, his expression blank.

"All right," he said, patting my shoulder. "Good man."

In the bedroom there were two bunks. She was on one of them, covered to her forehead with a green woolen blanket so that only her bobbed hair showed.

"What is this?" I asked.

"We need your help," Magnum said. "This has to disappear."

I walked to the side of the bunk, my hand edging toward the blanket.

"I wouldn't do that—"

She looked barely human, she'd been so badly beaten. She looked like a mutant in some kind of genetic experiment gone wrong, covered in blood, her bones smashed and twisted, her bruised skin a record of fingertips and the tread of boots. The stud was missing from her nose. Shaking, I forced myself nearer, listening for breath.

"There's no point in that," Magnum told me. "I'm not an idiot."

I wheeled on him. "What happened?"

"It was one of the cabana boys," Crewes said. "They've ordered up some girls before, which is what put the major on the warpath."

"And this time," Magnum said, "it got out of hand. He was alone with her; otherwise it would have been stopped."

"Where is he? Do we have him in custody?"

Crewes studied the linoleum floor while Magnum got the same amused look he'd had in the major's office.

"We're talking about your golden boy, right? César?"

"I asked for you," Magnum said, "because you seemed reliable. We've got some tough hours ahead of us, and the longer we spend talking, the closer daybreak is."

The protocol wouldn't come to me. An image of the warrant officer at the PX flashed in my mind. That's who should have been there, not me. I had no business at the scene of a murder, no business witnessing what was under that blanket. I looked from one man to the other, my features twisted in shock. Crewes wouldn't make eye contact. Magnum seemed disappointed, like he'd expected me to be made of stiffer stuff.

"What . . ." I said. "What do you expect from *me*?"

"We're going to need more blankets," Magnum began. "And some kind of conveyance so we can move her quickly and cleanly. Apart from the mattress, everything's taken care of, so no worries on that score."

The trash bags in the front room. *Everything's taken care of.* The evidence, he meant.

"You want to move the body?" I asked, incredulous.

"Lieutenant," Crewes said, his voice paternal and warm.

I had come straight over when the sergeant called, which meant I didn't have a side arm. Ordinarily I didn't. Magnum, if he'd been true to his namesake, would have had a Government Model tucked into the small of his back, but I hadn't seen one. Crewes had one, though, hidden under the leather flap of a duty holster.

My eyes rested on that holstered pistol, calmness shrouding me. In four years of military service I'd never been threatened, never had the opportunity to test whether I would bear up under life-or-death stress or not. But I'd known since I was a boy that I could be cold-bloodedly serene in times of danger. When the stress got so intense that others couldn't think, I could. And that's how it was that night. I saw the holster, envisioned the movement, and suddenly I made my move. I rushed Crewes, using my hip to knock him off-balance, opening the holster flap and drawing his weapon.

The two men watched me, frozen. I stepped back, then racked the slide, glancing down into the chamber in time to see the shiny full-metal-jacketed round slide into place. We all stood there, looking at each other.

"That's not what I was expecting," Magnum said, smiling so hard his laugh lines deepened into slits.

Crewes, disarmed, looked dumbfounded. "Lieutenant, now stop and think—"

"Stay where you are," I said, swinging the muzzle from one to the other. In my rush, I'd adopted a point-shooter's crouch, not so much aiming as jabbing the barrel toward them. I took a deep breath and squared off into the Weaver stance, letting them know I wasn't fooling.

I knew Magnum had to be strapped, so I turned the pistol on him. "You know the drill," I said.

He used two fingers to untuck his polo shirt, then raised it to reveal a belly-band holster, the butt of a small black automatic jutting out.

"Keep your hands in the air," I told him. Then, "Crewes, you take it out. Slowly."

The sergeant lowered the pistol onto the floor and kicked it over to me. One glance down confirmed that Magnum was playing the role to the hilt. His pistol was a Walther PPK, the original short-gripped version that could no longer be legally imported into the country. The weapon James Bond carried in the movies.

"Now what?" Magnum asked. "It's your call."

"If you see that man," the major had said, *"if he asks for anything or seems to be engaged in any activity out of the ordinary, I want you to inform me immediately."*

I turned to Crewes. "Get Major Shattuck down here."

He shook his head. "You're making a mistake here—"

"You'd better do it," Magnum told him. "He's liable to shoot us both."

"I'll do what I have to," I said. "And I *won't* do what you're asking. You said you could measure a man up. Well, the sergeant here might think nothing of covering up a murder, but you made a mistake when it comes to what side I'm on."

"We're all on the same side here."

"Tell that to the major."

After Crewes left, Magnum went to the bed and pulled the blanket up over the dead girl, watching me the whole time to ensure my approval. Then he pulled a wooden chair away from the wall and sat down. He checked his watch, then motioned for me to have a seat on the empty bunk opposite the girl. I stayed where I was.

"We don't have a lot of time," he said. "You're sure this is what you want to do? All right, then. The thing is, I had you pegged for a different kind of guy—and I wasn't kidding when I told you I was a good judge of character."

"Is that right?" I spat the words out.

"Maybe you're the one who doesn't know himself."

"I do now."

He was studying me the way a climber might study a rock, looking for a way up, trying to assess whether the attempt was worth making.

"What's your real name?" I asked. "Everybody calls you Magnum."

"On account of this?" He stroked the mustache and shook his head. "You can go on calling me that. Doesn't bother me."

"Tell me something. If you're such a good judge of character, how'd that girl end up dead? Are you sure you've got César pegged? Maybe it's him that has the measure of you."

"A man in the throes of passion will sometimes get carried away. He gets angry. He does something like this. Does that make him a bad man? An evil man? Or just a man like any other? I've seen a little bit more of the world than you have, son, and I'll tell you this: I've never met a man who wasn't capable of something like this."

"I'm not capable of it."

"You might tell yourself that." He gets a faraway look in his eyes, maybe reminiscing about his own transgressions. "I judged you wrong, Lieutenant March, but I don't think I'm that far off. You're the one standing there with the gun, after all. I haven't killed anyone tonight and I don't plan on it. What are *your* plans, if you don't mind my asking?"

"I plan on bringing you to justice. You're aiding and abetting a crime. You're trying to cover up the evidence. And I plan on slapping the cuffs on César, too. If he thinks he's getting a pass on this—"

"I'm only doing my job. And I told you already, I'm building relationships here that are going to last a long time. When you walked in and saw that girl, what went through your mind? You were horrified, weren't you? So was I. But something else occurred to me. I've been watching these men. I've been looking to see which ones will last, which of them will rise to the top. When I saw this, I thought, *he's the one*. The man who did this, if he doesn't self-destruct, will go far. Trust me."

"Shut up," I said. "You're not gonna talk that way with her lying there."

I made him rise and walk down the hallway into the front room. I made him untie the garbage bags and dump out their contents on the floor. Up to that point, he'd been easygoing, as calm under pressure as I was. But emptying the bags got to him. His cheeks flushed with anger. The sides of the mustache curled down.

"You're a student of history, aren't you, March? That's what you were checking out at the bookstore, if I remember. I'm more of a literature man myself, but as a historian, maybe you can appreciate this. There are certain historical events that, if you understand the relationship between them, will unlock the way of the world. You know what I'm talking about?"

"I think you're insane."

"You ever studied the French Revolution? Liberty, equality, fraternity, all of that rot. The whole of modern history is just footnotes to the French Revolution. In 1789, when the people started guillotining their masters, that got the slaves down in Haiti thinking, If you guys are all about freedom, then how 'bout giving us a little? Now, in Europe, the French were all about exporting the revolution. Every monarch on the continent started itching around the collar. But when their own colony starts talking about the rights of man, what do you think happened?"

"They suppressed it," I said.

"That's right. The ideas you champion for yourself become a threat when they're embraced by the people you need to subjugate. You overthrow your tyrant, but you still have to make friends with tyrants everywhere. You have no choice."

"You can choose not to subjugate anyone."

"Can you?" He seems genuinely surprised. "That's not as easy as you might think."

Outside in the corridor, I could hear footsteps. Then Crewes's voice. Then the voice of the major. I pulled the door open wide, leaving the pistol aimed at Magnum.

"Sir," I said.

Major Shattuck strode through the doorway with Crewes in his wake. He ordered me to lower the gun and I did. Even Magnum stood straighter, halfway to attention. The major looked the room over, then turned to me for a report.

"There's a dead girl in the bedroom," I said. "One of the cabana boys—one of the Latin American officers—raped her and beat her to death. When I arrived, Sergeant Crewes and Magnum—and this gentleman—were in the process of cleaning up the scene. They expected me to help them remove the body, sir."

Shattuck glared at Crewes. "Is this true?"

"Yes, sir. Lieutenant March took my side arm and threatened to shoot me if I didn't come and fetch you out of bed. So that's what I did. Sir."

"And you?" He faced Magnum. "Anything to add?"

"Only that if we don't do something about the body in there, this could get very ugly very fast. Like I told you before, we have to extend every courtesy."

"There's a limit."

"Maybe so," Magnum said. "But this isn't it."

Shattuck pondered the situation with a taciturn expression. As he did, I felt a weight drop from my shoulders. I had not only proven myself, I had defined myself. I had declared which side I was on. Years later, at the bed of a victim I'd been unable to help, a reverend by the name of Curtis Blunt would quote some Scripture at me, to the effect that cops are God's instruments for doing justice, and only the wicked need to fear them. Setting aside any delusions of grandeur, an instrument is what I was. A servant of the abstract idea. "Justice," I'd said to Magnum, and with a straight face, too. And I still believe it. The same fire burns in me, muffled though it is by cynicism and failure and the passage of so many years.

The pistol in my hand felt so heavy that when the major asked for it, I was happy to give it up. He ejected the magazine, drew back the slide, and released the chambered round. It thudded to the floor. He handed the pistol to Sgt. Crewes.

As soon as he did, Magnum sprang forward.

I never saw the blow coming. But there it was. The crack against my cheek, my neck twisting, my eyes clenched shut in agony. When they opened, the world was decked in gauze and I was reeling. I must have staggered back against the wall, because there I was, sliding down to the floor. I was down and out, and Magnum's fist was already recocking for the next punch.

The last thing I remember seeing was Sgt. Crewes pistol-whipping the CIA agent. He crumpled and went down. Maybe I'm fooling myself, but the way I remember it, my eyes stayed open a moment longer than his.

CHAPTER 26

I don't have to get out of my car or even roll the window down. Like the white van, I just drive straight through, one of the hundreds, maybe thousands of tourists crossing back and forth across the border today. All the precautions were seemingly for nothing, though it brings me no relief. The sound of Charlotte's voice still rings in my ear. The Rio Grande might as well be the Rubicon.

Three bridges over the river connect Brownsville to Matamoros, and we have taken the middle one, which feeds onto a fingerlike promontory wrapped by a bend in the river. The northbound lanes, like the ones at Sarita, are backed up with Americans heading home. The rush into Mexico must slacken by early evening, because once we're through the checkpoint, the cars in front of me accelerate at a brisk pace. Keeping the van in sight, I scan the sidewalks for any sign of Jeff among the stream of pedestrians.

He slips through the crowd, jogging into the street just ahead of me with a silly grin on his face, reaching for the door handle and slipping inside.

"That was anticlimactic," he says. "It seems you don't need a passport at all to get *into* Mexico. This guy on the bridge told me, it's getting back that's the problem."

"We'll worry about that when the time comes."

He nods toward the van. "So they just drove straight through?"

"That could be typical. I don't know. It's not a chance I would have taken with all those guns, though. Either they're the most cold-blooded risk takers in the world, or they know something we don't."

"Or the Feds just waved them through," he says. "If what they told you is true, it's not like they have a problem with the guns going south."

I glance over at Jeff, whose walk across the bridge seems to have left him feeling refreshed, wondering whether he didn't already know he could get across without a passport. A more cynical man might wonder if his little detour served no purpose but to insulate him from any consequences if my car had been searched and the weapons underneath discovered.

He sees me looking at him. "What?"

"Nothing," I say. "Now the hard part begins."

Although the transition from Brownsville isn't jarring—apart from the signs in Spanish and the different license plates, this city isn't all that different from the one I've just left, equally shabby and run down, with a superficial lipstick for the sake of the tourists—there are a few buildings here and there you wouldn't find across the river, including a stately mustard-colored place, pure Bourbon Street, with wrought-iron balconies and ornate windows shut away behind weathered shutters. A few street vendors are still working on the corners. Many of the shop fronts, however, are already hidden behind roll-down metal doors.

The white van makes a turn, travels a few blocks, then turns again. We follow them through a verdant city park, the slope dominated by a crazy sculpture that looks like two twists of red licorice rising out of the ground. They stop the van and get out.

"Here we go," Jeff says.

I pass them and drive back onto the street, pulling into an empty space where we can watch through the back window. A minute later, a silver Toyota turns into the park and rolls up beside them. A tingle runs through me as Brandon Ford exits the passenger side, coming around to shake hands with the two men from the van. He slides open the van door, peers inside, then snaps it shut. The three of them exchange a few words between the vehicles; then Ford motions them toward the Toyota.

"They're gonna leave the van here. Someone else is picking it up."

"What do we do?" Jeff asks. "Stick with them or wait around?"

I tap the steering wheel, indecisive. Ford is why we're here, but leaving the van's cargo for pickup by the cartel would be an inexcusable breach. The handoff I'd envisioned, a classic guns-for-money trade going down somewhere secluded where we might have a shot at interdiction is clearly off the cards. I have to choose between Ford or the guns.

"I can't let them have those guns," I say.

Jeff, half turned in his seat, gets a constipated look. "Forget about the guns. We stick with Ford. That's why we're here."

"I can't do it. I thought I could."

"Listen. We have to stick with Ford."

"I hear you, but I'm not letting the cartel have those guns."

We're crossing all the lines. We're doing things we've got no business doing, taking risks we've got no business taking.

"They'll get more guns," he says. "That's not a real problem for them."

His cheeks are flushed with color, his voice thin, reminding me of his emotional reaction earlier on the road. He has a stake in this, too. His attachment to Nesbitt is what's driving him, not any loyalty to me. He wants Ford, simple as that.

"Yeah, they'll get more guns," I say, "but they won't get them thanks to me."

"So you're gonna let him go?"

I nod, hardly believing it myself.

"It's unacceptable."

"Even so—"

"All right, listen. Here's what we'll do. You stick with Ford. Don't let him out of your sight, no matter what. Leave me here and I'll take care of the van."

"Take care of it how?"

"I don't know," he says. "I'll hot-wire it and catch up to you."

The Toyota pulls out of the park, flashing past us down the street. Jeff pushes his door open, rushing to get out.

"Jeff—"

"Call me when you know where he's going. I'll catch up to you when I can."

He slams the door, then beats his palm on the roof a few times until I finally get going. As I race to catch up with Ford, I see him in the rearview, running toward the van, moving like there's a bomb to defuse and the timer's ticking down.

The geography of the city is wholly unfamiliar to me, just a half-remembered jumble from those college visits, which means that after a couple of turns I'm lost, with nothing but the Toyota's taillights to guide me. Even now, I couldn't explain to Jeff by phone how to catch up to me, and maybe that's for the best. If he keeps his word and takes care of the van, if he manages to hot-wire it or just flags down the *policía* to report a suspicious vehicle, then he'll have justified my trust and ended his exposure to danger all at once.

Down darkening streets and brick-paved alleyways I follow Ford's car from a safe distance, cutting through the heart of the city, past old, arcaded squares and glass-fronted, garishly painted storefronts with tatty striped awnings. Past bars and restaurants, *farmácias* and *paleterías*. They finally come to a stop halfway down a neon-lit side street, reversing into a curbside parking space and walking two by two to the mouth of a pedestrian alley.

I stop a block away, waiting for them to turn the corner before doubling back. Before locking the car behind me, I peel my jacket off and toss it onto the backseat. I free my shirttails and roll up my sleeves, trying to look as casual, as nondescript as I can.

By the time I reach the alley, picking my way along the congested sidewalk, Ford and his men are standing twenty yards away, killing time in front of a cantina entrance and checking their watches every couple of seconds. They seem to be waiting for someone.

I call Jeff from the end of the alley, reading the street markers phonetically.

"What are you doing?" I ask, unable to hear anything in the background.

He chuckles. "What do you think I'm doing, March? I'm driving."

As I hang up, a knot of men approaches from the far side of the alley, moving with enough deliberation to part the crowds. The way they carry themselves, I don't have to wait until they're close enough to see the ink on their skin or the telltale bulges under their baggy shirts. They're with the cartel, and on the streets of Matamoros they don't have to hide it.

There might be ten or twelve of them—it's hard to keep count—and in their midst walks an older man, more distinguished, with silver hair and a patrician bearing. He wears a guayabera the way American politicians wear plaid western wear, more as a symbol than an article of clothing, or the way a generalissimo might don mufti to travel incognito.

Ford advances to greet the man, making a little bow and waiting for the silver-haired man to offer his hand before extending his own.

"You made it," the man says, or at least it appears that way from the movement of his lips. He shakes Ford's hand in both of his, a gesture of warmth that, seen from a distance, conveys just the opposite.

Ford turns to introduce his companions, looking slightly unsettled. Perhaps I misinterpreted the old man's remark. He must have said something that got under Ford's skin. As the seconds pass, his expression goes from concern to panic, then shuts down completely.

For his part, the silver-haired man seems disinterested. He uses the opportunity of each proffered hand to edge closer toward the cantina door. Once the niceties are concluded, he motions them down two shallow steps and into the bar, waiting to have a word with his entourage before following. They disperse to take up positions against the wall, staring down passersby. The boss pauses in the doorway, removes a plated case from his pocket, and withdraws a slim cigar. He puffs a few times, the light of the flame revealing a dark mole on his weathered face.

César.

The words reverberating in my head are my own, spoken years ago to Nesbitt when I only knew him by the nickname Magnum. *I plan on slapping the cuffs on César, too.* And there he is, surrounded by minions, smoking a cigar in the warm evening. Whenever I'm tempted to congratulate myself on being a good cop, a careful gatherer and logical analyst of concrete evidence, something like this happens to remind me all I am is an instrument. A blunt instrument of fate.

César disappears down the steps. I wait and watch, wondering whether his men will let me pass. After a frozen moment, several people approach and enter the cantina without being molested. I follow their lead, doing my best impression of a hapless tourist. Their eyes bore through me, but the gang proves as lax as the border agents, making no move to stop me.

I step down, grasp the door in my hand, and pull. A blast of muggy air hits my face, accompanied by a woman's laughter and the strumming of guitars.

————

From a spot I've elbowed my way into at the far end of the long bar, I watch the round table where César holds court, flanked on his right by Brandon Ford and on his left by a tall and shapely blonde with big eyes and a tiny dress. Either she arrived early or she came with the table. Apart from the old man, no one at the table takes much notice of her. They can't afford to. This is business, pure and simple.

Did César somehow rise through the ranks of the cartel, or did Nesbitt plant him here? I suspect the latter. Whether all the pieces fit or not, I can't tell, but a theory rumbles like thunder through the back of my head. Nesbitt uses César to infiltrate the cartel, then César decides he doesn't need Nesbitt anymore and uses Magnum's own people to take him out.

At the table, Ford does most of the talking, leaning in and gesturing emphatically with one hand. Insisting on something. César dismisses all this with a slight shake of the head, as indifferent to Ford as a horse is to a fly. He steals glances at the blonde beside him, takes drags on his cigar and sips of tequila neatly from a glass at his elbow.

Increasingly desperate, Ford turns to his men for confirmation of whatever it is he's saying. They have their backs to me, but I can see their heads nodding. One of their voices carries over the hum of conversation and music.

"We left it where they told us to. If it's not there, how is that our problem? Is this his city or isn't it?"

So that's the problem. César has already discovered the absence of the van. Now the deal is falling through before my eyes.

Sweating *cerveza* in hand, I notch out a new position for myself down the bar, close enough to hear what's happening at the table without being too obvious an eavesdropper. César hasn't aged well, but he has retained the graceful manner I recall from our encounter more than twenty years ago. He studies the cherry of his cigar, letting Ford's words bounce off him, then raises his hand as if to summon someone from across the room. I follow the motion with my eyes. He looks at me. Looks away. Then his eyes cut back to me. The hand lowers.

"Gentlemen, excuse me," he says to the table. He rises and makes for the rear exit, the blonde bouncing her way behind him.

Ford and his men exchange glances, dumbfounded.

"You'd better go after him," one of them says.

"Fine. You sit tight."

Ford peels away. The others make no move to follow him. Before he reaches the exit, they're already calling for drinks, content to let the boss sort everything out. I scan the crowd for any of the gangbangers César brought in with him, but I'm not sure who's who anymore.

Ford disappears behind a black-painted door.

Over the din I hear an electronic chirp and feel the vibration against my leg. I reach for my phone. The number on-screen is Jeff's. His voice crackles, but it's no use. I press the phone tight against my head and clamp my free hand over the opposite ear.

"Say that again."

"Out back," he says. "They came out back. They're leaving. I have to go."

The volume climbs as I move forward. Maybe it's the thumping of the pulse in my head. I hear something crash on the floor and look down in time to see my beer bottle rolling around just as I kick it. The bottle spins, gurgling foam, but I keep pressing toward the door. I pull it open and duck through, down a dimly lit hallway, dodging a waitress with a tray of empties over her shoulder. I reach a door with a scarred kickplate and a grimy push bar.

SALIDA.

The breeze on the street is cool in comparison to where I've come from. There's a lonely sidewalk and a few parked cars and at the end of the road—which is so narrow it must be one-way—I spot the brake lights of the white van.

I run. In contrast to the din inside the cantina, out here there is nothing but the sound of my feet on the pavement and the hum of traffic out on the thoroughfare beyond the van. I reach the back bumper as the van rolls forward.

"Wait!" I yell, slamming my hand against the side.

The van lurches and halts. I wrench open the passenger door, only pausing an instant to confirm that it's Jeff behind the wheel. He motions me inside with an impatient curse, then mashes his foot down on the gas. I fall heavily against the back of the seat, the force pulling the door shut.

"Thanks for the ride," I gasp.

"We're cutting this too close. I told you to stay with him. You better put your seat belt on."

"Yes, sir."

According to the clock on the dashboard, it's already a quarter past eight. The fact that he's here, and that he managed to take the van, fills me with wonder. Behind me, a mountain of long canvas duffels lie one on top of the other like a stack of body bags. I slip through the seats, steadying myself against the side of the van, and stagger toward the nearest one, pulling the zipper open. Inside there are smaller nylon cases, the same kind I saw in the icebox inside the storage unit, with pouches on the side for 30-round magazines.

Jeff yells at me to sit down, then yells again for me to hold on as he turns.

"You got them," I say. "You got all the guns."

"Do you have *your* gun?" he asks.

"It's still under the car."

"Great. In that case, you can make yourself useful and see if there's any ammo back there. Otherwise we're taking a knife to a gunfight—assuming you have a knife."

"Who says anything about a gunfight?" I ask, crouching between the seats.

"When they came outside, there were guys waiting. They grabbed Ford and stuffed him into the trunk of the car. Whatever we're heading into, I'd just as soon be ready."

"They kidnapped Ford? The old man was with him?"

"The old man was in charge," he says.

I slump to the floor, feeling the hum of the wheels underneath me.

"It doesn't make sense," Jeff says.

"I think he recognized me."

"Who, Ford?"

I ignore the question. "They were supposed to pick up the guns. But you took them instead. And now Ford's got some explaining to do."

"So it's *my* fault?" he asks. But he's not angry. He's laughing.

While Jeff struggles to keep up in the traffic, I feel my way around in back, opening bags, digging through their far recesses in search of ammunition. *Water, water everywhere.* And not a round to fire. I have to empty each of the duffels, patting down every empty magazine pouch. There must be a hundred rifles in total, maybe more, some of them rattling around loose in the canvas bags, but most tucked inside the soon-to-be-discarded Cordura cases.

At the bottom of the second to last bag I find an odd-looking case. It's similar to the others, only longer, like it was made for a full-size rifle, and it's olive drab with stained leather tabs on the corners, the surfaces scuffed from use. There are no magazine pouches on the outside, but when I unzip the case, I find not a brand-new flattop M4 but an old-style CAR-15 with the carry handle on top, the bluing around the sharp edges all but worn away. Nestled in the space between the grip and the bottom of the case are four stubby plastic 20-round magazines. I grab one, pleased with the weight. Running my finger along the top of the mag, I feel the sharp point of a full-metal-jacket round.

"We have ammo," I call out. "But not much."

In all those straw purchases, one of Ford's middlemen must have bought this off a private seller who'd delivered up the goods already in a case, with his loaded magazines forgotten inside. I like the well-used look of the CAR, so I slap one of the mags inside and tuck a second into my front pocket. Then I load one of the M4s for Jeff, sliding it between the seats with the last of the four magazines alongside.

When I crawl back into the passenger seat, we are no longer driving down city streets. The lights are all behind us and a dark stretch of highway looms ahead, the running lights of several cars just visible about a mile in front of us, the cone of their headlights casting shadows on the swaying palms. Jeff's face, illuminated by the console, is grimly set.

"I'm trying to catch up," he says.

They could stop anywhere, I realize, dragging Ford out into the dust, leaving nothing behind for us but a bullet-riddled corpse. We'd have his body and nothing else. The end of the road and not a thing to show for it. No answers and no explanations.

"How many guys did you count?" I ask. "Are we about to do something stupid here?"

He shrugs. "Maybe five or six? There's a woman, too. And the old man."

Nesbitt said he would go far and he certainly has. Nesbitt said he would take care of it, that César was his problem, not mine. But Nesbitt is dead and César isn't. What did he expect me to do? What was in that packet he gave Jeff for me? An apology? A confession? An entreaty urging me to finish the job he barely started?

"César," I say. "He's the boss. He's the reason Nesbitt dragged me into this. Don't let them get away."

"What does it look like I'm doing?"

Jeff is exasperated, but I don't care. I watch the red lights on the horizon, willing them closer. Not for Ford's sake, not anymore. The generalissimo with silver hair, the old man, the big boss. The one who plucked the cigar from his lips, his once-handsome face, and smiled. César, he's the one I want. He's always been the one. But he was untouchable until now.

CHAPTER 27

There are two cars up ahead. Our headlights flash on the trunk of the rearmost car, gilding random bits of trim, casting a glow into the cabin. In the backseat, a round-faced man with black hair and an old scar down his cheek turns to squint at us, and makes a rude gesture with his hand. The figures up front are only silhouettes obstructed by the headrests. I can see the driver fiddling with his rearview mirror, trying to cut the glare.

"He's in that one," Jeff says.

The car in front, a sleek Teutonic sedan, contains César, the blonde, and a couple more of the foot soldiers.

We're racing down a divided highway, two lanes heading south and two north, with scraggly palms swaying in the median. Just beyond the grass shoulder on our right a metal fence runs parallel to the road, backed by a screen of lush, shadowy scrub, while on the left the bare prairie is interrupted every mile or two by modest signs of habitation—a garish motel, a lonely Pemex gas station, a walled courtyard hiding a cluster of squat houses. I hold the CAR-15 in my lap, the barrel pointing toward the floor between my feet, my hand resting on the cocking handle. My window is rolled down, the wind thundering in my ear.

In the backseat of the car, the scarred man is yelling to his companions, jerking his thumb in our direction. He twists himself around and starts waving a chromed semiautomatic in the air, warning us off.

I glance down at my untrembling hand, feeling disassociated from my physical self, a hovering watcher, calm and detached. As my options pare down, so does my indecision, leaving behind the hard but simple equation of survival: kill or be killed.

The man lowers the chrome gun, his expression transforming from one of menace to wide-eyed surprise. And he's not paying attention to us anymore. His eyes are cast down. I lean across the dash, trying to see what he's seeing.

The trunk lid bounces as the car hits rough pavement, rising a foot in the air, opening up a gap for our headlights to shine through. Under the lid I glimpse a section of forearm before the trunk settles down.

"It's Ford! He's opened the trunk—"

The driver hits the brakes, bathing us in red, and the back end starts to slide. The trunk lid rips free of Ford's grasp, flapping wide open, revealing his hunched body like Botticelli's goddess on an oyster shell. His skin is washed out by the shine from our high beams, but the rictus of fear is unmistakable.

Jeff has to brake, too, swerving into the next lane to avoid a collision. The car's brakes let up and it gains speed on us. Jeff hits the gas, pitching me back. In the trunk, Ford is writhing, afraid to jump out and afraid of missing his chance, too. I can almost read the thoughts running across his face.

"He's gonna jump," I say.

The van veers again, just as Ford makes his move. He rises on his haunches and rolls forward, more of a fall than a dive. I lose sight of him as he hits the road. Jeff mashes down the brake, hurtling past the spot where Ford landed. We shudder to a halt with the screeching of wheels. Ahead of us, the car stops, too. They're about thirty yards away, cocked sideways on the periphery of our headlight cone, the open trunk screening their movement.

I open the door and slip onto the pavement just as the first shot is fired. There's a loud pop, a muzzle flash from the side of the car, and a *thunk* near my left ear. A bloom of broken glass. Then silence. I hear voices, then footsteps scraping across the pocked asphalt.

By the time they start shooting again I'm already on the move, circling behind the van for cover, drawing back the charging handle and letting it slap a round into the chamber. Hunched at the rear bumper, I wheel around and bring the muzzle up. There are three of them crossing the gap between their car and the van, the scarred one in front with his chromed gun at the ready. Our headlights throw enough light on them to make a sight picture easy. I line up the post on the lead man, lowering my finger onto the trigger.

Jeff scuttles around beside me, breathing hard, the M4 in his hand. "Was there another mag?" he whispers. "I felt around but I couldn't find it."

"I put it next to the gun," I say, not taking my eyes off the target.

He mutters something under his breath, then rises. "I can see Ford. He's—"

I pull the trigger. At the last moment I drop the muzzle and put the round in the scarred man's leg. He drops his pistol and doubles over, clutching his thigh. The other two bolt back to the car, leaving him there. He staggers backward a few feet, then falls to the ground and emits a terrible wail.

Jeff puts his hand on my shoulder, making sure he has my attention. "Hold them off. I'm going after Ford."

As he scuttles off into the night, I glance back after him. He's heading toward the dim lights of a roadside settlement a quarter mile down the highway, just a concrete block wall with a sheet-metal gate and a couple of small shacks on the other side. An amber streetlight marks the entrance. Squinting, I realize it's not the settlement he's making for but an inky form limping toward it, trying to conceal itself in the shallow ditch running alongside the road. Ford.

A burst of gunfire erupts from the direction of the car. Dull, metal hailstone thuds rock the van, sending showers of glass onto the pavement. I put some distance between myself and the bulk of the van, still keeping the cover between us. I need a new firing position and my best option looks like the ditch, where I can hunker down and fire from around the front of the van while they're looking for me to poke around the back.

The wounded man rolls on the ground, alternately clutching his leg and reaching for his dropped gun. He calls to his comrades for help.

"*¡Cálmate!*" a voice shouts from behind the car, sounding annoyed at the distraction.

I can't tell exactly where they're standing, and they've stopped firing, so I aim in the direction of the sound.

A double tap: *one, two.*

Pause to let them look up. Then another two: *tap, tap.*

Before they can return fire, I'm on the move, running in a crouch, staying as low in the ditch as I can. By the time I draw level with the back of the van, they're pouring fire on the front, so I just keep moving.

I don't see Jeff anymore. Or Ford. The faster I move, the harder it is to see anything at all apart from the streetlight. Over my shoulder, the gunfire subsides long enough to hear the lead car doubling back. I can't turn around. There's no time.

They can race ahead on the highway, cutting me off, and if I lay down some fire to try and slow them down, my muzzle flash will give away my position. So far there's no evidence they have anything but handguns, meaning that if I put enough distance between us, my carbine will have the advantage. Until then, I can't count on keeping enough heads down with my unaimed fire to prevent one of them from drawing a bead on my position and dropping me.

My lungs swell with the effort of running, only I don't feel winded. I don't feel my age, either. The adrenaline is pumping through me, and while my mind may be clear, my body seems to exult in the challenge. No pain, no constraint even. I'm alive, so alive that I feel like laughing. Then they start shooting again and I have no time to feel anything. The engine roars and the tires squeal.

There's no choice now but to drop. I hit the ground, swing the carbine around, and fire a string of rounds at the approaching car. It's the lead car, the one the silver-haired man was in according to Jeff. The windshield shatters, the car dips to a halt, then reverses eagerly until it reaches the cover of the van. I get up and start running again, accompanied by the crack of handgun fire. They must not have spotted me, though, because none of the shots come close.

I can't hug the road anymore; there's not enough cover. So I sprint into the darkness, picking my way across a flat expanse, exposed, all aglow with moonlight. I cut through a hedge separating the empty lot from a kind of shantytown, where some brightly colored corrugated huts are concentrated. No one is there apart from a barking dog, which rushes toward me in the dark. For a moment I panic, holding the carbine in front of me like a baseball bat to ward off the dog. But a taut leash pulls him up short.

"Next time, *amigo*," I whisper, and keep running.

When I reach the walled enclosure where Ford was heading, and Jeff after him, I sink down and catch my breath. Back on the highway, the two cars are rolling forward slowly, bumper-to-bumper, with their headlights doused. Apart from the drivers, the men are crouched on the far side of the cars, using the ditch for cover. If I had more ammo, if Jeff were with me, we could make short work of the soft-skinned vehicles. Under the circumstances, this tactic makes a kind of sense, though they'd be better off taking to the darkness—or leaving the field of combat entirely. But who wouldn't?

Some trouble you face out of necessity and other trouble you seek out. To see the one through without backing down is a sign of character. To persevere in the other, though, is nothing but pride, the stubborn arrogance that leads men to double down on disaster in the hope that everything will right itself in the end. They could run, then fight another day. But on the other hand, so could I. To risk my life, outnumbered and outgunned, for a cause no better than to keep Ford alive long enough to answer my questions, to preserve an outside chance of reaching César . . . if that's not the height of hubris, I don't know what is. How did Gina Robb put it? *"He waits and waits until everybody's basically dead."* Somewhere in the night, she's bringing new life into the world. And here I am.

If it were just me in this, maybe I'd vanish into the night. Probably not, but there's always hope that in middle age, a man might still learn. There's Jeff to think about, though. I can't leave him in the lurch. With that thought to hold on to, I sling the carbine and find a handhold on the top of the wall, hoisting myself up.

This section of wall, well outside the reach of the anemic streetlamp, is bathed in relative darkness. There's some crushed glass on the top of the cinder blocks in lieu of razor wire, but it's scattered loose on the surface and easy to clear aside. The moment of risk is when I'm perched on the rim, silhouetted against the sky. No one shoots, and I manage to drop to the ground with a quiet thud.

There are four buildings inside the perimeter. Three little bungalows are situated around a dirt circle, two of them with bulbs burning over the front doors. No lights on inside, which means the occupants probably went to ground when the shooting started. The fourth building looks to be a kind of ribbed metal barn with a big louvered door up front large enough to accommodate a tractor. There's a side door, too, which stands open and reveals nothing but darkness within.

I see no sign of Jeff. Maybe he didn't make it this far. Maybe he caught up to Ford in the dark and they're still out there somewhere. With my flanking run I could have circled them without realizing. Or they could be inside one of the buildings. Somehow I can't bring myself to break cover just to knock on the door.

"*Jeff?*" I hiss.

Nothing. I can always call him. I slip my phone out, feeling ridiculous the whole time. The line rings, but he doesn't answer. Of course not. Before I put it away, there's another call I should make. It's time. We're holed up without much ammunition in country that is unfamiliar, with an unknown number of cartel shooters converging on us. If there was ever a time to phone the cavalry . . .

I pick the number out of my recent calls, pressing down on the glass. Several rings, and then her voicemail picks up.

"For what it's worth, just so somebody knows, I'm down in Mexico," I say. "On the highway south of Matamoros. I left it too long to blow the horn. And maybe I'm a fool to trust you, but what choice do I have? Brandon Ford is here somewhere. And the ringleader, César. If nothing else, there's a murder you could pin on him from 1986. There's not going to be a paper trail, but . . ." My throat tightens up. "Anyway. We're about to get into something ugly. I guess I should've said something sooner. It's up to you now, Bea."

I should call Charlotte, just to say goodbye. I'm about to push the button when the cars on the highway roll past the open gate. They're in the far lanes, across the median, pointing in the opposite direction of traffic, though there's little traffic to speak of. I rush across the dirt circle toward the gate, taking cover right at the edge. The concrete blocks afford pretty good cover against small-arms fire, and this is as good a place as any for a showdown. I'm not sure how many rounds I've fired, how many are left in the magazine. I swap it for the fresh one so as to put off the need for a reload as long as possible.

Then it's time. Game on.

The cars have stopped, and a couple of the men are advancing over the median, trying to use the thin palm trunks as cover. I pick the one most exposed and line up my sights. The carbine bucks and he slumps to the ground. The rest of them drop flat or start rushing back to the cars. *Tap, tap.* Another man falls. And then a hurricane of return fire pelts the wall, pinging on the metal gate and kicking up dirt a few feet away. I glance around the compound for a new shooting position. That's when I hear the scream.

Even under the circumstances, with my heart thumping and the task of keeping alive activating the problem-solving centers of my mind, this is a scream so primal and horrifying that I am yanked out of my cool efficiency. I don't just hear it; I feel it in my spine, the way a kid in a spook house, even though his brain knows the haunts are fake, surrenders himself over to terror. Despite the gun in my hand, despite my will to live, that scream puts fear in me.

My first reaction isn't to investigate. It's to run away and hide.

I fire a few rounds to keep their heads down out there, then force myself to sprint across the open dirt, clearing a gap as another storm of bullets zings against the gate. The sound came from inside the metal barn. I pause at the entrance, fumbling in my pocket for the tiny Fenix flashlight I always carry.

Inside, the smell of oil couldn't be more overwhelming if I were crawling through an engine. There's ragged breathing coming from the back of the barn, a rhythmic, feral pant. I advance along the right-hand wall, keeping the carbine at hip level, holding the flashlight high and to the left in case it draws anyone's fire. There's a yellow combine or tractor to my left, and behind it a pegboard draped with greasy tools. A shop light hangs from a hook in the corner, casting a sterile white halo over the space. I can't see around the tractor, but the sound is coming from here.

"You've seen what I'll do," a coaxing voice whispers. "Why make it so hard on yourself? This can end right now, if you'll just tell me where to find him. Give me a name. Give me an address. Is that so hard to do?"

I click off the light near the back of the tractor.

"March," the voice says. "We're back here."

I step into the halo, my finger on the trigger.

The first thing I see is Jeff's hand, slick with blood. He stands beside a heavy wooden workbench, feet apart, with his M4 resting, muzzle up, against the bench leg. In his glistening hand he holds something flat and shiny. A sheaf of black zip-ties peeks out from his jeans pocket. He smiles at me with a smile I hope to never see again.

Brandon Ford kneels at his feet, his back against the bench and his arms extended along the table edge. His wrists are secured to the thick wood legs with plastic ties, and he looks like he's been beaten badly, probably from jumping out of a moving car onto the highway. His black curls are matted with sweat, his face and throat and bare arms displaying the drained pallor of marble. His feverish eyes dart toward me an instant, then wander back to the site of trauma.

At the end of his outstretched left arm, on the back of his hand, a flap of skin hangs uselessly to one side to reveal the teeming redness beneath.

"He's close," Jeff says. "He can't take much more." He gives Ford's cheek a gentle pat, almost affectionate. "Give me a second and we can get out of here."

"*Are you insane?*"

Before he can answer, another volley of gunfire explodes against the gate outside. They must be advancing.

"I don't need much more time, but if you don't get out there . . ." He says the words slowly, like he's instructing a child. The tip of his knife catches his attention and he turns it in the light. Just an everyday lockback knife with a clip on the side and a grooved nub on the back of the blade to make one-handed opening easier. It's no different than the kind many people carry clipped inside their pockets, only the edge is honed razor sharp.

"You're the one? You killed the man we found in the park? *Why?*"

"We don't have time for this," he says. "They're coming."

I raise the carbine. "*Why?*"

"At the time, I thought it was *him.*" He flicks the tip of the blade in Ford's direction. "And they went through quite a bit of trouble to make it seem that way, too, don't you think? After the fact. The thing with the DNA. That was for my benefit, wasn't it?" The question is addressed to Ford and punctuated by a slice across the cheek. Ford winces and I take a step forward. "Never mind. Now we're back where we started and it's time for answers. He knows who Inferno is, and he knows where to find him. And if he doesn't tell us, well"—Jeff's smile widens—"he knows what to expect."

Voices outside, then more gunfire, this time closer. They're inside the gate and it won't take long to figure out where we are.

"And Macneil, that was you, too?"

He appears to be straining to remember. "You mean the guy in Argentina? That was a favor for Mr. Nesbitt's new friend. The one who was supposed to help him bring Englewood down. Supposedly he'd stashed a lot of money somewhere, but he must have spent it all. Otherwise, by the end, I think he would've told me."

"There's something wrong with you."

"There's something wrong with the world. At least I'm honest enough to see it for what it really is. You, on the other hand, are a disappointment."

"Nesbitt thought so, too."

"I don't know what he expected from you. I mean, look at you."

"You have to understand, Jeff. Nesbitt unleashed something he couldn't control. He thought I could finish it."

"I'm the one who will finish it."

"Your way isn't what he had in mind. He was hoping to make amends."

"Look," he says, desperation in his voice, "there's a back door here. We can slip outside and disappear into the night. But not until Brandon here tells me where to find his friend. So what do you say, Brandon? Do I have to ask the question again?"

He extends the knife toward Ford's maimed hand, the blade gleaming.

"Jeff—"

The barn's metal hull amplifies the gunshot. Then there's the ding of my spent casing bouncing against the wall. Jeff bends at the waist, letting the knife fall, twisting as he tips toward the ground. My round struck his hip, probably shattering it. I had no choice but to shoot, but I couldn't bring myself to aim for center mass.

"*You shot me*," he wails.

I pick up the knife and cut Ford's torn hand free. Then I loose the other one. Hands are pulling at the barn's roll-up door, looking for a way in. As I cross to the shop light and rip the plug from the outlet, a shot rings out from the open side door. They're in the barn. I take Ford by the scruff and start pushing toward the back exit.

"March," Jeff moans.

I pause over him. "I *trusted* you." This has no effect on him in his state, and there's no time for speeches anyway. "Listen, your rifle is where you left it. They're coming for you. What you do about it is your choice."

Then I'm pulling the door open, pushing Ford through, and closing it behind us.

Outside, he starts to mumble his gratitude, which I don't want, then says he's able to walk if I'll steady him a little. We stumble toward the concrete perimeter wall, with Ford's good arm slung over my shoulder and his injured hand clutched to his chest. He sucks in breath through his teeth with every step. As I mount the wall and reach back to help him over, the barn turns into a live firing range. The explosion of gunfire, the projectiles punching through steel—it's like a roll of quarters tossed into a clothing dryer, clattering free as the dryer spins.

"*Don't leave me! March! You can't leave me alone with them!*"

The sound draws more fire.

I don't stop to think about the men advancing through the dark on either side of the tractor. I don't stop to think about the dwindling number of bullets in the M4's magazine.

I drop to the far side of the wall, reaching up to cushion Ford's landing.

Then we head off into the darkness, pushing forward, ignoring injury and fatigue, ignoring the all-too-real possibility of a bullet in the back.

"What are you even doing here?" Ford mutters, barely loud enough to hear.

"I came for you. Did you think I wouldn't?"

"You took the van—you and *him*?"

"Don't talk. Just keep running."

"What happened to your partner, that's not on me. He got the jump on us coming out. Drew down. Lodge started shooting before I even knew what was going on."

I stop in my tracks. Try to catch my breath. I hear gunshots, distant and intermittent, engines revving.

"Keep moving," I say.

"We couldn't trust the cops," Ford says, "not after what happened to Nesbitt. For all I knew, you guys were out to punch my ticket." He starts coughing. "Tonight you almost did."

"Shut up," I tell him. "Just shut up and keep moving."

We run, holding each other, kicking our way past underbrush, stumbling and rushing on, until Jeff's voice is gone and the sound of gunfire is gone and everything's gone but the scrape of our feet through the scrub. That and the tortured breathing of the man beside me, Bea's lover, with his flayed hand.

CHAPTER 28

It takes me a while to remember the crossroads where the cantina is situated, the street where I left my car, and I have to repeat the names several times before the Mexican in the pickup nods with comprehension and tells me to sit back. He's a small man with a contented smile who shows no qualms about having stopped for us, despite our condition, and waves away the wad of cash offered in compensation for the ride, as if assisting gringos in distress comes so naturally to him that he wouldn't dream of taking a dollar.

Ford slumps between us, his hand in a hastily improvised wrap, slick with sweat, eyes closed, murmuring under his breath. Before we reached the road, he went through a phase of feverish delirium. When I wouldn't agree to getting in touch with his men, he said there was one other person in Matamoros who could help, one other person who'd have the incentive since tonight's escapade would put his own life in danger.

"Inferno," I say. "It's not César, is it?"

"What? No. Inferno was Nesbitt's secret weapon, the guy who made sure César rose to the top. Only César used him to wipe Nesbitt off the board."

"If you know that, why are you doing business with him?"

"I'm trying to stay alive," he says, gesturing with his mangled hand. "And I don't *know* anything. You never do with these people. Look, it's Inferno you want anyway, not me. We can make a trade. Just let me walk out of here and he's yours."

On our way into the city, we come across a column of police vehicles advancing in the opposite lane. If it weren't for the flashing lights, it could pass for a military detachment. They seem to be heading to the location of the gunfight. Hopefully they'll arrive in time to take possession of the van and its contents.

The streets of Matamoros have gone quiet in the intervening hours, apart from a lonely drunk here and there, or a couple on a late-night stroll. There are also ominous trucks full of young men crisscrossing the intersections, prompting the Mexican to shake his head and release a spew of words under his breath. What he's saying is all a jumble to me, but the gist seems clear. The cartel has turned out in force. Probably looking for us.

Before hitching a ride, I had to dump the carbine—I stripped it down and threw the parts in different directions, keeping the bolt with me until I found a soft bit of ground in which to bury it—so we'd be defenseless in the event of a confrontation. It's not uncommon out on the highways for the cartels to set up roadblocks, but here in town they seem to content themselves with cruising around at high speed with a menacing air. The cops are out and so are the gangs, and I don't want to run into either of them.

The pedestrian alley in front of the cantina is empty when we pass by, most of the neon signs now doused. If I were being extra cautious, I'd have the man drop us a couple of blocks away from my car, but the injuries from his fall, the cut on his hand, and our breakneck run have all taken a toll on Ford. I doubt I could hustle him two blocks without prompting a collapse.

"*¡Gracias!*" I say.

The Mexican wards off my thanks just as he did my money.

Once the truck drives off, I settle him in the passenger seat, buckling him in. Then I check the street to make sure nobody's watching, then duck under the car. Feeling around, I locate the Browning and the nylon bag, slicing the zip-ties with my knife. The rifle I leave in place—it's too big to conceal. I clip the holstered pistol onto my belt, adjusting my untucked shirt to keep it covered, and then get behind the wheel.

When I start the engine, a blast of cool air-conditioning envelops me. I'd almost forgotten what it's like. It feels too good. I'm exhausted. My limbs are heavy, my joints on fire, and I could close my eyes right now and sleep for ages.

Here's what I should do: I should leave Ford at the nearest hospital, then get out of here. Get back across the border, get a hotel room somewhere, go home first thing in the morning and forget any of this ever happened. I've dug myself into a deep hole, but apart from that message I left for Bea, there's nothing that can't be undone if I leave right now. That would mean giving up on Ford, giving up on bringing César to justice. It would mean forgetting about Inferno, too. That's what I should do. I'm out of my depth and have been for a while. It's a miracle I'm still alive.

Ford stirs next to me. His eyes open. He starts to look around.

"I recognize this," he whispers. "We're not far away."

I put the car in gear and pull onto the street. "Tell me where to turn."

I'm not going back, not now. Whether it's from the top down or the bottom up, whether it's my genes or my destiny, I'm determined to take this path as far as it goes. The line was crossed long ago, and now that I'm on the other side of it, there's nowhere to go but forward, no matter what awaits me there.

———

The place Ford takes me is a second-floor apartment behind a shop. I walk down the alley to a narrow set of metal stairs bolted into the brick, ascending to a landing that wraps around the building's corner, hiding the apartment from the street, and onto a veranda shaded by a vine-wrapped pergola, the deck full of colored metal outdoor furniture. Across the veranda, the apartment's front door is made of louvered glass—a jalousie window, I think it's called. The apartment windows are louvered, too, the glass panels frosted for privacy.

Through the glass I can make out a table lamp inside, the shadowy outline of a chair back. The faint drum of music filters through the slitted windows. I pause to listen. It's a crackly recording of some melancholy chanteuse, maybe Billie Holiday, I don't know. That sort of thing, anyway. Maudlin stuff.

Ford volunteered to stay in the car, not wanting to climb the stairs, and put up only verbal resistance when I reached into my briefcase and produced a pair of handcuffs. He's beat, as far as I can tell.

I rap a few times on the glass. I hear weight shifting in a chair, then footsteps approaching. A man's silhouette against the fronted louvers. The handle turns and the door swings open.

Standing on the threshold, his shaved head silhouetted by the lamp inside, Reg Keller blinks twice and then smiles coldly. He holds a big-bore Smith & Wesson revolver at hip level, the hammer cocked back. When he glances down at my Browning, aimed at his gut, the smile broadens a hair.

"It would be funny if it wasn't so serious," he says. "A Mexican standoff."

"Hello, Reg. I had a feeling it might be you."

"Congratulations, then. You're the last person I expected to come gunning for me. You're supposed to be one of the good guys, March, not some cold-blooded assassin."

"People change," I say. "Mind if I come in?"

He steps back carefully, keeping the revolver between us. I enter the apartment, taking a moment to glance around. It's a nicely appointed pad, with luxe furniture, a flat-screen television, and a gleaming wood-cased stereo. But there's something sterile about the place, like a pre-furnished executive rental whose occupant changes every other week. Beside the chair near the stereo, there's a cocktail pitcher beaded with condensation. As I circle around, the melting ice shifts inside. The highball next to it is packed with ice and topped with fresh mint. Reg goes to some trouble when it comes to his drinking.

The only thing in the living room that seems out of place is the standing birdcage in the corner behind him. My arrival must have agitated the sleek white bird inside. Its yellow Mohawk of feathers stands upright, and it flaps its wings helplessly.

"My companion in captivity," Reg says.

"You're the contact inside the cartel? That doesn't seem possible."

"I made the wrong kind of friends and this is what happened to me."

"You went to work for Nesbitt."

"It's a long story, March, and if you're going to pull that trigger, I'm in no mood to tell it. Why don't we get this over with. It's been a long time coming. I just don't care anymore."

"I didn't come here to kill you. I didn't know it would be you."

"I'm supposed to believe that?"

"Believe what you want. Just put the gun down."

"I don't think I can do that."

"I'm a cop," I say, "not an executioner. Some of us still know the difference. Now put the gun down so we can talk. The next knock at your door won't be so accommodating."

He thinks this over, then points the revolver at the floor. When I don't react, he lowers the hammer and waits to see what I'll do.

"Okay," he says. "I'll play."

He walks to the built-in unit housing the TV and sets the revolver down, raising his hands in mock surrender.

"So tell me what you're doing here," I say.

This brings a bitter smile to his lips. He spreads his arms to encompass the room, the street, the city. "March, can't you see? I'm in hell."

He was always a lithe, muscular man. Even when he left the streets and donned a coat and tie, he retained that tough beat-cop vibe. Now he seems gaunt, the creases on his face have deepened, and his reptilian eyes are deeper sunk than before.

"Are you working for Englewood," I ask, "or Nesbitt?"

"You know about Englewood, huh? It kind of surprised me that you never cottoned on back in the day. I'd known him a long time, so when I got the idea of putting my company together, he was a natural source to turn to. But then Macneil disappeared and I quickly discovered I'd made a bargain with Satan himself. These guys, when they get their hooks in you, they don't let go. Englewood turned the thumbscrews and, little by little, I found myself turning with them. I couldn't even recognize the man in the mirror. When things got too hot for me in H-Town, he whisked me away. But after that, he owned me."

"And the only way to get free was to betray him to Nesbitt?"

"Very good," he says. "That was the idea, anyway. I needed money more than anything, so I called Nesbitt and made a deal. If he'd find Macneil and shake him down, I could give him the blueprint to Englewood's operations."

"You could deliver on that promise?"

He shrugs. "Maybe I exaggerated the extent of my knowledge. He failed with Macneil. The kid he sent to do the job is some kind of psycho. He got nothing, and left a body behind that people naturally assumed was my handiwork. To make it up to me, Nesbitt offered this job, and I was stupid enough to take it. Between the two of them, they sucked me in."

As he talks, he makes a cautious move toward the chair, easing himself down and pouring a cocktail. I circle away, keeping him at gunpoint.

"Mojitos," he says. "I don't suppose you want one? No, you've sworn off the sauce on account of your little girl. Good for you. In my case, it's the least of my worries. Englewood. Nesbitt. Two years off the grid. All the brutality. They've hollowed me out, March."

"How did you penetrate the cartel?"

"That was simple. The new *Jefe* was a protégé of Nesbitt's from the old days. César Soto-Andrade, that's his name. If you can believe it, this guy used to be high up in the Mexican military establishment, and now he's a drug lord. Go figure. That's how it works down here. So what happened was, he reached out to Nesbitt. He knew what the American intelligence capability looked like and what he wanted was a countermeasure. Somebody who knew the way the DEA and the FBI operate and could help him outwit them."

"And that was you?"

"That was me. The secret weapon, Nesbitt said. I coached him through the process of getting the old boss arrested, then helped make sure that when the new leader was chosen, it was César. While I was advising the *Jefe*, I'd be funneling back information to Nesbitt, who'd make a killing selling all that intel back to the Feds."

"But César was finished with Nesbitt by then."

"The crazy thing is, it all made sense to me at the time. Nesbitt held this out like it was a path to redemption. Once they were hooked on the intel, the government would be all too obliging when it came to making my legal problems back home disappear. Instead of a pariah, a wanted man, a cop-killer. Anyway, I went along with it. And for a while it was working. César set me up with this place, I had a chauffeur to drive me around, and whenever I wanted anything—money, women, booze—all I had to do was ask. Nesbitt's man Ford would come around every so often, and I'd give him something new. Life was good."

"So what changed?"

"What didn't? First of all, Ford got ambitious. He shows up one day and says all these reports of mine aren't earning me any credit back home. The people getting them don't even know it's me doing the work. And Nesbitt has no intention of letting me leave. He's gonna use me until I'm all used up. But Ford would help me out, he said, if I was willing to help him, too."

"And you believed him."

"I didn't have to trust Ford to know I could count on his ambition to serve my purpose. If I could raise the scare back in Houston, make Nesbitt think he was in real danger, then he'd have an incentive to get himself clear and hand the business over to the FBI. Then I could deal with them direct. I explained to Ford how the hook would need to be baited, and he did the rest."

"You had Nesbitt killed? César put you up to it."

The question surprises him as he's taking a sip. He spits his drink back into the glass. "Is that what you think? Then you really have drunk the Kool-Aid, March. Nesbitt got himself shellacked because the fear got to him. If I had people back home willing to assassinate on my orders, you really think *you'd* be walking around today? But I'll admit," he says with a mirthless laugh, "things couldn't have worked out any better for me. César was happy being a drug lord and wasn't interested in helping Nesbitt dismantle the cartel. He wanted Nesbitt out, and Nesbitt got out. So what if I took the credit? Then the Bureau stepped in and Ford tells me all they want is one last favor."

"The arms trade?"

"You got it. Are you familiar with Operation Gunrunner, the ATF's attempt at stopping the flow of guns to Mexico? Huge failure. They didn't bag any of the big fish, for all their posturing. This would be different, though, because César is a hands-on kind of guy. He'd want to do the deal himself. I knew him well enough at that point to make it happen."

"And that was supposed to go down tonight?"

"Well," he says, throwing his hands up in frustration. "Things started going crazy after Nesbitt's little psycho got into the picture. He killed one of Ford's men, thinking he was Ford himself, only the guy didn't know anything. If Ford had come to me, I would have walked him through the situation, but he got this lunatic idea of passing the dead man off as himself—and to do that, he needed major assistance. He went to Englewood. The thing you have to know about this Ford guy is, he thinks he's a player. I can sympathize. I thought I was, too. But these guys are snakes; you can't handle them without getting bit. Englewood turned him out just like Nesbitt did to me, and since then it's been a roller coaster."

"The deal was tonight," I tell him, "and it all went wrong. Which means the *Jefe* knows you're not on his side, and he'll be coming for you."

"Consider this, March. If the deal was tonight, then Ford would have had backup waiting to swoop in. Where are they? I don't see any flashing lights."

"Don't let that fool you," I say, hoping he won't call my bluff.

He doesn't. "What do you want from me, March? I can sense an offer coming."

"I want César. And I want Englewood, too. Can you deliver them or not?"

"Are you asking, will I testify against them?" He shakes his head dismissively, but then a strange look comes over him. Realization dawning. "You're offering me a lifeline, is that it?"

"I'm not offering you anything. But if you can help me bring those men down, then I'll get you out of here somehow. Otherwise, I'll just walk you into the nearest police station. You make the call."

"Can I take a moment to think it over?"

"Go ahead."

He pours himself another drink, the tinkle of ice against glass. My mind fills with the logistical impossibility of smuggling an injured man like Ford and a wanted felon like Keller back into the country. I don't trust the local police, who'd have too many questions about my presence, and there's no one I can call to part the waters on my behalf. Even Bea couldn't do all that—and if she could, I doubt she would. Bringing all this into the light was never part of her plan.

I could always gun the engine past the Mexican side of the bridge and then turn myself in at the other end, like Cold War asylum seekers jumping the Berlin Wall.

What am I even doing here? Cutting a deal with Reg Keller? Risking anything for this man is insane. Maybe I'm the one who's been sucked too far down, my moral compass spinning. How do you reckon which is the lesser of all available evils? Nothing makes sense but to flush them all down, and myself along with them.

Prosecutors cut deals like this all the time, I tell myself. But that's the reason I could never stomach working as a prosecutor. I don't want to cut the deals. It's not in me.

Big Reg gets up out of the chair, the ice sloshing in his glass. He crosses the room, giving the revolver a wide berth. His pet bird starts flapping as he approaches. Downing the dregs of the mojito, he flips the cage door open. "Fly free, little man."

"You've made your decision?"

He turns to face me. "Get me out of here, March, and I'll do it."

I hate myself for saying the words: "It's a deal."

Under my watchful eye, Keller takes two minutes to pack a bag and then leads the way out. Despite the open cage, the bird still twitches on its perch inside, afraid to come out. Reg pauses, shaking his head.

"Goes to show," he says, walking through the door.

From the top of the stairwell I can see down the alley to my car parked on the street. It's lit from behind by a pair of headlights, though the other vehicle is out of view. My passenger door hangs open, but there's no sign of Ford.

I reach my hand out to keep Keller from descending. He stops just as two men step into the mouth of the alley. One of them raises a hand in greeting, and I recall him from the crowd of heavies outside the cantina.

"These guys with you?" Keller asks, turning on the step.

I'm already raising my pistol as the first man fires.

CHAPTER 29

The only thing that saves us is that our sudden appearance at the top of the stairs is as much a surprise to them as their entry into the alleyway is to us. They loose the first shot, but it's fired in haste and zings past my left ear. My answer comes in a wild, unaimed volley, spraying and praying, the flash of the muzzle in the darkness temporarily blinding me.

Somehow I grab a handful of Keller's shirt with my free hand, dragging him back up the stairs. The other end of the alley explodes, bullets tearing past us.

As I pull him off the landing and onto the veranda where we're shielded from view, Keller flinches and slaps his hand to his neck, as if he's swatting a mosquito.

"Are you—?"

My voice chokes off as the first pulse of blood drains through his clenched fingers.

I stick my gun around the corner and fire down the stairs. The bricks near my wrist burst open, showering me with dust. I pull my hand back before they shoot it off, hustling Keller back into the apartment.

The lights are still on, so I waste precious seconds flipping the switches and kicking the lamp's power cord free from the wall socket. Moonlight pours in through the glass louvers, making the blood down the side of Keller's neck and down his shirt look black as oil. With both hands on the wound he lumbers down a short hallway into the lavatory.

Alone in the living room, I crouch at the corner of the window farthest from the door, which affords the best view of the top of the stairs. I push the louvers open, wide enough for the muzzle of my gun. From here I can see them before they spot me, and when they return fire, the apartment wall should afford some protection. My hand goes instinctively to my belt, searching for the spare magazine loaded with 9mm hollow points. I switch mags again, just as I did at the gate on the highway, so no matter how one-sided the fight is, at least I'll be going into it with a fully loaded weapon.

Footsteps on the stairs. It's hard to tell, but in my imagination it sounds like more than two men ascending. From my vantage point, the veranda runs parallel to the apartment wall, dead-ending at an L-shaped turn that leads to the landing at the top of the stairs. When they come up, they'll be silhouetted against the building across the alley, having to cross my field of fire to reach the veranda. The numbers are on their side, but the ground is mine.

The first of them reaches the landing in a low crouch, gun extended. I let him come. He creeps over to the veranda, bending lower to inspect something on the ground. Probably Keller's blood. A second one appears, and then a third. There are more footsteps on the stairs behind him. The Tritium inserts on my gunsights shine bright in the dark. I line them up over the first man, let out my breath, and fire.

I don't know whether I've hit him, or anything else for that matter. Once the shooting starts, there's nothing but the flash of the muzzle and a barrage of earsplitting concussions. All I can do is try and match my shots to the map of targets locked in my memory. How many rounds I let off, I don't know—the shooting goes on forever, uninterrupted, like a stage of fire on the range.

And then the louvers shatter down on top of me, raining glass everywhere, and I have to crouch to the floor, hands over my head, to keep from being hit. Something burns against the side of my neck. I panic, thinking of Keller's wound. When I cover the spot with my hand, though, I find one of my own spent cartridges. It must have kicked back from the ejection port and landed inside my collar.

I crawl along the base of the wall toward the next window, then the one nearest the door. From the corner I can see two men on the landing, emptying their clips into my original position. Another is coiled on the ground, clutching his guts. Very close to the window someone is whining pitifully above the roar of the guns.

Lining up my sights on the two shooters, I open fire. One of them drops like his strings have been cut, and the other stumbles backward and pitches over the side of the railing, falling to the alleyway below. When I crouch for cover, there's no return fire, just the wet mewling of the man on the veranda and the echo of feet descending the stairs to regroup.

My pistol is smoking in my hand, the slide locked back. The 17-round magazine is already empty. I eject it to the floor and seat the other mag, dropping the slide to chamber a round. I don't know how many times I fired in the first engagement. The mag could be mostly full or nearly empty and there's no time to stop and check. Already I can hear them coming up again, this time with an unnerving deliberation, as if they're pausing to get the next attack right.

"Hello in there?" a voice calls from around the corner. The English is clear, only lightly accented, with a friendly, paternal timbre. "We would like to have a word."

"It's him. The *Jefe*."

I turn to find Keller at my side, hunched down with a seeping hand towel against his neck, secured in place by what looks like a rolled pillowcase with a jaunty knot on the side opposite the wound. In his fist, the shiny revolver, its hammer cocked back. The thought of him lurking there behind me, the snub nose in hand, sends a chill through me.

"I believe," César says, "there is a misunderstanding. We have not come here for you, whoever you are. It's Meester Keller we want. Send him out and we will go, you have my word."

In my ear, Keller whispers: "Don't engage with him."

"What did you do with Brandon Ford?" I call out.

"*What did I just say?*"

"We had a matter to discuss with Meester Ford, I am afraid. But you? You are no one. If you like, you can put down your weapon and go."

The voice hasn't changed at all. Hearing him speak, I'm back in that Leesville parking lot, my fists cocked ready to beat him down. One thing in my favor: Magnum was teaching torture techniques to the cabana boys, not combat tactics. The apartment isn't exactly a fortified position, but with the advantage of the wall and the confined open ground the cartel shooters have to cover just to reach us, we can hold out as long as we have ammo. If they keep rushing us like they did before, we have a chance.

In the distance, I hear the faint ring of sirens. They could be miles away or just blocks, it's hard to tell. I turn to Keller, who hears them, too, but doesn't look encouraged. He shakes his head. "The police around here, they're in his pocket."

"I have a proposition," I call out. "Why don't we discuss this man-to-man, out in the open? I'm not afraid. Are you?"

It's a silly idea, but I'm grasping at straws. If I can shame him in front of his men, call his machismo into question, then maybe . . . But no. Keller's shaking his head again, disappointed in my maneuver. And in spite of the dire situation, I find his censure irritating.

"If you have anything better to suggest . . ."

The sirens are sounding louder. They echo down the nearby streets. I want to believe Keller's wrong about the local police, that all I have to do is buy time. My gun hangs heavy in my hand, and when I glance down, I find that I'm trembling.

"Well, what do you say?" I yell.

"This is a very interesting proposition. Allow me to think it over."

He speaks with exaggerated courtliness, inserting long pauses between the words, his conversational tone wholly unsuited to the circumstances. The man is confident, I'll give him that. The approaching sirens don't seem to worry him at all.

But perhaps I'm not the only one buying time.

I motion Keller to be quiet and sit tight. Then I creep backward on hands and knees, between the couch and chair, passing the cocktail pitcher. Back at the far window where I started, I pause at the perimeter of broken glass, listening intently.

"Now, *señor*, I have a proposition for you."

Just outside the window I hear the faint crush of glass underfoot, the sole of a boot pressing down and twisting slightly. While César was talking to me, they must have sent someone to climb up over the veranda railing. Not bad. I listen to his progress and as his head breaks the plane of the sill, I raise the Browning and light him up.

The man pitches back into the shadows, a vaporous cloudburst erupting from his brow. Keller screams and starts firing his revolver two-handed through the window, each loud, throaty bang accompanied by a long tongue of flame. They're rushing us again, spilling onto the veranda, and the six rounds in his chamber won't hold them for long. I scramble along the wall, firing through each window as I pass, then shouldering the door open to empty the last of my clip point-blank into the writhing mass.

Flashing blues and reds cast their glow down the alleyway and the sirens are right on top of us, right inside my head, threatening to burst out. I am slung sideways against the doorframe, my pistol shot dry, looking back at Keller as the hammer of his revolver snaps down on one spent chamber after another. He can't tell the gun is empty, because he's still yelling at the top of his lungs, his eyes clenched shut.

On the veranda, men are crawling on top of each other, stumbling back down the stairs in retreat. A pair of blank eyes stares up at me from right at the threshold. I reach out and twist a cocked .45 from his hand. I'm running cold again, my trembling gone. I emerge into the night, stepping over the bodies of the dead and wounded, ignoring the carnage. The landing is slick under my feet. At the top of the stairs, two bloodstained men hold a third between them—silver-haired, in a sodden guayabera. I reach down, taking César by the collar, pressing the borrowed gun into the ear of the carrier on his right.

"Leave him," I growl.

They spring back, dropping the *Jefe* against my leg. The one under my muzzle just runs, while the other lets a stray round fly. I snap the .45 toward him and fire. He goes tumbling down the stairs.

Then I start dragging César back, grunting with the effort, my whole body radiating, enflamed. I drag him across the landing, leaving contrails in the blood. I drag him across one of the wounded, who crawls away with a frightening gasp. I drag him across the threshold and into the apartment, kicking the door shut, releasing his shirt.

He sprawls facedown before Keller, who stares at me wide-eyed.

"*You're insane*," he says. "Are you trying to get yourself killed?"

"You're under arrest," I say to the silver-haired man. "You have the right to remain silent. Anything you say—"

"March, what are you doing?"

"This man is under arrest," I say. "For murder."

He edges toward me empty-handed. "What are you trying to say? Are you hurt?"

I sink back against the wall, lowering myself onto the floor like a man relaxing into a hot bath, feeling so wet, so utterly poured out as I break the surface.

"This man," I say, then stop. "This man is guilty of murder. He beat a girl to death at Fort Polk, Louisiana, in the summer of 1986."

An amplified voice thunders through the alley in syncopated Spanish that I don't understand. It sounds official, though, and very soothing. Everything feels very soothing. Keller scoots toward me, reaching out, taking the front of my shirt in his hands and ripping it open, letting the two sides drop. His mouth gapes open at what he sees.

"Are you religious?" I ask. "My wife is. Charlotte. Do you think there's anything out there? Besides the stars, I mean. Or is there nothing but nothing?"

His hands feel warm on my skin. He's pushing down on me, pushing me back against the wall.

"I don't think there's nothing," I say.

Up close, I can see the waffle texture of the dish towel tied to his neck, damp with his own blood. Big Reg is covered in blood, all over his hands right up to the elbows, and his breath is foul and he's panting right over my face.

My head lulls and I notice there's an unfamiliar gun in my hand. I open my fist and let it tip onto the floor. Above me, Reg is saying something and his voice is as loud in my head as the sirens were before, only none of the words make any sense, like he's forgotten to leave spaces in between. They run together into a melodic jumble. Is Big Reg singing? That can't be right.

The door opens and there are men in balaclavas with automatic weapons, men shining flashlights everywhere and coming in through the broken windows. Reg pulls back, raising his hands over his head, and the farther away he goes, the fuzzier he gets.

"Reg," I say.

To my left, there's a white bird. It shuffles uncertainly across the floor, wings canted outward in an avian shrug. A ridge of yellow feathers stands along the crest of its head. This bird is watching me from the corner of its eye, and then the wings spread wide and the bird flaps its way through the open door and up into the sky. Everyone watches, the people around me smudging as they gaze upward.

The bird, though, I can see clearly, every feather perfectly articulated. As I watch it ascend, I have this funny idea that I'm watching my own soul. Which would mean I have one, or at least I did. And I don't want it back. Don't come back. Keep on going until you reach whatever's up there.

A boy crouches over me, his body dwarfed inside a Kevlar cocoon, a spike of matted hair jutting from his forehead. He puts a cool hand against the side of my face, frowning mightily. When he gets up, he starts to yell, but in a woman's voice. "*We need a doctor here . . . doctor, how do you say doctor in Spanish? Now!*" I know this voice. I try to get up.

"Stay there, March. You're going to be all right. Don't try to talk. There's gonna be plenty of talking to do, don't worry about that. But not now, not yet. You just hang on, you hear? You just hang on."

"I know you," I say.

"Don't try to talk."

"It's Jess, isn't it?" I say. "They told me you were dead." My lungs inflate with joy. I try to raise a hand and pull her toward me. "They all told me, but I knew. I knew it wasn't true. Why did they tell me you were dead?"

The boy's hand is on my forehead now, and there are people above me, doing things to me. I watch them with far-off benevolence. There's something over my nose and mouth. I feel myself levitating. The ceiling of Keller's apartment sinks away to reveal a heaven full of stars, a million constellations, all of them swirling in a clockwork dance. And circling in among them, wings outspread, is a white cockatoo, and in my ears the cooing of doves.

INTERLUDE : 1986

"Cheer up, sir. This is what you wanted."

Crewes stood in my doorway, arms crossed, watching me toy with the plastic alligator, staring pensively at the clock on the wall. More time had passed, and after the first morning neither of us spoke about Magnum or the dead girl again. It was Major Shattuck who issued the orders. The unnamed suspects in the girl's death had all left the country—they'd been spirited away before Magnum even summoned the MPs—but he had been given assurances (presumably by Magnum) that the incident would be reported to the appropriate authorities in their home country. And that was that. On the sly, Crewes informed me that a little rough justice was in the cards. On the flight home, one particular cabana boy would be making an unexpected snorkel dive in the Gulf.

I pretended to believe him, because it seemed to make him feel better. But I remembered what Magnum had said. Seeing the body, he'd thought, *This is the one.* There was no way he'd lift a hand against that particular killer. César. He had high hopes for the man back home.

Besides, what I'd said to Magnum the night of the murder was right. He might think César was his puppet, but César had other ideas. The

316

ease with which he'd done the deed, knowing he was under surveillance, knowing I had seen him with the girl, made that perfectly clear.

So the clock ticked down, my enlistment ran out, and before long I was sitting with a plastic gator in my hand, pondering the whole course of my life up to that moment. Ironically, during my whole hitch with the MP battalion, I'd never once considered a future in law enforcement. The uncle who'd raised me was a cop, invalided out in a wheelchair, making his living by running a Richmond Avenue gun shop where he cut all his HPD buddies a good deal. That was never a life that appealed to me.

Now I rarely thought of anything else. That feeling of being in the right, of being the only person left to stand up for the dead—I liked it. It suited me. Though it would be a while before I'd see another corpse, and a long while after that before I'd be responsible for bringing a killer to justice. I had found my purpose.

I made the first phone call from my desk at Ft. Polk, first to my uncle and then to his old commander, who by then was a shift lieutenant in the patrol division. After my discharge, I took some time off, did a little traveling, spent a few weeks on the Gulf with some fishing buddies I'd stayed in touch with off and on since college. Then it was back to Houston, the academy, the badge, and the mean streets.

The last time I saw Magnum was the day of my discharge. On base, we assumed he was long gone after the night of the murder. Maybe it was just convenient to tell ourselves that. I'd already taken care of business at Ft. Polk. All that was left was wedging the last of the things at my off-base apartment into an already-packed car, then driving the four hours to Houston.

Before I left town, I stopped at the cemetery where the dead girl was buried. All that my heroics had managed was to ensure that her headstone bore her name. That she didn't just disappear without a trace. Maybe that was enough. I crouched down beside her grave and tried to remember everything about her. I'd only spent a few minutes in her presence, so it didn't take long. If I had realized she was only the first, one of a long line of victims, mostly women, whom I would mourn without knowing, whose killers I would hunt and sometimes catch but never bring to justice in any ultimate sense, my intention to become a cop might have ended right there. Nicole Fauk, stabbed to death by her high-flying husband. Hannah Mayhew, killed for staying true to her friend. Evangeline Dyer, whose body rests in the unfathomable depths of the Gulf, and Simone Walker, copycat victim of a psychopath whose career was nipped in the bud.

There are so many, some without names, and behind them all, haunting my sleep, the little girl I could never save, my own daughter, Jess, taken by chance while I was miles and miles away. Hunched beside that grave in Leesville like Atlas taking on the first of his weight, I had no idea what was in store for me or I would have run.

Then again, maybe I wouldn't have. This is the way I was made. I came from the factory with a sense that time was out of joint and had no Shakespearean qualms about being the one to set it right. Righteous indignation ran in my veins long before I had any reason to feel it. All that's happened since has only confirmed what I knew from the cradle. The world had long since fallen into the ditch, but that didn't mean we belonged there, caked in mud.

As I walked back to the car, I found Magnum leaning on the bumper.

He had his arms folded, the right hand tucked under his suit jacket casually. Probably gripping the butt of a pistol.

I stopped.

"I could kill you from here, if that's what I wanted," he said, flashing his grin.

"All right, then." I closed the distance between us, pausing a few yards off. "You've got a gun under that coat, and this here's a cemetery, but I'm not to read anything into that?"

"Read whatever you want into it."

"You're just here to say your goodbyes."

"Is this goodbye? What makes you think that?"

"For one thing, I'm leaving. For another, I'm gonna be a cop. Since you're an accomplice to murder and probably a murderer in your own right—"

"Hold on, there, partner. There's no need to get worked up. You've got the wrong idea about me entirely. I'm on the side of the angels. The world's just not as black and white as you seem to think."

"That girl out there," I said. "Maybe you ought to pay your respects while you're out here. Didn't see you at the funeral."

"The thing is, March, I was telling myself there was still hope for you. The way you handled yourself that night . . . I was impressed. I know a lot of guys with resumés that would put yours to shame who couldn't pull off what you did. What I'm saying is, I think we ought to have a talk."

"I think we already did."

"Don't blow this off. That would be a mistake. There are opportunities that come only once in a lifetime. I'm talking about the major leagues here. The big show. There's no glory in it, no recognition to speak of, but that kind of thing doesn't matter once you've looked behind the curtain."

"I already got a peek back there. Didn't like what I saw."

"Come on, now. I'm not going to throw myself at you—"

"Is that what all this is about? You're trying to recruit me? This is how it works?"

He wasn't smiling anymore. He looked at me with a strange fierceness. "This is my core," he said. "This is my inner sanctum I'm opening up to you. You have no idea what I've seen. No idea what's happening all around you every day. Men like you sleep at night because men like me don't. All I'm saying is, you made a bad move back there, but it revealed something about you I hadn't seen before. Now I know."

"Now you know what?"

"I know I can make something of you, March."

"No thanks."

The suddenness of my answer surprised him. It surprised me, too. There was a time not long before that I would have jumped at the offer. To hear a man like him saying these things about me would have galvanized me. Now it meant nothing. I'd seen his world for what it was, and I couldn't unsee it.

"I don't care who you are. I don't care what you've seen. I don't care what's behind your curtain. If we cross paths again, I'll put you in cuffs as an accessory to murder."

"That's not even an option," he said. "Those rules don't apply."

"We'll see," I told him.

I opened the driver's door and got inside. He motioned for me to roll down the passenger window, then leaned in for a final word. His hand wasn't under the jacket anymore. And he was smiling like his usual self.

"I'm gonna keep an eye on you," he said. "Maybe I'll drop in and see how you're doing from time to time. This isn't goodbye. I'm taking the long view when it comes to you."

I waited for him to pull back so I could roll up the window.

"You ever read Conrad, March? Joseph Conrad. You should. I told you I was more of a literature man. There's a book of his—it's great. It starts with a guy blowing up some Russian aristocrat's carriage; then he hides out with this second man, more of a law-and-order type like yourself. And he can sense the judgment coming from your guy, just like I can sense it from you. So I'm gonna tell you what he tells the guy in the book."

"Fine, go ahead."

"Here's what he says: 'Men like me are necessary to make room for self-contained, thinking men like you.' You understand? Say what you want—and believe me, I've heard it all before—but men like me are necessary. But maybe men like you are necessary, too. I'm keeping an open mind about you, March. One of these days, maybe I'll find a use for you after all."

And then he was gone.

CHAPTER 30

In the end it is politics, not virtue, that saves me. Even as the surgeons perform their ethered miracle inside my chest cavity, a narrative begins to take shape. Bea Kuykendahl tells the story in the presence of Federal agents as they number the bullet wounds in Brandon Ford's recovered corpse. According to this account, Ford died in the line of duty, and so did I nearly. Though I don't remember it this way, I am later told that when the *Federales* burst into the apartment, they found me bleeding out with a pistol in one hand and the scruff of drug lord César Soto-Andrade in the other.

I am a hero.

Not only that, but at the time I was apparently operating with the blessings of the Federal Bureau of Investigation, in full knowledge of the Mexican authorities, who not only sanctioned the operation but played a significant role in its accomplishment. The first photo of me to hit the wire is snapped at my bedside with my torso swathed in bandages and my chin covered in stubble. I'm shaking hands with a uniformed Mexican military official while members of Bea's team, including the old-timer who'd warned me off, look on in stony silence.

There would be many more photos, many hospital-room interviews, many tight-lipped congratulations from law enforcement officials who had a good idea what had really gone down. But politics is politics, and none of them could deny the bounty: a high-profile cartel boss, a thwarted arms shipment, and a dead FBI rogue contractor in need of posthumous apotheosis. Is there any other kind? All the bent and broken rules, all the red tape, all the fodder for an international incident—with the wave of the political wand, it all just vanishes.

All that's required of me is to keep my mouth shut. For once, I do. Whether Bea is a snake or not, I can't tell, but if so, she's the snake that saved me.

The real story goes something like this. When they found me, I was short of breath and coughing up a fine mist of blood. The bullet had entered my chest and collapsed a lung, which made my blood pressure drop rapidly. Keller put pressure on the wound to try and stop the flow of blood, but by the time the paramedics reached me, I had slipped into shock.

Bea says I was rambling incoherently, that I mistook her for a boy at one point, and for my deceased daughter at another. It pains me to hear this.

After they stabilized me, I was rushed into surgery, spent the night on a ventilator, and woke up with a blank space where my memory of the night before should have been. I was flown back to Houston and discharged after a week free of complications. The doctor who signed off on my papers told me I was lucky.

He had no idea.

While I was in the hospital, Charlotte posted herself beside me, scrutinizing everyone who came in. Officials in search of photo ops she sent packing unless I insisted, not realizing that after my string of misdeeds, nothing but a dam of publicity was holding back the tide of consequences. Cavallo came, paving the way for a state visit by Wanda Mosser, who poured on a treacly layer of kindness for the cameras before giving an interview out in the hallway, stressing her commitment to interagency cooperation. Before she left, Wanda conveyed her thanks to Charlotte and whispered in my ear that from now on I should direct any inquiries from reporters to her desk. I agreed wholeheartedly. Cavallo stuck around awhile after she was gone, angry with me for what she called my "rampage," but grateful and teary-eyed that I was still alive.

One evening after visiting hours, Charlotte managed the thing I wanted most.

After disappearing for half an hour, she returned with Gina Robb holding a swaddled baby in the crook of her arm. Carter came in behind them, looking askance at my chest tube, almost afraid to come close. I beckoned them forward. Their baby girl was pink and translucent and beautiful in every way, with a downy cap of dark hair on her crown and a pinched little face. Gina bent low and offered to let me hold her, but I was afraid. It didn't feel right somehow, touching such innocence with these hands. I stared at that little girl, and when I looked up, all three of them were gaping at me, triggering a memory of Keller's exclamation of shock when he saw the ragged hole in my chest.

But it was my eyes that set them off, my eyes goggled with tears.

———

A secret world had opened up to me, sucking me down through its many layers, and instead of swallowing me at the last moment, it coughed me up.

The official record had been not only tidied but heavily redacted, leaving behind a series of notable omissions. Jeff's body must have been recovered from the barn out on the highway—I'd seen the column of police heading in that direction with my own eyes, and it was common knowledge that the van full of M4 carbines was recovered—but in the official version, he never existed.

All that's left of the killer I brought to Mexico with me is a tattered copy of *The Foxhole Atheist*.

The murder of Chad Macneil remains unsolved, as it was in the beginning, and the headless victim he left in the park with its ominous finger pointing to the place Nesbitt died is still identified for the record as Brandon Ford. The man I knew as Ford was buried with honors under the name of Robert Johnson—the idea being, I suppose, that false identities are interchangeable.

The last time I saw Reg Keller was in his apartment in Matamoros. He is no longer a part of the story, either. As obliging as Bea proved in the aftermath of my shooting, whenever I brought up Keller's name, she cocked her head in incomprehension. There will be no more confidences, she told me, never saying a word.

The week after my release from the hospital I eat a burger at Five Guys before driving out to the cemetery where Jerry Lorenz is buried. A riding lawn mover whirs in the distance, and I have to hold my breath to walk through a cloud of gnats. All the trees have been planted on the perimeter, leaving the cemetery grounds to bake and boil in the Texas sun, and me along with them. I press my hand to the back of my neck and it comes away damp. I'm cold-blooded by nature, and even in high humidity it takes more than a stroll across a gently rolling graveyard to raise a bead of sweat on my skin.

Either the heat is astronomical or what's changed is me. I'm not the man I was, not so resilient. The ice water in my veins is starting to melt, and maybe I should take that as a sign.

The tombstone lies flat on the ground, a gleaming black slab incised with an ancient tablet and the inscription BELOVED HUSBAND, FATHER, FRIEND. I kneel down at the edge of the still-fresh grave, feeling a slice of pain through the back of the thigh. My old companion making an unwelcome return.

What do you say to a fallen partner? What do you say to a man you started off despising and came to grudgingly respect, whose death is on your conscience and whose absence you're only beginning to feel? I'm not a good mourner, despite all the practice.

I press my hand flat on the granite, leaving a fleeting impression behind on the stone.

His last thought was for his kid, as mine would have been, as mine *was* in the confusion of shock when I mistook Bea for Jess. It was Lorenz who first thought that the finger must be pointing, Lorenz who later worked out what it was pointing at. And I've come without even a conclusion to offer him, no killer behind bars, no clearance on record.

Just death. At the end of the day, Lorenz and the man he was hunting are both equals in the grave, their differing moral weight apparently balanced in a zero-sum game of nonexistence.

If there's anything in religion I want to believe, kneeling beside this beacon in a sea of markers, serving no ostensible purpose but as a focal point of memory and remorse, as a blaze cut into the bark to let us know something's rotting underneath, it's that the dead and disembodied will rise again before the cosmic judge, that the zero-sum game will give way to the balance scales of an unblindfolded justice. That a cool psychopath like Jeff will be weighed and measured and found wanting, and someone will tell Jerry Lorenz that he didn't die for nothing after all. Which is more than I can do, hovering without words over the silent grave.

———

At first I fear the ripping sound signals some new injury of the flesh, that I've popped some stitches in my chest or my taut sciatic nerve has finally snapped asunder. But the gashed seam isn't inside me; it's between my legs. The seat of my pants has snagged on the fence around Jeff's vacant garage, the threads giving way. On the ground I make a quick inspection. An inch or so of frayed fabric gaping wide, nothing more.

The desiccated hulks of the once-treasured muscle cars haven't moved at all since the last time I was here. Everything's the same. There are no migrants congregating in the parking lot across the street, but otherwise the clock could have reset to the moment before my ill-judged southward journey. When we left, we were both in a hurry, and I distinctly remember Jeff pausing at the door only long enough to lock one of the dead bolts. With that lock in mind, I've brought along a crowbar. In thirty seconds I'm inside the garage.

I turn on the window unit A/C and the upright fan. The stifling heat doesn't abate one bit. If anything, the thin sliver of refreshing air makes the rest of the space burn hotter. My shirt sticks to me, my imperviousness gone.

From my jacket pocket I remove *The Foxhole Atheist*, setting it on the table. Then I snatch it up again and start ripping the pages apart. It's a fat little book and the dismemberment takes some effort, leaving me with an ache in my chest and the usual prickling along the sciatic line. The book's pieces lay clumped around my feet. The idea of stomping them comes to mind, but my anger has already run through me like a fever and is gone.

My footsteps slap against the concrete. My soles stick a little before lifting. The surface is tacky with grease. I pace around the reclaimed corner of living space, noticing a film of dust over everything. It wasn't so different before. Though the garage was fitted out for primitive occupation, were there signs that Jeff was really living here? Try as I might, I can't recall. Looking at it now, the place seems long unoccupied, more of a clubhouse than a bedroom. Things were not as they seemed. If I'd been looking closer, I might have realized.

The gaping hole in the floor left by the removed lift is rimmed with oil-blackened track and random debris. I bend down to examine the abyss, which gives off a smell not unlike an overheated engine when you first lift the hood. At the bottom of the hole, jutting up from the floor, there's a metal remnant of the lift, a shaft maybe four feet tall that splits into two arms at the top, like a gently curving iron T. When I slide down into the hole for a closer look, marking my pant leg with grease, I find the shaft is socketed into the floor but jiggles around freely in its mount. Cords dangle loose at the end of each arm, secured at one end by complicated-looking seaman's knots.

I don't try it out, not wanting to mark my shirt, but I can imagine a man leaning forward against this shaft, his arms stretched just as I saw Brandon Ford's arms back at the barn in Matamoros, wrists secured at the end of the metal arms. Remembering Jeff's makeshift dissection, I feel light-headed. Queasy.

Removing my flashlight, I peer along the grimy floor for any signs of blood, but if they're here, they are hidden from the naked eye. A forensics team could find them, I'm certain of that, and they'd match the telltale grease stain on the back of the corpse's leg to some piece of railing in the pit. He would have been filthy from dying down there. Jeff would have had to drag him up, then over to the bathroom for a wash. I look for an axe, just in case, but there's no sign of one.

Climbing up to the floor, I retrace his probable steps, ending in the small, dank restroom. The sink is gray from oil. The trash basket beside the basin bursts with fetid gray rags.

The night he rescued me from Ford's men, it wasn't home base Jeff brought me to, not his refuge. He brought me to his killing ground, his carefully appointed torture chamber, then spun a story so he could gauge my reaction and determine how much I knew. I'd felt so grateful to him for the unexpected deliverance that I wasn't really on my guard. Not psychologically, and certainly not physically. If he'd wanted to, if he'd decided I could be of more value to him down in the pit than up here on the surface, I have no doubt Jeff would have killed me. After seeing him standing over Ford with the glistening knife, I have no doubt at all.

I spin and stumble, reaching for something to steady myself on. My hand rests on the edge of the table where Jeff stacked his many books. His books. I'd imagined him reclining on the army cot, reading his paranoid literature until the wee hours of the morning, unable to sleep. Now I can picture him coming up out of the hole for a break, a little rest and relaxation, leaving his victim down below to linger in agony. I see him reading while a moan ascends from the abyss, a private smile on his lips.

I don't rip the books apart or even lash out at them. All I do is push them one by one, with the slightest pressure of my fingers, over the edge and onto the floor. Each one drops with a satisfying impact that sends a thud reverberating through the garage. I move the books over the edge like so many beads across the wire of an abacus, counting an arithmetic of hidden shame. The whole place should burn. It should be razed to the ground. But it's not up to me to see this done. None of it is up to me anymore. I was not born to set this right. Not this.

The last book left is a thick old paperback with a creased black spine. The pages curl upward from repeated reading, their edges brown with age. On the cover is a detail from a medieval painting, a horned demon with serpents projecting from his head, the bare legs of a half-consumed man dangling from his mouth. All around him, naked bodies writhe in bubbling oil vats. They are stoked by pitchforks, their bone-white faces twisted in pain. This is a thousand-year-old vision of the depths of hell, affixed to the front of Dante's *Inferno*, a place Jeff didn't believe in but brought to life.

I snatch the book up, the same copy Magnum was reading the morning I jogged past him at the picnic table. *Can you keep a secret?* And to my surprise, in blue ballpoint just inside the cover is written the name ANDREW NESBITT.

That confident trickster and talent spotter, grooming future dictators for the good of democracy, a would-be puppet master whose own paranoia became his undoing, who never settled the debts he owed to justice and didn't live to see the red harvest his deeds put in motion. Like a jeweler gazing through his loupe, he had seen something in me all those years ago, some flaw of character that led him to believe I would go along with concealing a woman's murder. And then he'd seen something else and, after a lifetime, sent me a message by way of his torturer, hoping to put that second flaw to use, my willingness to travel on the other side of the line that keeps good men on the path and bad ones in check, to balance his sheet while avenging the death of a nameless woman in 1986, and every woman who came after her, and all the rest. I look in vain for a place to set the book down. Finding none, I take it with me. Full circle and a fitting end to a story I never intended to be a part of, let alone to tell.

AUTHOR'S NOTE

Life imitates art, and vice versa. *Nothing to Hide* was inspired by a true story. Houston police really did pull over a man who claimed to be a retired CIA agent, the man really was shot and killed by the officers who stopped him, and a bit of a mystery ensued when the government denied all knowledge of him—despite the fact that he'd been active in the city's network of former intelligence officers for years. Andrew Nesbitt, of course, is pure fiction. When I decided it was time to send Roland March into the murky waters of the paranoid thriller, the true story served as inspiration. What do I make of the *real* mystery? I have no idea what to think.

Books are written long before their publication date. When I completed the manuscript for *Nothing to Hide*, I had no idea that Bea Kuykendahl's reckless gunrunning operation would prove so prescient. Though it was inspired by my research into the ATF's Operation Gunrunner, which Reg Keller mentions just before the bloodbath in Matamoros, I worried that plot would strain credibility. Then reality came along and lent a hand. Throughout 2011, following the death of a DEA agent in a cartel-related shooting in Mexico, details emerged of Operation Fast and Furious, a Gunrunner-related sting that supplied American arms to the cartels. The fallout from the resulting controversy is just beginning.

Throughout the Roland March novels, details from real life have been woven into the fictional world March inhabits, starting with the crime lab scandals that plagued Houston law enforcement for so many years. Television crime fighters have it so easy. From their slick accommodations to their up-to-the-minute technology, the flawed reality of modern law enforcement rarely intrudes. For March, by contrast, homicide has always been a hard slog. He is, to borrow Henry V's phrase, a warrior for the working day. I like him all the more for it, and I hope you will, too.

J. Mark Bertrand

Autumn, 2011

J. Mark Bertrand has an MFA in Creative Writing from the University of Houston. After one hurricane too many, he left Houston and relocated with his wife, Laurie, to the plains of South Dakota. Find out more about Mark and the ROLAND MARCH series at *jmarkbertrand.com*.

More from
J. Mark Bertrand

Rogue Houston homicide detective Roland March has been given one last chance. But between battling a new partner, a corrupt investigation, and the demons of his past, getting to the truth could cost March everything. Even his life.

Back on Murder
A Roland March Mystery

It's Christmas in Houston, and homicide detective Roland March is on the hunt for a killer. A young woman's brutal stabbing in an affluent neighborhood bears all the hallmarks of a serial murder. The only problem is that March sent the murderer to prison ten years ago. Is it a copycat—or did March convict the wrong man?

Pattern of Wounds
A Roland March Mystery

If you enjoyed *Nothing to Hide*, you may also like...

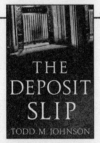

When 10 million dollars goes missing, a down-on-his-luck lawyer is given the case of a lifetime...if he can stay alive long enough to win it.

The Deposit Slip by Todd M. Johnson
authortoddjohnson.com